Misled

A Death Dwellers MC Novel
Book One

By

Kathryn C. Kelly

Misled by Kathryn C. Kelly

Published by Makin Groceries Media
24200 SW Freeway, Suite 402, #353
Rosenberg, TX 77471
https://www.katckelly.com
https://deathdwellersmc.com

LCCN: 201895213
ISBN: 978-1-7325889-1-2 (ebook)
ISBN: 978-1-7325889-0-5 (paperback)

Misled Blurb

Outlaw.

It's not just his name, it's his lifestyle. Explanations aren't necessary.

He presides over a club in chaos after the death of their longtime president and his mentor, Joseph "Boss" Foy. Outlaw is trying to keep everything with the club in his control. His world of sex, violence, and betrayal is closing in on him and there's a target on his back and hell on his heels. A year of sitting at the helm of the Death Dwellers MC has hardened him, and now, Big Joe Foy's daughter threatens to change him in ways he never thought possible. He hides a horrible secret that has haunted him and thrown his club into chaos. When Megan finds out, she'll hate him. She's a distraction he doesn't need. She's too sweet, too sexy, and too young. Worse, she brings out protective feelings Outlaw doesn't like.

Meggie.

Her father's been murdered, but she doesn't know it... yet.

Megan Foy seems to be the only daughter in a perfect little family, but appearances can be deceiving. Her abusive stepfather makes her life a nightmare and her mother has given up. She needs her father, so she runs. Big Joe is her last chance to save her mother. But her hunt leads to the new, dangerously handsome MC President, who makes it clear he doesn't want her around. He's difficult to ignore and impossible to forget. As she waits for a father that she's unaware will never return, she sees through Outlaw's tough exterior. He might want her gone, but Meggie wants him—and she'll fight for what she wants, not knowing the man she's fallen in love with is her father's killer.

Will love conquer all in the world of bikers and revenge?

Dedication

Mom, this one's for you.

Brenda Joyce, one of my favorite authors I've always wanted to meet, who created one of the best Saint/Sinner duos in Rick Bragg and Calder Hart.

Chapter One

I N EACH OF US LIVES GOOD AND EVIL. THE CONUNDRUM we face as a society is recognizing those we pigeonhole as evil and those we applaud as good. That's the grossest mislabeling in the world, the greatest injustice. Have we not heard of the fable of *The Wolf in Sheep's Clothing*? Do we yet misunderstand how deceptive appearances can be? The sun casting a golden gleam upon us doesn't shield us from the rain. Good and evil are wrapped in illusions we're determined to create.

The man society views as acceptable…you know the one…? He gives up his seat to little old ladies. Attends church. Sings carols with good cheer. Gives a handout and a help up. That man, too, has evil lurking in the depths of his soul. Perhaps, he's more evil. This man can charm and smile and manipulate the world to see his goodness. When, in fact, he's the scariest of all.

He's a wife-beater and a child molester. He tears down under the pretense of building up.

I know him well.

He is my stepfather.

Chapter Two

Meggie

EMERGENCY LIGHTS BOUNCED OFF THE SURROUNDINGS on the night-darkened street in a dizzying pattern that hurt Meggie's eyes. Blue. Red. Blue. Red. The colors flickered endlessly from the three patrol cars that had responded to her '911' call.

Her shoulder throbbed. Thomas's hit had been particularly vicious tonight.

Blinking, Meggie stared at the sky, missing the neighborhood she'd grown up in, with its swath of trees and simple beauty. Still, she was able to pick out Venus, the brightest star in the heavens. For some reason, the memory of Dinah singing *Twinkle, Twinkle Little Star* swirled in Meggie's head.

They'd been so happy then. Her daddy had visited more often. Dinah had smiled all the time. Meggie had felt protected and loved. She'd had dreams.

Earlier, when she'd been out with her friends, enjoying the 4th of July celebrations, she'd somehow pretended her life was still good. She'd pushed away the relief and despair that mingled together whenever she sank a razor or a blade into her flesh, stealing a semblance of control in her own way, while the world around her went mad. She'd felt *normal* because she'd been allowed to spend a day out with her best friends. Most of the time, she could only spend a night out for a sleepover at Lacey or Farrah's house, and that after strict assurances by their parents there would be no excursions away from the home.

This morning, Megan had awakened with such hope. So stupid on her part. But today was her father's birthday. When she'd acknowledged it with a text and much love expressed in heart emojis, she'd thought he would've responded. He had last year. But it had been months since he'd texted back. He hadn't even contacted her for any of the past holidays. If she thought hard, she didn't believe she'd heard from him since her last birthday.

Before that…had he contacted her for her sixteenth birthday? She couldn't remember. She only knew between her fifteenth and sixteenth birthdays, Dinah had gotten the courage to leave Thomas a second time. Meggie had wanted her mother to go to Big Joe for help. She'd refused.

What else was new? Dinah had the unerring ability to ignore every suggestion Meggie made that might see them to safety and then lean on Meggie to patch her back together after one of Thomas's violent rages.

Her mother brushed past her, opened the door and leaned inside. A moment later, the porch light came on before Dinah returned to the officer she'd been talking to.

This was the third time in the last month Meggie had called for help. It seemed as if this response would go much the same as the others.

Her burning, thumping scalp reminded her how Thomas had grabbed a fistful of her hair and dragged her down the hall and back to the living room. The moment she'd walked into the house, she'd heard Thomas screaming at her mother and she'd only wanted to get to her room before he saw her.

She hadn't succeeded.

The porch light worsened Meggie's headache, a glaring testament to a scene too often repeated. Her mom standing on the second step, speaking in measured tones, a smile plastered on her face. Her stepfather off to the side, affable and laughing, talking to the two male police officers who'd pulled him to the side.

The coolness of the evening washed over Meggie's face. If she'd still been crying, the breeze might have dried her tears. But nothing could calm her fears. No one cared anymore. The neighbors no longer bothered to come outside when the cruisers swerved up.

"I'm so sorry, Officer Landry," Dinah said in a calm, self-assured tone, so far from the truth of her personality that Meggie sometimes wondered if her mother had a split personality. "Girls my daughter's age are so emotional." She trilled laughter.

Meggie flinched at the high-pitched sound.

"I'm around them all day, five days a week during the school year."

Officer Landry returned Dinah's driver's license. "You're a schoolteacher?" she asked.

Dinah nodded, stuffing her ID into the pocket of her modest skirt. "An assistant principal."

A burst of male laughter rose into the air, momentarily drowning out Dinah and Officer Landry's conversation. Meggie tuned into her stepfather's words.

"The more her mother and me try to rein her in, the wilder she runs," Thomas Nicholls said. Affable. Convincing.

Lying.

Why hadn't she slept at Farrah's house again?

"She snuck off to some 4^(th) of July event after we told her she couldn't go." He glanced over his shoulder, glaring in Meggie's direction. "She comes home spoiling for a fight because her good-for-nothing father hasn't called her. My poor wife bends over backward for her. We give her everything."

Anger surged through Meggie. She'd heard enough. She'd *had* enough.

A small sound escaped her, because suddenly everyone fell silent. "He's lying," she said, not caring how angry her mother got. One day, Dinah would thank Meggie. Thomas would end up killing them.

"That's enough, Megan Foy," Dinah said in the stern voice she used on her students.

Meggie should know. She attended the same high school that Dinah served as assistant principal, next door to the middle school where Thomas taught math.

"Momma, enough—"

Dinah caught Meggie's arm. "May I take my daughter aside for a moment, Officer?"

"I don't want to listen to you," Meggie snapped before anyone spoke again.

"Do you see how disrespectful she is to her own mother?" Thomas lamented.

"*Die,*" Meggie snarled.

"I'll have you know, young lady, calling '911' with a false report is a crime," one of the cops who'd been talking to Thomas said. "If I talked to my stepfather the way you're talking to this fine man, my mother would've tanned my hide."

"You don't understand. It isn't false—"

"Meggie! Enough," Dinah said sharply. "Officer Landry, is it okay—"

"She's your kid, Dinah," Officer Landry said, eyeing Meggie with disgust.

"We're going to test your urine, miss," Thomas told her. "Make sure you don't have any more drugs in your system."

"Drugs?" Meggie gasped, so stunned by her stepfather's accusation that her muscles loosened and allowed Dinah to push her out of earshot.

"Please, Meggie?" Momma whispered, her eyes no longer lively but frantic and dull. Her lips trembled. "Don't do this."

"You stay," Meggie returned, her voice as low as her mother's. But she was shaking from anger and humiliation. She'd never touched drugs a day in her life. "I have to go. I can't stay here anymore with Thomas. You're letting him malign me. You know I'm not a drug addict. I don't smoke. I don't drink. I hadn't been home ten minutes before he hit me and continued beating you. He's your husband, not mine."

"Meggie, please. Don't leave me."

"Then leave with me."

"We've left twice. You know that. He found us both times."

The beating after their second escape attempt had been much more severe than the first.

"Don't ask me to do this."

"We're a team, you and me. I won't survive if you aren't here to put me back together."

Tears rushed to Meggie's eyes. "This is so unfair," she cried. "Why are you doing this to me?"

"You're my beautiful girl," Dinah whispered, no longer the self-assured woman she'd exhibited just minutes before. Fear wafted from her like steam from boiling water. She brushed strands of Meggie's hair aside. "You'd never forgive yourself if you convinced them to take you and something happened to me."

A sob broke free from Meggie.

"And suppose you are believed? What happens then? Thomas would be taken into custody. Possibly lose his teaching position. I would suffer untold humiliation. You'd be removed. Put in foster care. You're still three months from eighteen and we have no family to take you in."

Swiping at the tears falling down her cheeks, Meggie sniffled and lifted her chin. "I have Daddy."

"Big Joe?" Dinah scoffed. "We haven't heard from him in months."

"I wonder why," Meggie said with sarcasm. "You've barred him from visiting me more times than I can count. You sold the house he'd given us—"

"My allegiance is to Thomas, Meggie," Dinah spat. "I'm Mrs. Nicholls, *not* Mrs. Foy. Thomas didn't want to live in a house another man purchased for me."

"Daddy purchased that house for me, and you know it," Meggie blazed, hating Dinah the tiniest bit just then. Overwhelming guilt hit her, and she hung her head. "It doesn't matter, Momma. You gave Thomas the money from the sale, and he gambled it all away."

Dinah kissed Meggie's forehead. "I love you, Meggie. So very much. I'd be so lost without you." She shifted her weight. "W-wouldn't you miss me?"

"Of course!" Meggie said fiercely, the truth. She loved her mother so much. She just wished Dinah found the courage to break free of Thomas Nicholls.

"I'm going to send the officers away," Dinah said quietly, then turned away before Meggie responded.

Trembling, she stumbled to the edge of the porch to listen as Dinah fed Officer Landry a convincing lie. She wrapped her arms around her waist to keep from throwing up. She wanted to escape so badly, but what would happen to Dinah if she left? For that matter, *would* she end up in foster care?

"Meggie!"

She jumped at the sound of her momma's voice.

"The nice officer asked you a question."

"I'm sorry," Meggie said hoarsely, gritting her teeth at her trembling tone. "Can you repeat what you said, ma'am?"

The officer smiled, her face full of kindness. Meggie wondered what Dinah had said to change Officer Landry's attitude.

"Let me speak to you and your daughter a moment, Dinah," she said.

Meggie followed Dinah and Officer Landry to the same spot she'd spoken to her mother minutes ago.

"I understand if you don't feel safe enough to tell the truth within earshot of Mr. Nicholls," Officer Landry started, glancing between Meggie and Dinah. "Tell me now if there's cause to take him in, and we'll remove him from the premises."

Dinah placed a hand on her chest. "Michelle, your concern overwhelms me. I can't thank you enough for your interest, but I assure you we are fine. My husband is a big teddy bear. What happened tonight was just a misunderstanding. Meggie's angry at me because she thinks I'm keeping her father away. This was just her way of acting out."

Officer Landry folded her arms. "You're going to be a senior this year, Meggie?"

Meggie nodded.

"Any plans for college?"

"Yes, ma'am." She swallowed, not wanting to think about her mother's anger the time she'd confessed she wished for something completely different than a career.

"She wants to be a meteorologist," Dinah put in.

"Impressive," Officer Landry said, sounding as if she spoke the truth.

She dug in her shirt pocket, then handed Meggie a business card. "If you want to talk to me about anything—anything at all—give me a call."

Meggie glanced at the card, only then realizing the blue and red lights continued to swirl; all her aches and pain still beat against her nerve endings. Anger and determination had blotted both. Now, as her despair and hopelessness returned, so too did her awareness. She nodded to the officer. "Thank you," she said softly, offering a tremulous smile. "May I go inside? I'm very tired."

"Wait for me in the living room," Dinah instructed.

"Okay, Momma." She walked inside. Not having the energy to defy Dinah, Meggie veered into the living room instead of continuing down the hall and waited, forcing all thought from her head.

Why think about it when she knew what to expect?

Within five minutes, Dinah and Thomas joined Meggie in the living room.

Thomas snatched Officer Landry's business card from Meggie's hand and ripped it up.

"You little cunt," he snarled.

She'd forgotten to hide another razor blade underneath the sofa cushion. Why hadn't she remembered?

"Do you hear me talking to you, bitch?"

Peeking at Dinah, Meggie felt the plea in her expression. The need for Dinah to do something, *say something*, rose swift and hot inside her.

He glared at Dinah. "You never fucking learn, do you?"

"I'm sorry," Dinah blurted, tears already in her eyes. "But what did we do? We sent them away, so—"

Thomas struck Dinah across the face.

Meggie cringed, and still she waited for her turn.

"Shut your fucking mouth," Thomas yelled, hitting Dinah again, this time so hard she fell to the floor, where she stayed and sobbed.

"You think you're better than me, Meggie?" he asked.

Not answering, Meggie stared at Dinah, not truly seeing her, but unable *not* to see her.

He grabbed Meggie by the throat, then shoved her in the direction of the sofa. She landed nearby. Hearing Thomas unfastening his belt, she scrambled to her feet. If he began wielding that leather while she was on the floor, he might strike her face. As it was, the licks caught her back and legs. The T-shirt absorbed some of the blows, but her thighs and legs were exposed in the shorts she wore.

Ten heavy-handed hits later, Meggie curled in a heap, near where her mother still lay—still in tears.

Thomas dragged Dinah to her feet.

"No! Stop," she cried. "Meggie won't do it again. You've beaten her already. Please leave me be."

"Weak bitch," Thomas muttered in disgust, punching Dinah in her belly and watching as she fell to the floor again.

"It hurts, Meggie," Dinah whimpered. "It hurts."

Meggie blinked at the ceiling. "It'll be fine, Momma. I'll get you water and a pain reliever."

"Hurry."

"You don't need that," Thomas said, his voice changing to a disgusting croon. "Keep your daughter in line, Dinah. For now, I've taken care of her. Let me make you feel better."

"I-I'll feel better if you let me suck you. I know you'll feel good, my love."

Refusing to stay for the next sad act in this tragic play, Meggie crawled to her hands and knees, and willed herself to stand. She stumbled toward the hallway, just as Thomas dropped his pants and his pasty white butt cheeks bid her farewell.

Chapter Three

Seven Weeks Later...

Meggie

"**N**O! PLEASE. *STOP!*"

The crack of a hand connecting with flesh tore through the tension. Meggie jumped and wrapped her arms around her middle, her sob competing with her mother's pleas. She sat on the edge of her bed, body trembling, praying her mother would survive this latest beating.

Another lick. Dinah wept and Meggie's belly roiled at the tormented sounds.

"Please, Thomas," Dinah cried. "You've got to stop!"

Meggie nodded vigorously. Yes, he had to stop. One of these days he'd kill her mom.

Glass shattered and furniture banged. Dry heaves wracked Meggie at the heavy thud. She knew that sound—her mother was careening to the floor. Dinah screamed and Meggie doubled over, sweat popping off her skin, her mother's pain her own.

Surrounded by her white bedroom furniture and pastel green décor, Meggie wondered once more how her home life was such a nightmare. On the outside, everyone saw the perfect family—a woman, an assistant high school principal, finding happiness in her second marriage with the teddy bear of a middle school math teacher who'd stepped in as a father figure to the woman's daughter.

All those thoughts mirrored the ones she'd had seven weeks ago, except today Meggie was weeks away from her eighteenth birthday and days away from starting her senior year.

Once she graduated, she'd give her mother the option of leaving with her, but Meggie wouldn't stay under this roof one day longer. She'd spend the next nine months planting the seeds of escape in Dinah's head.

Maybe, that's where Meggie had erred. She'd demanded Dinah leave without warning. This way, while Meggie worked on graduating, she would get her mother used to the idea that they *had* to leave.

Dinah's scream coupled with tearing clothes. Though not in the den, Meggie had seen the situation play out enough to pick out the sounds and their meanings.

"Please," Dinah sobbed. "I don't want to."

She didn't want to have sex, she meant. Meggie bowed her head into her hands, wishing for the strength and fortitude to kill her stepfather.

"Let's go to the bedroom." Dinah's breath caught around a moan.

Thomas grunted. "I'm fucking you right here. Right out in the open."

Embarrassment competed with Meggie's fear and anger.

Her mother's next sob burned through Meggie, and she covered her face.

"Don't. Not in the den. I don't want Meggie to hear."

"Think she's not fucking?"

No. Meggie bit into her wrist, barely feeling the injury but tasting metallic blood.

"No," Dinah echoed through tears. "She's a virgin."

"No. She's not," Thomas sneered. "I should know."

Oh God. Oh God. Oh God. Meggie stared at her bite mark, oozing red, and shook her head in denial.

Silence met Thomas's lie and he took advantage of the stunning insinuation by taunting, "she's been coming on to me for months. I thought it best to keep it in the family."

"Wh-what?"

Meggie wasn't sure if she wanted her mother to believe Thomas or not. Dinah was too broken to defend her. She hadn't even allowed the police to haul Thomas away, a week ago, when Meggie had called 911 once again, something she hadn't done since July 4th. Unlike in July, Dinah had blamed her injuries on something asinine and stupid this time. For Meggie's attempt to defend Dinah that night, she'd gotten her bedroom door removed.

"You lying bastard," Dinah screamed.

Meggie drew in a sharp breath, her already aggravated pulse and heart rate throbbing in her ears. She spread her blood over her skin, attempting to refocus.

Thomas yelped and, for a few blessed moments, it sounded as if Dinah asserted herself and inflicted serious damage.

"You fucking bitch!" he snarled. "I'm going to kill you."

"Big Joe is coming for her," Dinah persisted in a wild, unrecognizable tone. "I called him! And I'm going to tell him. I'm going to tell him you've violated his baby. I'm going to tell him and he's going to kill you. He's going to chop your dick off and feed it to pigs."

Meggie cheered at the thought. Her daddy was coming. She'd been trying to reach him with renewed vigor for weeks. Left so many messages, it surprised her his voicemail wasn't full. He was very busy, so the fact that he hadn't answered wasn't really surprising.

Sometimes, it took her months to get a response from him. Before, he'd just blaze into town on his bike, the noise of his Harley pipes rumbling in the quiet suburb, blocks away. He took a lot of trips, something he called runs.

Ever since Dinah had barred him from visiting at Thomas's insistence, Meggie always imagined going on the road with him and his boys.

"You know how hard your fighting makes me, huh, baby?" Thomas crooned.

"Y-yes."

"I'm not letting Megan live with him. When he comes, tell him she's not interested in going with him." Thomas groaned and gasped. "Tell him she doesn't want to see him. Ever again."

Dinah moaned. "Right there, Thomas. Harder."

Meggie's cheeks burned and her stomach churned at Thomas's filthy response. And so the cycle continued, she thought, humiliated. She stretched to her pillow and retrieved the little knife she kept hidden under it. Pressing the sharp blade against her forearm, she sliced down, sucking in a breath at the brief burn and pain. Blood rushed from the wound and her tension and fear seeped away with it. The respite lasted a moment. The satisfaction dwindled in the amount of time it took the pain to recede.

Sniffling, she tightened her mouth and slashed again. Meggie swiped her tears once more and cut at the wrist she'd bitten.

"Ah, God!" She'd gone deeper than she intended and had to grab the sheet to staunch the flow of blood, the sounds from the den both sickening and infuriating. She wasn't sure if her mother truly liked Thomas's attention or if she just accepted it. In the end, no matter what Thomas said or did, Dinah gave him sex. Meggie didn't want to see her mother as a weak, pathetic woman because it went deeper than that.

Dinah had tried to run, Meggie reminded herself. Both times Thomas had found her and beaten her to a bloody pulp before using his fists on Meggie. Her momma had just given up and given in. She knew Dinah refused to risk Meggie being hurt again because of her escape attempts.

"Meggie?"

She raised her gaze at the sound of her mother's whimper. Dinah stood in the doorway, her face swollen and bloody, bruises covering her naked body. She clutched the wood molding, trembling.

The sight tore through Meggie and she shoved her knife under the bloody sheet. She stood and swallowed; her chin wobbled. Both she and her mother were wrecks, but she couldn't add any stress by allowing her injuries to show. She stepped forward, arms behind her back. "Momma."

Dinah went sprawling and Meggie hurried to the door. Thomas stood inches away, naked, too, and smelling of sweat and alcohol. Unable to hide her derision, Meggie glared at him, her cheeks burning at the sight of his flaccid penis and hairy testicles. Not that she hadn't seen him nude before, but the spectacle always repulsed her.

The back of his hand shot out. Meggie didn't jump away fast enough. Stars danced in front of her eyes at the slap.

"Please. Not Meggie," Dinah whined, prone on the squeaky-clean linoleum.

Thomas kicked Dinah's thigh and she whimpered again. Meggie growled and launched herself at Thomas, buoyed by the thought of her father coming for her, not caring if Thomas beat the crap of her. She'd learned to cover her pain and bruises, but she wouldn't have to. She could show each little hurt to her daddy and he'd find a way to make them go away. He'd make *him* go away.

Her fingernails dug into Thomas's cheek and she drew them down, drawing blood just like he drew her mother's blood and sometimes hers. He grabbed her upper arms and slammed her against the wall. Meggie bounced and stumbled onto Dinah, who lay silent and still, but warm, the rise of fall of her back assuring she lived. Thomas yanked Meggie to her feet by her hair. She kicked, connecting with his penis and he dropped to his knees.

Meggie blew out puffs of air, not having much time. Steeped in drunken insanity, Thomas's meanness and strength rivaled a dozen men. She doubted he'd even feel a bullet.

Stupid bull of a man.

Ignoring her pain, she scrambled to her mother and latched onto her hands, pulling her forward. "Come on, Momma. Help me."

She needed to get them to Dinah's bedroom. Just until Thomas drank himself into a stupor and passed out. If she couldn't convince Dinah the wisdom of leaving while Thomas slept off the vodka and bourbon, then, at least, the latest danger would pass. Thomas would be sick for a day and sober for a couple more. Sometimes, he even went a week without drinking. Sober, his hits lacked so much viciousness and murderous intent.

Meggie pulled Dinah another inch and her mother groaned. Thomas roared to his feet. She didn't want to leave her mother, but her sense of self-preservation took over. Dropping Dinah's arms, Meggie stumbled toward the nearest door, the half bath right next to her bedroom. His arms encircled her waist. He lifted her off her feet. Meggie screamed, struggling in his arms.

He stepped over Dinah, a firm grip on Meggie, and walked into her bedroom. Reaching her bed, he slammed her down. She sprung up and barreled into him, the maneuver useless. When his hand neared her, somehow, she dodged it and, instead, sunk her teeth into the fleshy side.

"Bitch!" he yelled, crashing his fist on the side of her head and her world went black.

Meggie ached everywhere – her face, arms, hands, belly, thighs, knees, legs and feet. Even the top of her head and her breasts throbbed. Wincing, she lifted herself on her elbows, the moonlight reflecting on her bare body. Blood and bruises glimmered in a grotesque sheen, and she shivered, her skin burning, her insides cold. Whatever sick twist in the universe sent Thomas into their lives wrapped itself tighter and tighter.

Feeling the pain of Thomas's rage sweeping through her body, she understood her mother's decisions. It was the other times. The times when she only listened and witnessed, she resented Dinah's inaction. She sniffled and fell back onto her pillows, tears slipping down her cheeks. The two of them gave bodies of evidence a literal meaning. On them lay a wealth of substantiation Thomas was a violent pig. Then, again, on them a mountain of proof validated Dinah had bad taste in men.

Meggie thought her mother had all types of demons to contend with. While she could always judge Dinah, tell her life happened, she knew so many other factors were in this twisted tale; therefore, her inaction could be overlooked and excusable. Meggie's couldn't.

Dinah never battled her husband. Meggie's sense of outrage overwhelmed her at times, and she couldn't help but fight back but there was absolutely no winning with Thomas. Unless they ended up on an outpost in Antarctica, he'd always find them and hurt them. One day, he'd kill them if Meggie didn't do something.

That her mother had done one small thing and telephoned Big Joe was enough. Thomas wasn't going to allow her to leave. No, he wanted to sever all ties between her and her father. But Meggie couldn't allow that to happen. Her father would protect her and rescue Dinah. No matter what else had passed between him and Dinah, he loved Meggie enough that he'd want to see her mother safe.

She swiped the backs of her hands across her cheeks, pain shooting through her at the skim over her welts, bruises, and self-inflicted injuries. "Ow!"

It was the weekend, so Momma had the day off but they'd both returned to work a few days ago. Meggie's school year began in under two weeks. At one time, Thomas was cognizant of time and place.

Every now and then he'd deliver slaps and punches in a place where bruises couldn't be hidden. Mostly, he'd kept his abuse below the neck on them. Now, he no longer cared where his hits landed. His drinking and gambling were out of control and his wild violence was intensifying.

The overhead light flipped on, and Meggie blinked, the sudden brightness hurting her eyes. She curled her knees into her chest, praying for the ability to disappear. By the time she came to, Dinah and Thomas had been locked in their bedroom. Meggie had dragged herself to her bed, just over an hour ago, taking comfort in her surroundings, which reminded her of happier times. All around her were items she and her mother had chosen when Meggie turned thirteen. A redecorated room in their old house had been her birthday present. No expense had been spared, courtesy of her father. Meggie loved Monet and had a replica of *Renoir Painting In His Garden* hanging on her wall. Another wall had a framed print of Minnie Mouse with the words *Explore the Magic Inside*. Pretty lame, she knew, but she really liked Minnie Mouse.

Not long after, they moved into Thomas's place. She'd been so relieved that her mother allowed her to bring all her new decorations and furnishings.

"Girl."

Gritting her teeth, Meggie pretended she didn't hear Thomas, just as she'd zoned out the glare of the light when he'd walked in. Pink roses entwined with green vines were etched on the scalloped headboard on her bed. The footboard wasn't so fancy.

Meggie huddled closer to the wall, searching for her knife but finding the razor blade she'd stashed a week ago.

Thomas's heavy breathing polluted the air and grated on Meggie's nerves. She clenched her teeth, pretending he wasn't there, and raised the front of her gown. Thin silvery lines crisscrossed her outer thighs, mapping all the places she controlled what happened to her body. He was moving around in the room, but she didn't care. She knew what was coming, so she pushed his presence out of her head and ran her fingers through her pubic hair. It was so soft, unlike Thomas's. She swallowed, held her breath, and dug the blade into the flesh on her hip, slicing straight, neat and not very deep, moaning at the pressure, the sting. The hurt.

"Scoot over."

She did as instructed, shuddering when he pulled her into his arms and pinched her nipples. She dragged the blade through her upper thigh, the new wounds mingling with the older ones, and blessed numbness embracing her. He shoved her nightgown above her waist and bit into her shoulder. In her head, she recited the words to her favorite song, fisting the blade in her hand, the pain tearing through her just as Thomas inserted his finger...*there.*

"Your ass is made for fucking," he breathed.

Warm blood ran down her hand, joining the dried blood from earlier. He fumbled in his pajamas, his finger going in and out of her.

She remained quiet, still, the song beating through her head, her blood sliding down her skin. The overhead light reflected against her window, but Meggie concentrated and found the prettiness of the night. The clear, velvety brightness of the sky. The...

He shoved his flaccid penis against her, and Meggie whimpered, unable to stop it. One day, he'd be sober enough to get a real erection. One day, he'd hurt her rather than just humiliate her. If she didn't act. She trembled, her body a desert of pain and a tundra of shame, layered, hot on top of cold and cold on top of hot.

His hand fluttered across her belly and teased her pubic hair. Cutting her other wrist, Meggie closed her eyes, able to cope and pretend this was a man she *wanted* to make love with. The man who'd love and protect her. He'd listen to Bruno Mars and Miley Cyrus and Adele and Alicia Keys with her. He'd overlook her shame and what she couldn't control and what she willingly did.

God, please. She *would* find that man. She *had* to.

Thomas's fingers squeezed her clitoris and Meggie tensed, his alcohol-laced breath fanning across her cheek. She was as much a coward as her mother. If she had courage, she'd slice Thomas to pieces. Kill him with her bare hands, all five feet eleven inches and two-hundred-fifty pounds of the mean pig.

"I'm gonna fuck you soon."

Revulsion turned her stomach, competing with all her other emotions and aches. Dinah didn't know how far Thomas had gone with Meggie over the past few months and she worried, if she told her mother, Dinah would be too frightened to do anything about it.

"Your stupid bitch Momma refuses to put you on the pill." He licked her ear and snickered, pulling back before slamming against her again. "I bet she will now after I kicked her ass tonight and showed her how I intend to fuck you."

Big, overgrown tyrannosaurus rex. Under the guise of trying to free herself and knowing she couldn't, Meggie jerked her elbow back and thunked his nose. The sharp intake of his breath made the hard slap against her belly he punished her with worth the pain.

He removed his hand from her clit. "Cold, fucking whore. Can't even come when I'm rubbing your pussy."

The scent of alcohol seeped through his pores. His sweat dripped onto her face, mixing with her tears. She wouldn't allow this man to ruin her. Never. She hadn't ever lived anywhere except with her mother, but she had to get to her father. It didn't matter that she'd have to drop out of high school in her senior year. Neither did it matter that her father headed the Death Dwellers' MC, a club of motorcycle enthusiasts. He'd welcome her and he'd get her mother away. She'd call and, if he didn't answer, she'd leave a message and tell him she'd come to him. He didn't have to pick her up.

Thomas grunted and then stiffened before shuddering and relaxing his grip on her. A moment later, he yanked her face to the side, almost breaking her neck. He planted his mouth over hers and shoved his tongue past her lips.

Thomas cupped Meggie's sex and squeezed. "I want all that innocence between your legs. Your father will never get you. Never. You're mine."

Though she should've known better, she couldn't help her resistance, which only infuriated Thomas more. He cuffed the side of her head and stars danced in front of her, lulling her to the darkness. She resisted, refusing to give in so completely. If she didn't run away, he'd ruin her before finally murdering her. Dinah had married this pig. Meggie hadn't and determination to get away from his sick perversions possessed her.

He leaned in and Meggie spat in his face, then threw her hands over her head to protect herself. He shoved her onto her back, ignoring the cuts she'd done because they were interspersed with bruises he'd caused. He stretched out on top of her, and her body screamed in pain. Hatred flowed between them, and she almost wished one of them would end it for the other.

But she didn't want to die. Not really. She just wanted to escape and be in control of her body. She wanted someone to love her and shield her. Until she got to her daddy, though, responsibility for her well-being fell on her shoulders. She tried to gulp in air, but her lungs struggled for oxygen, Thomas's heavy weight crushing her and placing her well-being in dire jeopardy.

Momma, please, where are you?

Beaten and brutalized and in her bedroom.

Meggie brought her blade to his cheek, furious. Caught off guard, Thomas clutched his cheek and fell to her side. She scrambled over him and off her bed, just managing to evade his grasping hands.

"You little fucking slut! I'm going to kill you."

Blood dripped from a variety of wounds on her body, so she couldn't hide in the secret cupboard she'd found. A trail of blood would lead him straight to her. Instead, she ran into the bathroom and locked the door.

Meggie rushed to the window over the sink. She kept it unlocked for this reason, learned from almost five years of living with this. Thomas kicked at the door and she shuddered, sorry she hadn't told her father the truth when Dinah first barred him from visiting anymore. He'd asked her the last time he stopped by.

"Talk to me, Meggie. Is there anything I should know?"

"No, Daddy. I swear, we're fine."

His blue eyes, so like hers, took in every last detail of her features, then he nodded. He seemed old in that instant, tired, and so sad Meggie wanted to cry.

"So your momma just want to cut me out like that? All because the asshole she married don't like me."

"I guess, Daddy," she whispered. The truth lodged in her throat, right on the edge of her lips. Big Joe looked tall and intimidating, his blond hair reminiscent of a Berserker rather than a modern-day motorcycle man. If nothing else, he'd take her with him. But then, she'd have to leave Dinah behind, and she couldn't bear to think of her mother being alone with Thomas. "They just told me last night." She mumbled the fib.

Big Joe crouched to her eye level, a feat considering she was five feet, and he was over six. "You don't lie good, sweetheart."

She lowered her lashes, embarrassed she'd been caught. Her arms throbbed from her cuts. New ones. Old ones. Partially healed ones. Her long sleeves hid the wounds from her father, but the guilt of the injuries weighed upon her.

Another moment of silence went by before he turned on his heel and headed for his bike. Before climbing on, he shoved money into her hands. "Go shopping. Cheer yourself up."

Shopping sounded good. She nodded and embraced him, her world a train of dominoes collapsing at a reckless speed.

"You need me, call. I'm a phone call away. Remember, you're my *daughter. No matter what that asshole says to you, don't believe shit. The problem is his, not yours."*

Thomas's words weren't the problem. It was his actions.

"If the fucker does anything," Big Joe continued, like he'd seen her thoughts, "that's when he's going to have real problems. Understand, Megan?"

That had been the last time she'd seen her father and that conversation haunted her. So much could've been different if she'd spoken up.

Meggie climbed onto the bathroom counter and wriggled through the window, feet first. Another exercise borne of desperation. Just as the door crashed open, she landed on the ground outside. Grimacing at the pain, she headed to the clearing behind the house.

"Megan! Where the fuck are you?" The call, through the open window he couldn't fit through, resounded in the quiet night.

She reached her favorite tree, the smell of the spruce and bark and grassy earth calming her, soothing the exhaustion overtaking her. Thomas would pass out soon enough.

Meggie just had to bide her time and wait.

Chapter Four

THREE WEEKS LATER...

Meggie

DARKNESS SLITHERED AROUND MEGGIE, THE 'L' shaped alleyway her last means of escape. She paused to hurl her ballerina flats in the direction of her pursuers. Cold pierced her feet, reminding her she no longer had a jacket or socks. If she got away, she'd freeze to death.

She stumbled past a dumpster and the scent of garbage and urine turned her stomach. Had she eaten any substantial meal recently, she would've puked it up. Blackness colored the sky. No moon. No stars. Just a blanket of darkness that made the buildings close in on her. Fear chilled her blood and the frigid air seeped into her pores. But nothing mattered now, except escape. Not the glass shards strewn about in the alleyway and stabbing her bare feet or the icy weather.

Her instinct of survival, the need to outrun her pursuers, made everything else seem little more than trivialities.

Her heart pumping, Meggie rounded the corner. Her lack of familiarity with the area hindered her and she skidded to a stop, air escaping her lungs in short bursts of breath. Some of the men chasing her were already there, blocking her exit, waiting for her. To rape her. To kill her. She wasn't sure, and she had no wish to find out.

Panicked, she glanced over her shoulder. The other three men were closing in on her and blood roared in her ears.

The smell of beer and sweat twisted around her as the men circled her.

Pain careened through her frozen, cut feet, most of her hope gone. But she had a mission, one to save her mother *and* herself. She couldn't fail. She wouldn't.

"Where's the money, bitch?"

"I-I don't know what you're talking about, Rack." Her stomach growled.

"The money, Meggie. Not only do I want my money, I might help myself to whatever other coins and bills I find on you."

She didn't have money. They knew that. That's why she'd followed them into the bar and lifted the five-dollar bill. Should she hand the cash back or deny she had it? The money rubbed against her breast, a guilty weight inside her bra. What was the code of the street, anyway?

After a month of being a runaway, her exhaustion claimed what her stepfather hadn't been able to: her hope and determination. She wanted to live, but she barely had the strength to hold on. Instead of sneaking away to find her father to demand he help the morning after Thomas's last degradation, she should've remained at home and allowed her stepfather to molest her and continue to watch him beat the crap out of her mother until Big Joe arrived. She'd been so sure leaving was the right thing to do. Head off Thomas's determination to keep her away from her father while saving herself from him. She shouldn't have left her mother's house. She could've dealt with

Thomas. Anything, *anything* rather than the animalistic way she'd been living.

A hand gripped her forearm and she looked up. Rack hacked a cough, then sent a stream of spit near her bare feet. *Big ass.* She couldn't discern his features tonight. The dark alleyway swallowed his black hair and beard.

He shook her. "Where. The. Fuck. Is. My. Money?"

Her body trembled. She hadn't eaten in two days and today, her eighteenth birthday, she wanted food from McDonald's. She shouldn't have stolen, especially from her father's, um, men, but he'd repay them. She just needed to *find* him. "I'm hungry," she said quietly. She didn't mention her birthday to Rack. He wouldn't care.

"How the fuck is that my problem?" he sneered.

Meggie had met him the first night she'd gone to the compound to find her father. Rack had been locking up and refused to allow her entrance. She'd begged and pleaded for him to summon Joseph "Boss" Foy. He hadn't listened, just told her that wouldn't happen.

One night, not long afterwards, as she'd passed by a dive, she'd noticed several motorcycles lined up outside the establishment and decided to go in, thinking, perhaps, one of the bikers would know her father. It wasn't a big city, but a small town in Washington State, along the Columbia River. How many other big compounds on the outskirts of town housing a notorious MC with a morbid and creepy name like the Death Dwellers were in the place?

The moment she'd entered the bar, she'd run smack dab into Rack and introductions had been made. She'd only given her nickname— Meggie. His guarded study of her had raised her suspicions and she'd decided against identifying Boss as her father. *Then. Now* was a different story. Unlike the night she met Rack, he wore his vest with the patches proclaiming him a Death Dweller.

They wouldn't want to hurt the daughter of the club's president. Would they?

Meggie licked her lips. "It might be your problem if you hurt me."

He pressed his nose against hers. "Ya think? This shit should be interesting. I'm all ears."

"Boss…Joe Foy—" She frowned at the snickers.

"Yeah?" Rack prompted. "Boss…Joe Foy…what?"

"My daddy. He's m-my daddy," Meggie whispered. And, this time, her voice did tremble.

OUTLAW

Outlaw growled in approval at the pink flesh descending toward his hungry mouth. His tongue met wet pussy, his fingers digging into the hips of the other bitch riding his dick. The one on his mouth wiggled and he lapped her juices, satisfied at the identical squeals and moans the two were making. She hammered her pussy against his lips. He thrust his tongue into her entrance and swirled, matching the thrust of his cock and the quick swivel of his hips.

Fuck, but these bitches were good. He'd been fucking the two of them almost exclusively on a regular basis for six months and saw no sign of tiring of them. Kiera and Ellen, Club Ass with a long history with the club. Dweller Girls he'd randomly picked one evening to be his, out of sheer boredom. They thought to change his mind and wanted him to pick one.

Nah, bitches. They'd be in his bed his way or no way, a point they'd quickly picked up on. After the first night of fucking, he'd left it up to them to decide. If they wanted to continue to fuck only him and be called 'his', they'd have to tag team him. Otherwise, they could move the fuck on and so would he.

They'd chosen wisely.

In the background, Hendrix's rendition of *Voodoo Child* played on repeat. Outlaw thought the song the most appropriate since them two bitches had used their pussies and mouths to put a spell on him and his dick. Truth was, he had a soft spot for Kiera with her olive complexion and black hair long enough to cover the aureoles on her very delectable breasts.

Kiera was so easygoing. If she hadn't fucked most of the other brothers, Outlaw might've considered throwing Ellen aside and making Kiera his old lady. She was twenty-five, a perfect age to his way of thinking. Still young enough not to hear the tick-tock of the internal clock women freaked over, but old enough where she'd lived a little, had her own job and her own place. She was faultless, but for her whoring. Sharing a bitch was cool, but Outlaw refused to bring said bitch to meet his ma, knowing Patricia's feelings. Most of the club knew the feel of Kiera's pussy, so she remained just pussy to him and he'd keep it that way.

Ellen, on the other hand, was only two years younger than he was. She'd started intruding on his space and time *without* Kiera. Her actions and growing possessiveness just showed Outlaw the bitch had no loyalty to a girl she called a sister. Ellen smiled in Kiera's face, fucked her when Outlaw ordered, while steadily trying to move her out of their ménage-a-trois. She also sucked good dick and did whatever shit Outlaw or any of the other boys asked of her.

Was he really fucking thinking about this shit *now*? With his dick in Kiera and his tongue in Ellen? Well, fuck. Maybe, the charms of their pussies were wearing away. Determined to focus on fucking, Outlaw nipped Ellen's clit and she squealed, grinding her pussy against his mouth, starting to come. She finished with a harsh groan, then fell in a weightless heap next to him. Outlaw raised his head, met Kiera's dark eyes and gave her a half-smile. He wrapped an arm around her waist and turned over, readjusting her long legs so her knees were on her shoulders. He sank deeper into her, his growl matching her soft sigh. He slammed into her harder and she came, crying out, pumping against him to milk his own release.

Outlaw grunted, cum shooting from him in a hot spurt. Kiera

giggled, then pressed a barely-there kiss against his sweaty neck. Unable to help himself, he smiled down at her and brushed a few damp, dark strands of her hair behind her ear. Drawing in a couple more deep breaths, he withdrew from her and pulled the condom off his dick.

Fuck, he had nothing to wrap it in. He'd have to take care of the shit later. Right now, he intended to prime the girls for their next fuck. This time, Kiera would fuck his mouth while Ellen rode his dick. He reached over and set the condom on the table next to the bed.

A pound came on his door. "Outlaw!"

Raising his head, he scowled. "Get the fuck away from my door, Rack," he snarled. He didn't feel like fucking with that motherfucker right now. He wanted to empty his balls a little more. That door served as the dividing line between *him* and *them*. Them being the motherfuckers plotting his demise. He just hadn't been able to weed out who refused to pledge their undying loyalty to him.

He guided Kiera onto her back and rolled a nipple between his fingertips.

"This have to do with Boss," Rack called. "I need you out here, now, brother."

Boss? *Fuck*. Sitting up, Outlaw scrubbed a hand over his face. He stared at the bare brick wall, on the other side of the bed, praying the motherfucker was burning in hell. Even dead, Joseph Fucking Foy fucked with him. If he could kill the assfuck again, he'd dig him up piece by piece and fuck him up just because he'd been such a motherfucker.

But Rack hadn't mentioned Boss to him since the man's death last year. For him to do it now, coming upon his one-year anniversary, and in such an urgent voice meant something not good. He started to rise.

Kiera caught his arm. "Don't, baby," she whispered, her eyes huge and pleading. "Rack still got beef with you for what went down with Boss. This may be some trap or setup."

No shit. But Outlaw hadn't ever run from shit and wouldn't ever run from shit. He hadn't run from his reason for existing—the rape of his gentle mother—or the cloud that'd hung over his head for years because of that. Her father had seen him as the reason for all the woes in his mother's life. Not the motherfucker who'd forced him into his mother's belly. No. *Him.* So, no, he didn't run from shit. He hadn't run from fucking Boss in life, so he sure as hell wouldn't run from the motherfucker in death. He kissed Kiera's temple and sat up.

"Fuck! Outlaw! Get the fuck out here, man."

"Hold your fuckin' fat balls," he growled. He navigated around a sleeping Ellen, grabbed his jeans and pulled them on. Picking up his piece, he shoved the barrel into his pocket. He grabbed a lighter and his smokes, then sauntered to the door and threw it open. Not bothering to look at Rack, he lit up. A nicotine fix would get him through the next few minutes. He drew in, then released the smoke through his nostrils. Throughout his display, Rack remained quiet. He sucked on the cigarette again. "Boss," he said impatiently, playing the motherfucker's game and breaking the silence first. "What 'bout the assfuck?"

Rack attempted a sneak peek into Outlaw's room, but he wouldn't give the fuckhead the satisfaction. *Motherfucker.* Now, there was a name for Rack. Yeah, Outlaw should rip the VP patch off and replace it with Fucked up Fucking Fuckhead. Perfect.

"You ever hear Boss talk about his other kid? A girl about sixteen, seventeen, some shit like that?"

Although Outlaw didn't want to remember, he did. At one time, whenever he and Outlaw went on a run, Boss talked about her. A beauty, he always bragged, who wanted to become a meteorologist.

"She's a beauty. Like Dinah, her Momma. My girl has my eyes, though. You'd know she's mine just by those blue orbs of hers."

Outlaw smiled at the reverence in Boss's voice and awe in his eyes. He clearly loved the two. Until Boss, the only other man who'd shown him any fatherly attention was his sisters' dad. His maternal grandfather had hated him, and his father had been a piece of shit.

Boss reared back in his seat. They were in the office, just the two of them, sharing a drink and going over profit and loss in cash and bodies. It was midday, quiet, everyone sleeping off the prior night's events, over at the warehouses prepping gun and drug shipments, or out on club runs.

"Whatcha beauty name?"

"Don't worry about that, asshole. She ain't for this life and you ain't for no other life."

No, he wasn't. He knew that. He knew he shouldn't have been born. He'd come from scum, and he'd become scum. It was a fact of his life, one he'd accepted a long time ago. He looked out at the bright sky, high above the tall trees edging the back of the property, a restful view framed in the office window.

"Didn't mean that the way you takin' it, son," Boss said gruffly, slamming his empty glass down. He grabbed the bottle of tequila and filled it to the brim. "I just meant my girl is my little princess. Give her whatever she wants whenever she wants. She even got my last name, just like my boy."

As usual, Boss was right. The bitch wasn't for him. She sounded like a spoiled little cunt.

"Give Dinah whatever she wants, too." He frowned, downed half the contents of his glass. "Or I did 'til she met the asshole she's married to."

Outlaw didn't say shit, but fuck him, if Boss didn't sound like a lost puppy when he mentioned this bitch.

He smiled, his eyes red-rimmed. "Don't need Snake finding out about my girl and I know you two assholes are friends when you aren't involved in pissing contests." He sniggered at Outlaw's scowl. "Boy has enough issues. Don't need him finding out about a little sister I never told him about."

Outlaw grunted, not bothering to comment. Snake didn't take surprises well.

Outlaw's resentment spiked toward Boss. He should've known he couldn't keep his fucking mouth shut about the bitch. Even if he hadn't said anything to his psycho son, he sure as fuck told Rack about her. Just more evidence he'd never been special to Boss, like another son, with secrets shared only between them. The confidences Boss shared with Outlaw was just a lie. No, he'd said all that bullshit to get Outlaw under his thumb.

"Outlaw? You hear me?"

"What 'bout the bitch?" he asked, dragging on his cigarette again.

How many other people knew about the little cunt? *Great fucking going, Boss.*

A scream rose above the music and laughter humming in the background. Then silence. Complete and utter silence. Rack winced. Outlaw pulled his nine, a reflex reaction, and started down the hallway. Light reflected off the gigantic mural of the Grim Reaper, his scythe dripping blood, his eye sockets burning red.

"Daddy!"

The wail pierced the sudden stillness as he rounded the corner. A little blonde urchin barreled into him, and semi-peaceful waves kicked into his brain. She stopped, his gun inches from her head and he loosened his grip.

He stared into familiar eyes. Blue. Intense. Brilliant. A perfect mirror of the former president of his MC. Only these eyes were *un*familiar. And not because of the dark circles ringing them.

They were the eyes of the daughter of the man he'd killed.

Chapter Five

Meggie

A GUN. MEGGIE HAD A GUN IN HER FACE, POINTED at her head. The man holding the gun could be a sex symbol women all over the world drooled after. Muscles swelled from his tatted arms. Broad shoulders and a wide chest narrowed to ripped abs and…and he stood, tall and tempting and all but naked. Despite her best effort, her eyes insisted on roaming to his unfastened jeans. Black pubic hair and part of his penis showed.

The gun should be more important, but she'd never seen such a beautiful man before. A beautiful, nearly unclothed man. The one man she *had* seen naked…*God. That* man and this one was worlds apart. Her stepfather reminded her of the Pillsbury Doughboy, soft and pudgy. This man had muscles rippling from his broad shoulders down his flat stomach. They defined his biceps and abs. The tattoos on his arms and chest flexed with power. A Grim Reaper with burning red eye sockets and a bloody scythe floated on his left bicep, sliding onto the Celtic cross wrapped in roses on his forearm.

But his penis kept drawing her attention.

"What the fuck you want?"

Meggie blinked and jumped. The edge in the words hardened his voice, made him appear scary. She'd come this far, though, escaping whatever Rack intended for her over five measly dollars. She made herself meet his green gaze and ignore the weapon. "I want my daddy."

A heartbeat pulsed by before he lowered his gun and stuffed it partially in the front pocket of his jeans. His thick, black hair lay in complete disarray, swatches of it falling onto his forehead. Her errant gaze refused to stay on his face and insisted on traveling down to his penis and upwards over his perfect six pack to his amazing face. He smiled, a wicked gleam in his eyes, as if he knew how he affected her.

She limped a step back and winced at the pain. The heat sweeping through her body, pulling at her belly and nipples had nothing to do with her foot injuries.

"Boss your pops?"

She swore recognition flashed in his eyes when he first saw her. Obviously, she'd been mistaken. She nodded. "Yes."

He tipped her chin up, his fingertips rough against her skin. Stubble shadowed his strong jaw. Coupled with his enticing lips, he had a dangerous aura. He smelled of musk, smoke, and something wild and ripe, mixing with the underlay of his unique scent.

He rubbed his thumb over her lips, and they parted, her heart jumping and her breath shortening. His fingers slid through her hair and exhaustion pressed in on her. She was so tired and so hungry, she could've stood beneath his scrutiny forever.

He traced the tender skin under her eyes. She was so glad she'd stuffed a toothbrush and toothpaste in her backpack when she'd run away. Bad enough she wore the same, smelly clothes she'd had on for a month. At least her teeth were clean.

The man nodded. "Yeah. I fuckin' see he your old man."

She leaned into his touch, and he stiffened. "I need to see him," she whispered, regretting the loss of his nearness when he pulled away and stepped back.

Another half-smile curved his full lips, this one cold and mean, not reaching his green eyes. He folded his arms and mockery twisted his face. "He ain't here."

She refused to panic. He seemed to be waiting for her to fall into a screaming heap. Although she *wanted* to fall into a screaming heap and have him pick her up and take care of her until her daddy returned, she wouldn't humiliate herself in front of all these men. Men who looked up to her father. Her weakness might somehow be broadcast upon Big Joe. Her stomach growled and her feet throbbed, like they had a direct connection to one another. In a way they did since both of them were causing her such distress and misery. She stiffened her spine. "When's he coming back?"

He laughed, the sound as ugly as he was beautiful. And he was very beautiful. "Probably never."

Women's cackles and harsh male snickers followed that announcement.

Meggie pressed down on her lips. If she didn't, they would begin trembling. Okay. *Now* she was on the verge of breaking down. It was all just too much. All of it. Her father had been her last chance for her mother to escape Thomas. Now, Meggie either had to go back home or live on the streets forever. She'd called her father's cell phone, over and over, and he hadn't answered. She couldn't understand why. She'd clearly heard her mother say they'd talked about Meggie living with him.

"Why isn't my father coming back?" she demanded. "Where is he? And why won't he answer his cell phone?"

He lifted an inky brow at her but didn't answer. Instead, he started to turn away. She lurched toward him, grabbing his forearm. He narrowed his eyes and jerked away from her.

"Never, *ever* putcha fuckin' hands on me. *Ever.*"

Desperation made her reach for him again. Let him hit her. So what? Her stepfather was a huge fan of whippings and he knocked around her mother on a regular basis for nothing. If this man could provide her father's location and give her something to eat, he could do his best.

He raised his hand and Meggie flinched, despite her bravado, unable to stop her own hand from shielding her face while tightening her grip on him with her other hand.

"Please," she said in a rush.

"Put your fuckin' hand down. I ain't a woman beater."

"Well, my stepfather is," she mumbled, lowering her hand and her eyelids, but refusing to lose her hold on his right forearm where he had a tattoo of a heart surrounded by colorful flowers, a banner slicing across and angling on a diagonal with the word 'Ma'. On his bicep were two battling snakes, another Celtic cross rising between them, their entwined bodies hidden by red roses with pretty green leaves. Big Joe had tattoos too, but she'd never taken as much time to study his as she did this stranger's. She swallowed and met his emerald gaze. "I just want directions to where I can find my father." Her stomach growled. "And I want something to eat."

His nostrils flared and the black fury on his face reminded Meggie these men were part of an MC named the *Death Dwellers*. He looked as if he could mete out death without a second thought while the Grim Reaper painted on the wall appeared as if he'd step from the mural and hack everyone into tiny pieces at any moment. The inescapable work of art slapped you in the eyes the moment you stepped through the door and looked to the right. But her father always said his club just had a frightening name. In reality, they were only a group of guys who didn't agree with society's rules and who loved motorcycles.

"Rack, bring this bitch to my office. Get her somethin' to eat then get her the fuck outta here." He glared at her and pried her fingers from his arm, shoving her away. "If you know what the fuck good for you, stay the fuck away from my fuckin' club."

Rack grabbed her arm and yanked her toward the hallway. She hobbled as fast as she could behind him, peeking over her shoulder. Rack was dragging her in the opposite direction from which the other man went, and disappointment sank into her like a heavy stone. Rack opened the door and flipped on the light. Meggie noticed the word, 'President' painted on the shiny wood.

"Sit, you thieving little bitch."

As if she had a choice. Not with Rack manhandling her and shoving her down onto a brown leather sofa. He slammed the door closed and Meggie sagged in exhaustion. Now that her adrenaline was dipping again, the pain was returning. She settled one ankle on her knee and studied her foot. Dried blood, dirt, small glass shards and gravel coated the bottom. She needed to see to her feet, remove the glass, but she was just so tired. It had been a long, long month, and she'd survived by a thin thread, living off chips and cinnamon rolls the guy at the minimart gave to her after she'd traded her coat in lieu of giving him a blowjob. She drank water from the creek, the place where she spent most of her time.

She hadn't thought of the possibility of not being able to contact her father since her mother told Thomas she intended to send Meggie to Big Joe. Perhaps, he'd gone on a run. Or, maybe, they'd crossed paths. She'd been running to him in Hortensia, and he'd been hightailing it to Seattle to pick her up.

Frustration made Meggie want to scream. The adults in her life were driving her insane. She'd had to leave when the opportunity presented itself. She hadn't been able to wait for her father's arrival. In the span of twelve hours, Thomas had clamped down on where Meggie could go and who she talked to. Since her mother had spoken to him, her father should've been expecting her. Or, at the very least, her call.

When she'd last seen her daddy, he said he still lived at his club, where he'd resided for the past fifteen years after he and her mother separated.

The adults—

Meggie sank back and rubbed her temples. As of today, she, too, was an adult.

The door slammed open, and Megan jerked her head up. The beautiful man sauntered in, carrying a tray with something steaming from a bowl. She'd expected Rack's beady face again, not the big, sexy biker whose smoldering green eyes took in every inch of her. After using his foot to close the door, he sat the tray on the desk, then stopped in front of her, leaving her eye level with the tease of his penis.

She flushed. His penis pressed urgently against his jeans, waging a war with the zipper.

"Wanna see all the motherfucker?" he asked. His words were clipped, and anger lingered in his eyes, but laughter curled around the offer.

She gazed up at him, searching for a sign of trouble. She was all alone with him, and he might be perverted just like Thomas. She shook her head. "Would you zip your jeans?"

He mimicked her and shook his head. "Nope. Ain't wantin' to ruin your study of my cock."

The burning tips of Meggie's ears rivaled the heat in her cheeks. She told herself she was leery of this situation, but the lie mocked her. She wasn't leery of *him*. Not. At. All. She wanted to study every inch of his tanned skin and explore the entirety of his hard body. She wondered how her breasts would feel if he touched them with his rough fingertips.

Without warning, he pulled her to her feet and began patting his hands down her body. She gasped when his hand landed on her chest and unbuttoned her shirt. She was hungry and hurting and wouldn't be able to fight his intentions long, but she *would* fight. He dug his fingers into her bra and Meggie threw the full weight of her body against him. Other than a brief widening of the eyes, he didn't budge.

His hand slid down to her jeans and she balled her fists, but he saw the hit coming and grabbed her wrists, pulling her to him.

"What the fuck you doin'?"

She struggled against his hold. Her stomach roiled and her vision blurred. She hated that she'd felt safe for some crazy reason, but he was no better than Thomas. "You know what I'm doing. You want to force me to have sex with you." She kicked out and he lifted her off her aching feet. He threw her down on the sofa and landed on top of her, holding her hands above her head.

"I fuckin' told you I ain't fuckin' hurtin' women," he growled. "I ain't into stealin' pussy when so much thrown at my ass for free. Even if my cock the loneliest motherfucker, *your* pussy yours. I ain't got no right to it unless you givin' it the fuck up."

The fight was draining the last of her strength and energy. If she didn't have something to eat soon, she'd faint. She licked her lips, her mouth dry and her head pounding. "What are you doing if you aren't—"

"I'm lookin' for your fuckin' ID, to see your goddamn name."

"You're feeling me up for my *name?*" she hissed. "Why didn't you just ask me, you moron?"

He stilled and narrowed his eyes, a muscle ticking in his jaw. "You just call me a fuckin' moron?"

God, nothing beyond the meal he'd promised her ran through her brain. If she'd been rational, she wouldn't have bitten the hand promising to feed her by calling him a moron. "I'm sorry. Please. I'm hungry," she said. She cleared her throat, appalled at the heat pooling in her belly and centering between her thighs with his hard body pressing into hers. "May I eat the food you brought in?"

He continued his unnerving contemplation of her before removing his body from atop hers. Getting to his feet, he walked to the food, then brought her the bowl. He stood there, not moving out of her personal space. Her knees brushed against him, and she felt...safe within the bubble of his zone. By his own doing, he'd swept her into his orbit, and he had to know what an overwhelmingly sexy, virile man he was. Meggie figured he was trying to unnerve her on purpose, though she didn't detect any menace behind his actions. Just pure sin and wickedness. Had she been a different type of girl, she would've done whatever he wanted her to do. She wasn't at all like her two best friends. Farah went into graphic detail about how she'd did most of the high school football team and Lacey made no secret of her sexual fluidity.

Meggie kept her head bowed, slurping up the soup like the starving maniac she was.

She'd been tempted by men before, but her temptations always focused on the cute male teachers rather than the student body, so she'd kept her mouth shut and enjoyed the male attention she got from boys her own age. She couldn't risk sleeping with anyone, though. High school boys could be so juvenile, and she'd get a reputation for whoring around even if she didn't deserve it. And, of course, with her mother being the assistant principal at the school Meggie attended, she couldn't risk that. If her mother found out, then Thomas would inevitably find out since Dinah found it necessary to tell him every little detail of both their lives.

Her spoon clanked against the bowl, and she frowned. She'd finished? Already? God, she'd just gotten started.

"How long since you last ate?"

A sexy voice to go with a sexy body and magnificent face. Meggie shivered at the timbre, promising to memorize his voice so it soothed her to sleep at night and banished the memories of Thomas's voice and actions. "Two days."

He grabbed the bowl from her. "Ain't givin' you no more. You gonna hurl if you stuff your stomach with food after not eatin' so long."

"But I'm still hungry," she protested, hating her whiny plea. "And I haven't had anything hot to eat in days."

"Your ma ain't feedin' you or somethin'?"

"She can't since she's in Seattle."

That startled him. His eyes widened and he cocked his head to the side. Meggie squirmed beneath his intense scrutiny. Their gazes locked and she wondered at his impression of her. Electrical currents raced through her veins, and she parted her lips. From her head to her toes, her body reacted to him. The memory of her last night in her mother's house replayed in her mind and she closed her eyes.

His voice broke through her misery. "Why the fuck you here and she there?"

"Because my father is *here*, and her husband is *there*." She didn't want Thomas inflicting any more damage to her psyche or her person. She pretended the sheer horror of his actions didn't affect her. In reality, she hurt to her very soul. Recognizing the sickness in Thomas consoled her but left her with two choices. Allow his brutality to rule her or acknowledge the problem for what it was and keep her life on a forward motion.

To counteract her reaction to the biker's proximity, she refocused on her feet, deciding to give up the argument about more soup. Her stomach was already starting to hurt. He touched her foot, his hand dark against her white skin. Crouching in front of her, he checked one foot and then the other.

"You cut your feet?"

"Rack didn't tell you?"

He crouched in front of her, his brow raised. His thumb caressed the high arch of her foot, almost stealing her ability to think and talk. "Ain't givin' a fuck if he did. I'm askin' you."

She winced at a spot he touched. "Um, I stole five dollars from him. I wanted a hamburger, fries, and a milk shake tonight." To celebrate her birthday.

He didn't stop his investigation of her feet. "Five dollars ain't enough."

"For a kid's meal it would've been," she countered, gasping when he squeezed her upper sole.

"You that? A kid, I mean."

Not as of today. "I'm eighteen," she said softly, taking advantage of her unfettered access to him and touching his scruffy jaw before combing her fingers through his silky hair.

Her touch angered him and he glared at her. "I told you don't fuckin' touch me."

She narrowed her eyes at him. "You've been touching me. Why can't I touch you?"

He got to his feet, and she looked away, not wanting to defy him. Whenever she or her mother stared at Thomas, he took that as a challenge. But this man said he didn't hit women. And? What man admitted to domestic abuse? Thomas certainly didn't. He didn't even admit it behind closed doors. He blamed everything on either Dinah or Meggie.

She sat still, not raising her gaze when she heard the biker rambling around through a drawer. A moment later, he stood before her, wrapping his big hand around each ankle, one at a time, to wipe first one foot and then the other with a wet napkin. Done, he threw it aside. He picked up a long medical tweezer and narrowed his beautiful eyes in concentration.

Meggie grit her teeth as he carefully removed glass shards from each foot. Focusing on his face helped to alleviate the discomfort of his ministrations.

"Fuckin' surprisin' you was fuckin' able to walk," he told her, sparing her a brief glance before returning to his first aid.

For the first time, she noticed the medical supplies next to her. "I didn't exactly walk," she muttered.

He frowned at her. "What the fuck that mean?"

"Rack didn't let me go once he caught me. He swore very painful revenge if it turned out I was lying about Big Joe. I suppose he thought I'd escape once we got here. Just like he manhandled me onto his bike, he hustled me into the club. Yes, I'd come here once when I first arrived in town, but I came from a different direction, so by the time we got here this evening, I was completely lost. Even if I'd wanted to escape him, I didn't know where to go."

He grunted and returned to caring for her feet without commenting. Once he threw the tweezer aside, he sprayed peroxide on each foot, dried them off, and spread a layer of ointment before covering them with medical tape.

Who knew an MC had such things? She supposed it was necessary given all the alcohol she'd noticed, and the temperament of the men involved.

"By the fuckin' way, what the fuck *is* your name?"

"Megan," she answered. She didn't have her ID. It was in her backpack, and she'd left it in her hiding space at the creek. "Meggie."

"Got a last name, Megan?"

"Same as Big Joe," she said, slumping against the sofa. "Foy. My name is Megan Foy."

He drew in a deep breath and his green eyes shuttered. Jaw clenched, he nodded. "Where your shoes?"

"In some alleyway, I guess. I threw them at Rack and the others," she added when she saw his curiosity.

"Shit."

He left her in the room, leaving the door open, so she saw the long hallway with lights from the main room shimmering against the brown wall. With the door open, the overwhelming noise made her head hurt. The smell of cigarette smoke thickened the air. Everything she should've observed while the man mesmerized her, she was noticing now. But he engaged all Meggie's senses, her ears warmed by the sound of his voice, her eyes fascinated by the sight of his face and body, her nose filled with his scent and her skin consumed by the feel of his hands.

As he stormed back toward her, she rose to her feet. Standing up, she wouldn't feel so vulnerable. He still loomed over her, but, somehow, she seemed like a frightened little girl when she sat down and let him intimidate her.

He threw socks at her, and she noticed a burly, baldheaded man behind him. A teardrop was tattooed beneath his left eye. She sat down to put the socks on. They were terribly big and colored the type of gray that once was white.

"Val, escort Boss daughter the fuck outside the compound."

"No!" Meggie said. "C-can't I stay here until—"

"No," he barked.

She set her jaw and raised her chin. "My daddy won't be too happy when he finds out you made me go."

"Ain't as if I give a fuck, but I appreciate your concern. Ain't gotta worry, babe, I know just how to handle Boss."

The man named Val snickered, but the other man's warning look shut him up.

"I can't go back out there. Please? I won't be any trouble. I promise to behave until my daddy gets back. I'll even tell him how nice you were to me."

The more she spoke, the angrier the man seemed to get. She didn't even know his name. He signaled to Val, who grabbed her arm and started dragging her out the office.

Tears rushed to Meggie's eyes. "Please," she whispered, looking over her shoulder at the other man.

In response, he slammed the door shut, smashing the last of her hope that he might soften toward her and allow her to stay within the safety of the club.

Chapter Six
OUTLAW

THE NEXT MORNING, OUTLAW SCOWLED AT RACK as they sat at the table in the meeting room. "I ain't ever wantin' no lil' bitch comin' in my club, tellin' me my boys went after her for five fuckin' dollars," he snarled.

He couldn't get the girl's fascination with his dick out of his head. She should've had *virgin pussy* stamped somewhere on her. She was that fucking innocent. A fool could see she was fucking trouble. Not only as Boss's daughter—and Outlaw had killed the motherfucker— but because the thought of plucking her cherry appealed to him. He knew whores and he knew innocents. Her big, blue eyes had been completely taken with his cock and not because it was *large*. No. A chastity belt clamped on her pussy wouldn't have proclaimed her inexperience as loudly as her expressions had.

Virgin or not, though, she was a feisty little thing. Determined to have him listen to her, she'd touched him even when he'd ordered her not to. Her conversation in his office had been engaging and lively. Every now and then, her eyes sparkled and snapped, fascinating him. Her eyes were so much like Boss's and Snake's, hinting at the little hellcat hiding within the frightened girl.

But she'd left Seattle because her stepfather lived there. Outlaw didn't like the unspoken words. The things she hadn't said must've been bad as a motherfucker for her to have sought out Boss for help.

Outlaw fucking wanted her. He wanted inside of her. He tried to drum up disgust at the thought but couldn't. He couldn't blame her because her father had turned into a murdering, lying, drugged-up dickhead. He doubted she was even aware of what the man had become.

"I can't allow nobody to get away with lifting my shit. I don't fucking care if it's a penny—"

"You fuckin' heard me, Rack. When she told you she was Boss's kid that shoulda ended it. You shoulda put her on the back of your fuckin' bike, bought her whatever the fuck she needed and been fuckin' done with it."

"Oh yeah?" Rack snapped, planting his forearms on the table and leaning forward. "You're so concerned with Big Joe's daughter when you stopped being concerned about *him* months ago?"

Outlaw looked at Mortician, who shrugged. His dreads were queued and the skull ring on his brown fingers reminded Outlaw of how the man had earned his patch. He'd rewarded himself after being patched in and he'd earned his patch by helping Outlaw bury a motherfucker alive.

If anything pussified Outlaw, it was that shit. He'd never forget the horror frozen on the assfuck's post-mortem face when they'd dug him up. It had taken Outlaw months to sleep in the fucking dark again. That had been some intense and fucked up shit. He swallowed. After all these years, he wanted to hurl. Other kills had been much more gruesome. Fuck, the buried-alive-motherfucker's disposal had been grislier. Something about digging the motherfucker up instead of letting him stay the fuck smothered by dirt fucked with Outlaw.

They'd had orders, though, and they'd had to follow them.

"I ain't discussin' what went down with Boss, brother," he said as nice as he could, when he wanted to rip Rack's throat out.

"Nothing new there, *brother*."

"Yo, Rack, if you have a problem, you need to get gone," Val advised, chewing on the straw he'd just used to slurp up beer and thrusting his chin toward the door.

"We not here to dig up old shit," Digger advised, then laughed, although Outlaw didn't find nothing funny. "Get it? *Dig*?"

"Shut your dumb ass up, bruh," Mortician growled. "With your Winnie-the-Pooh ass."

"That was Trigger," the man amended.

"You mean *Tigger*, dumb ass," Mortician corrected his brother. He rolled his eyes, reached over and slapped Digger's arm. The two men shared a strong family resemblance, but Digger was slightly taller than his older brother.

"Shut the fuck up. All you," Outlaw said. He focused on his vice president again. "Heed my fuckin' words, Rack. You wanna pick on a motherfucker, find somebody your own fuckin' size. She was hungry. You shoulda fed her."

"She's also homeless," Rack said with a smirk. "I didn't hear you inviting her to stay here. And you lucky I decided to bring her here and not take my money out of her ass."

Bitches came and went. Every man in the club had his favorite piece of ass and many of them had their old ladies. But the thought of Rack putting his big paws on that gorgeous little piece infuriated Outlaw. He shot from his seat, knocking it over, and grabbed Rack by the throat.

"You fuckin' touch her, Ima let Digger shovel outcha grave and give Mortician a shot at you with all his special lil' tools. We clear?" He pressed his fingers into the motherfucker's neck until his eyes started bugging out, then he abruptly released him.

Rack slumped into the chair, holding his throat and gasping for breath.

"Who the fuck else was with you?"

Rack threw him a dirty look and tightened his lips.

"That's the way shit goin', huh, motherfucker?" Outlaw didn't have time to deal with a young bitch who had more spunk than sense. However, he intended to impress upon Rack what a wise decision it would be not to harm her if he ever ran into her again. "I'll deal with you later. Right now, we gotta get ready for distribution and collection."

Outlaw braked his bike before killing the engine and toeing the kickstand down. The creek languished beneath the sun, the glare bouncing off the placid gray water. He stared at nothing, enjoying the warmth on his face, though it was as cold as a motherfucker. Lighting up a smoke, he walked to the water's edge. He needed the peace and quiet, the beauty of nature. He had some hard shit facing him and if he didn't survive, he hoped his last thought would be of this place. The serenity to be found here.

God knows, he'd had little enough of peace, quiet, or serenity. Not in years. And, from a young age, he'd killed God knew how many dumb fucks. He'd stolen shit from rival clubs. He'd run guns. He'd moved drugs. He'd gotten himself and his brothers out of some pretty fucking tough spots. His time was ending. Motherfuckers just couldn't keep fucking with dangerous shit and stay alive. Sooner or later, luck walked the fuck away, leaving a poor assfuck with a knifed or bullet-ridden body, then small parts of them buried deep in forests and shit.

Or buried the fuck alive.

His cigarette was almost burned out, but he took a drag anyway. He gazed to his left where lush vegetation mingled with tall trees before sloping to a flat carpet of grass and the creek. He stilled. For the first time, he noticed a bundle curled up beneath a tree. He squinted, angled his head, first one way and then the other. That didn't look like just a discarded jacket.

"Fuck," he said, releasing the smoke from his lungs and throwing the butt aside.

When he reached it, he saw that, yeah, infuckingdeed, the figure was real. He couldn't see her face, but he saw the small foot and delicate arch identifying her as female. This bitch had to be whacked out of her fucking mind to be out here without shoes. He should leave her the fuck here. If a bitch wanted to freeze the fuck to death, who the fuck was he to stop her?

He grunted at the thought, his conscience pricking him. He had a mother, sisters, and nieces. He'd want a motherfucker to help one of them. The bandages on the foot registered.

"Fuck."

With another curse, he brushed aside the jacket and revealed a head of golden blonde hair. Long and thick, it covered her face. He turned the bundle over, almost afraid to have his suspicion about her identity confirmed.

"Fuckin' motherfucker."

Her eyes were blackened and her lip and nose bloody, but he recognized Boss's daughter. Even without the bandages, he would've. A motherfucker had worked her over. He really, really, really didn't need this bullshit. He should leave her right the fuck here and let her go and join her fucking father in the afterworld.

Outlaw felt the pulse at her throat. Weak and reedy, but there. He hated to look at her, hated to see Joe Foy in her gorgeous features. Whereas the male members of her family were big and masculine— but even Outlaw had to admit handsome fucks—this girl was little. She reminded him of how much her father had betrayed Outlaw— the entire club. He'd looked up to Boss and loved him like a father. Only to be stabbed in the back and have to face the decision of choosing his own life over Boss's.

He *hated* that assfuck. Would never, *ever* fucking forgive him.

Outlaw stood, spat near her head. His conscience had deserted him when he'd made his first kill, determined to move from Probate to a fully patched in member. He'd been a kid, but responsible for looking after a houseful of females. He'd appreciated the brotherhood, the loyalty, a place where he could find his own species—men. His uncle and cousin had been around, yeah, but in his *immediate* household, he'd been surrounded by girls. A ma and five sisters. And, later, as his sisters fucked with dickhead after dickhead after dickhead, a ma, five sisters, and three nieces. Fuck him, but his family couldn't seem to produce dicks to save their fucking lives.

Boss, K-P, and back then *Rack*, had accepted him for him. They hadn't blamed him for all the woes in his ma's life. He'd been able to forget the pitiful circumstances of his conception. They'd let him do that when no one else would.

Now, gazing at this battered girl, he wanted to walk the fuck away, but he couldn't fucking do it. Away from the male-infused atmosphere of the clubhouse, Outlaw could hear his a's voice, see her beloved features. She'd want him to help this girl. She'd *raised* him to help. She was good and kind and loving, and if he could do shit over again, he'd do so much fucking different. He wouldn't have fucked a swath through a battalion of women. He wouldn't have lied.

He wouldn't have killed.

But he'd found Boss and his brothers and gotten the acceptance and male influence he so craved. At the clubhouse, he could belch, fart, fuck, pick his nose, curse at the top of his lungs, and do whatever shit he felt like without having to worry about female sensibilities.

Crouching down, he scooped her into his arms. She weighed next to nothing. A strong wind would knock her the fuck over. She pulled in a deep breath, half gasp, half sob.

He could always take her to town, put her up in a motel, keep her pockets flushed with bills until she figured out what to do. That was the sensible thing to do. Motherfuckers were gunning for him, meaning he didn't need the distraction of virgin pussy. Because, fuck him, he'd done a lot of shit, but, as far as he knew, he'd never fucked a virgin or such a young bitch. Bitches at least had to be legal drinking age to get in his bed. He just couldn't get her cock study out of his head, though. Her fascination with such a cherished part of his anatomy tempted the shit out of him.

Fuck it. He'd take her to the clubhouse. It was going to be a fucking tedious ride with her barely conscious. The clubhouse was closer than town, anyfuckingway.

Twenty minutes later, Outlaw was striding into the clubhouse carrying Boss's daughter. Early in the day, not many people were around. Most of them were preparing for tonight when brothers from a smaller club rolled in to pick up the shit for distribution. The Dwellers didn't need to dirty their hands with drug distribution and gun running no more unless it was special circumstances. They'd paid their dues. *He'd* paid his dues. So had Mortician, Digger, and Val. Even Johnnie, his cousin, who wasn't a full patch member anymore.

After Boss tried to fuck them up the ass with another club and after Outlaw put him to ground and been elected president, he'd had to decide if the club would wage war with the smaller club or if they could somehow work together in a way to benefit both organizations. He'd moved his ma out of her house and relocated her to the place he owned two hours away, though he'd long lived at the club. Motherfuckers knew where his ma lived in Hortensia, so he'd had to wrap away any thoughts of retaliation against him through her by removing her out of danger. Fortunately, though, they'd come to a peaceful resolution.

For now. Shit could change any time, so whenever the other MC members set foot on Death Dwellers' property, his boys turned out in force.

He headed for his room, glad Kiera and Ellen weren't in his bed, and laid the girl down. He frowned, swore, suddenly recognizing the oversized jacket on her. *Rack.* After he'd told that miserable motherfucker to stay away from her. He'd deal with that fuckhead for disobeying him.

Outlaw went to his private bathroom and grabbed a pan, filling it with warm water and his bar of soap. He got some towels and returned to her. It didn't take him long to strip her and he stared at the thin silvery lines crisscrossing her arms, thighs, legs and belly. Healed cuts.

What the fuck?

His mind searched for answers about why Megan Foy looked like she'd been used as turkey carving practice and breathed to talk about it. What stupid motherfucker had sliced Boss Foy's daughter? The Death Dwellers weren't no bitch ass, fly-by-night club. The good deeds they bestowed upon the community allowed for some very positive press. Their crimes were either overlooked or so well covered no one could ever accuse them. Fuck, yeah, rumors persisted but no motherfuckers was insane enough to openly accuse them.

Which meant all Megan had to do was identify her father and that should've been enough to deter such sadistic marring of her beautiful skin.

Outlaw grunted. Those slashes and her ass beating wasn't all that was ailing her. The outline of her ribs pressed against her skin. Either she was anorexic or she'd lost a shitload of weight due to starvation. Her shoulder blades and breastbone stuck out, making her breasts rounded and fuller, topped by tight, little red nipples. Golden pussy hairs matched the golden hair on her head. He wanted to spread her legs and lick that blonde-covered perfection for hours, lose himself in her sweetness.

Despite her scars and bruises, she was one gorgeous fucking bitch. His dick swelled and lengthened. Sometimes, a conscience fucked you worse than taking the low road. Like now, for instance. He represented everything bad, beginning with how he'd been made. She was good, an angel amid hell. If he hadn't brought her here, he wouldn't have such a brutal fucking cockstand. He could've called Kiera and Ellen and fucked the afternoon away until time for the meeting came. But, no, he'd brought this girl here, to his room. He must be going fucking soft.

Shaking his head and sighing, he decided to get to his task. Wasn't no use delaying what he had to do.

As careful as possible, he cleaned the dirt and blood from her face, hands, and poor, abused feet after removing the dirty bandages. She groaned and Outlaw noted a rush of pink replacing some of the paleness in her cheeks. He laid a hand over her forehead, finding her warmer than she should be. Rack. He needed gutting for doing this to her. Outlaw could only be thankful the fat balled fuckhead hadn't raped her. Then, again, no matter his threats of taking his money out of her ass, Rack knew Outlaw *would've* gutted him. Her color was returning, but she'd be in a lot of pain and needed rest, a place to heal. He picked the first T-shirt he put his hands on and dressed her in it before tucking the covers around her. He didn't know if she was asleep or unconscious or a combination and, really, at this point, he couldn't do anything more for her. He couldn't migrate too far from the clubhouse today, so he'd be able to check on her and make sure she was comfortable. She'd either live or die. He'd gotten her out of the cold, cleaned her up, warmed her up.

Everything now depended on a God he'd stopped believing in years ago.

Chapter Seven

Meggie

"YOU AWAKE."

The husky words resounded in Meggie's brain the moment she opened her eyes. She blinked and coughed, trying to get her bearings. As lucidity returned, so did her pain. She moaned and clutched the side of her face.

Had Thomas found her?

She hurt all over. Not surprising because pain and tears had been Meggie's constant companions since her mother's marriage five years ago. She tried to lift her head and found her sight narrowed to one slit in her right eye. She couldn't see anything out of the left one. It throbbed with nauseating fierceness. A sliver of light beamed off the brick wall she faced, and she frowned, too late remembering any small movement would aggravate her pain receptors. She tried to take in her unfamiliar surroundings but couldn't fathom her whereabouts. She *knew* she was inside, in a bed.

"Megan?"

The voice sounded like *Outlaw's*. Impossible. He'd thrown her off the premises and the last thing she remembered was Rack and the guys he'd been with when they'd cornered her in the alley, exacting revenge, they said, because Outlaw had battered Rack thanks to her big mouth. Amid their fury and listing all the reasons she deserved what she'd get, one of them had finally revealed the big, sexy biker's name.

She lifted herself on her elbows and noticed movement. "Outlaw?" she asked, hoarse. Her throat felt tight and scratchy. She sneezed and bit her lip to keep from crying out in pain. She hurt in no particular place. Agony blanketed her body.

He lifted a brow but didn't comment about the fact she knew his name. "Yeah?"

More movement and the sound of boots thumped to the floor from where he sat on a chair near the bed.

She cleared her throat. "What are you doing?" She was still hoarse.

"Puttin' my fuckin' feet on the floor to stand up," he answered. A moment later, the bed dipped as he sat next to her. His warm fingers gripped her chin and turned her face this way and that. "Lay back."

She complied, grateful for the comfort of the bed. He dropped his hand away, resting it on her belly. She scooted closer to him, not sure what compelled her to touch him every time he was near her. "Where am I?"

"At the clubhouse. In my room."

In his bed. Her heart rate increased at the thought, and she placed her hand over his.

"Do you gotta touch me all the fuckin' time?"

Her head was already pounding something awful, and his growl only worsened the pain. "Unless you wish to stop touching me," she countered, hoping he didn't take her challenge and move away.

He grunted and narrowed his eyes, trying to intimidate her, she supposed, through two sneezes and a cough. She refused to look away. A curse accompanied his scowl. Fatigue still pulled at Meggie, but, more than that, she felt like a lost little girl. The way her body responded to his, though, wasn't in the least childlike. Besides, she'd grown up the moment she'd stepped out of her mother's house to find her father on her own. Hortensia, Washington was relatively safe, tucked between Camas and Victoria, along the Columbia River. She'd found a spot near a creek to sleep and bathe. Although Rack had found her hideout, she'd gone unharmed for a month.

Now, she was hurt, alone and afraid. Outlaw reminded her of her father—a frightening, overwhelming figure. But, like her father, he had a softer side. With them, what she saw was what she got. With Thomas, well…

Meggie burrowed against Outlaw's chest, her cheek rubbing against the soft leather of his vest. He stiffened for a moment, as if he considered pushing her away. A cough racked her, and he sighed his favorite curse word. He pulled her into his arms. It hit her she didn't have her jeans or her panties on. Or her shirt. Whatever she wore, dirt and perspiration didn't stiffen it. "Where are my clothes?"

"Should be in a shit pile, but they gettin' washed. Now, I got a question for you."

She tried to breathe in his scent but couldn't through the stuffiness in her nose. "I have another one for you."

"Megan—"

"What's your name?" she interrupted, repositioning herself to get a better focus of him. As if she really needed to see him to know the raw and perfect angles of his face, his inky hair, and his green eyes.

"Outlaw."

"Your *real* name," she huffed.

He adjusted their positions until they were eye-to-eye, his nose nearly touching hers. He ran his fingers through her hair and Meggie wanted to die of mortification. Her hair probably resembled a rat's nest. Not to mention how her face must look. With the way her lips and eyes throbbed, she had to be a swollen mess. She also needed to brush her teeth. The thought made her back away. He caught her before she went very far and pulled her closer again.

He sighed, ending on a very vivid curse word. "Name's Christopher." He swallowed. "Christopher Caldwell."

She caressed the side of his jaw, the dark stubble bristly beneath her fingertips. "Was that so hard?"

He didn't answer and asked instead, "Why you got all them scars?"

Frowning, Meggie pulled away and, this time, he didn't try to stop her. She scooted closer to the wall, her sneeze giving her time to make sense of his words. Once she did, she avoided his scrutiny and pretended she didn't know what he meant. "Scars?"

"Fuckin' cuts. You know what the fuck my ass talkin' 'bout, Megan. I see it in your fuckin' face."

She didn't have the energy to argue, nor did she have the vigor to think of a good excuse. "Go away," she ordered.

"Ain't fuckin' happenin'," he shot back.

She'd never felt so awful in her life, and she didn't need his interrogation while she felt so feeble and cold. She might weaken and confess what she did to herself in order to cope with Thomas and her hellish home life. Since she'd been away from that house, she'd experienced twinges of need to float away from reality. But it was different.

"Well?"

She sagged into the comfortable pillows. If he wouldn't go away and she couldn't ignore him, she'd turn the tables on him. Whether she understood her attraction to him or not, she studied every little detail about him, listened to every change of cadence in his sexy voice. Just like she had family secrets, he had his, too. "Is Caldwell really your last name?" she asked around a sneeze.

"What the fuck you ask me?"

"You heard me. You're right next to me."

"You ain't gettin' to ask me 'bout me. It ain'tcha fuckin' business."

She wheezed in a breath and bit her lip, wanting to make everything about him her business. But fair was fair. "Then you don't get to ask me about me. It's not your business."

His eyes widened at her announcement, but he snapped his mouth shut. Meggie hoped he'd open up, even a little, but silence stretched between them, broken only by her sneezes and shivers.

"Fuck me, but I should kick you the fuck outta here." He dragged her closer and pulled her into his arms, wrapping his body around hers, his heat enveloping her, curling around Meggie and bringing her warmth and a sense of safety. "If I answer you, I wanna fuckin' know where them cuts on your beautiful skin come from."

That wasn't the way this was supposed to work.

"Underfuckinstand, Megan?"

No one had ever said her name with such raw sexuality and rough command. Although barely an inch separated them, she drew herself closer to him. The moment she did, he pushed her on her back and said, "Face the wall."

Obeying without question, Meggie pressed her back against his front, rewarded when he pulled her closer, allowing her to feel every solid plane of his big body.

"Unfuckinfortunately, yeah, Caldwell my real fuckin' name. Your turn."

"Why, unfortunately?" she pressed.

His body tensed against hers. "Megan—"

"I want to know. Please?"

"Look, I ain't fuckin' knowin' you and I ain't sharin' my personal business with my close friends, let alone a bitch who gonna be here only long 'nuff to get well."

He was right. They didn't know each other and, once her father returned, they'd probably never see one another again. Just because she felt an attraction to him didn't mean he felt one to her. She caressed his knuckles and remembered she had to keep her end of the bargain. Though she should give the same reason to him he'd given her, he had, at least, given her a small tidbit. Her fingers roamed over his forearm and he sucked in a breath.

"I…" Her voice trailed off. What should she say? She'd gone through great lengths to hide what she did to herself. She couldn't dismiss her own pain and shame, so the thought of the revulsion others would turn upon her chilled her soul. Especially someone like him—older, in control, and unafraid of anything. God, she just wanted…

What? What did she want?

She sniffled. Safety. She wanted safety most of all. She wanted to know her father still loved her. No matter what happened, he had no excuse for just forgetting about her these last two years then promising Dinah he'd get Meggie but disappearing on club business instead. If she hadn't heard her mother's words to Thomas, she wouldn't have left until after she graduated high school. She thought her father wanted her with him.

"Them cuts, Megan," Christopher cut in with impatience. He untangled himself from her and Meggie missed his nearness immediately.

"It doesn't matter," she whispered, tired, and wishing for a bath. She wanted to talk to her mother and her friends. Maybe, Big Joe had arrived in Seattle and Meggie had already left. Maybe, he was returning to the club at this very moment. "They're just cuts. Nothing for someone whom I won't ever see again, after I'm well, should bother with."

"You know what, babe—" He cut himself off with a curse and bolted from the bed.

Meggie rested on her back again in time to see him thrust his fingers through his hair. He pulled out his cigarettes, maneuvered one partially out of the pack, then grabbed it between his lips, not once taking his green gaze from her. He flicked the lighter he also got from his vest. Once he'd taken a few puffs, he tried again.

"You gonna drive some poor motherfucker, huh?"

"Drive?"

"Up a fuckin' wall. To the edge of fuckin' violence. Just plain fuckin' crazy."

His observation stung her because, in essence, he thought her difficult, and she wasn't by any means. He puffed in nicotine, then huffed out a breath.

"I can't fuckin' stand the name Caldwell cuz the fucker who made me shoulda been castrated for what he did to my ma. I'm here cuz of a fuckin' rape, Megan. Conceived in violence, live in violence, and Ima fuckin' die in violence. Ain't a day went by when my grandfather ain't remind me of how I ruined my ma's life." He sucked on his cigarette again, his eyes glittering with anger and other emotions. Hurt. Humiliation. Shame.

He might very well deny he felt either, but Meggie herself had lived with everything she saw in his expression.

"No child asks to be born," she pointed out. "No matter how it's conceived. *You* didn't ruin your mother's life."

"What the fuck ever," he snapped. "I ain't told you that shit to get fuckin' pity. I ain't gave a fuck in years." He pointed a finger at her. "Don't ever fuckin' tell that shit to *no*fuckinbody. So, now, you lil' pain in the ass motherfucker, fuckin' spill. Tell me the fuckin' truth 'bout those fuckin' cuts and not fuckin' bullshit. Because you know what the fuck I think, Megan?"

"No, but I'm sure you're about to tell me."

He threw his cigarette to the floor and, Megan assumed, stepped on it to put it out, as he stalked to the bed, climbed in, straddled her, and pinned her arms above her head. She tried to draw in air, to smell the leather of his vest, to smell *him,* but mucus still stuffed her nose, continuing to block his scent from her.

"You fuckin' right I am." He paused and pulled back to allow her a cough. "I think," he continued, "you fuck yourself up. Ain't no fuckin' cuts another motherfucker givin' you so fuckin' straight and neat. Them some precision fuckin' cuts on you. I cut motherfuckers in methodical ways but they move and shit. Squirm. Tryna get the fuck away. That shit ain't allowin' for straight fuckin' lines. And another thing. When other motherfuckers cut you? Wounds a lil' fuckin' deeper. Unless you dealin' with a fuckin' pussy, your wounds ain't deep efuckinnuff for another motherfucker to do that shit."

Meggie's eyes burned and her entire chest ached, not from the flu or a cold or whatever. Christopher's harsh words compounded her gut-wrenching shame. The raw, no-nonsense account from a man who hadn't hesitated to point a gun at her head held an inescapable truth. Her father always insisted his innocuous club involved just a bunch of guys who loved motorcycles and gave money to children's charities. The Death Dwellers were no such thing. They were *real*. They were violent. They were scary.

So what did that make Big Joe? Christopher?

"Fuckin' spill," he demanded.

She shook her head, wretched to her soul.

He released her arms and studied her. She wanted to crawl somewhere and never come out again.

"Your ma know you fuck yourself up?"

"No," she admitted, her voice barely audible. A question was easier to answer than stringing together words.

"How long?"

"T-two years." After the last time they'd run away, and Thomas found her and beat her and her mother so terribly. "I called Daddy and he never came. He always came. Always," she said, wanting to lean into this big, strong man and know she'd be safe.

He backed away from her. "Jesus."

One word. So much meaning in it. Regret. Annoyance. Anger.

He rubbed his eyes and stretched out next to her again, as if he were unsure if he wanted her close to him. "Who the motherfucker worked you over?"

His sudden change of subject left her reeling, though she acknowledged her relief he'd stopped questioning her about what she did to herself. But he went from one uncomfortable topic to one equally as provocative. Her brain searched for an answer to satisfy all parties concerned. If she told the truth, she didn't know what the consequences would be. He mightn't believe Rack capable of such violence. "Who's here?" She had to know. Because if he did believe her and confronted Rack…Meggie shivered at the thought. "H-has my father returned, by any chance?"

"No."

Her father seemed to be a sore spot with Christopher. "Christopher," she blurted to test how his name sounded on her lips. A strong name for a strong man.

"Yeah?"

"Nothing," she whispered, feeling like an idiot for just wanting to say his Christian name. "Um, who's here?"

Christopher contemplated her and Meggie squirmed against the hard length of his body. Awareness of how little she wore seeped into her and her entire body flushed. She wriggled and he tightened his grip on her.

"Keep fuckin' still," he growled.

"I-I've never had the choice to be so close to a man like you in bed before." She felt as breathless as she sounded. His erection pressed into her belly, and she rubbed against him. Her nipples ached.

"One more fuckin' time, Megan," he snapped through gritted teeth. "You got one more fuckin' wiggle against my dick. *One more,*" he repeated, like she was some type of moron. "You move afuckingain and Ima fuck you."

"Umkay." Meggie's feminine core burned with heat and she felt her body slickening. If she moved again, she *was* a moron but the idea of making love to him sent her hormones into overdrive. He seemed so sexual and so sure of himself. "Will you fit inside me?"

"Motherfucker." He shoved her away and jumped out of the bed. He thrust a hand through his hair and glared at her. "You wanna fuck, lil' girl?"

"No. Yes. I-I don't know."

He paced for a minute before lighting a cigarette. "You ain't ever been fucked."

He almost made it sound like an accusation. She wished she hadn't been worked over so she could return his glare. She stared at the ceiling, preferring to be *fucked* on her terms rather than her stepfather's. "And?"

"What motherfucker hit you?"

"You're not going to answer me?"

"My answer relievin' you of your virginity."

At least, her virginity would be relieved with someone she wanted.

"And that shit ain't a fuckin' answer at all," he went on.

"Are you sure you're a biker? You can be really sweet and considerate."

Somehow, her observation insulted him. He stiffened. "I ain't no pussy, Megan."

"I didn't mean—"

"I just got fuckin' sisters, nieces, and, most of fuckin' all, a ma."

"Christopher—"

He kicked the chair against the wall, and she jumped, unable to stop her cry of fear. She shielded her head.

"Stop callin' me that! I ain't takin' your pussy. Case fuckin' closed." He drew in deep breaths and changed the subject. "In your fuckin' words, exfuckinplain why Rack workin' you over like this? What'd he say?"

"You know?"

"Contrary to the fuckin' girly bullshit swirlin' in your head 'bout me, I live a hard, fast life. If I ain't knowin' motherfuckers, I end up with a real fuckin' knife in my back."

Her stomach sank along with her mood. "You think that's what happened to my daddy?" she managed, envisioning her father in a situation where someone close to him had put a real knife in his back. She trembled and tears rushed to her eyes. She was just a wreck.

"Stick to one motherfuckin' subject at a time. You jumpin' from one conversation to the next and we ain't finished a fuckin one. Why did Rack—"

"Do you think—"

"I ain't got time to fuckin' run through scenes 'bout why your old man ain't here. He either turnin' up or he ain't and you gonna know."

"And I'll know," she echoed on a sob.

"Fuck, Megan. Don't cry."

The bed dipped again, and the warmth of his nearness enveloped her. She sniffled, trying to control her tears but her confusion, fear, and pain made it difficult. She had no one. No matter how safe Christopher...Outlaw...*him*...no matter how he made her feel, he didn't even want her to say his name in any of its forms. She'd never felt overwhelming sexual desire before, but she knew she wanted to be in his bed. Not that he cared what she wanted. Besides being cranky and disagreeable, he didn't like her.

He gathered her in his arms, and she buried her nose in the crook of his neck, sobbing harder.

OUTLAW

Outlaw gritted his teeth against the feel of Megan in his arms and the sounds of her sobs. His dick throbbed and his tight balls ached. Fuck his conscience for beating him to a pulp. No matter how fucked up his past, he just couldn't bring himself to do anything to hurt this girl. Boss's daughter. Her presence should've had him jumping for fucking glee as another means to exact further revenge on the man who'd turned Outlaw's life upfuckingside down. However, he wasn't that much of a dumb fuck. Fuckhead Foy was dead, so using his daughter for more revenge wouldn't do nobody a whole fucking lot of good. It wasn't like he was around to know, and Outlaw knew Snake wouldn't care since he'd known fuck all about her existence.

Megan's fucking youth and innocence awakened a restless energy within himself. The way she said his name made him want to hear her say it while he moved deep inside of her. It made him remember how it felt to be called by the name his ma had gifted him with. She, his cousin, Johnnie, and his sisters were the only ones who called him 'Christopher'. His grandfather had called him everything but a child of God, a fact he tried hard to forget.

Something he'd never shared with anyone outside Boss, K-P, Johnnie and his closest motherfucker's—Mort, Val, and Digger. And, now, Megan. Fuck, he'd wanted her to know he wasn't worth the time of day. He certainly wasn't worth the way she looked at him. As beautiful and as smart as Boss always said his girl was, if Outlaw wasn't careful, *he'd* be the motherfucker Megan drove insane.

He didn't want anyone to hurt her, including herself. He didn't know much about self-injury, other than remembering one of the whores who came through the club did it.

"You wanna fucking die, you stupid slut?"

Outlaw couldn't believe the wild light in Boss's eyes, directed at a woman who clearly needed kindness. He might not have understood why she was naked in the middle of Boss's bed, holding a razor blade dripping with her own blood from the fresh cuts on her breasts and belly. They weren't deep and he knew what she'd done because she'd once done it when she was with him. He'd smoked. She'd sliced.

"Lemme take care of this bitch for you," he offered. His heart pounded in his chest, hurt at how far gone Boss was. The man had been like a father to Outlaw and, now, drugs was eating Boss alive, taking his soul and all the compassion he'd ever had in him.

Whatever else the Death Dwellers might be accused of, physically harming women wasn't it. Boss kicked the shit out of any of the boys who hurt a woman. If it happened on the down low and Boss never found out about it, then fine.

"Get the fuck outta here, Outlaw. I don't need your fucking help with this whore."

"You need to sleep it off, Prez. I promise you, Ima take Summer outta your way and give her a good talkin' to."

Outlaw glanced at the girl, frozen in horror at being caught; Prez slid deeper into the pit of hell with each passing day, where no one escaped his drug-fueled wrath. Outlaw, Rack, or Snake barely reached him anymore.

"You fucking her? That's why you wanna get her the fuck outta here?"

Not anymore. *Not that Outlaw would mention that or remind Boss most of the boys in the club had tapped Summer's pussy. Outlaw wanted to see another sunrise. He wanted to find a way to help his idol and mentor.*

Raising his hands, he edged toward Summer, not wanting to play on Boss's paranoia. His dilated eyes watched Outlaw. He'd lost a shitload of weight. He barely ate or slept. Outlaw covered for him, having to take over most of his duties. Though Outlaw and Snake danced around each other, they'd bonded for the common cause. The two of them, along with Rack, shielded their Prez, but it had to stop. He had to come back to himself.

Slowly, Outlaw sat on the bed, feeling the weight of that intense stare. He wanted to look, make sure he wasn't pulling his piece to blow Outlaw the fuck away, but the man would take even that as a challenge.

Outlaw reached over and grabbed the razor blade from Summer's trembling fingers. He did it quick. He wanted to do it all quick. Grab her and run the fuck away until…when Boss returned…FUCK…would Boss ever be normal again? Did the man even want to be? Grasping Summer's arm, he dragged her to his lap.

"She scared, Prez. I'm just doin' the same thing you'd want a motherfucker doin' for your girl."

Boss's eyes lit up. For a moment, Outlaw glimpsed his old hero, the one who put his daughter up on a pedestal. "My beautiful girl. What's her name? I can't remember her name. Her beautiful face. It's all gone." *He chewed on his lip, his eyes filling with tears, and covered his face with his hands. All too briefly. He lowered them again and stepped forward. Tears tracked his gaunt cheeks, but pure hatred filled his eyes.*

Risking his own life, Outlaw stood with Summer in his arms. He'd never felt a girl tremble with so much fear. He wanted to reassure her, tell her he'd get her out of here. But, then, Boss stepped in front of Outlaw, blocking his path and pulling his blade out of his boot. Before Outlaw could beg for Summer's life, beg for Boss to remember his code, he'd slit her throat. As Outlaw held her. Blood poured from her and, if he moved his hand, her head might fall off with the deep, ear-to-ear slit.

Boss backed away, threw his knife on the bed. "Now take her the fuck away," *he ordered and stormed out of the room.*

Jesus Christ. Megan cried for *that* man. Outlaw had known Boss's treatment of those girls, but he'd never had to physically clean up after one of his rampages. He'd see Digger and Mortician's haunted eyes, watch them lose themselves in women, weed, and booze. Wonder how they could do what they did to get rid of those women's bodies on behalf of Boss. Then, he'd done it. Because he'd loved that motherfucker. Because he'd wanted Boss. Wanted the stupid motherfucker to recognize he had people in his corner. People who loved and needed him and would do anything for him.

Then, a few weeks later, he'd put Outlaw in that same position. Only this time, Outlaw had flat out denied him.

"I ain't buryin' no more girls, Prez, and you ain't killin' no more neither."

They were in the meeting room and Boss'd just called Outlaw out to go get the bitch from his bedroom for entertainment before disposing of her like they did Summer.

Boss got right in his face. "You fucking sure about that, motherfucker? Maybe, I should fucking kill you and then any bitch I want."

Snake, Rack, Val, Mortician, and Digger were silent, shifting in their seats, swallowing, sweating. Praying. Outlaw should've known Boss was up to this shit when he'd given Sinner, Tex, Guardian, and the other motherfuckers brave efuckinnuff to still come to the club, orders to make a run, then called the rest of them to church.

"You fucking hear me, motherfucker? Now, you go get that bitch, so we can fuck her and then bury her."

Outlaw swallowed, his hands flexing to keep from reaching for his piece. He could deny, as much as he wanted, Boss would never hurt him, but Outlaw knew better. After seeing Boss's destruction over the past months, he realized Boss stood a hair's breadth from putting him to ground.

"Sorry, Prez. I ain't mean to tell you what to do. Killin' girls ain't us." It ain't you, *Outlaw wanted to add.*

He'd seen some scary motherfuckers and stood up to them, but, Jesus, the maniacal light in Boss's eyes frightened him. In that moment, he knew. One or both of them would die. Boss was too far gone, had too much innocent blood on his hands and wanted more. It didn't motherfucking matter whose blood he spilled, either.

Boss thumped his chest. "I'm not asking you to kill those sluts. I do the killing. You do the disposal."

Outlaw backed away, his heart shattering into millions of pieces. He wanted to live. He wanted Boss to live. He wanted everything to be the same as before. Because, if he somehow managed to get out of this with both their lives intact, he was turning in his patch. And that hurt as much as anything. This club represented everything to him. His fucking entire life.

"Now go get the bitch."

Rack stood. "Boss, calm down. Give the brother a break. I'll get the fucking bitch for you and do to her whatever you want me to afterwards."

"I want this asshole. My VP," he sneered. "I chose this motherfucker over my own flesh and blood." He pulled his gun and shoved it against the bridge of Outlaw's nose. "He owes me. You all fucking owe me."

"Dad, put your shit away. You'll never fucking forgive yourself if you hurt this motherfucker."

Even the pretense of Snake and Outlaw having a friendship was stripped away. They'd always tolerated each other to make Big Joe happy. Now, they only wanted to survive.

"I chose you, Christopher," Boss screamed. "You told me the fuck like it was. I respected that. You were a man of your word and cow towed to no one." Spit slid from the sides of his mouth, the hand holding the gun shaking. "But if you defy me, you're a dead fuck. I'm sick of your bullshit anyway. Whining about me and what I need to do. FUCK YOU. I do what the fuck I wanna do."

After a tense moment, he lowered the gun and everyone breathed a collective sigh. Boss narrowed his eyes, studied each man, then laughed and pulled Outlaw into a chokehold, his idea of affection. "I love ya, boy. You're like a second son to me." He thrust his chin toward the door. "I think I'm gonna get some rest. We'll party another time."

Unless they had church or support clubs were visiting, no one hung out in the main room much anymore. Nowadays, they partied in small groups and in the rooms of the brothers who lived on premises. Most of the brothers had even given up their old ladies to keep the bitches safe. Boss was a loose cannon and no one wanted to set him off. After the near disaster in the boardroom, everyone scattered. Outlaw was exhausted, though, and he wanted to be alone. He didn't want to see or hear no bullshit.

How unfortunate for him.

Just when the alcohol and Aunt Mary started buzzing through him, a girl's scream ripped through the quiet. What the fuck was going on now? Grabbing his nine, he sprinted out the door and down the hall toward the sounds. He skidded to a halt and stared at the half-opened door.

Boss's room.

Fuck.

"No! Stop! It hurts. Please, please, please."

"Open, you little slut."

The next scream went through Outlaw and he knew he had to breach the lion's den. This girl sounded so fucking young. Too young. He didn't know how he knew it because he'd dealt with bitches who were eighteen and nineteen, thanks to Boss. But Summer was the oldest bitch Boss had been with in a while and she'd been twenty-two.

"Help me! Please!"

The unmistakable sound of flesh connecting with flesh decided Outlaw. He opened the door fully and stepped in. On the bed, Boss lay between a pair of pale white legs, his pants still on, just pulled down. With each thrust, the girl screamed, and Outlaw gripped his nine, knowing he had to be ready to fire, even though he kept his hand slack at his side.

He cleared his throat. "Yo, Prez."

Big Joe went still and looked over his shoulder, his weight bearing down on the girl under him.

"Get the fuck out."

"This ain't our style," he said quietly. "You hurtin' her. I heard her screams down the hall."

Boss pulled away and roared to his feet, bringing up his pants as he did. Before he closed his fly, Outlaw saw Boss had as much blood on his dick as the girl had smeared on her thighs. Grabbing his .45 from the nightstand and stuffing it in his waistband, Boss stalked to Outlaw.

One glance at the trembling girl on that bed told him all he needed to know. He'd been in enough bitches to recognize when he saw one who shouldn't have some dirty old motherfucker using her the way Boss had. He hoped the gun stuffed in his pants went off and blew his fucking dick off.

Outlaw hated Joseph Foy, in that moment. He couldn't take this shit anymore. First thing tomorrow, he'd turn in his VP patch and stomp on his fucking cut.

Boss cold-clocked Outlaw, who'd been so lost in his thoughts he never saw it coming. Before Outlaw had a chance to recover, Boss hit him again, sending him to his knees.

Boss gripped handfuls of Outlaw's hair. "I told you stay out my shit."

Fighting to remain conscious, Outlaw's hold on his gun tightened. "Let her go. I doubt she even legal."

"She'll be legal in about four years," Boss sneered. "That isn't your fucking business."

Outlaw wanted to argue, but the time for arguing had passed. It all happened too quick and, yet, the girl's head exploding, Boss turning the gun to Outlaw, and Outlaw raising his own piece and pulling the trigger while diving for cover seemed to go in slow motion. Painful, heartbreaking, life-changing slow motion with no rewind button to do shit over, to make whatever had gone wrong right. To bring this girl back.

But it was too late now. She was dead.

And Boss was dead.

Outlaw blinked and snapped back to the present, wanting to forget everything about Joseph Fucking Foy. But now, his beautiful girl needed him, and Outlaw didn't fucking know what to do with her. If he could fucking hate that motherfucking Boss a little more, he did just then.

Sighing, he buried his hand in her beautiful golden hair. He needed to get her the fuck away, but he didn't know where he'd put her. She made him weak and regretful. He'd always liked his given name, but it just didn't fit in these surroundings. His surname, though, he fucking detested. He closed his eyes and kissed the top of her head.

"What went down with you and Rack?" he persisted.

"He c-came there…um…" She sniffled and sat up, her firm little ass grinding against his cock. "How long have I been here?"

"Two days." Two days of hell, too. He'd gotten just about fuck all done, barely focusing on the logistics of the merchandise their support club had picked up for distribution. The distraction of knowing she was in his bed and his fucking worry that she might wake up or, worse, stay unconscious had not only pissed him the fuck off but shocked the fuck out of him too. Especially since seeing to his club was second nature.

She'd been feverish, racked with shivers and coughs, and thrashing through nightmares. He'd kept her cooled off with wet towels, dribbled water in her mouth, and acted like a nurse.

Though pale, she was awake, and Outlaw took that as a good sign.

She swiped the back of her hand over her red, runny nose and nodded. "Then, two days ago. You told him about going after me for the money."

"Yeah," he confirmed, studying her bruised and battered face. "What you did, stealin' his money, wasn't good but it was only five dollars, and after you told him you was hungry, he shoulda pulled back. No, he shoulda fuckin' gave you more money so you coulda got somethin' decent to eat." He narrowed his eyes at her. "Wait. You sayin' that motherfucker hunted you the fuck down the same fuckin' day my ass warnin' him away from you?"

She shrugged. "I don't know. When he saw me he was really angry."

Outlaw's mind spun. He needed to get Rack the fuck out of the Death Dwellers, but he had a lot of the brothers in his corner and, if Outlaw disappeared Rack, he might face even more anarchy. He didn't consider himself a bitch ass punk, but, fuck him, it took a heart of steel and balls the size of an elephant to run this shit. And he'd been fucked in the head for months, losing more and more control of everything because of all the hatred he carried for Big Joe.

Outlaw scowled at the admission. He stared at what he knew could become his greatest weakness. "This the deal, Megan." He stood and folded his arms, determined to ignore the outline of her breasts in his shirt. "I gotta go to a meetin'. Ima bring you some food. You take a shower after you eat and get some rest. I'll see you in the mornin' and we'll figure out shit then."

Megan frowned at him and sneezed. "Are you going to sleep at your house?"

He'd call Ellen so she could meet him at Kiera's house, then fuck the two of them 'til his cock punked out. "Nope. Besides, *this* place my house."

She hesitated. "Oh," she said in a small voice as if she knew he'd leave her to go to another woman.

So what if she did? All the better. Sighing, he rubbed the back of his neck. He remembered something else he'd noted on her driver's license when he'd found her backpack and verified her identity.

"Happy belated birthday."

She smiled at him and, though her lips were cracked and swollen, he swore her look reached out and touched his heart.

"Th-thank you," she whispered. "That's why I took the five dollars. I wanted to celebrate with some French fries. Treat myself and try to forget my first birthday alone."

A girl like her would see birthdays as special. A man like him acknowledged the day with herbs and pussy.

Her coughing reminded him he needed to buy some over-the-counter medicine for her. If she hadn't improved by tomorrow when he returned, he'd have to suck it up, bring her to the hospital, and hope his sister wouldn't be on duty.

"Stay in here."

"Okay."

A sweet voice to go with a beautiful face. Yeah, he was fucked if he didn't get his dick in some bitch tonight and get Megan the fuck away from him as soon as possible. "We'll see 'bout gettin' you somewhere."

She swallowed. "Is there anywhere you can send me? I-I mean a place where people know you?"

"My ma but—"

Jesus, the hope in her barely opened eye twisted him up.

"But?" she whispered.

"But I ain't talked to or saw my ma for 'bout a year."

"Why?"

He cracked his knuckles before jerking his head from side-to-side and cracking his neck. "Cuz I…" His voice trailed off and he clenched his jaw. He'd wanted her safe.

Thinking on it now and looking at Big Joe's girl, Outlaw recognized his other reasons. These were deeper. So much more fucked up.

He'd felt tainted, unworthy to be in her presence. He'd broken the Bikers' Creed, committed the ultimate betrayal, when his patch bound him to always take care of his brothers and their families. Respect them. His ma didn't know about most of the shit he did, but she *did* know how he admired one certain man.

"Chris…um—"

He stalked toward the door. "Stay the fuck in here, Megan," he snarled over his shoulder, beating a hasty retreat out of the room.

Chapter Eight

Meggie

COUGHING RACKED MEGGIE AND SHE WANTED to rest and heed Christopher's words. Truly, she did. Neither did she want to run into Rack or any of the others who'd been with him in the alley or at the creek. But her empty stomach made her desperate. The last time she'd eaten was the soup she'd had the night she met Christopher.

She glanced around but found no phone or any other way to communicate beyond the walls of this room. Grumbling at the awkwardness of the side she slept on being against the wall, she crawled out of bed. Removing herself from bed took work thanks to her stuffy head and achy body.

On her feet, she stood still, allowing the dizziness to recede and the pain to settle into dull throbbing. She hobbled forward, heading toward the door across the room and to the right. Relief sighed through her lips when she realized she'd guessed correctly and found the bathroom.

After taking care of more basic needs, she forced herself to gaze into the mirror, crying out at the sight of her face and hair. Bruises, swelling, snarls, and tangles. When put together, it equaled the hot mess who stared back at her.

Maybe, she should remain in the room. The next time, Rack might kill her. What did three-day-old hunger compare to another beating? As if to ridicule her, her belly grumbled and ached.

To do something to take her mind off her hunger pangs, she opted for a shower. She'd always gone for a swim at the creek to forget her wish for food. She peeled off the ridiculously big top and hung it on the hook of the cupboard door. Inside, she found towels. Before stepping into the bathtub and turning on the showerhead, she made sure there was soap and shampoo.

Finding both, she stepped under the warm spray of the shower and let it wash away weeks of dirt that swimming in the creek didn't. She soaped her body, shampooed her hair and tried to forget the sight of Christopher and how it felt to be in his arms.

He'd left for the night and she didn't want to consider what that meant. She might've retained her virginity by a thread, but she'd been exposed to sex thanks to her friends and her home life. The look in his eyes when he'd said he'd see her in the morning had been the same look Lacey had when the girl she sometimes slept with caught her with the guy she really wanted to be with.

Christopher was going to some woman. Meggie supposed his look had been worry because he didn't want her to cause any trouble between him and whoever.

The soap and shampoo burned over her cuts. Worse, a bout of coughing and sneezing seized her. She hoped she'd developed a bad cold and not pneumonia. Instead of taking her to a doctor, he'd nursed her himself. While sweet, it meant she lacked proper medical attention.

Her stomach growled.

Or the proper nourishment.

She'd make do. Find something to distract herself. After she finished cleaning herself, she'd go through the CDs she'd seen in Christopher's room and listen to music. Her plan settled, she turned off the shower and wrung out her hair, pushing the shower curtain aside. She shivered, though she felt as if she'd go up in flames. The cool air hitting her wet skin brought another round of coughing.

Meggie moaned, feeling sicker than a dog. She knew she couldn't leave her hair uncombed, so, for a time, she focused on her task, detangling it little by little until it curtained her back and shoulders. Then, she parted it down the middle and styled it into two braids. Between the shower and the hairstyling, exhaustion settled into her and she swayed.

She focused on the door on the opposite side of the bedroom, hoping to find a closet since the only other door stood straight ahead and opened to the hallway. Another rush of heat burst through her and she thought she'd erupt into flames at any moment. She'd kill for a glass of water.

Maybe, Christopher sleeping somewhere else was a good thing. She didn't want him catching whatever she had. She let the towel drop to her feet and fanned herself, licking her dry lips.

The bed seemed so far away. Didn't horses sleep standing up? Meggie palmed her eyes and scowled. If not horses, some animal did. Maybe, she could, too. Just stop and close her eyes and sink into unconsciousness.

And slip to the ground and conk herself into oblivion.

The door swung open and three men barreled into the room, then came to a screeching halt. Their gazes fell on her and their mouths fell open.

She squeaked, dropping her focus to where the towel lay on the floor. Too much distance. She blinked and, through her hazy heat, recognized Val with his stocky build, bald head, and tear drop tat beneath his left eye. The two black guys with dreads, diamond studs, and light brown eyes, she'd never seen, though.

The shorter one slapped the other's arm. "Check yourself, fuckhead," he snapped. "If you don't stop staring, Outlaw going to pluck both your fucking eyes out."

"He's staring, Mortician," the man snapped, pointing to Val.

Meggie swallowed and stumbled back.

"Er, um—"

Her thoughts exactly. She didn't need to echo Val's words when he said them with such eloquence.

"I'm Digger," the tallest one said, the one the man named Mortician slapped.

"I'm Meggie," she said, her ears ringing.

He ignored her. "We came to see about you." As he spoke, he concentrated on her face or some place over her shoulders. "Outlaw said not to disturb you too much. I wanted to know what you want to eat. My brother, Mortician, wants to show you around the club and keep you company while you out there. And, Val's riding out for a minute. If you need something, he'll pick it up while he out."

She sneezed and saw double. She reached out to balance herself. To her, it seemed as if the men stepped back. "Food would be great," she got out, somehow staying on her feet. "Something to wear, too. Guiding me to a chair or the bed would be even better."

"I like breathing, Megan," Mortician remarked.

Stars danced in front of her blurry vision. "Meggie," she wheezed.

Mortician ignored her, too. "I'm not fucking touching you while you buck ass naked, girl."

She opened her mouth to speak, not release the hideous squeak. The room, the faces, whirled around her, mixing with the stars and the fuzziness in her head. The concrete rose to meet her. She reached out and two strong arms caught her, saving her from an indignant fall to the floor.

Chapter Nine

OUTLAW

PAUSING OUTSIDE HIS BEDROOM DOOR, OUTLAW frowned at the sound of Mortician's voice coming from his room.

What the fuck?

A pissy mood already possessed him after he'd barreled through the main room feeling the weight of everybody's stares boring into him. It wasn't so much *him* as it was the punk ass shiny balloon with the words '*happy birthday*' and the ridiculous fucking teddy bear he'd carried while gripping a grocery bag in the other hand. Thank fuck, his brothers hadn't seen the cupcakes and birthday card inside.

He intended to bring this to Megan, then get the other bags from his pickup—the pair of boots he'd bought her as a gift and all the shit for colds he'd bought at the drugstore.

A squeak caught his attention, followed by concerned yells.

Outlaw pushed open his door and halted. Closed his eyes. Counted to three. Opened the motherfuckers again. Found the same scene. Two assfucks, Val and Digger, staring at Megan naked and in another assfuck's arms. Mortician swallowed and Outlaw saw the stupid motherfucker contemplate releasing his hold on her. Yeah, Mortician *really* thought about letting her fall to the fucking floor— because clearly, she wasn't awake with the way her arm fell like a limp noodle. Even though Outlaw intended to break Mortician's fucking fingers for holding her—continuing to hold her—he'd kneecap the assfuck if he dropped her.

"One of you better fuckin' start talkin'."

Surprise turned to shock when they saw what he held. He stopped long enough to set the teddy bear and balloon on his table, then grabbed Megan from Mortician, stalked to his bed and laid her gently down.

Fuck him…he swallowed, his body tightening at the sight of the golden curls between her thighs, her flat belly, her round breasts. Her pigtails hardened him even further, made her look sweet and untouched and vulnerable. Her flushed skin percolated with heat, the smell of his soap and shampoo rising in dry waves from her body. He liked that she smelled like him, but he wanted her to smell like *him*, his cum, his sweat.

"She got fever," Mortician said, standing across the room and out of Outlaw's reach. "I caught her on her way to a meeting with the concrete."

Outlaw touched her forehead, ran his knuckles along her lower lip. "How you get in here while she naked?"

Silence. Absomotherfuckinglute quietness. He glanced over his shoulder, narrowed his eyes. "I fuckin' told you, assfuck, ask her what the fuck she wanna eat and give her my other fuckin' messages 'bout these two fuckin' morons. Seem a big fuckin' leap between my instructions and what I'm seein'." He stalked to Mortician. "All I'm sayin' is some fuckin' body better start explainin' or bodies gonna shatter. Ima pause at the cock tip and end with brain matter. Speak," he roared. "*Now.*"

"We wasn't thinking, Outlaw," Digger started. "We just wanted to tell her who we was and let Meggie know what each of us was here for."

They exchanged glances. Val drew in a breath and stepped forward, head bowed, all but cowering in submission. If the motherfucker had a tail, it would've been tucked between his legs.

Outlaw folded his arms.

"We didn't knock. Not out of disrespect," Val swore and rolled his shoulders. "We just wasn't thinking. I was anxious to get the fuck to my bitch and I didn't want Megan holding me up, so we just barged in."

"In my fuckin' room. Knowin' she was *where*? In my fuckin' room. You fucks did this on purpose."

Digger shrugged. "Ain't like the bitch yours."

"Yeah," Val agreed, grabbing onto Digger's words like a lifeline. "I mean she's Boss's daughter."

Something he wanted to forget. Will away. Find a fucking genie and wish it wasn't so.

He clenched his jaw and stalked to his chest-of-drawers, finding a T-shirt for her. He slid it over her head and got her arms through the short sleeves, making sure clothes covered her. His shirt reached her to her knees. He scooped her into his arms.

Whether he liked it or not, Megan had to go to the fucking hospital. He only hoped his sister wasn't working.

As Outlaw sped toward Hortensia General, Megan opened her eyes a moment before they slipped closed again. She was flushed and her labored breathing didn't ease his mind at all. He swerved his pickup in front of the ER entrance and screeched to a stop, barely remembering to put the truck in park so urgent was his fear for her. Jumping out, he rushed to her side, opened the door and lifted her into his arms.

Her eyes slitted open as coughing besieged her, stealing what little strength she had. By the time she quieted and her head lolled back, he was at the intake desk. Either they'd seen him coming or heard her coughing or saw her go limp or…fuck all of the above, because an attendant barreled through the double doors that led to triage and rolled a gurney next to him.

"Lay her down, Outlaw," the man said.

Outlaw did as instructed, ignoring how the motherfucker was taking in the patches on his cut.

"I'm Marion, by the way," he continued, preparing to roll Megan in the back. "My momma was a John Wayne fan."

Outlaw didn't answer, starting behind the gurney.

"I'm sorry," Marion said, stopping him at the door as someone out of Outlaw's line of vision grabbed the other end of the gurney and wheeled Megan out of sight. "You can't come back there yet. She seems pretty bad off—"

"I ain't lettin' her outta my fuckin' sight."

Marion heaved in a breath. "By the time you're finished with the paperwork, her initial assessment will be completed."

Paperwork. Fuck. Right. He didn't want to leave her side, but Outlaw nodded. Once the doors shut, he stared at them, reminding himself she was young and strong. She'd be fine. Besides, the only reason he was so worried about her was because she was all alone and if he had allowed her to stay at the club the night Rack brought her she wouldn't have gotten so sick.

She was a fucking stranger to him, so fuck her. It wasn't his fucking place to worry about her.

"Outlaw?" a female voice called.

He glanced behind him and saw a pretty, dark-skinned woman with close-cropped hair, smiling at him. Her wine-colored, form fitting dress paid justice to her magnificent tits, small waist, and curvy hips.

"We need to register the patient," she said, her voice silky and smooth. She glanced at him through her lashes. "Follow me."

When she turned and added an extra wiggle to her already sexy walk, he grinned. Once he sat at her cubicle, he lit a cigarette.

"Boy, you know you're not supposed to smoke. This is a hospital."

"If it wasn't a fucking hospital, Carissa, my ass wouldna been here," he retorted, taking another puff and blowing the smoke out of his mouth.

"Fine," she said with a sigh. She slid an ice-filled Styrofoam cup to him. "Your ashtray. If my ass gets fired, I'm filing unemployment with you."

He snickered, flicking the ashes onto the ice. "Always been a witty bitch."

"Still a single bitch, too," she lamented. "Pussy in need of some good dick." She leaned forward and dropped her voice. "The way you let me sit on your face and ride your tongue last time, I'll even make an exception for you and suck your cock."

"Nope," Outlaw said, shaking his head and taking another drag on his cigarette. He'd give her a minute more before he made her focus on Megan. "Ain't makin' you do shit you ain't gonna enjoy, babe."

Her eyes lit up and she licked her lips. Before she responded, two girls stepped next to her and stared at him.

"You're Outlaw," one of them breathed.

He drew in a deep breath, but he nodded and inhaled again, wishing it was Aunt Mary instead of a regular smoke. He flicked more ashes into the cup.

"I wasn't here last Christmas when the Death Dwellers sponsored the Toy Drive," the other said.

"Marion said the Dwellers sends in money for several events," the first new bitch said.

"Would you two skedaddle?" Carissa ordered. "Let me get back to my business with Outlaw."

"I'm so jealous," one of them pouted, but they took their giggling asses away.

He tamped out his cigarette on the ice, then abandoned it in the cup.

"Now, where were we?"

"Seein' to Megan," he said, trying his best not to lose his patience. She was a cool chick that he'd met at a Dweller-sponsored hospital event several years ago.

She was a year older than him, but what she wanted and what he wanted had been completely different. His club came first. Case fucking closed. Like all good, solid bitches, however, *she* wanted to be number one.

"After we see to her, meet me at my house. I get off in three hours."

He shook his head. "Ain't leavin' her to fuck you or no other bitch, Carissa."

Surprise marched across her face before understanding settled into her eyes. "Have you gone and fallen in love?"

"Nope. Ain't believin' in love. Befuckinsides, she a good girl like you. What the fuck she wantin' with me ass? And fuckin' finally, I ain't been knowin' the lil' pain-in-the-ass motherfucker long efuckinuff to feel nothin' for her."

Her eyes mocked him. "Okay, bad boy, if you say so." She turned to her computer. "What's her full name?"

"Megan Foy." He dug into the pocket of his cut and grabbed her ID. "Put the club address as her place of residence."

She studied the ID, then looked at him. "Foy? Is she related to—"

Outlaw's nod interrupted her. "She Big Joe baby girl."

"Boss was good to the hospital," she said on a sigh, glancing at the screen again. "He put me and a couple other girls through college."

It sounded like something the Big Joe of old would've done.

"It tore me apart, hearing about how he was found." She cleared her throat. "*Parts* of him was found."

Outlaw's stomach turned at the memory. "Ain't up for discussion—"

"That was a big news story, Outlaw," she said. "You don't have to say anything. I read about it and heard about it. Coverage went on for days."

Coverage that meant jack shit since the circumstances had all been fabricated. Val had erased the club footage from that afternoon. Johnnie and K-P had taken the bodies, while Mort and Digger had cleaned Big Joe's room from top to bottom. Once video evidence was deleted and K-P returned to the clubhouse, they'd joined Mort and Digger. Outlaw had ordered them to clean more than just Big Joe's room since the chemical smell only there would've been a dead fucking giveaway.

"Do you have her insurance card?" Carissa asked, bringing him to the present.

The memories were so vivid that Outlaw had to take a moment to compose himself, allow the hatred for Big Joe to swirl up again and settle back into his gut. "She ain't got no insurance."

"I'll have to let them know," she said with regret. "Once she's stable, she will be released."

Christopher narrowed his eyes. "My fuckin' club give a mint to this motherfucker."

"She isn't a club member. I'm sorry," she added. "I don't make the rules, baby."

"Put my ass as her guarantor," he grumbled.

She nodded. "Just so you know, you'll be responsible for the entire bill. Treatment, doctors, tests, room if she is admitted. Just the ER will cost several thousand dollars."

"You hearin' my fuckin' ass gripin' 'bout the goddamn cost? Ima pay the fuckin' bill, Carissa. Case fuckin' closed."

"Okay." For a moment, she fell silent as she typed, then she pursed her lips. Stared at the screen. Hesitated.

"Christopher Caldwell," Outlaw gritted.

Her gaze flew to his. "How'd you know?"

"Cuz you once asked my fuckin' name and I told your ass you ain't needed to know and if you insisted, you ain't ever hearin' from me afuckingain."

"I'm surprised you remember that."

It happened at the last club New Year's Eve party before Big Joe went completely off the rails.

She typed again. "Club address for you too?"

"Yeah."

"How are Miz Patricia, Kiera, and Ellen?"

He couldn't say how Ma was. As a matter of fucking fact, she was another subject he didn't want to discuss. "Ki and Ellen fine. You met other girls that night. Why single them two out?"

"Neither your mother or Kiera and Ellen liked me," she said with a shrug. "Miz Patricia looked at me like I was dirt. Kiera kept trying to hook me up with a dude named Reptile. And Ellen would've slit my fucking throat if she'd had an opportunity."

"Motherfucker name Snake," Outlaw corrected. "I gotta idea why you thinkin' my ma treatin' you like that and it ain't nothin' 'bout how you look, Carissa. She ain't likin' no club girls and she mighta thought you was one."

"Fair enough."

"Howfuckinever, Ellen and Ki probably ain't likin' you cuz you was there with me and it wasn't no secret we fucked right before the party and we was fuckin' as soon as we got to my room."

"You can come back there now," Marion said, stepping next to Carissa.

"Not yet," Carissa said quickly. "You still have to sign."

A flashing light angled across the waiting room and Outlaw looked over his shoulder. Hospital security was inspecting his pickup. He'd forgotten all about the motherfucker.

"Go park my truck," he told Marion. "Motherfucker still runnin'."

"You can run out and do it," Carissa said, even though Marion was halfway to the exit to follow Outlaw's instructions.

He shook his head. "That's just gonna make me take longer to get to Megan."

Carissa nodded. "I just need a couple more minutes of your time, then I'll buzz you back."

Not responding, Outlaw decided it was a good omen that no one had mentioned Zoann.

Or maybe fucking not.

He didn't know why he bothered with wishes. The last time one came true was when he was twelve and his ma bought him a skateboard he'd wanted.

Zoann *was* on duty. Even worse, she was Megan's ER nurse.

When she stepped into the curtained-off space where Megan lay on the gurney, she paused.

"Christopher?" she whispered and rushed into his arms. She'd turned twenty-five in August, the third of his five sisters. She had big, brown eyes and rich brown hair, a beauty, a bitch, and a bother. Unmarried with no kids, she kept her nose where it didn't belong.

He barely remembered the man who'd fathered his sisters. Vague instances of care and concern, from an average-sized man with average looks, came to his mind on rare occasions. An encouraging smile. A game of flag football. Bicycle lessons. Like everything good in Outlaw's life, all too soon the man left, while his mother was still pregnant with Ophelia, his youngest sister.

After that, the girls started spending more time with their grandparents, a place Outlaw hated. No doubt, their grandfather contributed to Zoann's self-righteous bitchiness.

She pursed her lips and sniffed. "Where've you been? Mama—"

"We gonna talk," he interrupted, not wanting to discuss their ma. "Look after Megan first."

"Okay," she said softly. She worked in silence for a few minutes, broken only when she asked about Megan's illness.

He knew he was in for a grilling. Questions brimmed in Zoann's eyes. She'd always been nosy, and he suspected curiosity kicked the fuck out of her right now.

"And you said you don't know who assaulted her?"

"Nope. Sure the fuck ain't knowin'."

She rocked back on her heels. She didn't believe him. He didn't give a fuck. It just reminded him of another reason he hadn't brought Megan in. She didn't know the score, so she might blab Rack's involvement. Not that Rack didn't need handling, but Outlaw wanted to do it his way and after he found out who the fuck else worked with Rack.

He should've just left Megan by that creek. Or thrown her the fuck in so she could join the father she searched for. Then, again, maybe no. Boss was burning in hell. Megan deserved a place in heaven.

"Don't gotta get law enforcement in this," he warned. "Hear me, Zoann?"

Her mouth drew in like she'd sucked a lemon. "I'll see what I can do, Christopher."

His ass she would. He narrowed his eyes at her. "Just remind them some lil' kids in this buildin' who want that fat fuckin' bastard in the red suit bringin' 'em toys. Last I remembered, my club plunked down a few Gs to get it done."

She nodded and turned to leave, then stopped and drew in a deep breath. "I have two hours before my shift ends. Would you meet me so we can talk?"

Outlaw frowned. "I'm hangin' 'round 'til Megan's ready to leave."

"She's been admitted. Didn't the doctor tell you?"

"She that bad off?" He glanced at Megan. She looked so fragile.

"Yes. She is."

As much as he hated hospitals, he supposed he was stuck there for a while.

By the time Zoann's shift ended, Megan had been moved to a room, antibiotics dripping into her, and oxygen hooked to her while machines measured her blood pressure, pulse, and heart rate. The constant beeping worked Outlaw's last nerve and, more than anything, he needed a smoke.

To him, hospitals ranked up there with being buried alive. It wasn't for him.

Zoann pushed opened the door and stepped in, letting in a moment's glare from the bright hallway lights.

He stood as she tipped to the bed and stared at Meggie.

"Are you bringing her home to meet Mama?"

Wary, Outlaw eyed his sister. It was always a mistake to take Zoann's words at face value. "What the fuck you talkin' 'bout, Zoann? It ain't like that between Megan and me."

Zoann bit her bottom lip. "Then why are you her guarantor? Responsible for paying her bills."

"Her ma in Seattle, that's why."

"Her last name is Foy. Is she related to Big Joe?"

"Jesus, Mary, and all that's fuckin' holy, you a nosy bitch." He thrust his fingers through his hair, surprised when her face crumpled. "Fuck, Zoann. Yeah. This Big Joe girl. She lookin' for him."

She cocked her head to the side. "Where is he?"

"Zoann—" He clamped his mouth shut, not wanting to argue with his sister or say words he'd regret.

"You know where he is," she accused. "I know you do. Big Joe disappeared and you suddenly decided to turn away from us. The two are related. I know they are. It's your business if you want to throw your life away. But you've hurt Mama. Where is he, Christopher? Where have you been?"

"I ain't needin' the third fuckin' degree from you. Club business, club business. Case fuckin' closed."

She fisted her hands on her hips. "Isn't it time you left that miserable club? While you still can. Before something bad happens."

A mountain of fucking bad already happened.

"Mama's so sad. She just wants to hear your voice."

If he was honest, he missed his ma, too. Something he could ignore to protect her. He'd caused enough damage in her life. He didn't want to taint her by all the other shit he'd done.

"Ima call her when I got time."

"You have Mama living two hours away, Christopher," she stormed. "Shit has to be bad."

It had gotten much worse in the two years since he'd moved his mother to the house he owned on the Pacific Coast. He glanced at Megan. He needed to speak to her, find out just what the fuck was going on with her stepfather. If he couldn't send her home to her ma, maybe he *would* send her to his.

"Johnnie got out," Zoann persisted, referring to their cousin. "You can, too."

Not really. John Boy had gone Nomad. He now ran their medical laboratory. His preppy look made him the perfect choice to work at the lab. They made legitimate money because doctors found all kinds of reasons to order blood work, and piss and shit samples. So while their relatives believed Johnnie was out of the life, the club family knew better.

"I ain't leavin'," he growled. "For you. Ma. No fuckin' body."

"No, because you're nothing but a piece of trash like Granddaddy always said," she spat.

He was used to these words from various members of his family. Zoann was once his favorite. They even had nicknames for each other. He'd called her Bitsy and she'd called him Christy. Not that he gave a fuck about that anymore. Zoann thought she had a valid reason for her anger for this latest wrong. He'd dropped out of sight and hurt their ma. That still didn't give his sister a right to spit out the words she knew had always hurt him the most. "Get the fuck outta here, bitch."

"I always hated when they said that about you. But watching Mama this past year, I knew they had you figured out."

Outlaw's skin crawled in humiliation. Long ago, he'd pushed those years aside, all the hurt and shame he'd always experienced. Now, Zoann pulled up those memories and teased him with them, waving a red flag in front of the angry bull he'd become. Megan, a girl he'd never met until three days ago, offered a form of comfort. Whereas Zoann, the bitch he'd known all his life, scorned him.

He drew to his feet, fists balled at his side, and she stepped back, meeting his gaze.

"Please, Christopher. Do what's right for once in your life and get out of the club. Give Mama some peace."

Her voice had softened, turned wheedling.

"Is this why you wanted to fuckin' talk to me?"

She bristled. "Partly."

"Well, speak the other fuckin' reason and get the fuck outta my sight."

After a moment, her brows drew together. "I had a dream," she said. "All I saw was blood. *You* covered in blood. Unmoving. Dead."

Fuck Zoann and her dreams. She shouldn't be a fucking nurse. She should be a fortune teller. She'd had a dream about him being swallowed by dirt. Less than ten days later, he was burying a motherfucker alive.

He glared at her, opened his mouth to tell her to get her jinxy fucking ass the fuck away, but Megan moaned, and he forgot whatever the fuck he was going to say.

He rushed to Megan's side, took her hand in his, and sagged in relief when she opened her eyes and turned her sweet little smile on him.

Chapter Ten

OUTLAW

"HOW JOHNNIE?"

Accepting the bud Mortician handed to him, Outlaw took a draw, held the smoke in for a moment, then exhaled before answering. "Good as far as I fuckin' know, Mort. Ain't hearin' from him in a minute." He grinned, passing Aunt Mary to Val. "He still a preppy motherfucker."

"Always was," Val agreed, inhaling the good ganja and taking another hit.

"Mort, why you sitting here?" Digger asked, walking to the table and snatching the roll from Val. "For that fucking matter why you and Val here, Outlaw?" He nodded to where Kiera and Ellen played pool with K-P, Tex, and Sinner. "I got it on good fucking authority Ki and El ready to fuck your brains out and your tongue numb."

Outlaw snickered, glancing across the room to the railed pool table area. That way also led to the bathrooms, one for chicks and the other for dicks, designated with signs on each respective door.

Kiera was so fucking pretty with her olive complexion and long dark hair. Ellen was a good-looking bitch herself. Her hair showed more strawberry than blonde. Unlike Megan's softer gleam, Ellen's blue eyes were icy and flecked with gray and green. Ellen had such a hard fucking edge; it dampened her beauty more than her tough life ever could.

"Bruh, if you don't want them, I can do my duty to the club and fuck the shit out of them," Digger added. "They haven't been in my bed since you took them."

"Shut the fuck up," Mortician snapped. "Prez still want them for himself right now."

He did. Had. For six fucking months, he'd been satisfied with their fucking arrangement. But he felt out of fucking sorts, and he knew it was because of that little pain in the ass motherfucker currently in the fucking hospital. She'd been there five fucking days already, and he couldn't stay the fuck away. Every fucking day, he went to see her. He told himself it was because she was here alone, searching for a father no longer alive.

A motherfucker he'd killed.

Assfuck deserved it.

That didn't mean shit, though. Not where Megan was concerned. She only knew she needed that motherfucker's help.

Kiera squealed and bounced up and down. She wore a long-sleeved crop top without a bra. Each move she made, her tits followed suit. "I win," she announced.

Outlaw smiled at her happiness, accepting Aunt Mary from whichever motherfucker handed him the roll.

K-P Andrews left the pool area and headed to the table. He lifted a brow at Outlaw, snatching the bud from him and dragging on it. "Why the long fucking face, runt?"

"Maybe, he need a little loving," Kiera said, sitting on Outlaw's lap and kissing him.

"You're so fucking sappy, Ki," Ellen snapped, hot on her heels. "Always wanting to kiss. *Blegh.*"

Lifting her head, Kiera grinned, her lipstick smeared. She thumbed the edges of his mouth.

"Lipstick, huh, babe?" he asked, wishing he'd feel something other than a hard cock. At the least, he usually felt some anticipation of getting into their pussy. Even excitement at times. Tonight, nothing, and he hadn't fucked since he'd brought Megan back to the club last week.

"You want to go to your room?" Ellen asked, gazing at him through her lashes.

Kiera laid her head on his shoulder.

"Up, Ki," he told her and nodded to Digger when she complied. "He wanna fuck." He shrugged. "I ain't in the fuckin' mood."

Kiera and Ellen, Mort and Val, *all* the motherfuckers at the table stared the fuck at him like a cock suddenly sprouted the fuck out of his eye.

"Uh…" Kiera rocked on her heels. "I…" She opened her mouth, then closed it, searching for something to say. She glanced at Digger. "I haven't forgotten how you like your cock sucked." Her eyes flickered back to Outlaw.

"Ain't takin' the bait, Kiera," he told her. "You fuckin' him or suckin' him up to you."

Her shoulders sagged but she nodded.

"Aww, Kiera, baby, don't look like that," Digger said gruffly. "Outlaw going through menopause or some shit. Maybe, his cock not working."

"Kiss my motherfuckin' menopause ass, assfuck," Outlaw said, but he laughed. "My cock doin' fine."

Ellen licked her lips. "Can I see?"

"Nope," he answered, getting his pack of cigarettes from his cut and lighting one up. "Ain't you heard what the fuck I said?" he asked around plumes of smoke.

Her lips tightening, she turned. "I'm ready to go home, Kiera. You're my ride, so let's jet."

Taking one last shot at changing his mind, Kiera wiggle-walked to Digger, wrapped her arms around his neck and kissed him, long and deep. "Let's go to your room for a quick fuck," she breathed.

Digger nipped her bottom lip, then took her hand and started off. "Come on, Ellen. Join our party."

Ellen stood silent for a moment, staring at Outlaw, waiting for him to say something. When he lifted his brow, she huffed a breath, then stomped behind Digger and Kiera.

"Prez, you okay?" Mort asked.

"Fuckin' fine. Why?"

"Cuz you just sent away two bitches with the hottest pussy for miles," Val offered.

"I ain't in the mood for them two," he barked. "You want them, go join Digger. Or fuck them tomorrow. Fuck, it ain't meanin' I ain't ever gonna wanna fuck them again."

Mort got to his feet. "I'm going back to bar duty. Stretch doing a good fucking job for a Probate, but that bar mine."

"Mort, you ain't got to serve no more," Outlaw said with a shake of his head. "You the fuckin' enforcer. Yet you guard that motherfucker like you gave fuckin' birth to it." He glanced at the brown-haired assfuck serving the brothers. It had been years since he'd sponsored a motherfucker. Not since Val. Fuck, usually, he didn't even bother with fucking Probates.

"Talk to me, boy," K-P ordered, and Outlaw realized Val and Mort had left the table to go to the bar. Mort took position behind it, while Val slid into a stool in front of it.

"Whatcha want my ass to fuckin' say?" Outlaw demanded.

"How's Meggie?"

Outlaw clenched his jaw. Of course, K-P knew about Meggie. At one time, him and Big Joe had been real close. "She gettin' better. Probably bein' released tofuckinmorrow or the next fuckin' day."

K-P nodded. "You're letting her come back here?"

"For now. Where the fuck else she goin'?"

"Boss would want her here with you," K-P said quietly.

"The fuck that motherfucker would." Outlaw told K-P about the conversation he'd had with Big Joe when he'd first mentioned Megan. "He fuckin' said my ass ain't good efuckinnuff for her."

"Joe was protective of her. She was a child when he said what he did to you. But he said several times, he needed to whip one of you into shape for her. He…Dinah had him in a bind. He loved the fuck out of her. She was a good woman. Just like my daughter's mother. Bitch one of my closest friends to this fucking day." He stopped and grinned.

Outlaw lifted a brow.

K-P snickered. "She wouldn't much appreciate me calling her a bitch. I think I might tell her, just to hear how many different ways she can call me a motherfucker."

"You soundin' like you still feelin' her," Outlaw said, chuckling.

"She's a good woman. Spirited. Humorous. Loves life. We were so fucking good together. I'll always regret losing her. As tough as she was, she couldn't take the pressures of club life." A dark look crossed his face. "It didn't help that Logan was around in those days."

Logan Donovan was a worse motherfucker than Big Joe could ever hope to be. Outlaw scowled at the mention of his grandfather.

"Rack—" K-P grimaced. "Or *Wally Bart*. Motherfucker's civilian name," he added.

"He ain't lookin' like a Wally."

"What about Wallace? That's his actual name. He just preferred Wally."

"I prefuckinfer Ass Fuck Face Fat Ball Motherfucker."

K-P guffawed. "He's that and more. But he loved Boss. Rack admired his bravery and his fucking audacity. That makes him dangerous, Outlaw. He's grieving for Big Joe. Deeply."

Pain sliced through Outlaw at K-P's gruff tone. Rack wasn't the only motherfucker grieving for Big Joe. K-P was, too. Mortician, Val, and Digger. Even John Boy. "Fuck Big Joe," he spat, hating the catch in his voice. "I hate that fuckhead."

Instead of censure, K-P nodded. "It's okay, boy. You did what you had to do. Joe would've expected no less. We both know he should've been kicked out long ago. Or put down well before you were forced to do it."

Though he wanted to talk about anything other than Big Joe, his curiosity got the best of him. "How you met them two black-hearted motherfuckers, K-P? That day on Johnnie tenth birthday when we was with Bitsy—" His sister wasn't that sweet girl to him anymore. Fuck her, too. "Zoann," he corrected. "How long was you knowin' them?"

K-P glanced away, lost in thought for a moment before he met Outlaw's gaze again. Agony shadowed his face. "A long time, boy," he said quietly.

"So you was knowin' Boss befuckinfore he met Megan ma?"

"Yeah. I was with that motherfucker the night they met. Fuck, at that party, he was headed to where Roxanne was and I was going to Dinah. Arrow pissed Roxanne off and she threw a goddamn drink in his face and cussed him the fuck out."

Arrow was K-P's younger brother that Outlaw could leave or take. He was a Dweller too, a former president of one of their Midwest chapters, gone Nomad.

"Lemme fuckin' guess. Arrow started threatenin' motherfuckers in her life or some shit."

Eyes twinkling, K-P nodded. "But I went to rescue *him* from *her*. She was threatening bodily harm to him. Or as she put it, threatening to *cut a bitch*. She had a blade about yea big." He used his fingers to measure about four or five inches. "Arrow was so fucking shocked, he didn't know what the fuck to say."

"Fuck, where the fuck was you at?" Outlaw asked, laughing along with K-P. "Badges come out?"

"We were at an event Sharper was throwing."

At the mention of Mort and Digger's old man, Outlaw's humor fled.

"Both Dinah and Roxanne were there with their respective churches." K-P snorted. "Paying homage to the great Reverend Sharper Banks."

Outlaw completely fucking agreed with the disbelief in that sound. A fucking devil like Sharper Banks posturing as a minister.

"He'd tapped Joe, me, and a few other brothers to serve as protection. He had open bars and shit, but no one questioned him. Flush with his wife's money and gifted with gab, he was already on the rise."

"If he ain't put your future bitch the fuck out, he musta still had a lil' fuckin' soul left in him."

"Sharper? Nah. I got to my brother and Roxanne before it got too out of hand."

"If ever two motherfuckers sharin' the same blood was more fuckin' different, you and Arrow is."

"Famous last words," K-P said with a straight face.

"What the fuck that mean? I ain't got no fuckin' brothers."

K-P cleared his throat. "You have sisters, and you couldn't be more different from them."

"They ain't countin'. We was born fuckin' different. I got a cock, they got pussies."

"You're right," K-P agreed easily. "I prefer talking about the night we met Dinah and Roxanne."

"And how Boss movin' in on the bitch you wantin'." Big Joe was a motherfucker like that.

"Well, I moved in on the woman he'd been eyein'. It worked out the way it was supposed to, boy. I saw Dinah from afar and thought she was what I needed. Just based on her looks. She's a little older than Roxanne, but she put Joe through hell. Understand, Outlaw? I never formally met her. What I knew about her was from what Joe shared. Listening to him, I always got the impression she was so much more fragile than Roxanne. Joe wanted Dinah happy, so he backed away, instead of stepping in and eliminating certain issues."

"Such as?"

K-P shrugged. "Shit," he said on a sigh. "Shit." He rubbed his bald head. "Meggie's here now. I heard all about her first night here. You're a good man, Christopher."

"She a fuckin' pain in the fuckin' ass, K-P," Outlaw snapped. "Already causin' me more fuckin' headaches than any fuckin' bitch I ever met. And she fuckin' eighteen years old." He leaned closer. He'd known K-P since he was a child. "More fuckin' important, I fuckin' killed him." It was his burden to bear. Since she'd arrived, it weighed on him more than ever. "Shit like that ain't forgivable."

"It never will be, if you don't forgive yourself first," he admonished. "The fucking club's falling apart, boy. You know it and I know it. You're suffering from what Joe left you no choice but to do. Rack is waiting to fucking pounce, even more so after you avenged Meggie's beating. Snake lingers in the shadows. In a few days, it'll be one year since all that shit went down. There's us and there's them. You have people who believe in you, Outlaw. Mort, stingy motherfucker that he is, pumped a lot of fucking money into this club when he got his hands on that safe. Val admires the fuck out of you. Digger would do anything for you. Johnnie, for all his college education and your grandfather's admiration, looks up to you, too. You did what the fuck you had to do. If Rack and Snake get a foothold, those of us aligned with you are dead. *You're* dead anyway. After all you did to *live*."

"Fuck, motherfucker gotta die someday. Maybe, Big Joe shoulda lived and not my fuckin' ass. He had the fuckin' stomach for this. I ain't got it."

K-P leaned back. "You were the fucking enforcer at one time, you little runt, so fuck you. Don't hand me that bullshit. You have the stomach for it."

Outlaw didn't say anything.

"Strike before they do," K-P advised, then fell silent for a moment. He must've seen Outlaw's hesitation because he decided to open his fucking mouth again. "Don't think about us for right now. Think about Big Joe's baby girl. What happens to her if anything happens to you?"

Resentment flared up at that statement. "How the fuck I suddenly got responsible for her lil' ass?"

"At least get her healthy before you send her away."

"You so fuckin' worried 'bout her, *you* watch over her."

"I have my own baby girl to look after. And, fuck, being with me might be a bigger danger for her. I have my own skeletons. Should they catch up to me, I'm fucking dead, too."

As brothers went, K-P was one of the most amiable and even-tempered. "Ain't even imaginin' your shit so fuckin' bad, a motherfucker wanna fuck you up." He nodded toward the hallway, in the direction of Rack's bedroom. "Afuckinside from that fat-balled fuckhead."

"It all goes back to Logan," K-P admitted.

Outlaw threw K-P a dark look for bringing up Logan again. "He fuckin' dead and suckin' off Satan. Ain't no longer a worry to you or no other motherfucker."

A fleeting expression crossed K-P's features. Outlaw swore it was guilt but before he could think on it, K-P got to his feet.

"Think about what I said, runt."

"I'm six fuckin' feet and four fuckin' inches. You 'bout five-eleven. How the fuck my ass the runt?" Outlaw said, snickering.

"You were a runt when I met you," K-P responded. "A fucking smart-mouthed ten-year-old."

That didn't explain why he referred to Mort, Val, and Digger as runts. They'd been almost full-grown when K-P first met them.

"Get your shit together, Outlaw," he said. "If you can't fucking do it for the club, then do it for Meggie. At least until she's healthy enough to be sent away."

Refusing to commit to K-P's request, Outlaw stood.

"Going find some pussy?" K-P asked. "That's what the fuck I'm about to do before I hit the fucking road to visit my daughter."

"Nope. Ima go to my fuckin' room and fuckin' rest. Hospitals wear on a motherfucker and if Megan ain't released, my ass stuck there another fuckin' day."

K-P grinned. "Of course, Florence Nightingale."

Outlaw flipped him off.

"How's Bitsy?" the man asked, still referring to the name Outlaw had given to Zoann ages ago.

"Bitch fuckin' there," Outlaw grumbled. "Still meaner than a motherfucker." He was through talking about any of this shit, finished reminiscing, tired of questioning his ability to restore the club to what it had once been and fucking over thinking about fucked up motherfuckers better off fucked up. "Later," he said, and sauntered the fuck away.

Chapter Eleven

Meggie

MEGGIE SAT IN THE MAIN ROOM AT THE CLUBHOUSE, grinning like an idiot. Three days ago, she'd been released from the hospital after spending an entire week there. Christopher had ordered her to bed the moment they set foot in his room. Though much better, she still felt weak and tired. Thankfully, her lungs were now clear. Even better, the swelling in her eye had gone down and her bruises were fading. Not long after she'd arrived, she'd fallen asleep, but a noise had awakened her, and she'd realized Christopher had returned to the room.

She'd remained quiet for a moment, studying the play of muscles beneath his white T-shirt and leather vest. He thrust impatient fingers through his inky hair, a scowl marring his brow. His tan skin combined with his black hair and green eyes gave him an exotic look. His masculine beauty coupled with his big, strong body and I'm-your-worse-nightmare attitude made him every woman's fantasy. A bad boy with a good heart and as many emotional scars as she had. As if he had any control over being born. He had more sense than that. But, when something was pounded into the psyche day after day, it became the gospel truth. Especially when it was the psyche of a young and vulnerable boy.

Meggie hurt for him and wanted to take as much care of him as he had of her. He'd seen to her safety and well-being, and she couldn't remember the last time someone had taken care of her.

"Christopher?" she'd whispered.

Her voice seemed to surprise him, and he'd paused whatever he'd been doing. "Yeah?"

"Thank you."

He answered with a curt nod, knowing what she thanked him for without her saying the words. They'd fallen silent and she thought he'd leave. Instead, he'd picked up a balloon and teddy bear and brought them to her.

"Happy belated birthday, Megan," he'd said gruffly. The soft lighting from the lamp couldn't hide the red in his cheeks.

He was blushing. But more than that... "You bought this for me?" she asked. Her heart raced at the unexpected gesture.

Another brusque nod. "My sisters into this kinda bullshit." He shrugged. "You a girl like them bitches, so I fuckin' figured you likin' it, too." He set the teddy bear with the sagging balloon on his nightstand and shoved his hands in his pockets.

Her smile had faltered at his disappointing explanation. "Oh. Right. Of course." Not that it wasn't sweet. He could've allowed her birthday to pass without comment. She just wished he'd given her the things because of *her*. She wasn't his sister and didn't want to be. Every day she'd been in the hospital he'd visited her, spending hours each day just talking to her. Somehow, it never got truly personal. He didn't like talking about Big Joe. Even when Meggie asked had he called her father to let him know she was sick, she realized he'd evaded answering. He was very adept at steering the conversation away from topics he didn't want to discuss.

Since her release, he'd hung around the club, escorting her to the main room and allowing her to leave his door open when he wasn't with her. She'd been in heaven.

Then, earlier today, he'd come to the room with an unwelcome announcement.

"I gotta make a run," he'd said after a moment. "Mortician bringin' you somethin' to eat. He not just bargin' in, either. So you ain't got to worry."

Meggie frowned. "Why would I?"

Menace marred his features. "Just in case you would."

Meggie had narrowed her eyes at him, not buying his explanation. "What—"

"Fuckin' drop it, okay?" He'd headed to the door. Opening it, he'd paused, then turned, the darkness in the hallway throwing him into shadow. "Rack ain't touchin' you, so go wherever the fuck you wanna." Stomping back into the room and swearing a blue streak for reasons unknown to her, he lifted two bags from his table and threw them to her. "Ain't thought 'bout wrappin' paper or nothin'." Not giving her a chance to respond, he'd stalked out and slammed the door behind him.

That happened a couple hours ago. After she'd found a pair of black motorcycle boots, leather pants, leather jacket, and a sapphire blue sweater, and before he'd returned with two chocolate cupcakes. "These replacin' the ones some motherfucker ate while you was in the hospital."

Now, she sighed in pleasure, closing her eyes as the rich flavors of dark chocolate icing combined with the creamy milk chocolate center. The noise of laughter and music bounced off Meggie. The overwhelming cigarette smoke aggravating her cold, and the abundance of women hanging around the bikers, couldn't dampen her mood. For her, only she and Christopher mattered, and her focus narrowed on his proximity to her.

The attention he was bestowing on her right now felt different, more intimate.

"Yo, Megan. Fuckin' chocolate on your nose," Christopher said with a laugh.

She swiped at it with her finger, then sucked the chocolate off. He followed her every move and his eyes darkened. His hand holding his cupcake paused mid-air. He drew in a breath and bit into the sweet, reversing their roles. Now, instead of his finger, he licked the icing from his lips, and *she* followed the movement of *his* tongue. She squirmed in her seat and bit down on her lower lip. Without thinking, she reached over and thumbed a tiny drop of chocolate from the corner of his mouth.

As aware of him as she'd ever been, she slid her tongue along her fingertip more than she had to to remove the minute bit of chocolate.

"Fuck me," he groaned. He leaned toward her and pushed her hair over her shoulder, securing it behind her ear. Then, he took her face between both hands and bent his head to kiss her.

A voice interrupted him, and Meggie wanted to scream in frustration.

"You morphing into Boss or something, Outlaw? Fucking young girls and shit."

Meggie jerked at the hard, female tone, already aggravated at having her near-kiss interrupted. As the words penetrated her disappointment, she sucked in a breath. "What?" she asked. Another dose of outrage piled on top of the accusation against her father when the woman planted her mouth over Christopher's and took from him the kiss meant for Meggie. She got to her feet and tugged Christopher's hand. "What's she talking about?" she demanded, her stomach churning at the lingering kiss. "I need to talk to you."

He allowed the other woman free rein with his mouth, only looking at Meggie when the strawberry blonde pulled away and smirked.

"I need to talk to you," Meggie repeated, the careless expression on Christopher's face cutting through her. "Who's this?"

He narrowed his eyes and his jaw clenched. Meggie became aware of the growing silence, the attention turning their way. Warning darkened his eyes and her contentment evaporated. With the regard Christopher had been showing her, she'd been satisfied to wait here a few more days for her father. But not only did this woman touch Christopher as if she had every right, she spoke of Meggie's father with derision and hate.

"Who's she? What's she talking about? Where's my father?" The questions flew out of her mouth.

Christopher winced and cursed. Meggie's stomach dropped at the remorse flashing on his face.

"What's going on here, baby?" another woman asked, stopping on Christopher's other side.

She was pretty—no beautiful—with her dark hair, dark eyes, and olive skin. Her breasts strained against the long sleeve shirt she wore, the black leather pants and black motorcycle boots carbon copies of Meggie's. The casual way she kissed Christopher and placed a hand on his shoulder, the way she glared and bristled at the strawberry blonde, led Meggie to believe she stared at Christopher's girlfriend.

Meggie glowered at him. "Where's Boss? Where's my father?" she snarled.

The strawberry blonde's mouth curled in a distasteful smile. She opened her mouth, but the other woman shook her head.

"Shush, Ellen," she ordered.

Not taking his eyes from Meggie, Christopher nodded. "Listen to Kiera, Ellen." He stood and wrapped his arms around Kiera's waist, leaning to kiss her just as Ellen had kissed him.

His look challenged Meggie to gainsay him. Without thinking, she grabbed his mug of beer and threw it in his face. The outflow caught Ellen and Kiera, as well, for which Meggie was grateful.

"What the fuck, bitch?" Ellen yelled.

Her father always told her no one could shove her into an emotional mire unless she allowed it. As best she could, Meggie had held onto that through her dealings with Thomas, knowing *he* had the problem. She didn't. Of course, that reasoning seemed well and good in her head. Putting it into effect was something else entirely. She'd found other ways to cope. It might not have been the best way, but it was *her* way and she'd gotten through it. More her father's daughter than her mother's, she wouldn't be cowered.

When Ellen came at her, bypassing Christopher's furious advance, Meggie shoved her back with all her might. The move caught Ellen by surprise, and she smacked into a barstool, landing hard on her butt.

Christopher jerked Meggie toward him. She balled her fist and managed to graze his jaw, earning her freedom. She scooted around him and headed for the exit, not knowing her destination, just knowing she had to leave.

"Sit your fuckin' ass down, Ellen," Christopher called, hot on Meggie's heels. "Dontcha walk outta that fuckin' door, Megan."

"Bite me," she yelled. "You overbearing, conceited rhinoceros."

His arm looped around her waist, and she struggled against his hold. Since he was as *strong* as a rhinoceros, it didn't do any good. He plunked her down near the shattered glass and wasted beer.

"You fuckin' cleanin' this."

His tone told her arguing would be a mistake, but she felt hurt, disappointed, angry, just a walking stew of emotions too numerous to list. She drew in a breath, hating how close to tears she was. To counteract sobbing her heart out, she decided to face him. She narrowed her eyes. "I'll clean it if you tell me what she meant about my father having sex with young girls."

"This shit ain't up for negotiatin', Megan."

She stomped to the table where she'd been having such a wonderful time and sat in the chair Christopher had vacated. She began untying the laces on her boots. When she had one off, she threw it at Christopher and hit his stomach. He didn't flinch.

"Whatcha fuckin' doin'?"

She got the other one off and aimed for his head. He sidestepped it.

"You don't like shit on your feet too much, huh, babe?" Rack called, the amusement in his voice indicating his extreme enjoyment of this scene.

They had become the night's entertainment. As the club president, Christopher wouldn't allow anyone to disobey him. In private, it would've been horrible enough. Being in public made it ten times worse. But Meggie didn't care.

"Do what you will to me. I don't care! I'm not staying here and I'm not cleaning anything. I'm not wearing the same boots you bought for your girlfriend. You must've gotten a 2-for-1 special."

The more she spoke, the blacker Christopher's mood turned, until the force of hell surrounded him. He balled his fist, stepped closer to her. Meggie swallowed, determined to stand her ground.

"You ain't stayin' here, bitch. You fuckin' right. Go back to your fuckin' ma where lil' girls like you befuckinlong."

"Go back to hell where mean, cantankerous men like you belong," she countered.

He grabbed her arms, lifted her to her feet and shook her. "Shut the fuck up. I mean it. You testin' my patience. If you was anyfuckinbody else, you'd be flat on your fuckin' ass. Knocked the fuck out. Not wakin' up for a fuckin' month." To emphasize how little he held onto his control, he shook her again. "Now, Ima fuckin' tell you nice. Clean this fuckin' mess."

"No. If you want to hit me, do it," she spat. "But I'm not my mother. I fought her husband when she wouldn't. If he ever finds me, I'm going to fight until I can't anymore. Either he'll win or I'll win. So do your best."

"Sit down," he ordered, setting her on her feet, his voice echoing in the deathly silence.

"No."

Christopher kicked over the table they'd spent the evening at. "Goddammit, you fuckin' lil' piece of baggage. Sit the fuck down. *NOW!*"

Meggie sniffed but slid into the chair without another word.

Christopher paced, thrusting his fingers through his hair. Everyone tracked his movements, not speaking, remaining still. He paused a moment and pointed a finger at her. "That's why you lookin' for Boss, yeah? Your step fuckhead tryna take your pussy?"

Her lips thinned and she pinned him with an accusing gaze. "You're crude."

"Ain't givin' a good fuck whatcha think 'bout me, Megan. So you might as well fuckin' answer me."

Her stomach dropped. As long as she fought back and didn't think about it, as long as she reminded herself her father's DNA infused her blood, as long as she insisted Thomas's violence wouldn't rule her life, she coped. She laughed. She flirted and desired the angry man before her.

Most of all, she *survived*.

Now, Christopher insisted she admit to one of Thomas's basic motivations—his sick determination to have sex with her.

Nausea churned in her and she shook. She had to hold herself together in front of these people. In front of Rack, Ellen, and Christopher's girlfriend.

He crouched down in front of her and took her chin between his thumb and forefinger in a gentle but firm grip. "Look at me."

Exhausted, she raised her gaze to his and gave him the barest of nods.

"What the fuck his name?"

"Thomas Nicholls," she croaked. The same focus and kindness he'd exhibited before Ellen and Kiera walked in returned. That was the hardest to swallow. The way he made her feel, the desire, safety, need and want. The way he *knew* he made her feel and gave so little thought to toying with her and then kissing two other women senseless.

He rose to his feet and pulled a pack of cigarettes out of the inside of his vest pocket. "I ain't got whatcha call a girlfriend," he began, after lighting a cigarette and taking a drag. "Second, if you ever fuckin' actin' like a psycho bitch, Ima strip you to nothin', lay you over my lap, and beatcha bare lil' ass."

She glowered at him. He took another drag of his cigarette, unaffected.

"Next, Ellen ain't had no business openin' her fuckin' trap 'bout Boss." He threw an evil look at the woman, who flushed and looked away.

"My father—" She paused and the thought hovering in the back of her head broke free. She sucked in a breath and clutched her belly. "Young girls," she whispered, and her voice shook. "My father." She swiped away the tears she couldn't stop and pressed down on her trembling lips, determined to control herself. She started over. "My father isn't like Thomas, is he? I-I mean the whole world looks at Big Joe and sees a biker. They don't even try to see the real him." She shuddered. "They look at Thomas and see a math teacher. A wholesome, all-American citizen. But…but he isn't. He's worse than my father could ever be. With Big Joe…" She swallowed, blinking rapidly. Thomas was vile, evil, the very bottom of humanity, preying on the weakness of women and children, a sociopath, who didn't penetrate her because of her mother's one stand against him, her refusal to put Meggie on any sort of birth control. He'd still hurt her, humiliated her, and held her down to exercise his will. Her father couldn't have been that man. He just couldn't have been. "With my father, what you see isn't all there is to him. He isn't…my father wouldn't—"

Everyone shifted uncomfortably and exchanged meaningful glances before all the attention converged and focused on her. She felt their feelings like a heavy hand pressing into her.

Christopher stared at her in brooding silence, smoking his cigarette. When he finished, he walked to the bar and tamped it out into an ashtray. He released the last bit of smoke.

"Shit, Megan." He leaned on the bar and thrust his hands through his hair. "Shit, shit, shit."

Another more horrifying thought occurred to her. Until then, she'd been too stupid to put the pieces together. "Christopher," she breathed, shaking her head in denial. "Why are you in his office? Why do you wear the president's vest?"

"Cut," he inserted.

"Cut?" she echoed.

He nodded, holding her gaze, his own guarded. "The vests called cuts." He rubbed the back of his neck, then scratched his jaw. "Fuck, Megan. Fuck, fuck, fuck."

And, suddenly, she knew. Dread and horror pitched through her, and she rose to her feet, everything in slow motion. "He isn't coming back, is he?"

No one moved or said a word.

She barreled to Christopher and jabbed a finger in his chest. "He's gone, isn't he?"

Chapter Twelve

OUTLAW

HOW THE FUCK WAS HE SUPPOSED TO ANSWER the desperate plea in Megan's voice? Her beautiful eyes filled with anger, fear, and dawning grief. Tears spiked her long lashes and disbelief parted her lips, her cheeks flushed with all the emotions rushing in her.

He felt like choking the shit out of Ellen. The stupid whore had gone too fucking far this time. Her words, as much as her fucked up display that led Megan down this path, pissed him the fuck off. His part in this entire fucked up affair saved Ellen's fucking ass.

He wanted to forget Zoann's words, but they'd opened up old wounds. As determined as he was to keep his hands off Megan before speaking to his sister, he'd doubled his efforts afterward. Even K-P's talk hadn't changed his mind.

His brain told him he made the right decision. His dick, however, had different ideas and wanted to fuck Megan with as much resolve as Outlaw wanted to resist her. Worse, she wanted him and wasn't making it easy for him to do the right thing by her when he'd hurt so many other people. When almost everyone else, outside of his brothers, saw him as a piece of shit.

The thought chilled his blood, humiliating him with the freshness of Zoann's accusations. But, fuck him, if the way Megan looked at him didn't reach into his loneliness, make him feel as if she saw past the man the world saw. The killer that he was.

If Ellen's arrival hadn't interrupted him, Outlaw would've kissed Megan and not stopped until he had her in his bed. She'd been fucking teasing and tempting him all evening. He hadn't expected Ellen or Kiera to cause problems. He'd fucked other bitches in the time he'd been fucking them. A few weeks ago, he'd even shared them with his cousin, Johnnie. First off, they were family *and* the motherfucker was still a member of the club, Nomad or not.

Outlaw paced again, buying more time. Megan made him feel all sorts of new shit. Maybe, because, she was innocence and sex, a dangerous combination. He'd felt the sweet touch of her fingers in the corner of his mouth all the way to his balls.

But he pretended he didn't give a fuck and kissed Ellen back, hugged Kiera and kissed her, too. And fucked up more than anyone else. Because all he did was piss Megan the fuck off. All it did was make him want her pussy more. Make him want *her* more.

Somehow, he had to convince her about Boss. What, he wasn't sure.

He glanced around the room, noting the sympathy in Digger, Mortician, and Val's faces. They were his friends. They must've recognized how different he treated Megan. He glared at Rack's smirk. The assfuck knew Outlaw, too. He was older, had been a man Outlaw looked up to as much as he did Boss. Rack would also recognize the difference in the way Outlaw treated Megan. He was probably considering how to clue Megan in about his suspicions over the role Outlaw played in her old man's death before Outlaw blew Rack the fuck away.

Maybe, Outlaw should end this sick fucking game between them once and for all. Megan didn't have to worry anymore, though. The words *Megan can't be touched* was carved on Rack's fleshy, hairy back. The wounds were superficial but had made a fucking lasting impression. As had all the screaming when Outlaw had poured rubbing alcohol over the fresh cuts. So, yeah, that motherfucker carried all kinds of hate for Outlaw. But, fuck, sometimes, he didn't fucking know if he was coming or going.

Decisions had always come so fucking easy to him. Except now his brain felt leaden, burdened with anger and regret. Boss had groomed Outlaw to lead the club, and he'd moved through the ranks. Member. Enforcer. Secretary. Enforcer again. Treasurer. Sergeant-at-Arms. Vice-President.

President. Because he'd killed Big Joe.

Swallowing, he crouched in front of Megan. Might as well get the shit out in the open. Well, part of it. Then, he could get her somewhere away from him. Jesus, he had to. He wasn't for her. She wasn't cut out for this life. And he wasn't cut out for no other.

"Boss ain't comin' back, Megan. *Ever.*"

A strangled gasp escaped her bloodless lips, her complexion turning sheet white. "No," she got out, a whisper-sob. "*No.*" The tears slipping down her cheeks brightened her eyes and stripped away all her defenses, leaving behind pain and denial.

If Outlaw could resurrect Boss, make him be the man he once was, he would. For Megan. Just to take away her heartache. That meant he might not be standing here, memorizing every feature of her perfect face. But who the fuck would miss him? Even Boss, in all his fuckuppedness, had people who'd loved him and needed him. Namely, his beautiful baby girl.

She blinked, a rapid movement of her eyelids. "He's dead." No question, just a blunt, heartbroken statement.

Outlaw nodded, determined to have that point clear. *Gone* to her might've meant something different than *dead.*

"How? When? How? What happened?"

Her trembling words shot straight to Outlaw's heart.

"I don't know," he lied after a tense moment. Since he was confessing, he should tell all. But he couldn't bear to see her look turn to anything other than the one that made him feel like he owned the world. He'd send her away, but he wouldn't send her away hating him. "I wasn't there when he died, so I ain't able to answer what happened. We comin' up onto the one year mark." Tomorrow.

"Where's he buried?" she asked around a pitiful sob.

He deflected the answer by giving her what she wanted, pulling her into his arms and kissing the top of her head. She buried her nose in his neck and cried so hard Outlaw felt like a complete bastard, so unworthy of Megan that he was glad he hadn't fucked her.

He scooped her up and she wrapped her arms around his neck. Bringing her to his room, he got her into bed and held her in his arms for a few minutes. He thumbed her wet cheeks, caressed her soft hair. She stared at him out of liquid blue eyes, pleading for comfort, something he couldn't give her. Her flushed cheeks and parted lips told him what else she wanted from him, something he was fighting like a motherfucker *not* to give her.

He got out of the bed and her entire body sagged, as if his rejection punched the last of her fight right the fuck out of her.

Pretending to ignore her, he slammed the door behind him and stalked to the bar, his dick hard and heavy for her. The mood had changed since he and Megan first sat at the table several hours ago. In the short time he'd been gone only a handful of people remained. Ellen sucked on a bud before passing it to Mortician. A filled shot glass sat in front of her amidst several empty ones. Mortician rested his forearms and elbows on the counter. She stood on the stool's footrest and leaned forward to whisper something in Mortician's ear. She laughed, a harsh, raw laugh that Outlaw had never liked. Val was cleaning up the mess of broken glass and spilled beer that Megan had made, the table Outlaw knocked over had been righted again and pushed to the corner. Her boots stood on the far end of the counter. So, maybe, he was wrong to get Megan the same boots he'd bought for the other two. He could only be thankful Ellen hadn't worn hers. Megan would've flipped.

He nodded to Digger, who was busy removing bottles from the other tables and near the pool table and dart board area. Kiera had disappeared altogether. At loose ends, Outlaw headed for his office, allowing a crack in the door. He pulled out a fifth of vodka from his desk cabinet, along with his stash of Aunt Mary. Nothing like a little Herb and Al to get his mind off shit.

After preparing everything and saving his shit away, he leaned back. He alternated between taking hits and swallowing vodka. Tomorrow couldn't come and go soon enough for him. It was the day he'd had to make a split-second decision to choose his life or Boss's. Outlaw saw to it that everyone would be extra fucking busy. He'd stay extra busy as well. He didn't want to think. He didn't want to feel. And he didn't want to hurt.

He took another hit, unable to get Megan out of his head.

"Outlaw?" Ellen pushed the door open before he answered.

He swigged from the bottle, watching her advance with dispassion.

She stopped next to him and gave him a nervous smile. "Wanna fuck?"

Yeah, but not *her*. He slammed the bottle on his desk and unzipped his jeans to pull his cock out. "Suck my dick then get the fuck outta here."

She dropped to her knees, and he closed his eyes, leaning his head back on the chair. Her tongue swirled around the head before she slurped half his dick into his mouth. The tip hit her throat and he grunted, holding her head in place, and thrusting hard, using her skills to release all his pent-up tension. It didn't take him long to come. Megan had him on edge and he either had to corrupt her or fuck other bitches.

He jerked and held Ellen's head in place and made sure she swallowed every drop of his cum before putting his cock away and throwing back more of his vodka. Ellen sat back and stared at him. Her nipples pressed against her thin blouse, and she pulled on them, her smile filled with promises.

"I wanna come, too," she said quietly.

He'd never seen nor heard such gentleness from her before. She almost looked soft, and Outlaw glimpsed the girl she must've been before life fucked over her. She wanted to be his old lady and she sensed how Outlaw was responding to Megan. She'd wanted him for herself before Megan arrived, played her hand at every turn to push Kiera out of the threesome. He turned away, stared at the old brown sofa.

"Whatever the fuck you got against Megan, the shit stoppin'. As long as she here you be on your best fuckin' behavior."

Ellen shot to her feet and stomped around the desk to face him. "That pissy little bitch shoved me."

"You wanna continue comin' here, get the fuck over it," Outlaw warned. "You got me?"

Her eyes widened. "You like her," she spat. "Sitting in here, smoking like the fiend you are, all alone. That's how Boss started. You're him all over again."

Outlaw shot to her and grabbed her by the throat, pinning her against the wall. "I told Megan I ain't no woman beater," he growled, his hand squeezing her slender neck. "Don't make me no fuckin' liar to her. Feel what I'm sayin', you stupid bitch?"

"Yes," she croaked.

"She leavin', but, in the meantime, if you ain't findin' it in your bitchy ass to be nice to her, you gonna deal with me. You a supreme fuckin' bitch to Kiera, but she been around. She used to bitches like you. Megan ain't. She ain't been around you bitches. Ain't had to put up with our world. If you ain't doin' nothin' else in your fucked up life, you should wanna help see this girl ain't hurt no more than she already been by all the fuckin' bullshit." He shook her. "That mean, bitch, you breathe one fuckin' word to her that don't sit right with her and Ima fuckin' put you outta your goddamn misery." He shoved her away. "Understand?"

She swallowed and nodded.

"If you or those other motherfuckers like breathin', then Megan better be left the fuck alone. She tell your ass to jump, you ask her how fuckin' high."

"You...you *do* like her." Her words no longer held malice, just genuine shock. She stared at him, taking in the hard set of his features, looking at him as if she'd never seen him before.

"Outlaw?" another voice interrupted.

"Val," Outlaw called. "C'mon, man. It's opened."

His Road Chief entered and paused when he saw Ellen.

"You headin' out with the dros?"

Val nodded. "Yeah. Should bring a nice buck. We killed it this growing season."

"Roll out then, brother."

Once Outlaw was alone again with Ellen, he nodded toward the door, just wanting to be alone. "If you wantin' some fun, go give Mortician some pussy. He been sweatin' you for fuckin' ever."

Mort liked Ellen and missed getting pussy from her after Outlaw took her out of circulation, but he suspected the motherfucker really had a thing for Kiera.

Ellen frowned. "You think him and Digger would come with me to Ki's?"

Outlaw shrugged. "Only way you knowin' is askin'. If Digger ain't goin' to Kiera with you motherfuckers, I promise you Mortician ain't gonna complain."

"What are you doing the rest of the evening?"

"Gettin' in my fuckin' bed." Next to Megan. He reminded himself not to get used to having her there.

The sooner he got Megan Foy the fuck away from here, the better for all concerned.

Chapter Thirteen

Meggie

LOUD SOUND AWAKENED MEGGIE, AND SHE BLINKED, wondering where Christopher was. Not that she cared. Nothing he did mattered to her. Two lamps were lit and the lone, unadorned window showed sunny skies. Groggy, Meggie recalled Christopher returning last night. He'd hardly spoken, and it had taken Meggie a while to fall asleep, wedged between the temptation of Christopher's sleek back and the brick wall.

She had to figure out what to do now that she knew the truth. Her father was *dead*.

Tears rushed to her eyes, the pain a sharp blade twisting in her. She'd never hear his voice again, telling her how much he loved and missed her. He'd never again take her for pizza. Ask about her grades. His promise to meet Farrah and Lacey and take the three of them shopping would never come to fruition.

Burying her head into the pillow Christopher had slept on, she breathed in his scent, sobbing in grief and misery. Her heart felt battered and bruised, like it had walked into a boxing ring and suffered a TKO. She'd be a complete liar if she insisted all her tears were for her father. Most of them were, but some were for Christopher, too. Why, she didn't know because he was little more than a stranger to her.

Like her father had been if they were telling the truth.

But the man she knew and the man they described…Meggie laughed bitterly. What *did* she know about her father? This club, these men, weren't as easygoing as he'd always insisted.

Rack had beaten her to a pulp over five dollars. Or the ramifications of her stealing the five dollars in the first place and then, telling Christopher.

Christopher didn't need her or want her. If she remained—if he allowed her to stay—she'd be in his way. Her problems were her own and her biggest one was also her worst nightmare. She couldn't return to her mother's house, but she had to try to get Dinah away from Thomas even though nothing short of a miracle would accomplish that. Meggie still had to try.

Her sudden resentment surprised her. She'd believed her mother's words about her father wanting Meggie with him. Dinah normally didn't fling careless lies about.

More tears slipped down Meggie's cheeks, and she curled into a ball. She wished she'd never overheard her mother. If only—

She couldn't finish the thought. Too many 'if onlys' to count existed in this sorry situation. Meggie breathed in deep, the chill of loneliness shivering through her, another sob escaping her.

"You motherfucker!"

The furious snarl yanked Meggie out of her thoughts and she bolted up, sucking in a breath. Oh, God. She'd forgotten a noise had awakened her.

"Fuck you."

The words boomed through the closed door.

She backed against the headboard, her trembling fingers clutching the bedspread. Gunshots. Shouting. Cursing. Doors were being kicked in. Vicious curses and threats peppered the air.

Her heart rate sped up and her pulse soared. Meggie stumbled to the floor, scrambling under the small space beneath the bed. More rapid gunfire, the *boom, boom, booms* getting closer and closer. Thumps, creaks and crashes resounded. She recognized the sound of doors being kicked open from when her mother showed a modicum of self-preservation and tried to lock herself in a room with Thomas hot on her heels.

Meggie's body shook just as the door flew open. She curled her lips inward to stifle her cry and focused on a pair of green and black boots. The black part looked like some sort of animal skin and the upper part—the bright green—had wings and a cross etched into the design.

No words were spoken. No warnings given. Just a rapid succession of gunfire. Not that she needed either. She'd never forget those boots or the fantastic amount of concentration it took to keep from screaming. If she'd taken a moment longer to get under the bed, she'd be dead.

Endless minutes passed while she waited for the intruders to leave. Thoughts of Christopher crowded her head. His smirking green eyes. The black hair that added sin to the temptation of him. She wondered if he was alive. No, he *had* to still be alive. She couldn't bear the thought he was dead, too. Though he could be scary and rude, he'd treated her nice.

She closed her eyes, afraid to expel the air in her lungs and afraid to move a muscle. Afraid to let herself consider the very real possibility that Christopher was dead. He was big and frightening and had an incredible disregard for modesty, but he'd saved her and taken care of her and…and aroused her. She couldn't imagine a man with such overwhelming masculinity as a corpse. Her brain refused to recognize he had to be hurt or grievously injured to allow these men the license to roam so freely through the clubhouse.

The boots made a three hundred sixty degree turn and Meggie held her breath, her heart jack hammering loud enough to give her away. She was going to die, too. They'd discover her and kill her. In the distance, glass shattered. The boots stepped nearer, so close Meggie could've touched them. Some guitar riff broke through the violent noise.

Christopher's cell phone. She'd heard it several times when he'd been with her at the hospital. A moment later, a loud bang almost deafened her. Wood and metal flew and crashed to the floor as bullets ripped apart the desk. Meggie guessed it was the desk since that's where the cell phone had been.

The boots pounded out of the room. Pausing in the hallway, the square toes turned toward her again.

"I plugged Rack," a voice called. "He taken care of just as we planned."

Whooping and hollering followed that.

"Yeah? Well, I popped Outlaw. Fucker. Told him I'd avenge my father."

The man grunted. "He shot me, too."

"I should go out there and make sure he's done. Blow his fucking skull apart."

"Why you still here?"

"Shit ain't right, Kit. I feel it in my bones. Like I'm being watched or some shit."

"Outlaw musta gave up the ghost and he's stalking you."

Boots started back into the room and Meggie pressed her nose to the concrete, nausea roiling in her belly. The floor tilted. If she wasn't already on the ground, she would've fainted at having her speculations confirmed about Christopher. She choked back a sob, praying they were wrong. But they sounded too confident and sure of themselves for her to have any hope.

"Yo, Snake!"

"Whatcha got, Relay?" The call halted his advancing stride and he backed out of the room.

Snake. He was the one who'd bragged about avenging his father by killing Christopher. If she wasn't so alone and vulnerable, she'd reveal herself and spit in *Snake's* face.

"Bags of powder, that's what. We got 'em next door, in the midst of preparing shipment just like we were told."

If I don't know motherfuckers, I end up with a real fuckin' knife in my back. The memory of Christopher's statement thumped through Meggie's head. Someone had set him up. But who?

"What about this place? Torch it?"

"No, Welsh," Snake responded. "Let's go next door and lift the sugar. Get it out of here. We'll return later to search. I'm sure there's more here. Haven't found the fucking bricks yet neither. We'll torch this shithole after I get what the fuck I want. Besides, Outlaw…"

The words faded into the air as they departed, leaving nothing in their wake but eerie silence. A minute later, a door slammed in the distance and Meggie jumped, her entire body shaking, jerking, adjusting to the fact that the immediate danger had walked away.

A vision of Thomas rose in her head. Compared to this, he *was* a teddy bear. Meggie squeezed her eyes shut, drew in deep breaths, counted sheep.

Her pulse banging in her throat, she slid from under the bed. Grabbing the edge to steady herself as she stood, she swallowed at the mangled desk and destroyed phone. Bullet holes decorated the walls and the door hung off the hinges.

She had to man up, *move.* Find Christopher.

Escape.

At the door, she peeked out glanced both ways down the hallway. The hairs at her nape lifted and goosebumps raised on her skin. The creepy quietness chilled her. She almost returned to her hiding spot, but she couldn't. Even if she found herself the only survivor, she *had* to get out of this room. And, somehow, the clubhouse.

Those men, Snake, Relay, and Kit, intended arson. If she didn't leave, she'd burn to death.

The dead men would be reduced to ashes.

Christopher…

Nausea twisted in her belly and a shudder rippled through her. Christopher *couldn't* be dead. She couldn't run, until she searched for him.

She couldn't move. Her fear atrophied her muscles. But the overwhelming, eerie silence reminded her she was once again alone. She could do this. Her father wouldn't stand down and neither would she.

Going right led to another hallway. She'd never gone further than Christopher's bedroom door.

She glanced to her left again, which led to the main room and Christopher's office. That way also led to light.

Despite the death and darkness in the building, the lights from the main room bounced off the wall, illuminating the Grim Reaper. She shivered, but she gnashed her teeth together and made herself ignore her pounding heart and overwhelming horror.

If Christopher was still alive, she'd find a way to administer enough first aid to save him and herself.

Forcing herself to put one foot in front of the other, she tipped down the hallway, covering her nose against the acrid smells in the air. Sulfur. Fear. Death.

When she reached the main room, with the long bar, the pool tables, the dartboard, and the huge television, she gazed all around. Not paying attention to where she walked, she tripped. She put her hands out to break her fall and landed on something soft. Part of a face reached her line of vision. The other half consisted of…nothing.

Meggie scrambled back, choking back a scream, too horrified to make a sound. Though she didn't know the man's name, she recognized him. She slid forward, on her knees, the floor wet and sticky beneath her, coated with blood and…and…Oh God! She shook her head wildly as if that would make it all go away. It didn't. She raised her blood covered hands, dizziness swaying her.

She cleared of the body, knocking over a small table. The loud crash reverberated around her and she longed for the safety of her mother's arms. But neither of them had been safe since her mother married *him*. When they were, usually Meggie made them safe. Her mother had given up, forcing Meggie to flee and find safety. Instead, it looked like she'd walked into a death trap. Into the bowels of hell.

She wasn't equipped to be a runaway, to survive a gun battle. She'd grown up getting whatever she wanted. While they hadn't been wealthy, they had been comfortable. What her mother couldn't buy her, her father picked up the slack. But, then, her mom had remarried when Meggie turned thirteen and everything changed. Her father no longer visited on a regular basis. Her mother no longer smiled.

Slowly, Meggie got to her feet, queasy and disoriented. A door opened and the bright sunlight flooding the room mocked the blood and gore surrounding her. She squinted, her hand flying to her mouth, the glare preventing her from seeing who'd walked in. She dodged into a corner, praying the shimmer an equal handicap for the other person. She crab-walked—ran—into the hallway and toward the office hoping to find Christopher there. Alive. Not dead. At the thought, she lost her balance, landing hard on her butt. She spun around, relieved no one had joined her and backed into the office, closing the door behind her. The lock was blown off but for the most part the door remained intact. She leaned her head against the cool wood, offering a prayer of thanks for her momentary safety.

A moan startled her, and she twisted. The gore greeting her sent the bile in her empty stomach hurtling out.

MORTICIAN

Lucas "Mortician" Banks sat the final package on the table in the club's warehouse where all the sorting and preparation was done. He couldn't wait until this fucking day was behind them. One year ago today, Boss was put down.

Despite what the motherfucker had become, the pain of his loss was real and deep. Mortician always thought he'd jump for fucking joy if Big Joe went away. The very day of Boss's death, Mortician had made the decision to jet. He just hadn't been able to take the fucking shit Boss insisted he do or the knowledge he passed to Boss who, in turn, had so long ago ignored.

Mort's stomach growled and he glanced at his watch. It was not yet noon and he'd been in the warehouse for hours after being awake all night fucking. *He* might've been tired and hungry, but his cock was very happy.

Speaking of satisfied dicks, he supposed Outlaw hadn't shown up to help because of Megan Foy. While it was shocking since Prez never let nothing and no one get in his way of running the club, his friend needed a diversion. Mort only hoped Outlaw saw everything there was to her.

An odd feeling settled in Mort's gut. For a moment, the silence overwhelmed him.

The ghost of Big Joe, he supposed.

Snickering, he went to the small office in the back of the warehouse, pulled a ledger out of the 2 drawer file cabinet and sat at the desk. He carefully jotted numbers into the columns, memorized thanks to the cheat-sheet he'd made of his hand.

Once he finished, he returned the ledger to where it belonged, not sure what to do next. He could take the back trail through the forest to the cave the club used for storage. Or he could return to his room. Despite the two warehouses standing between his current location and the clubhouse, he was closer to it than he was to the cave.

Except there he'd find a little peace. Here, as well as at the club, there were only memories.

"Fuck, man." He flipped off the overhead light and slammed the office door shut, then returned to the counter he'd been working at. The boxes were ready for their support clubs to pick up.

Normally, the packages stacked on the counters didn't bother Mortician. This morning, though, they seemed...*vulnerable.*

It came to him that Rack hadn't returned either. Motherfucker glued himself to the fucking warehouse during packaging and distribution. He always had. This morning, he'd stayed a couple hours, claimed he had another meeting, and left. Shortly thereafter, Sinner, the club's chaplain, and Tex, their treasurer, had gotten text messages and also disappeared.

What the fuck was going on—

"Mort, why the fuck you in here alone?" Digger demanded, his voice echoing in the big, cavernous space, as he walked back in. His kid brother had left ten minutes ago, happy to be through with a second round of preparation in just a week.

It had to be exact, and everything accounted for so the Dwellers received every dime owed them.

"Ready for another round of fucking Ellen and Ki?" Digger asked, unbothered that Mortician hadn't answered.

He shrugged. "Don't get too attached to fucking them again, fool. When Outlaw take them back, we going to be cut out again." He didn't mean to sound so fucking irritated.

Digger scowled. "What ant crawled up your cock? Why you worrying about what Outlaw might do instead of enjoying what he is doing? And that's letting us fuck Ellen and Kiera again."

"He's going to want them back," Mortician grumbled. "Once Megan disappear."

Digger blinked, too many times for it not to be both annoying and exaggerated. "What you mean by disappear?"

Fuck, what did he mean? No, he knew what the fuck he meant. They *both* knew. But she'd given Mortician no reason to suspect she was a threat, especially to Outlaw.

"Big Joe loved her a whole lot," Digger said with a sigh. "I feel you, though, bruh. If bitch here to fuck over Prez, we burying her." He winced. "She just so pretty and we don't hurt girls." His shoulders slumped and he bowed his head.

Mortician hated to see the burden of all they'd done on Digger's shoulders. He walked around to him and gave him a headlock-hug. "*We* don't hurt chicks and we never did."

"We never stopped him," Digger said, pushing Mort's arms away. They both knew the identity of *him*.

"Only motherfucker that had a chance of reaching him was Outlaw," Mortician said sadly. "Anyone of us even approached him and he would've shot the fuck out of us. He wouldn't have hesitated like he did with Prez. He would've pulled his piece, stuck it on the bridge of our noses, and fired."

Scrubbing a hand over his face, Digger nodded. "Is it bad that I miss him sometimes?"

"Nope. I miss him, too."

Digger shoved his hands into his pockets. "You ever mad at Outlaw?"

"No," Mortician answered without hesitation. "Outlaw knew Big Joe since he was a boy. If there was any other way for that day to be different, Prez would've done it."

"We didn't have the same amount of brothers we did before Big Joe got strung out but we had Snake and his friends," Digger continued. "Big Joe wasn't in his right head, but he still kept us together. Prepping for distribution wasn't such a monumental task with all the motherfuckers around to help."

All fucking true. Membership numbers had dropped dramatically. They just couldn't deal with Boss's bullshit.

"Nothing the same anymore," Digger said quietly. "Outlaw can't seem to get his head on straight to get the club straight."

"Prez grieving. Fuck, we all are."

"Outlaw hate Big Joe."

"Look what he made him do," Mortician snapped. "Outlaw *should* hate Boss."

"Then how the fuck he grieving, Mortician? You not making sense."

"I'm not fucking explaining to a grown ass motherfucker who a man knowing somebody since the age of ten can't grieve for that motherfucker even if he forced to bury him." Mortician glared at Digger. "Outlaw heart fucking broken."

"So's the fucking club, Mortician."

"In other words, you telling me you would've preferred if Boss shot the fuck out of Prez instead of the other way around?"

Digger's eyes widened. "What? No! Mort, no. Outlaw a good, solid motherfucker. I'm proud he include me in his close circle. But I thought he was the best man to be Prez. That's why I fucking voted him in. It don't seem like he is. Motherfuckers taking sides and ruining the Dwellers. Our club not our club no more."

"You had two fucking choices. Outlaw and Snake. If you voted for that psychotic motherfucker, I never would've forgave you."

Hurt flashed across Digger's face. "We had three. Rack was an unofficial contender."

Rack would've been as bad as Snake. Rack was dirty. Snake was soulless.

"Halloween coming up at the end of the month."

"Thank you for telling me that," Mortician said sarcastically, worn the fuck out. "I always thought October 31st came at the beginning of the month."

"Fuck off," Digger snapped. "I'm referring to the fucking party. I don't even know if I'm coming."

Mortician studied his brother. "You a grown motherfucker, son. I can't make your ass attend, but you have a fucking choice. If you with Outlaw, you got to be with him all the way. If you not, get to fucking stepping and don't fucking look back. He don't fucking need doubters."

"It's easy for you to stand so solid behind him. You always been a close friend to him. He trust me and like me, but I'm *your* brother, not my own fucking man. They wanted you to be sergeant, but you stepped aside to clear my way."

"What the fuck that has to do with you not thinking Outlaw should be Prez?"

"I didn't say he shouldn't be Prez, Mortician," Digger grumbled. "Don't twist my fucking words."

"I'm about to twist your fucking nuts. You been standing in this motherfucker for ten minutes complaining about Prez—"

"Not about him," Digger interrupted. "About the job he doing. Fuck, if he could somehow mourn a motherfucker he hate, I can fucking gripe about his leadership."

"This the fucking reason right here he can't get a fucking bead on the fucking club, motherfucker."

"No, he can't get a fucking bead on the club because of his indecisiveness and his fucking inaction. He killed *Boss*, Mortician. He need to take that same fucking gun and shoot the fuck out of Rack, Snake, and every other motherfucker against him."

"We live in a fucking democracy. None of the motherfuckers you name actually made a fucking move against Outlaw or the club. You want a fucking mutiny? Killing motherfuckers you *suspect* plotting against you is the way to do it."

Digger heaved in a breath. "Outlaw like another blood brother to me."

Mortician glowered. "You know what confused motherfuckers do?" he demanded. "Confuse other motherfuckers."

"I've been very clear about everything I've said."

"I'd hate to be your fucking brain. It has to bounce around in your big ass head and make sense of your fucking thoughts."

"I resent that."

"I don't give a fuck. I'm standing with Outlaw, Digger. If you blame him for Big Joe death and you don't think he the best thing for the club, then walk away. Otherwise, you a fucking weak link that Rack and Snake going to sniff out and turn you against Prez."

"No, never, Mort," Digger said with certainty. "I'm not going to betray Outlaw. I'm going to stand at his side through thick and thin. Besides, I damn sure wouldn't betray you." His shoulders relaxed.

"Now, I got a question about Megan," he said as if their serious conversation had never happened. "Aside from you not knowing if we putting her to ground."

"What about her?"

"Let's start with the bitches. A lot of gorgeous bitches hang around. Always have. Some of the regular girls, including Kiera and Ellen, don't have bitch fits over them. Why they fucking stressing over Megan?"

"With Ellen and Kiera, they been the top bitches for years. Even Big Joe saw them as special. Like you said, we have a bunch of hot chicks, but Ki been the reigning beauty queen."

"Yeah, that bitch badder than a motherfucker," Digger agreed. "And she know how to work her pussy—"

Mortician stiffened. "Shut the fuck up," he warned, low.

Digger grinned. "Moving on. Megan gorgeous, too. Fuck, that little bitch even prettier than Ki and that's saying a lot. And, fuck, she got a banging body."

"What's your fucking point?" Because, really, he didn't want to think about Megan's curvy little body.

"My point is one of the most beautiful chicks I ever saw been in our midst for fucking years and she, Ki, was just accepted into the fold. I'd bet a fucking g Ellen could kill Megan and not lose fucking sleep. She not the only bitch feeling that way and it got nothing to do with wanting to protect Outlaw. No, something about her making all the other bitches feel threatened and I don't understand how a bitch that's eighteen can intimidate *grown* grown ass women."

"It's the way Outlaw's protecting her."

"He protected Kiera when she first came around."

"Yeah, but he didn't keep her in his room to do it." Mortician sighed, hating to admit any of what he was about to say. "Megan a sexy little motherfucker. I was watching Outlaw with her last night and she...I haven't seen him smile as much since Big Joe's death. And, fuck, she not afraid. She was ready to beat Ellen ass. That even impressed me. She Boss's daughter. As exquisite as he was handsome and just as fucking tough. Despite all my suspicions toward her, she has my attention."

"She making quite an impression but I don't know if you reading her right. I don't think she knew anything about her daddy being dead. Suppose you do ice her? What will you tell Outlaw?"

What *could* he tell the man? Mort didn't have an answer, so he shrugged. "She not all that," he said. "The fervor behind her going to die down from bitches and motherfuckers."

"Once she leave," Digger said. "Can you imagine if Outlaw kept her? Motherfucker notorious for not wanting a old lady. Not only would Megan belong to Outlaw, but Big Joe her daddy. She would always be a target. For payback for all the shit Boss did and to hit Outlaw where it hurt the most."

Mortician didn't want to imagine such a scenario. It would be a fucking nightmare.

Digger changed the subject again. "Maybe, you can talk to Outlaw about Kiera. Take the bitch for yourself. You been pining after her for years."

"She want Outlaw," Mortician replied, not seeing a reason to deny Digger's accusations because they were true. He liked Ki a lot. "I'm not being with another girl wishing my cock was somebody else's."

"She like you, too, Mort. Straight up."

"She like me, but she love him."

"Outlaw not feeling her like that. Let shit settle down. We get over the Megan issue. Once he open her pussy to the rest of us, everybody'll see where shit stand. I can't wait to fuck her."

Mortician whacked Digger on the side of the head. "You going to be waiting a long fucking time. No matter how she end up, I don't think Prez ever releasing Megan to the masses. He just look at her different and that's why I'm worried he let his guard down too easy with her."

"You heard why she supposedly here, Mortician. For Big Joe help. We need to look into her fucking story and then decide."

He thought about the shock and pain on her face last night when Outlaw revealed Big Joe would never come. Her grief hadn't been pretense.

"Let's get back to the club. Fuck, we at the edge of the fucking property, in the last goddamn warehouse," Digger said.

"Outlaw texted and said where he at?" Mortician asked, following Digger toward the door.

"I assume he fucking Megan—"

"Val nowhere to be fucking found."

The voice carrying through the warehouse door sounded like Scissors, one of Snake's best fucking friends.

Before the thought fully formed, the door flew open and Snake, Scissors, and Bookman slithered in. By the time Scissors and Bookman processed Mortician and Digger's presence, bullets were flying and those two motherfuckers were caught in the crossfire.

Snake, the viperous psychopath, escaped into the forest. After sending Digger back to the club, Mortician gave a short chase behind Snake, then fell back. Mortician didn't know how many motherfuckers waited for Snake. Besides, they'd come to the warehouse as if they owned the place.

For that to happen, Outlaw had to be down.

With a cry of pain and fury, he turned on his heel and hurried toward the club. Megan Foy rose in Mortician's head. First, he'd check on his friend, then he'd take care of Big Joe's daughter.

Chapter Fourteen

OUTLAW

HEAT CONSUMED OUTLAW, SO FUCKING HOT he must be at the first gate of hell. He waited for that hoof-footed motherfucker to appear because, certainly, the devil would want to personally greet a motherfucker like him. But nothing. Just fucking heat and pain and a massive amount of fucking fury.

His shoulder and thigh burned like fuck. The scent of blood, piss, and shit filled his nostrils. Red and gray spattered a wall. He swallowed when Megan Foy crawled into his line of vision and shut the door behind her. Someone groaned and she turned. Horror filled her features before she leaned over and vomited.

He wanted to close his eyes but seeing her reminded him he had to live long enough to get her to safety. If she hadn't been here, perhaps, he'd close his fucking eyes and pray he never woke the fuck up. But the little hellcat needed him. Not since he'd killed Boss did he regret the choices he'd made in his life as much as he did now. Fuck, yeah, he'd had twinges of regret over the years, but not like this. She wasn't quite healed from her beating and her cold, and he had her dealing with this. He wondered if she knew today was the one-year anniversary of Boss's death.

Maybe, he moaned—though he didn't remember uttering a sound—because her gaze flew to his face. Outlaw gritted his teeth at her ghost-white features and eyes wide with fear.

So he really wasn't dead. Just shot. And pissed. Heads were going to fucking roll.

"Help."

That wasn't him. That croak was Rack's. He wanted to be happy the man had survived, but he didn't know if he should be. Outlaw had his suspicions and many of those motherfuckers pointed straight the fuck at *Rack*. Divided loyalties and high emotions left the Death Dwellers in fucking chaos. Motherfuckers jockeying for power and offices. They were imploding, destroying themselves from the inside out. Rack might like to draw motherfuckers as a form of special fucking torture, but it would be his fucking ass halved and quartered if Outlaw discovered his duplicity.

"Someone's out there," Megan whispered, shaking. "I-I was looking for you. H-he said he…he p-popped y-you. I-I th-thought y-y-ou n-needed m-me, n-needed h-h-help. And there's a m-man with half a face!" she sobbed. "I f-fell on him. A-and th-then someone came back in."

Tears slid down her cheeks and she stared at him. For comfort. For protection. To make sure he still lived. She visibly trembled. Jesus. Fuck. She needed him and she'd risked her life to find him.

Outlaw tried to rise and cursed at the pain careening through his body. Oh, yeah. He'd been popped in his thigh, too. Assfucks. Dizziness blurred his vision, and the metallic taste of blood filled his mouth. Slower than he appreciated, he rose to his feet and swayed. On her knees, she rested on her feet, breathing heavy. Fuck, she was bloody. She'd been shot, too?

"Y-you're bl-bleeding," she said, rising to her feet and rushing to him. Her hands explored his body in a frantic rush.

No. Not shot. She was too agile, showing no signs of pain. He worked out some of her babbling, the fact that she'd fallen on a man with half his head blasted off the most disturbing for her, in a day filled with fucking disturbances. Her frantic distress arrowed to his gut.

She finished with another, "You're bleeding, Christopher," in a stronger tone.

Outlaw clenched his jaw, the sound of his name on her lips spiking his resolve. "My ass shot, so, yeah, I'm bleedin'."

"I am, too," Rack said with a moan.

"I h-heard th-them t-talking," she sniffled in a low voice, pausing in her exploration to lean on his chest and wrap her arms around his waist.

Outlaw listened for sounds, zoning in on her beautiful face to keep himself upright. He told himself he was acting in the role of a big brother and would never lay hand nor tongue nor cock on any place on her body that might lead to fucking.

"A-and o-one of them c-came back," she continued, a little hysterically.

"Yeah?"

She pulled away to look at him, his blood covering her cheek. The quietness made it hard to believe another shooter wandered beyond the door. Whether they'd returned or not wasn't the point. Protecting her was.

"You heard them talk?"

She nodded. "Th-there were three m-men. One named K-kit. Another named Sn-snake. And R-relay. Sn-snake is the one who sh-shot you."

No fucking shit.

She kept her face turned to him. Any place else she looked, she would've seen brain matter and blood from the three other men in the room. Her thin voice and trembling lips told him how scared shitless she was. And, yet she wasn't screaming like a maniac or crumpling to the floor in a dead faint.

Strong under fire. Boss's genes. And, that motherfucking Snake's, too.

Outlaw crept forward, gripping the side of his desk, and reaching for his nine at the same time. His nostrils flared at the carnage. He was growing lightheaded and the wounds that had been burning like hellfire was growing numb. His eyes slid closed, but the sound of her voice popped them back open. He swayed.

"Th-they said th-they were taking the sugar s-so th-they would c-come back l-later to search the place b-before t-torching it."

They was stealing his shit, huh? He neared the door just as it began to push open. Painfully slow. Megan gasped and Outlaw thrust her behind him to make sure she stood out of the line of fire. Sweat beaded his brow. The door banged open, guns blazing.

Outlaw stood to the side and shoved his nine in the asswipe's temple. "Smile, motherfucker. You on candid fuckin' camera."

Pity it was Kit he was about to blow the fuck away and not Snake. "Hands up."

Without another prompt, asswipe raised his hands.

"Walk. And if you a prayin' fuckin' man, you better pray we ain't fuckin' runnin' into your brothers. *You* my shield, motherfucker. They shoot at me, you fucked first."

His brown ponytail swung with his nod.

"Rack?" Outlaw called, wondering if the last round of gunfire had killed him.

"Yo?"

He was alive.

"Getcha piece and come with me. Megan, stay the fuck put." Outlaw started walking out the door, backing the doomed fuckhead out.

"Pl-please d-don't make me stay in here with all these d-dead p-people!"

Outlaw ignored her, in another zone altogether.

The killing zone. He had some blood to spill.

Chapter Fifteen

Meggie

A S CHRISTOPHER LIMPED OUT, PAIN ETCHED INTO his beautiful features, Meggie wondered if she'd ever see him again. Was he walking to his own death after he'd survived the initial shooting? His shirt stuck to him, stained with his blood. That blood also leaked onto the floor. He couldn't survive a massive amount of blood loss.

It surprised Meggie when Rack staggered to his feet and followed Christopher out. Blood dripped down the side of his face. With all the blood on him, he looked as if he'd been shot, too, but she figured he'd only been grazed.

She needed to leave Christopher's office, get away from this gruesome scene. He might've told her to stay, but she couldn't, not with the horrific sight just behind her. No amount of pretending could remove the heaviness in the air. She pulled open the door and headed to Christopher's bedroom. As she turned the corner of the hallway where the bedrooms were located, more gunfire split the quiet and she ran the rest of the way.

She hurried past the broken door and halted, bending over and breathing heavy. She stared ahead, immobile, the frame of the window allowing her to see the beautiful day. Blue, cloudless skies with the sun gleaming through the pathway that cut through thick stands of trees. Pieces of the desk and cellphone littered the floor, and Meggie wanted to curl up in a ball. That wouldn't serve any purpose, however, other than giving into her fear and self-pity.

Maybe, she wasn't accustomed to such next-level violence, but assistance was still needed and *that* she was acquainted with.

Her hands shook as she began clearing the mess, focusing on the tasks at hand and losing herself in the back and forth of sweeping once she'd gathered the bigger pieces of the desk and set them in the hallway.

A hand landed on her shoulder and flung her around. Meggie covered her head with her hands, waiting to feel a bullet tearing through her body. Instead, another hand landed on the other shoulder.

"Ain't I fuckin' told you to wait in my office?"

She peeped through the triangle of her folded arms, wincing at the glower Christopher directed at her, his discarded shirt showing the blood still seeping from the jagged hole on his left shoulder.

She dropped her hands to her sides and set aside all the hurt, jealousy, and anger from last night. She didn't want Christopher to die as well. "You need to get to a hospital."

"I gotta see 'bout my fuckin' club."

"You won't be able to take care of anything if you're dead."

A black brow lifted, and he released her shoulders. "You worried 'bout me?"

"Yes." She wondered when her life would settle down, when there wouldn't be the threat of blood and pain chasing her and too often catching up. "I'm very worried about you. You need the gunshots tended."

Tenderness surfed through the pain in his eyes. He bent his head and brushed his lips against hers, his tongue gliding over the tears on her cheeks before taking her mouth again. Meggie stood on tiptoes, just wanting to assure herself he was alive and with her.

"Your lil' ass shoulda listen to me," he said gruffly, fisting her hair in his hand. "You shouldna left my office."

"I couldn't stay in there. Not with…with those men."

Sweat beaded his brow and discomfort brightened his eyes, the blood loss making him pale beneath the tan of his skin. She didn't know how long ago he'd been shot but he'd done a lot between then and now, including, as far as she knew, gotten the intruders off the compound. He moved slowly toward the bathroom, wincing, and mumbling more 'motherfuckers' and 'fucks' then she'd ever heard in her entire life.

He swayed and Meggie rushed to him, nudging her shoulder beneath his arm, almost bringing them both down because she didn't realize how heavy he was. And he wasn't even leaning his full weight on her.

"Whatcha doin', Megan?"

"Meggie," she said quietly. "Call me Meggie. And I'm tryin' to keep you from fallin'."

He staggered and Meggie clutched his biceps, finding no give, no softness, only hard muscle.

"I ain't gave you permission to touch me, yeah?"

"No, but I didn't ask for your permission," she countered, still gripping him, not under the false impression *she* held them up. Even wounded, his strength kept them upright. "You need to have your injuries seen to."

He scowled at her. "No fuckin' shit, genius."

She ignored his sarcasm and, instead, tugged him forward to the bed. He moved with her, but her hope of guiding him down in a smooth landing evaporated when he crashed onto the bed. She crawled next to him, exploring his naked torso. "Why haven't you had the wounds cared for yet?"

"Ain't nofuckinbody 'round able to dig out the bullets and sew me up or drive me to a hospital right now. Mortician and Digger doin' death fuckin' detail. Gotta get shit cleaned up and certain inventory stashed away." He groaned and closed his eyes. "Thought my ass was done for. Thought I ain't livin' to see my thirty-third birthday."

He still might not. His furnace-like skin and slurring speech warned Meggie she needed to do something for him soon. "Stay with me."

He gave her a crooked smile. "Ain't goin' nofuckinwhere."

She didn't respond, just hurried to the main room. The dead bodies had been removed, if not all the blood.

Digger and Mortician were in quiet conversation, their expressions grim, plastic gloved hands punctuating the discussion with gesturing. Rack leaned on the bar talking to several men Meggie didn't recognize. His face had been cleaned of most of the blood, but a deep gash marred his temple. She wasn't an expert on bullet wounds, yet she didn't see a hole anyway. He was also quite alert and narrowed his eyes when he spotted her.

"Get back in the room, Meggie," he ordered.

"Chris…Outlaw needs medical treatment right away."

"I can't—"

"He's lost a lot of blood," she interrupted, not quite understanding why they would let their president bleed to death. Wasn't MCs about loyalty and brotherhood? "You *have* to get help for him."

"Says who?" Rack's wintry gaze dared her to answer.

She raised her chin. "Says me. He's your president. You have to take care of him."

"Do I?" He stepped closer to her, his look unpleasant.

Meggie inched back, remembering his beating. She'd prefer not to deal with him, especially with Christopher injured. He needed her, though, and she refused to allow an overgrown Neanderthal like Rack to scare her into deserting Christopher.

"While you're worrying about our *Prez*, you seem to have forgotten all about your old man." He pulled keys out of his pocket and tossed them to her. "You want Outlaw seen to, take him your fucking self, bitch. I have to help put things back together around here."

Digger and Mortician materialized next to Rack. Digger lit a cigarette, took a drag then passed it to his brother. The smell swirled into Meggie's nostrils and her eyes watered.

Digger laughed. "Don't breathe in, girl."

Mortician puffed once, twice, sucked deeper the third time around. He held the smoke in before inhaling it in a puff. He nodded between her and Rack. "What's happening here?"

"Christopher needs to go to the hospital."

Rack's benign smile grated on her nerves. He clapped Meggie on the back. "Excuse me. I've got to get back to my work."

"Take him," Mortician agreed after Rack strolled away, whistling. "You need to be away from here for now, anyway."

Meggie started away, then paused. The hostility in Rack's voice had been unmistakable. "I heard the man—Snake—I heard him say the sugar was there just like they'd been told," she whispered. "This might sound crazy, like I just want revenge, but Rack doesn't act like a man loyal to his brothers. I'm not trying to overstep my bounds, but I think, as long as he's around, everyone's in danger."

"'Preciate the intel," Mortician said. "I'll keep that in mind."

He sounded neutral but his features were unconcerned, someone else who didn't intend to pay attention to her words. She'd done her part. It was up to them to do something with the information.

Chapter Sixteen

Meggie

CLUTCHING THE BLANKET TIGHTLY AROUND HER BODY, Meggie stared into space. Christopher had been taken into surgery almost two hours ago and, so far, she'd heard nothing about his condition. She wasn't a relative of his, but he had no one else there, so she'd been escorted to this waiting room, near the surgery unit, instead of being left in the general waiting area.

That meant something, didn't it?

She'd never been to a hospital for such a dire emergency. Until Thomas, she and her mother had been quite healthy. And happy. Her daddy...her daddy...

Was *dead*.

Grief hit her so fiercely that it made her dizzy. She didn't want to think about Big Joe as gone, even though she knew that he was. Too late, she realized he would've answered her desperate texts she'd sent in the days before she'd left Seattle.

Swiping angrily at her wet cheeks, Meggie sniffled. She had to keep herself together. Her father would expect it of her. He was gone, but Dinah was still alive—and still needed to get away from Thomas.

Then there was Christopher. He didn't seem to have anybody to look after him or truly care about him. Meggie was good at taking care of people. She'd looked after her mother for almost five years, ever since Thomas had come into their lives.

She wondered how Dinah fared. Now that she knew the fate of her father, she should go home. More than likely, Dinah needed her. Meggie could also get back in school and graduate in the spring.

More tears rolled down her cheeks. Once more, she glanced in the direction of the double doors they'd wheeled Christopher through. By then, he'd fallen unconscious. Actually, on the way to the hospital, he'd slipped into unconsciousness. Luckily, he'd given her proper directions and the hospital was almost a straight shoot from the club, once she'd turned off the dead-end street.

He was a strong man, seeming in the prime of his life. He could survive this. He *had* to survive. The moment she'd met him, he'd enthralled her, but when he brought birthday gifts to her, she'd become completely infatuated with him. That's why seeing him with Kiera and Ellen infuriated her.

Hanging her head, she heaved in a deep breath, unable to stop her silent tears.

Without warning, someone sat on the seat next to her.

Though she didn't lift her head, she saw the brown fingers wearing a skull ring and resting on a muscled thigh. Mortician. More than anything, she wanted someone to comfort her as she had Dinah so many times. The dynamics were different, however. Dinah was her mother and deserved Meggie's every consideration. She was nothing to any of these people. Even Christopher. Her chin wobbled.

"Is he going to live?" she asked, hoping Mortician had gotten news.

He stretched out his legs and sighed. His lack of a response alarmed Meggie, but she needed to know.

"Is he?" she demanded, her voice trembling.

"Probably not."

A sob broke free at the cool answer and she covered her face with her hands. "I didn't get him here soon enough," she cried. She shouldn't have confronted Rack. Christopher had needed her more and she'd failed him. She'd used up precious time with Rack, then taken up even more minutes by trying to convince Christopher he needed emergency care. "I didn't know what to do to make him come."

Beside her, Mortician stiffened and balled his hands into fists, then got to his feet and stormed away. Hanging her head, her hair swirled around her. She drew in deep breaths, trying to find the strength to calm herself. At home, alone with her hurt and humiliation, she used blades and knives as comfort. Here, she had access to neither. She only had her thoughts and recriminations.

Suddenly, Mortician was back, crouching in front of her, tipping her chin up, and thumbing her tears away.

"There a reason why you falling to fucking pieces over a dude you just fucking met?" he demanded, when her sobs quieted.

"I like him," she said around sniffles. She'd never met a more confident, sexy, *beautiful* man.

Mortician grunted. "You like fucking him."

Her eyes widened at the blunt words. "I-I've never...*fucked* him." She wanted to, though. It was strange to recognize her fierce yearning for him when she'd never felt it before.

"Who in the club or associated with the club have you fucked?"

She licked her lips, flushing with embarrassment. "No one. I-I've never had sex before."

Mortician drew his brows together. "What that mean?"

"I-I'm a virgin," she answered, his question so surprising some of her despair melted away, though she knew the big dummy understood what it meant.

Obviously, he was just as shocked, and his reaction challenged her previous assumption. As he stared at her, her embarrassment deepened, and her eyes flickered to the floor. He broke into loud laughter. She thought he'd lose his balance, but he didn't. He merely continued guffawing. Her emotions were so raw and overwrought. His amusement at her expense hurt her feelings.

He wiped tears from his eyes, then got to his feet and dusted off the leather he wore over his jeans. "Ahh, Meggie girl, I'm sorry," he said, composed again. "Let's go to the cafeteria."

Meggie wouldn't leave before she got word on Christopher's condition. "They might come out and—"

"How long ago they took him back?" he interrupted, sounding annoyed.

She shrugged.

He cocked his head to the side. "You should've just dropped him off."

"He might need me," she said, losing patience. "When he wakes up." The moment she said the words, despair hit her again. "He will wake up, right?"

"If he don't, where you going?"

"Somewhere." Where, she didn't know. Because as much as she knew she needed to go home, Thomas would be more brutal than ever to Meggie and Dinah wouldn't lift a finger to help her. She doubted Mortician cared about the details, so she had a question of her own. "What's it to *you*?"

"Fuck all," he admitted. "So you wouldn't go back to your momma?" he pressed, as if it meant a lot more than *fuck all*.

Folding her arms, she glowered at him and shook her head. "If that makes me a bad person, I don't care."

"Why would I think that?"

She swiped at her eyes. "Because I'm leaving my mother to him."

"Call the fucking cops."

As if she hadn't done that, but her mother never cooperated and backed up Meggie's story. "She'll deny everything like she has before," she explained in a broken voice. "And then…then he might hurt her really bad because I'm not there to get my punishment. He'd know it was me and he'd kill her. My daddy is…" Her voice trailed off and she swallowed… "*was* the only one who could've helped her."

"She a grown ass woman, Meggie. She can help her fucking self."

"She can't!" Madness seeped into her at his statement. Dinah should take care of herself, but she'd forgotten how. She couldn't even recall how to look after Meggie. "*I* take care of *her*. Even when he's punched me and stuff, before he gets to her, when I wake up, I go to her and clean her up. Why do you think I've never told anyone?" But hadn't she when Officer Landry had been there. She shoved that memory aside and continued her rambling. "Not even Farrah and Lacey and they are my best friends. My mom needed me and if I told, I'd be taken away. But then she said Big Joe was coming for me." She sounded just as she felt, on the verge of hysterics. "When I heard that, I decided to come to him instead. I couldn't reach him by telephone, and I couldn't get into the club and Rack wouldn't call anyone the night I arrived. Then, I stole Rack's money and he beat me up, too. But I was hungry and tired and dirty and afraid and I wanted a happy meal for my birthday and—"

"A Happy Meal?" Mortician interrupted, surprising Meggie. He'd somehow kept up with her babbling. "Like McHappy for McKids Happy Meal?"

Wiping her arm across her nose, she nodded, soothed by his calm demeanor.

"Prez know that shit?"

"Yes—"

"You want dick from him, you should've kept that shit to yourself, girl. That's some freaky sounding shit and he not into young bitches."

"I don't care!" she wailed. "I just want him to survive. That's it. I'll leave if I know he'll live."

Meggie wasn't sure if she could really so casually walk away from Christopher. Of course, she couldn't stay if he didn't allow it. More than likely, he wouldn't. He had his girlfriend who was both beautiful and experienced. Meggie had nothing to offer a man like him. Nothing except care and concern.

Bending, Mortician took her hand and tugged her to her feet. "Come on. Let's get you back to the clubhouse. You need to clean up."

"Can't I stay until he's out of surgery?" she asked, knowing he could force her to leave. Any of them could. For that matter, Kiera could arrive and send her away, too. "Please."

"Until he in recovery, then you go back to the club," he said. "For now, go to the bathroom and wash your face, while I run to the gift shop and get you a clean T-shirt. The one you wearing all bloody."

Meggie glanced down at herself, not caring about the shirt, but Mortician didn't sound as if he'd budge, so she agreed to his instructions without further argument.

Chapter Seventeen

Meggie

EVEN IN SLEEP, MEGGIE WAITED AND WHEN A SIGN finally came, she immediately roused. The groan penetrated her brain and she bolted upright as if a button had been pushed, swaying to her feet, and stumbling to Christopher's bed.

Yawning, she rubbed her eyes, scraping her fingers through her hair, blinking to clear her sleep away.

"Meggie?"

She started at the sound of her name being called and lifted her gaze. "Hi, Val," she croaked and cleared her throat. She looked at Christopher again, certain she'd heard him, but he remained the same. Unconscious. Stubble shadowing his jaw and chin. Hooked to oxygen, IVs, and all types of other monitors.

Last night had been excruciating. Once she'd changed into a clean T-shirt, she'd returned to the waiting room. Hours had passed before a surgeon finally came and said Christopher was in recovery, but he'd lost a lot of blood so his condition was touch and go. He was in a coma.

She couldn't wait to see him, but the men had other ideas. Mortician, now joined by Val and Digger, had taken her to the cafeteria. She hadn't been hungry. For that matter, neither had they because no one had eaten. They'd passed a flask among themselves, sending her curious looks. At some point, Val disappeared. It wasn't until the early morning hours that Mortician and Digger had finally escorted her to ICU, and she'd gotten her first glimpse of Christopher.

She'd given into exhaustion and fell asleep on the window seat she'd curled up on. Now, she stared at him, still and silent.

"Christopher?" she whispered, skimming her fingers along his hair-roughened jaw. "Come back to me. Please."

He didn't respond. Wondering if she'd imagined his groan, Meggie's chin wobbled. He might still die. It confused her why she was so torn up over a man she'd known mere days. But he'd taken care of her, acted as if he really, truly cared.

She sniffled and swiped away an angry tear. "He needs a shave."

A curious look on his face, Val nodded. He studied her. "What about the shooting?" he finally asked,

She paused her finger glide through Christopher's silky hair. Images from yesterday rose in her head and she shuddered. She didn't want to remember the dead bodies or their condition. "What about it?"

"I came back from my run to find Outlaw's been wounded and the club's been shot up."

His tone almost sounded accusatory, as if he believed she had something to do with the shooting. She dropped her hand to her side, lifted her chin, and gave Val a level look. "I don't want to talk about it."

He stiffened and narrowed his eyes. They were turquoise, very pretty, but nowhere near as striking as Christopher's. The teardrop tattoo had her so curious—she'd heard rumors about that particular design in that particular spot—but she dare not question him, especially now when he seemed so hostile.

"You can't go to the fucking cops," he growled into the tense silence, circling the bed and advancing toward her.

Panic hit her at his approach, and she widened her eyes. She was adept at escape when she chose to put off Thomas's beatings, so she ducked around Val before he caught her.

"I hadn't even thought about the cops," she snapped once she reached the other side and put some distance between them. She was much closer to the door. If he advanced toward her again, she'd leave. Hopefully, Mortician or Digger was around.

"Really?" Val sneered, searching her features, looking for...*something*. "Because girls from the outside usually would run screaming their fucking heads off straight to the fucking badges, so why not you?"

"I don't want to talk about it," she reiterated. Saying anything meant remembering men's splattered heads…

"You go to the cops, Outlaw gets arrested," he said flatly, breaking into her horrible thoughts.

Folding her arms, she glowered at him, wishing he'd leave.

"You want that?" he pressed.

Before she responded, the door opened, and Rack and Mortician walked in. Mortician glanced at Val and then at Meggie. His scowl surprised her, until Rack sauntered next to Val and glanced down at Christopher.

"What's—"

At the sound of Rack's voice, Meggie lost all reasoning. He was just like Thomas, pretending to be something he wasn't.

"You!" Meggie screeched, interrupting Rack and flying to him. She shoved him against Val, not caring about her past run-ins with Rack.

He would do what he wished to her anyway, whether she trembled in fear or spat in his face. Her mother's cowering only fed Thomas's brutality.

The thought made her angrier and she glared at Rack. "It's your fault he isn't waking up. You're responsible for this."

Rack pushed her back and poised to strike her. She raised her hands to shield her head, visions of kicking him and jumping up and down on his prone body dancing in her head.

The blow she anticipated never came. Val was there, jerking Rack's arm behind his back.

"I'll cut your fucking arm off and watch you bleed to death," Mortician promised, then turned to Meggie. "Come with me," he ordered.

They had to understand the danger Rack posed to Christopher. Possibly, all of them. Refusing to budge, she swallowed and pointed to Rack, wishing she had the power to incinerate him. "It was him. I told him to take Christopher to the hospital and he didn't want to. He even accused me of forgetting about my daddy because I was so worried about *Prez.*"

"Meggie—" Val began.

"You're a traitor, Rack," she went on, ignoring the warning in Val's tone.

Mortician looped an arm around her waist and lifted her off her feet. "Fuck."

"Ain't like that, Meggie," Rack swore fiercely. He looked and sounded so sincere, Meggie might've believed him, if she hadn't had experience with Thomas. "I swear. I'd never do anything to betray my club."

"Just leave," she snarled, struggling against Mortician's hold, and growling in frustration when he refused to release her.

"I almost got my ass shot off!" Rack fumed. "You think I'd set myself up?"

"Big, mean, stupid, rhinoceros looking morons like you do *anything.* You probably shot yourself." She looked him up and down.

"Besides, where's the bullet hole? You never looked wounded and you never acted like a man with an injury."

She ignored the shock on Val's face and Mortician's sharp intake of breath.

"Shut the fuck up," Rack ordered. "Who made you a fucking expert on fucking bullets or being in a gun battle?"

"*You're* still breathing, aren't you?" she continued, everything rushing back to her. The blood. The gaping holes. The green boots. "Those other men…they're all dead," she sobbed. "I saw their brains all over that wall. I *slipped* in a man's spattered head." She covered her eyes. "Oh my God."

The remembered horror was just too much. She twisted in Mortician's arms and sobbed against his chest. Still, Rack's stupid voice intruded. And, maybe, that was good. Before she became so entrenched in grief and horror that she would never lift herself out of the mire.

"You stupid little cunt. Outlaw's fucking alive. Want to see what that motherfucker did to my fucking back? If I was in on the shit that went down at the fucking club, he would've been fucking dead, wouldn't he? Since you fucking insinuating I have some type of beef with him."

"If I was you, I'd shut the fuck up, Rack," Mortician warned.

"And if I was you, I'd get that little slut out of my fucking face."

Mortician guided Meggie back to the chair and rubbed her back. "I'm saying this shit fucking once, brother. Meggie for Outlaw. More than that, she Big Joe little girl. If I don't protect her for one, I'm protecting her for the other. You fucking touch one hair on her and I'm fucking dismembering you with your heart still fucking pumping. Feel me, motherfucker?"

The words penetrated Meggie's brain and an overwhelming sense of gratitude hit her. No one had ever defended her in such a manner. She raised her watery eyes to Mortician, but he scowled at her, as if he didn't want her appreciation, so Meggie bowed her head.

"You know, motherfuckers, this is why we have to send extra fucking donations to the board of directors. ICU. Two fucking visitors. Any of you fuckheads familiar with that rule?"

The cultured voice reached Meggie, but she didn't bother to look at the newcomer. She didn't care who it was. She wanted Rack gone with the same desperation she'd wanted Thomas to leave.

She glared at Rack. "Stay away from Christopher," she ordered, hoping her eyes conveyed the hatred she felt. "I want you to leave."

"You don't have that motherfucking authority, slut. I can make you fucking leave quicker than the other way around."

"You think?" she demanded, livid, grief-stricken, and nearly out of her mind with worry. No one believed Rack presented a danger to Christopher, who was unconscious and unable to defend himself. "I'm not leaving him to *you*."

"Hold on, girl," Digger inserted. "You insulting me on the sly. I'm the sergeant-at-arms, so it's my job to protect Prez."

"Then do your job," she snapped, "and make him leave. You do that and Christopher's protected."

"Meggie, come and talk to me a minute," Mortician said in a soothing tone. "Calm down. You redder than a motherfucker, like Lucifer sprayed you in devil cum."

"I'm not leaving. I'm not talking. I'm not doing anything until Rack leaves," she screeched.

"So what? You Outlaw's bodyguard now?" Val asked in amusement.

Folding her arms, she straightened to her full height and nodded. "Yes," she hissed. "I'm not leaving until one of you makes Rack go away and stay away."

"What the fuck do you think I'll do to him, you stupid little bitch?" Rack snarled.

"Who knows what torture method you'll cook up in that putrid, diabolical mind of yours," she replied.

"What is going on in here?" Kiera demanded, walking to the other side of the bed, and staring at Meggie. "I heard you all the way in the fucking hallway, Meggie. Your screeching gave me a fucking headache."

"Then you should've kept walking to help your headache," Meggie said.

"You a flippant little motherfucker, huh?" Mortician said with a snicker.

Meggie ignored him, then focused on Rack again. "Get out."

"Let's you and me go somewhere and talk," Rack told her, his tone softening.

"Either you're out of your mind or you think I am. I've already talked to you alone and we know how that turned out, jerk."

"How did it turn out?" Kiera asked, his avid interest hard to miss.

Meggie glared at the other woman. "Bite me."

"Kiera, leave," Val ordered.

"But that's not fair!" Kiera protested. "I have more of a right to be here then she does."

"She brought Prez here, Ki," Digger said with strange familiarity. "He *let* her bring him here, so until he say otherwise, she get to stay."

"Mortician, tell them I can stay," Kierra said.

Mortician opened his mouth.

"Or tell her to leave if I have to go," she added.

"I say Kiera gets to stay," Rack said with a smirk. He pointed at Meggie. "Bitch, you leave."

Determined to hold her ground, Meggie plopped into the chair nearest Christopher's bed. "No," she said in a steely tone, and met Rack's astonished gaze. "Why do you want me to leave so much? As a matter of fact, why do you want to stay?" She smiled sweetly. "You were injured too. Shouldn't you be resting?"

"*Fuuuuuccccccckkkkkk,*" Mortician groaned, scrubbing a hand over his face.

"What are you implying?" Rack yelled, barreling toward her.

He was unable to reach her because of the barrier created by Mortician and whoever else had come in before Kiera's arrival.

Meggie stood. "I'm implying nothing. I'm *telling* you plainly you're responsible for what happened today. I don't know why...I can't figure out why you shot him the way you did—"

"I didn't fucking shoot him, cunt..." Rack's voice trailed off. Looking in Mortician's direction, he snapped his mouth shut, glowering at her.

"You didn't," Meggie said, loathe to agree with Rack on any matter. "A man named Snake did."

Rack smiled nastily. "Snake?"

She scowled at him. "Rack—"

"Meggie, baby, let me take you to the cafeteria."

Meggie startled at the sound of Zoann's voice. She'd been her nurse in the ER and, as Christopher later explained, his estranged sister. She didn't want to go anywhere with her. No one seemed to care about Christopher, or the danger Rack presented. But Zoann didn't give her a choice. She took Meggie's hand and tugged her toward the door.

Only when she reached the hallway did Meggie realize she'd been anticipating violence. Even courted it. Yet, she'd begged Rack not to beat her when he'd found her at the creek, just as she'd once pleaded for mercy from Thomas.

Maybe, too, she felt protected enough, especially by Mortician, not to bother with reservations. Or common sense. Or self-preservation.

She was coming unhinged, adrift without an anchor.

"Thank you."

Zoann's quiet voice reached through Meggie's exhaustion.

Realizing they stood side-by-side at the cafeteria's coffee station, she rubbed her eyes. "For what?"

"For saving my brother."

He wasn't saved yet, but she nodded and went about preparing her coffee in silence before finding a small table near the window to stare listlessly out.

…

…

"C'mon," Zoann urged, not waiting for Meggie to follow but heading toward a pair of locked doors. She pulled a key card out of her pocket and slid it over the magnetic reader.

Reveling in the cool fall breeze, Meggie headed for the stone bench sitting amidst shrubbery and trees. She sipped her coffee and then combed her fingers through her hair.

Setting her own cup next to Meggie's, Zoann opened her purse and rifled through it. She came up with a brush and handed it to Meggie.

A smile touched Meggie's lips. "That bad, huh?"

"No. I just thought you'd prefer a brush over your fingers."

"I don't have dandruff or anything," she said, taking the brush from Zoann and running it through her hair after setting her coffee aside.

"I didn't think you did."

For a moment, they fell silent. Even Meggie's thoughts quieted, until Zoann got to her feet, grabbed the brush and took over the brushing job.

It was a task usually assigned to close friends, immediate family, or lovers. Yet Meggie felt no awkwardness that Zoann was a virtual stranger. "You two aren't very close, are you?" she asked, silence weighted by sadness pressing between them.

Zoann's hand paused.

"Kind of like me and my daddy are...*were*," Meggie amended softly. "I didn't see him often, but I knew...I knew I could always count on him. But he's dead."

Instead of answering, Zoann dropped the brush into Meggie's lap, picked up her coffee again, and sat, facing the opposite direction. "Did you come for him?" she asked after a moment.

"My mom needed his help. *I* needed his help, I mean, *for* my mom."

God, her mom! Should she call her and tell her about Big Joe's death? Would Dinah even care?

"Thomas is going to kill her eventually," Meggie continued, "and I can't get her to fight back. I've called the police and she denies everything and that gets me in trouble with her husband. I can't make her do anything, but Daddy would. He'd at least get her to leave."

And there it was, her miserable story laid out. The horror, fear and grief enveloped her body again. The confusion over what to do. The guilt. It all blended together, each born from a different source, but all overwhelming.

Meggie rolled her shoulders, then leaned over and covered her face with her hands, her elbows on her knees, ignoring the brush as it slipped onto the stones.

"And you're with Christopher because you have nowhere else to go? Because you two are lovers? Why?"

Hiccupping, Meggie dropped her hands from her face. "He fascinates me." It was the simplest answer to give. She didn't understand it herself. "He...I've never met anyone like him. He's so amazing."

"He's an asshole," Zoann retorted.

Meggie sidled a glare at Zoann, affronted on Christopher's behalf. "Perhaps, he has a reason to be an asshole to you. I don't know you, so I'm not sure. But for every one of his actions, he has a valid cause."

"How long have you known him?"

Not long enough to insert herself into his life as she had. And not long enough to feel so attracted to him or protective of him. Yet, he seemed so alone, as if he had no one in his life to depend on. Even Kiera whom he'd greeted with such passion hadn't once come to visit.

Meggie noticed Zoann's look.

"A few days," she answered, remembering the woman's question.

"After a few days, you think you know everything there is to know about him? He's a fucking biker. Sooner or later, he'll walk away and leave you."

"I know," Meggie said slowly, realizing the world he lived in, one of violence and betrayal, left no room for love or even trust. "I don't know why you asked me about my reasons for being with your brother, but I'll be right at his side as long as he allows me. I swear I'll always take care of him."

At a rap on the door, Zoann gazed in that direction. When she groaned, Meggie glanced up, seeing an older woman standing there. Once she let the woman in, they both walked to where Meggie sat and stared at her.

Uncomfortable at the speculation in the newcomer's brown eyes, Meggie got to her feet. "Hello," she murmured.

The woman nodded but remained silent.

"I need to get back to Christopher." She didn't wait for a response, rushing away, anxious to return to his side.

Kiera

The handcuffs rattled against the metal headboard in Mortician's room at the club as Kiera Arnold felt him tug one of her wrists. She should never have agreed to the blindfold. Now, she couldn't see him, as sleek as a cat and just as stealthy.

His dreads brushed her thighs. She spread them wider, her ankles chains clanking, and tilted her hips. A moment later, he licked her clit and buried his tongue in her pussy. She arched her back and screamed at the pleasure rolling through her. The hard points of her nipples ached. He sucked her pussy with just the right amount of pressure, licking her seam, down to her ass, repeating the up-and-down motion over and over again, intent on driving her insane.

Each time he paused and sucked her clit, her thighs trembled, the stubble on his face abrading her tender skin. Straining against her handcuffs and ankle chains, she moaned. Gasped. Begged.

Her thoughts were as incoherent as her words. She wanted him to stop his torture. Her nerve endings were ablaze, ready to engulf her body in flames. She pleaded with him to continue, as if he'd paused. She rolled against his mouth faster and faster, her pussy soaked. He didn't let up, spearing his tongue in and out of her pussy hole, lapping her juices and moving with her wild grinds without taking his mouth away. Her eyes rolled back in her head and her body spasmed at his relentless pussy eating. She screamed and twisted, until she slowly came back to herself, shivering at his tender clit kisses.

Then, he moved from between her legs. She thought he'd remove the blindfold, if not the handcuffs. Instead, she felt the head of his dick stroking her clit. She shuddered.

He sucked her nipple into his mouth.

Kiera panted. "Mortician," she whimpered.

"Shhh," he whispered, sliding his long, thick cock inside of her and covering her mouth with his. She tasted her pussy, vodka, and weed. Her scent covered him, but underneath was the expensive cologne he favored, the one she'd always loved.

He slid almost fully out of her, then thrust into her, deeper, harder. She pulled at her restraints, tipping her hips up, wanting every inch of him inside of her.

"Let me at least look at you," she pleaded, her gasps in tune to his dick pounding.

He brushed his lips across her own, ever so tender. "You want the blindfold off?"

"Yeah."

Kisses rained along her hairline, along the curve of her face to her earlobe; he licked her neck. "Then beg me." He slammed into her again. "You do it so fucking good."

Her inability to touch him frustrated her. She loved to touch him when they fucked. Tonight, of all nights, she needed that connection. He fucked into her, slow and deep, grinding against her pussy and driving her wild.

"God, please! Please, Mortician. Let me see you."

"No," he said roughly, burying his face against her neck and pumping into her. "You like dick," he panted. "Maybe, this fucking way you'll remember whose dick in you."

"I do! I swear."

"Whose dick owning your cunt right now?"

"Yours, Mortician." She let out a little sob and pulled at her restraints again. "Yours," she hissed, arching her back, on the verge of coming again.

"You come and I fucking spank you *then* make you eat Ellen's pussy while I give her dick. You want that?"

No, not tonight. She couldn't bear to eat Ellen out or watch her fuck Mortician when she needed him right now.

Trembling, she shook her head. But she was so hot and wet, and he wouldn't stop grinding his cock into her, tapping against her swollen clit. There was no way she could control herself. He laid dick too good. She had to let go.

"Don't come," he growled again.

His rough tone tightened her belly and heated her insides. Her orgasm rocked through her and her pussy flooded his cock. He pulled out of her. Cold air rushed against her hot, swollen pussy, and she sighed, weightless and content.

Mort tapped his cock against her lips. Greedily, she gulped him in, lost in his taste, sucking him hard and drawing his cum down her throat.

As he slid his cock out of her mouth, their hard breathing combined. She was limp in her restraints, too sated to ask that he free her. And, yet, suddenly her hands were free.

She laid them against his taut ass cheeks, lifted her head, and brought her mouth to his balls, sucking each hot nut, licking his tender sac, before swallowing his cock down her throat again.

His hands brushing through her damp hair melted Kiera. When he untied her blindfold, she raised her gaze to his, and read the command in his pretty eyes that she not look away. But she did, only for a moment, wanting to take charge, even if she preferred it when he was in control.

Yet, she had to seize the upper hand with him, so he'd stop fucking Ellen.

She sucked hard on his cock, partly out of annoyance, but mostly because it always made him come. This time was no different.

After he unlocked her ankle cuffs, he laid beside her and drew her into his arms.

She snuggled against him, comforted by his warmth and strength. She'd always adored Mortician, but Outlaw was wild and unpredictable, always truly unattainable. He said what he meant, and he meant what he said. "Will he be okay?" she whispered after a long moment. Since he'd been shot, her world had seemed upside down, as if the sun would never shine again.

Mortician sighed, but otherwise didn't respond.

Four, agonizing days had gone by and Outlaw was still out. She needed him to open his eyes. Smile at her. Frown at her. *Anything.*

"I love him," she added into the silence.

"I know."

"What if he doesn't wake up?"

Tightening his hold on her, he kissed her temple. She knew Mort cared about her. Often, she'd wondered if he would ever consider having her as his old lady. For weeks, they hadn't fucked because Outlaw had decided he wanted her and Ellen for himself. Kiera hadn't once looked at Mort. Shamefully, she hadn't even thought of how it felt to be in his arms.

But then, that little blonde cunt had arrived, and Outlaw started encouraging her and Ellen to fuck everyone again. Maybe, Kiera should've been pissed like Ellen. Instead, she was crushed. Since Outlaw's injury, she'd slept with Digger, but she'd come to the club just to be in a place Outlaw loved, without having to look at that fucking girl. She'd planted herself at Outlaw's side as if she had a right to be there.

Tonight, when Mortician had walked in and Kiera saw him, she'd gone to him and kissed him. He hadn't denied her, for which she was grateful.

Now, reality was intruding. That stupid bitch was where Kiera wanted to be—with Outlaw; Ellen was somewhere on the premises. Kiera squirmed against Mortician's shoulder. "You really gonna make me fuck Ellen?"

"You disobeyed me."

Kiera's clit throbbed at his words. One drunken night, after wild fucking, he'd told her about his first girlfriend having particular sexual tastes. And just like that, Kiera and Mort's sexual relationship changed. She liked it more than he did. Mortician didn't have much patience for safe words, punishments, or orders. Much to her pleasure, when she 'disobeyed' him, he followed through on his punishments.

She was in a strange mood, and didn't want Ellen's pussy in her mouth. She had more important things on her mind.

"Is that girl staying?"

Reaching over to his nightstand, Mort l grabbed his cell phone. He sent a text, then threw the phone back where he'd gotten it. "Megan?"

She curled into him and nodded.

"I think so."

She did, too. Unless drastic measures were taken. "Can you fuck her and keep her distracted while I win Outlaw for myself if and when he wakes up?"

"He never offered her pussy to us."

At that astounding news, she drew in a deep breath and tears rushed to her eyes. She couldn't lose him. But how could she win him if he'd changed long-standing rules of a familiar game. "That isn't fair. Sharing is caring, right? Isn't that the way it goes?" For as long as she'd been associated with the club, that's the way it had been.

"Game look like it's changing," he said quietly.

Tears rolled down her cheeks, and she sniffled, her mind spinning. "I could tell him I'm having his baby." She swiped at her tears. "He'd keep me then. He wants a kid. If I was giving him one, she'd go away."

"That shit not guaranteed. When he found out you'd played him, he'd never want anything to do with your fucking ass ever again."

"No! My shot's due. If I forget it, I could get pregnant by him."

Shoving her away, Mortician sat up and glared at her. "Unless shit changed, Prez not fucking you without his dick covered."

She averted her eyes, guilt rising in her. "Condoms break," she said, defensive.

His narrow-eyed anger hurt her. "And bitches scheme. Sound like to me you'd have some random fuck make you pregnant and pretend Outlaw the daddy."

She sniffled, still refusing to meet his gaze. "I love him."

"Say that shit happen. You end up knocked up and you say Prez the baby daddy. You pitch pussy *every fucking where*. You think Outlaw would even believe that his kid in you?"

She burst into tears. Not only didn't she want to say she'd gotten pregnant by someone else, but she also didn't want to have to go through with it. She wanted Outlaw's baby. If he didn't fuck her, she couldn't trap him. In the last few days, she'd only fucked Traveler, Digger, and, now, Mort.

Sitting up, she threw her arms around his neck and sobbed against his shoulder.

Mort had always been such a steadying force in Kiera's life. He was so gorgeous and strong, confident. He meant more to her than he'd ever imagine. Maybe, one day she'd tell him, but right now her only focus was taking Outlaw from Meggie.

Mort caressed her back. "It's all right, girl."

His rising cock captured her attention. She rubbed against his hard dick before wrapping her legs around his waist and staring at him. "I love you, too." She'd told him before, but it might've been hard for him to believe since her actions never backed up her words.

He guided his dick into her, and she groaned, rocking against him.

"No fucking way to love two motherfuckers at the same time."

Gliding her fingers through his dreads and clutching his head, she kissed him. "I do love you," she breathed against his lips.

A knock sounded at the door. Kiera knew Ellen had arrived. She tightened her legs around his waist, desperation creeping into her.

"Up," he ordered.

"Please," she whispered against his ear, grinding on his cock. "Please send her away." She leaned against him and sobbed. "Just for tonight."

He ignored her plea. Lifting her into his arms and keeping his dick inside of her, he walked to the door and opened it. A naked Ellen stood there, cigarette hanging from her mouth. She scampered past him, and Kiera tensed, watching as her best friend set her cigarette in an ashtray and turned to them.

Ellen smirked at Kiera, her eyes cold and triumphant.

Kiera wanted to curl into a little ball when Mort pulled out of her and sat her on the bed.

Ellen stared at his cock. "Oh, baby," she said in a soft voice, "look at that big, pretty dick." She dropped to her knees and took him between her lips.

His ass cheeks flexed as he slid in and out of her mouth. Throwing his head back, Kiera watched the ecstasy on his face, admired his strong neck and big hands as he buried them in Ellen's hair.

Seeing Mort with Ellen usually didn't upset Kiera as much as it did when she had to witness Outlaw and Ellen. Tonight, Kiera felt intruded upon. Hearing Ellen whimper in protest when Mort pulled his cock out of her mouth, seeing his cum spraying her nose, cheeks, and lips...*knowing* she had to mouth fuck Ellen...

Mortician walked to his desk, got Ellen's cigarette and dragged on it.

Kiera wanted to draw the covers over her head and disappear. She didn't. Instead, she sat on the edge of the bed and saw Ellen's amusement even before she heard her coarse laugh.

Kiera shoulders drooped.

"Aww, babe. Don't be like that." Ellen wiped cum from her cheek and nose, then licked her lips. She sat on the bed and hugged Kiera. "Outlaw don't need bad vibes. He's gonna be fine and we'll be back in his bed before you know it."

Kiera didn't respond.

Ellen crawled toward the pillows, where she laid on her back and opened her legs. She massaged her clit.

Mortician scratched his jaw, glancing from Kiera to Ellen, his gaze unreadable. Even when he gave her a gentle smile, Kiera couldn't figure out his thoughts.

"Kiera," he said finally.

At his unyielding tone, tension filled Kiera. She drew in a sharp breath.

"Lie on your back and spread your legs. Ellen, get to your pussy eating, ass in the air."

It took a moment for his words to register. When they did, Kiera's anxiety burst, as sharply as if it had been jabbed with a knife. Throwing him a grateful smile, she switched places with Ellen and spread her legs, her heart speeding up as Ellen settled between her thighs.

"Fuck." Ellen dragged her tongue over Kiera's clit, slow and torturous. "Your pussy's so swollen and wet. It's just been fucked, huh, baby?"

"Yes," Kiera gasped, tweaking her nipples, and opening her legs wider. She pushed Ellen's head against her pussy, arching her back and rolling her hips.

"Oh fuck," Ellen groaned.

Kiera lifted on her elbows to watch Mort and Ellen fucking.

She sucked in a sob, and Kiera rested her head on the pillow again, smiling as Ellen adjusted to Mortician fucking her in the ass.

"Big dick bastard," she gasped. "Fuck me hard and fast, until you make the pain become pleasure."

"Then you tongue Kiera's pussy until she comes and don't stop making her come until I tell you to."

"Anything, Mortician," she swore, and sucked Kiera's clit between her teeth.

Chapter Eighteen

OUTLAW

"CHRISTOPHER, WAKE UP."

"I'm here, my beautiful boy."

"You have a high fever, Christopher."

"Meggie, babe, I didn't mean nothing by what I said."

"Please, Christopher, don't leave me."

"It's Zoann, Christy." A sniffle. "*Christopher.* We're all here. Mama, me, Ophelia, Bev, Nia and Avery. All of us. Squeeze my hand. Let me know you hear me."

"It's Digger. What the fuck you doing, bruh? Wake the fuck up. Enough enough, Outlaw."

"Christopher, please."

"Prez, this Mort. You got to come back to us, Outlaw. We been through too fucking much for it to end like this."

"You're a traitor, Rack."

"Ain't like that, Meggie. I swear. I'd never do anything to betray my club."

"Just leave."

"I almost got my ass shot off. You think I'd set myself up to be shot?"

"It's John Boy, Christopher. Aunt Patricia is in the waiting room. If you die, I think she'll die with you."

"Time to get the fuck up, you little fucking runt. *Now,* Outlaw!"

"You haven't opened your eyes since I left, Christopher. Come back to us. To me."

Outlaw. Christopher. Back and forth the names went, penetrating the black void of his mind. Christopher. Outlaw. Two men, in a single body, one soulless, the other lost.

"Christopher?"

Each time he heard that soft tone, he battled to respond. It was like a siren's call, willing him to fight. He yearned to be Christopher. For her. To her. Yet, he couldn't be but his brain was too foggy to understand why.

"I'm here. I'm not going anywhere."

Why?

He struggled to open his eyes, tried to speak. Question her. She needed to know that he could never be Christopher.

Could he?

He barely remembered how to be Outlaw. The man who'd turned him into Outlaw was gone, and it was his fault. Wasn't it?

A symphony of voices harped through Christopher's head. In and out, consciousness lured him but then darkness pulled him back. His awareness didn't last long enough for anyone to notice, leaving Christopher with vague outlines of people and wondering which conversations he imagined and which of them were real.

Despite the cacophony, he responded to the sweetest sound of all. Her voice pulled him out of his medicated stupor and allowed everything to rush back.

He cursed at the burning pain in his thigh and shoulder. Megan jerked her head in his direction. Luminous eyes drank him in, studied him as though he was the only man on earth. The man she needed and wanted above all else.

Christopher

"Christopher," she breathed, dragging her chair closer and taking his hand into hers. She kissed the back of it before laying it against her cheek. "I have to call your nurse and let her know you're awake."

He struggled to sit further up, the beeping noises of the various monitors irritating the fuck out of him. The antiseptic smell collaborated with the taste of medicine to turn his stomach.

"Before you do—" He paused to clear his scratchy and aching throat.

"Shhh," she soothed, putting a finger to his lips. "They removed the breathing tubes last night." She reached for the device to call the nurse.

He grabbed her hand again and swallowed his discomfort. "I got a coupla questions. Answer, then call."

Wariness entered her eyes and she combed her fingers through her hair, blanketing him with the scent of his shampoo. She didn't seem inclined to listen. As usual. He tightened his hold on her.

"My ma was here or I dream that?"

"You didn't dream it," she confirmed. "She was here. So were all your sisters. Only Zoann is still here. The others left."

He nodded and groaned. "Rack?"

She wrinkled her nose and sniffed, providing him all the answer he needed. She nodded. "Yes."

The ice in her tone also reassured Christopher that Megan *had* accused Rack of betraying the club. He wasn't sure if he should praise her courage or yell at her for her stupidity. She, of all people, should know Rack wasn't a man to accuse of wrongdoing. Then, again, with the carved words still healing on Rack's back, he might've realized the foolishness of harming Megan. Because if Christopher hadn't been able to protect her, Digger, Mortician, and Val certainly would.

But, fuck, Megan needed to think before she acted. Her impulsiveness combined with her temper was a lethal mixture.

He didn't have the strength to take that argument on now, so he went on with his original questions. "Digger?" he asked, deciding the sooner she left, the better.

"And Mortician and Val."

"My cousin?"

She shrugged. "I think. If your cousin's name is Johnnie, then yes. But I wasn't here. When Ellen and Kiera visited you, I left."

"Why?" he asked to goad her, her flashing eyes and flushed cheeks hard to resist.

"I just did," she snapped, refusing to meet his eyes.

Christopher stifled the grin threatening to breakthrough despite his fucked up pain. He knew girls and he knew jealousy had run Megan away. He refrained from mentioning that. "So while you was gone, Johnnie visited?"

"Yes. According to Val."

He dropped her hand. Annoyance thinned her lips and stirred Christopher's blood. He ignored the satisfaction he felt at having her face the first one he saw when he awakened. Though he'd been wounded, his cock was in perfect condition because, in spite of the pain and the promise he made not to touch her, his dick hardened. Yeah, well. Shit was about right. That was the power of pussy to a pervert like him. In pain like a motherfucker but still wanting to empty his balls dry inside her.

He groaned and shifted. Megan eyed the length of his body, her face turning red when she saw his erection.

Her complete and utter fascination with his dick punched him in the gut. He opened his mouth to tease her, ask her if she'd like to see it, but shut it immediately. Reckless little bitch that she was, she'd say yes.

"Ain't you seen enough cocks in your life?" he growled.

She frowned. "I've only seen two."

Two too fucking many since neither of the motherfuckers she'd seen was his. The jealousy tearing through him pissed him off even more. He glared at her. "And here I thought you was a fuckin' virgin."

"I am!"

"Then how the fuck you seen two cocks?"

"Really, Christopher? We're talking about this *now*? Really?"

She reached for the remote to call the nurse, but he used all his strength to yank it from her. Fatigue was setting in and, with each passing minute, his pain grew. He fought off the tiredness and burning pain in his body to talk to her. By the time he went to sleep, he hoped he'd have gotten his point across, and she'd agree to leave. Tomorrow, he'd tell Val to set her up somewhere and make sure she wanted for nothing ever. Right now, Christopher fought the oncoming fog and suffering to memorize her face and bask in the warmth of her scrutiny.

He swallowed, cold sweat beading his brow. The excruciating pain had even limped his dick. He trembled and blinked. "Answer me, Megan."

She folded her arms. "I didn't have a say when you walked out with your zipper undone," she chirped sourly. "And my stepfather didn't give me much choice, either."

If he'd intended to keep her around, he would've made finding her step fuckhead a priority. By the time Christopher finished with him, he'd be squatting to piss for the eternity he'd spend in hell. Not much more a man could do dickless or headless.

"May I call the nurse *now*?"

Christopher gritted his teeth, disgusted at how his conscience always intruded where Megan Foy was concerned. It couldn't be her home life. He'd known women with much more terrible childhoods, abused from the time they came into the world until the day they ran away, preferring life on the streets to the horrors at home. Neither could it be her temper and her fearless determination. It worried him that when the time came to turn her out, he wouldn't be able to.

He could only appeal to her self-preservation.

Dizziness whirled in his head and he squeezed his eyes shut. Fire blazed through his throat, his thigh, and his shoulder. "Look at me." The demand came out as a croak. Fuck, the look in her eyes made his heart beat faster and his stomach clench. She didn't see *Outlaw*. She didn't give a fuck that he detested the name Caldwell or the reasons for it. If he allowed it, if he opened up to her…

Those thoughts were not his. They weren't real. *She* wasn't real. Or, maybe, because of his injuries and fading attention he imagined the awe in her eyes.

"Christopher," she whispered, rubbing his brow. "Please. Ask me whatever you want when you feel better. I'll be here."

No. No. *No.* He had to make her understand what would happen to her if she stayed. What he'd demand of her. "I'm your worst fuckin' nightmare," he got out. "Stop thinkin' I'm some goddamn hero cuz I ain't." He paused, deciding to voice his intentions if she remained with him—the very reason she *couldn't* stay. Words flowed from him in a weakened tone. He hoped she still heeded them. "I wantcha pussy." He panted and blinked, the heart of the matter staring him in the face. "The shots coulda killed me and I woulda left without a kid to carry my name. Ain't never been particularly fond of the name 'Caldwell' either," he admitted grimly. "My old man was a family friend who raped my ma then had the fuckin' nerve to insist I got his last name."

"Shhh."

This time when she placed her finger over his lips, he kissed her fragrant skin before pulling her hand away and holding it.

"I ain't ever gettin' married," he rasped. "My kid…if I knocked you up…my kid would getcha last name. Foy a fine last name. Havin' a kid with Boss genes, *your* genes, would be fuckin' great. When he was sane and lucid, he was a solid motherfucker. Big Joe was good to me and, Megan, I miss the fuck outta him." He drew in a deep breath and squeezed her delicate hand. "I wanna fuck you 'til you can't walk. Come in you 'til I'm empty. Put my dick in you and fuck you s'more." He slurred the last word.

She took a step back, eyes wide. He wanted to laugh at her shock. He wanted to cry at her loss. She was finally getting the fucking picture. Even worse than what he wanted to do to her was another harsh fact—*she* could've been killed. Bullets didn't have names. Somehow, she'd escaped Snake's assault and survived. He had to get her away. A girl like her deserved better than a man like him. Now, to put the nail in the coffin, use the last measure of his conscience, strength, and decency.

"Leave. I ain't wantin' you here with me. Underfuckinstand?"

Jesus, the hurt creeping into her eyes knifed through Christopher, more painful than a dozen gunshot wounds.

"Get the fuck away from me. *Now!*"

She stared at him, caught between disbelief and fear.

"Get the fuck outta here." He turned his head, a dismissal.

When the snick of the door opening and closing came, Christopher felt as if the sun had walked out of his life and sank into oblivion.

Chapter Nineteen

Meggie

"HE'S AWAKE," MEGGIE CALLED TO THE STARTLED nurse, not pausing to answer any of the woman's questions. After five and a half days of hell, wondering why Christopher hadn't opened his eyes, after the hours he'd spent in surgery to remove the bullets, he'd awakened and sent her away. She hadn't slept well without him next to her the one time Digger and Mortician convinced her to stay at the clubhouse. They'd ordered pizza and ate with her in the main room. Along with Val, Digger and Mortician had taken her to a room along the building's third hallway, where a big TV had been set up. She wasn't in the mood to watch anything, so they'd taught her a couple of card games. When they finally escorted her to Christopher's room, it was well after midnight. She'd taken a quick shower and fallen into bed, exhausted. Nightmares about the attack plagued her with dead bodies and gore. In her dream, she'd stumbled over one and realized it was her daddy.

A scream had woken her up. *Her* scream. She'd sat in Christopher's bed, sweaty and trembling. She'd allowed the small lamp near his entertainment center to remain on, but it hadn't helped. Terror tore through her. Mortician, Digger, and Val had rushed to see about her. The enforcer had even sat with her a little while, until she'd insisted she was fine and sent him away.

She hadn't been fine, though. Tired of her tears, she'd done the only thing she could do. Discovered a small knife next to the CDs and found relief and peace. A channel for all her fear and grief.

Her thighs stung from the fresh cuts, but she wished she had something with her. All the emotions converging on her would burst free, like air being released from a balloon. She had to get to the clubhouse. When she packed her stuff, she'd take that knife, too.

She turned a corner, heading for the elevators. A blond man leaned against the wall, talking to Ellen and Kiera. She'd never seen him before, so she didn't think he'd recognize her. And, she figured, even if the women did, they wouldn't speak to her.

Averting her eyes, she intended to rush past the small sitting area outside ICU without a word. Instead, she ran smack dab into Val. He grabbed her arms to steady her.

"Meg—"

"He's awake," she blurted. She started around the big biker, but he pulled her by the arm to the seat he'd vacated and pushed her into it. Mortician, Digger, Rack, and Zoann, occupied the other seats.

"Where're you going, babe?" Val asked carefully.

"I'm leaving."

"Now?" the blond man asked.

God, he was gorgeous. Almost as tall as Christopher with silver-gray eyes and a dangerous air. Muscles popped through his clothes as he moved toward her with effortless grace. Christopher had a harder edge with none of this man's laugh lines. He stopped in front of her, and she gripped the sides of her chair.

"You intend to leave now? When he's finally awake."

Meggie lifted her chin. "Yes," she hissed, "*now*. As soon as you let me by." She got to her feet and forced him back. He refused to give her too much ground, so her body still brushed against his. She scowled at him. "Who are you, anyway, that whether I leave or stay is any of your business?"

"I gotta admit this bitch got fire," Ellen said. A hint of grudging admiration laced the words.

"Yes, she does." A slow smile started across the mouth of the man who stood in front of her. "I'm Johnnie, by the way. Outlaw's cousin."

"Whatever." She squirmed past him, unable to fathom why she noticed anything about this man when she felt so hurt over Christopher's treatment of her. And his words…she hated to admit they appalled and enthralled her in equal measure, although she was certain his current condition caused him to speak about making love to her and getting her pregnant and all of the other crazy, outrageous things he'd said. Though she had no means to support a baby, the idea held appeal to her for her own selfish reasons. He wanted a child to carry on his genes. She just wanted someone to love her. "If you'll excuse me," she threw over her shoulder, determined to get to the elevator. She didn't owe any of these people an explanation. Let the lunatic in the hospital bed explain.

"C'mon, Meggie girl," Mortician called. "We had to force you to leave for one night to get proper Zs. After that, you left his side for all of four hours. You demanded a way be found to get you to stay in here with him. Not taking a brain surgeon to know Outlaw pissed you off when he woke up. Whatever he told you, though, he not meaning it."

Once she admitted to them that Christopher told her to leave, they'd have to let her go. For them, his word was law. "He told me to leave." She didn't mean to allow her hurt to come through. Neither was she sure why she *was* so hurt. Maybe, she'd attached herself to Christopher because he served as a link to her father. Or, maybe, to her, he epitomized a man who'd never force her to do all the things Thomas intended but wouldn't hesitate to take what she offered. He'd allow it to be on her terms. Or, maybe, the inherent goodness she saw in him, and the protection he gave to her when he didn't have to, made his rejection so crushing. She hugged her arms around her waist. "He doesn't want me around him anymore."

She moved to leave again. Johnnie stepped in front of her.

"Move!" she snarled, trying to shove him away.

Amusement lit his eyes. Genuine amusement, not the sardonic kind Christopher normally had.

"No."

He tweaked her nose and Meggie had the urge to cuff him on the side of his head.

"Uh, uh, uh," he admonished, wagging a long finger at her. "Violence gets you nowhere, Megs."

"If you don't move or shut up or both, I'm going to punch you," she vowed. The reprobate laughed harder.

"Christopher and Johnnie are the only two penises to be born into the family in the last thirty-three years," Zoann informed her. "Instead of making them gentlemen, it has turned them into complete dickheads."

Val chuckled. Out of the corner of her eye, Meggie noticed Zoann flush a pretty pink.

"You two pathetic," Mortician observed. "If I was you, Val, I'd keep my dick outta Zoann."

"Fuck you," Val snapped.

"No, thank you. 'Preciate the offer, though."

"May I leave now?" Meggie asked no one in particular, although Johnnie still blocked her.

"No."

The chorus startled her. "He doesn't want me here," she reminded them.

"Uh, yeah, he does," Digger said. "He been jonesin' for your pussy since you got here."

"It's not my pussy he has the problem with," Meggie mumbled.

"He wants the rest of you, too, girl," Digger called in exasperation.

Heat rushed to Meggie's cheeks that they'd overheard her comment.

"You just a young bitch," Digger went on, shifting in his seat and stretching his long legs out. "Feel me? Reckless, too. You have the makins of a real sexy bitch. A dude hit your pussy two, three times, you'll find your sexy and you gonna be one bad bitch."

Having been around these men for the past few days inured her to their unique phrases. She should've been insulted or embarrassed or both. She wasn't either.

Digger rested his hands behind his head and leaned back. "Outlaw got sisters so he try to do right by bitches. I think he know if he fuck you, he gonna say ba-bye to any other pussy. A man got to come to terms with just seeing one pussy the rest of his life. Know what I'm saying?"

Sorta. Kinda. *Still...* "That isn't true. Christopher already has a girlfriend, anyway."

Zoann frowned. "He does?"

Mortician folded his arms and threw her a mocking look. "Says who?"

Digger laughed so loud Meggie glanced around, waiting for security to arrive and escort them out. "Where the bitch at?"

Meggie pulled her attention away from Rack's silent scrutiny of the entire scene. She still didn't trust him, although she needed to take more care in her accusations, especially now, when she wouldn't have Christopher around to prevent Rack from harming her.

"Well, Megs, who is she?"

She nodded her head in the direction of Ellen and Kiera. "Kiera," she answered.

Ellen bristled. "You think?" she called sharply.

Meggie glared at the annoying woman.

Johnnie grabbed Meggie around the waist. "Slow down, hellcat. And, Ellen, keep the fuck quiet."

"Meggie, that's the stupidest fucking idea I done ever heard cross your lips," Digger snorted. "Them bitches don't belong to him. Kiera might give him pussy but she get dick from whoever else is willing to put it on her." He winked. "Most recently, me."

Ellen laughed while Kiera made a sound of distress as jealousy burned through Meggie.

Digger wasn't finished. "He not bringing no loose pussy home to Miz Patricia, his momma," he clarified at Meggie's silent question. "You, on the other hand, yeah. He'll bring you home and show you off."

"Mama wouldn't want loose pussy tainting her doors," Zoann pointed out with a sniff, glaring between Kiera and Ellen.

Ellen flipped Zoann off.

"Fuck you right back, bitch," Zoann snarled. "Better yet, let's take it to the parking lot so I can tear you a new fucking asshole, then drag you up and down the fucking concrete, smearing it with your blood along the way."

Ellen stared at Zoann, and Megan saw she was torn between disbelief and...*fear.*

"Good to know the fucking Donovan genes alive and well," Mortician said with a snort.

"Pull in your claws, babe," Val told Zoann, then looked at Ellen. "She not playing. She related to John Boy and Outlaw. So—"

"Don't fuck with her if you value your life," Digger inserted. "She not going to none of us to fuck you up neither. She'll do the shit her damn self. Now, as I was fucking saying when I was so rudely interrupted." He looked at Meggie again. "Mark my words about him bringing you to his momma. Not going to happen, though, if you skulk off like a frightened bitch."

Resting her fingers on Johnnie's forearm and leaning back against his chest, Meggie pondered Digger's words, unsure if she had the nerve to stay after Christopher's conversation. On the other hand, where else did she have to go? And, even after identifying Christopher as a certifiable madman, she wanted him. She wanted to feel as special as she had when he'd given her her birthday gifts and brought her the cupcakes. Though she hadn't wanted the boots since Kiera had the same kind, she had them on because she had no other shoes to wear. He'd at least thought about that. She wanted to snuggle into his side like she did whenever he decided to sleep next to her in his bed.

"She must feel good in your fucking arms, John Boy," Mortician said, scratching his jaw. His dreads tied back made the diamond studs he wore in his ears more noticeable. "Your arm been pressing against her tit for fifteen minutes now."

Without a word, Johnnie released her. His dancing gaze summoned the evil eye from her. He winked. She blushed.

Sitting down, she drew her knees to her chest, resting her head on them. She hoped she wasn't making a mistake by listening to Digger instead of heeding the words Christopher had spoken.

Meggie sighed. Only time would tell.

Chapter Twenty
Christopher

CHRISTOPHER OPENED HIS EYES, A STEADY BEEP resounding in his head. Pain careened along his nerve endings and an antiseptic smell gathered in his nostrils.

He wondered at the time. Kiera's head lulled as she sat in a chair next to his bed, her dark hair curtaining her features. The harsh taste of the various medicines filled his dry mouth and he groaned.

Kiera jolted up and blinked, glancing around as if she needed to get her bearings.

Finally, she turned to him, and a huge smile curved her mouth. "Hey, baby."

As much as he liked Kiera and had tried his best to always look out for her, he didn't want her with him right now. "Yo."

She jumped to her feet, leaned over the bed railing, and hugged him. "I been so worried about you." Her hands skimmed over his body, bypassing his wounded shoulder and traveling down his stomach. "I thought I'd never hear your voice again. Taste your dick again."

What the fuck? He'd gotten shot up and this bitch was worrying about tasting his dick?

He gazed around the room, searching for Megan and knowing he wouldn't find her since he'd sent her away. It disappointed him she'd listened to him *now*.

Fuck it. He'd sent Megan away for her own good. In the big picture, Kiera was a sweet girl, just the type of chick he deserved and wanted. Sweet but not innocent. Tough but not vicious.

He tried to imagine Kiera pregnant for him, but the thought didn't jive, refused to form completely.

She covered his mouth with hers, spearing her tongue against his. Christopher turned his head away, not really feeling Kiera at the moment.

"Whatcha doin' here?"

She reached over and thumbed his lips. "I been here all night. Everybody else left."

"How long I been here?" One of the questions he'd meant to ask Megan before he'd been a dickhead and sent her away. The nurse had come in, not long after Megan left, and told him he'd been there five and a half days.

What? "What the fuck you mean? A week?" he'd demanded.

"Just what I said," the nurse-bitch had said with a frown. "Five and a half days. Almost a week."

Since Christopher didn't know how long he'd been sleeping this time around, he wanted to find out.

"You've been here six days," Kiera said now.

He'd only been out a half day, this time. *Still*...he wasn't doing his club duties.

Fuck. Fuck. Fuck. Fuck. There wasn't no motherfucking way—

Fuck! He shoved the covers aside, intending to stand and find his clothes. Check himself the fuck out. Bullshit like a week-long hospital stay was just the shit Rack needed to assume control of the club.

"What are you doing?" Kiera cried, jumping back.

"Gettin' the fuck outta here. I ain't believin' this shit."

"You were shot—"

"I was fuckin' wounded. A flesh fuckin' wound."

"You lost a lot of blood and slipped into unconsciousness on the way here."

"How the fuck I end up unconscious for almost a goddamn week?"

She shrugged, the import of his absence escaping her. Of course, it would. What the fuck did she know anyfuckingway?

Monitors were beeping, the cuff of the blood pressure machine inflating. Numbers were blinking in red. He felt dizzier than a motherfucker, but so fucking what?

The door crashed open, and several nurses rushed in. "Mr. Caldwell! You have to return to bed."

"No," he gritted. "I gotta get to my fuckin' club."

"Christopher! Christopher, please settle down."

As two male nurses lunged at him to wrestle him back onto the bed, he glared at Kiera. "How the fuck I got in this fuckin' place any goddamn way?"

"That girl."

Megan, she meant. He slapped away the hand of one of the grasping nurses.

"Listen to me," she said urgently, turning a blind eye to Christopher's struggles. "Rack is your Judas. He's feeding information to Snake. I'm sure. Just like I know you been thinking."

"Don't fuckin' try to figure me out, Kiera," he snapped, elbowing the persistent fucks.

"Him and that girl was talking. I think she helped him."

That startled Christopher so much, he stilled, giving the two assfucks a chance to subdue him.

"No fuckin' way! Megan ain't doin' shit like that."

"Think about it," Kiera went on. "Her appearance out of nowhere. And she's Boss's daughter. She just happened to show up right around the first anniversary of his death. She's innocent, huh? Then why don't she question nothing about our lifestyle? She just took to it like a duck to fucking water."

Every cell in Christopher's body rebelled at the idea of Megan working with Rack, and, possibly, Snake. But, fuck him, Kiera had a point. Megan hadn't been born into this shit. Yet...yet, she'd just went with the flow.

"Calm down, baby," Kiera cooed.

Christopher would've responded but one of those nurse bitches pumped something into his IV. He only hoped he didn't get a fucking concussion when he hit the fucking floor. His last conscious thought was Kiera's yelp of pain and the blurry vision of her flailing arms.

Well, fuck.

The next time Christopher awakened, the room was dark and quiet. The opened curtains revealed the night. He couldn't see anything else, though. His head pounded and his mouth tasted as if his tongue was made of cotton. He covered his face with both hands and cursed. He needed to get the fuck out of here.

Yeah, you fucking genius, that shit already established.

Christopher scowled at the random thought. How long he'd been out this time? Another fucking week?

"Christopher?" a soft voice said, startling him, as a small bedside lamp flicked on.

Megan. What was it with this girl? Why the fuck couldn't she fucking *leave*? Why the fuck did he want her to *stay*? Megan was the wildcard. Boss's daughter, who'd arrived just a few days before Snake's attempted takedown. The shit Kiera said made a lot of sense.

He glowered at Megan. "Get the fuck outta here, you fuckin' bitch. You set me the fuck up."

Her gentle look vanished and her mouth fell open. "*What?*" she screeched, high color blooming in her cheeks. "Set you up? Like I worked with those men to have you killed?"

He nodded.

"Jerk!" she yelled. "If I'd set you up, I would've finished you when I found you all shot up. And I wouldn't have brought you to the hospital!"

The sudden glare of the light directly behind his bed made him blink. Once his eyes adjusted, he noticed her standing as still as a statue, to his right. He reached his arm out and pulled her closer. Her hair clipped up, she wore the clothes he'd bought her for her birthday. She looked tired and sad and alone. And young. So fucking young, he wondered if she had permission to be in the room with him. Of course, she did. He knew she did.

"You show up outta the fuckin' blue and—"

"It wasn't out of the blue, Christopher," she murmured, his given name coming from her lips the sweetest sound he'd ever heard.

His head pounded in confusion and he wanted to be alone, not have those blue eyes appeal to him like a beacon to his dark soul. "Stop fuckin' callin' me by my name."

A frown creased her brow. "W-why? Is there a warrant out for your arrest?"

Christopher rolled his eyes and snorted. Was she for real? "I been laid up in this motherfucker for how long? Under *my real goddamn name?* If there was a warrant out, chances high, somebody woulda been clued in 'bout my whereabouts."

"You've been here six days."

"Six fuckin' days too long."

"No, it isn't. Rack is looking after things."

Christopher just bet he was. "You shouldna took me here," he said in frustration. "I woulda been fuckin' fine."

"I had no choice but to bring you here. You were dying."

"And? You ain't fuckin' knowin' me. Perhaps, I wanted to fuckin' die."

She stared at him and Christopher braced himself for some inane bullshit. Words like, 'of course you don't want to die' and 'you don't really mean that'. The fuck he didn't.

"I understand. Recently, I've wanted to die, too."

That statement shocked the shit out of him. She was gorgeous, well-spoken, and brave. She had everything to live for. At this very moment, she should be out with some little preppy fuck, talking about college and careers. She shouldn't be stuck in this fucking hospital room with him.

As if she had any other choice. She had a step fuckhead who had to be taken care of and a dead father whose protection she needed.

"Yeah? Why?"

She shrugged. "I've never been away from my mother for more than a day or two. And—and I've never been on my own."

As much as Christopher wanted to punk out and go the bitch ass route by pointing the finger at Megan, he couldn't. A made up argument might get her away from him but it would put her right back in danger. No, the shooting at the clubhouse had been brewing long before Megan arrived.

"I had to leave," she stressed. "For the reasons you guessed."

She swallowed, frowned, looked away. Swallowed again, looking anywhere but at him, Christopher noted, admiration for her grit rolling in him.

"My stepfather. His groping had amped up from holding my hand against him. Um, his groin. To pinching my...my nipples and trying to..."

Her voice trailed off and she hunched her shoulders, but humiliation haunted her eyes and tightened her mouth.

"Tryna take pussy from you?" he finished for her, his voice neutral.

"Um, I-I suppose it would've ended up that way. He l-liked to put his hand in...in my panties."

Remorse hit hard. Boss had been destroying himself, the club, and his son. Of course, Snake was born destroyed, missing the gene that gave him compassion.

Christopher might've fucking went from one woman to the next. And, yeah, he might not have been a fucking gentlemen to bitches all the time, but he'd never killed one for the hell of it to get his rocks off. And he certainly didn't snort and shoot up the fucking merchandise. Payoffs to the cops had become more and more exorbitant because Boss was fucking up right and left. So Christopher began quietly lobbying the brothers to do an intervention. As the vice president, he wanted a coup. Overthrow Boss until the motherfucker got his shit right. Let him detox. Get all the killing out of him. Make him be the man Christopher remembered and admired.

He hated Boss for making him have to *choose* between their lives. He hated Boss for turning a blind eye to his son's actions, a stone-cold fucking killer. He hated Boss for turning weak and strung out.

Christopher knew the man had adored his daughter. Or had before his brain became fried. And, yet, Megan was clueless. She believed her father could've protected her. In the last eighteen months of his life, he hadn't been able to protect a club full of grown ass men. Not only that, in those last months, he hadn't once mentioned his little girl. How fucking pathetic.

"I didn't set you up."

Her fingers slid through his hair and she stared at him. All Christopher saw was innocence and longing. Yeah, she hungered for him, but her desire for him overrode the baseness of pure lust. Something had to stop this freight train of disaster, careening at Mach 2 toward Christopher's bed. He grabbed her face between his hands. "If you're fuckin' lyin' to me…"

"I'm not. I swear."

He believed her. Christopher knew bitches tripped. Kiera could deal with him fucking Ellen, but, apparently, she didn't like the thought of him being with Megan.

If he lived as long as Methuselah, he'd never understand bitches. Especially the one who currently faced him down, more fearless of him than some men.

Fuck, did it really matter to him whether or not Megan knew Christopher killed her pops? If he wanted her gone, *really wanted her gone,* confessing to his murder would send her the fuck away. But which way would she go? To the police? Back home, even though she was terrified of Thomas Nicholls?

He sidled a glance at her and squeezed the bridge of his nose. "Whatcha plannin' on doin' 'bout the shootin'?"

Her throat worked. "I-I don't know what you mean."

"Yeah, you fuckin' do." He saw it in her face.

She shook her head, met his gaze. "Nothing," she whispered. "Val explained things to me. How it works." She licked her lips. "With law enforcement and the Death Dwellers."

His nostrils flared and he searched her face for any signs she was having second thoughts about not speaking up.

"It don't bother you?" he questioned. "Motherfuckers died."

She looked away from him and shifted her weight. "This is…*was* Daddy's club. If he…he r-ran it…if he t-took care of…k-killed men who in-invaded his t-turf," she managed through sniffles.

"Megan," Christopher crooned.

She drew in a deep breath and he allowed her a moment to compose herself.

"This was his life, Christopher. Whether I like it or not. I'd never betray him."

He nodded and smiled at her. A small smile ghosted across her lips.

"Where you been livin' since you ran away? Before I took you back to the clubhouse."

"By the creek."

"In other words, you fuckin' homeless." Something he already knew, although he hadn't known she'd been fucking living in that park.

"You can say that," she mumbled.

Fuck. Whether he liked it or not, he'd just acquired a very beautiful, very sumptuous, eighteen-year-old to look after.

Chapter Twenty-One

Meggie

CHRISTOPHER "OUTLAW" CALDWELL WAS THE most ornery, insufferable man Meggie had *ever* met. Any minute she expected some law enforcement agency to storm the Death Dwellers' compound to arrest Christopher for intimidation and intent to do bodily harm to someone. Namely, his physician. He'd left the man no choice but to release him. *Or else.* Meggie didn't like the ominous tone of the 'or else' and neither had the doctor. Five days after he'd awakened and an hour after issuing the ultimatum, Christopher was on his way back to the clubhouse, refusing to let Meggie drive his souped-up pickup, even though she'd driven him to the hospital in it.

He'd stopped at a drugstore and loaded up on magazines, novels, and puzzle books. Meggie wasn't sure what they'd been for. However, the moment they arrived at the club, he'd grabbed the bag, ushered her out of the truck, then dragged her to his room. Once there, he'd shoved everything at her, told her "stay fuckin' put", and disappeared.

She liked crosswords and magazines, but she didn't like to have that as her *only* entertainment. And, not enough of them existed in the world to take her thoughts off Christopher's sculpted body or the need to have him touching her.

She hadn't seen him since and it was early evening. Her concern for Christopher made everything else insignificant. She knew he had club business—whatever that meant—but he was still recovering from gunshots and blood loss.

All outward signs of the rampage were gone. The bullet holes had been filled in and the furniture replaced. In Meggie's opinion, the new desk in Christopher's bedroom looked much better than the old one.

She stretched out on the bed, staring at the ceiling, bored out of her head, afraid to remain too sedentary, fearing her thoughts would overwhelm her. He'd said to stay put, but there were other things to do in his room than read or figure out crosswords. He had a bathroom. She could shower. She lifted her head, gazed around. His room wasn't filthy, but it could be tidied up. She could do that, then shower. If he still hadn't returned, she'd find him and demand he rest.

Christopher leaned against the counter, studying the wall of monitors, ignoring the throbbing pain in his shoulder and thigh. No motherfucking way Snake could've gotten on the grounds without being let in. The monitors were in perfect working order. He had grade-fucking-A visuals of the hallways, the perimeter outside, the board room, and his main supply room. Sinner had been on monitor duty that day. If he'd let Snake in, he'd paid for it with a bullet to the head.

But Sinner had always had his back, even when Boss was alive. On the other hand, Sinner had been Snake's friend, too. But he was dead, so he no longer presented a problem. Rack was the VP now and Christopher knew not only was he grieving for Big Joe, but he was also displeased he hadn't been chosen as the new president, though he'd sworn he'd do whatever needed doing for the good of the club. Val and Mort patched in at the same time. They'd wanted Boss gone the moment they realized what he was up to. And Mort and Val fucking hated Snake. What did they have to gain by betraying him? Tex, the treasurer, and Guardian, the secretary, Mortician, the enforcer, Val, the road captain, K-P, the kitchen bitch, and Digger…fuck, who cared?

Out of his officers—Sinner, Mortician, Digger, Val, Rack, Tex, and Guardian—only Mortician, Digger, Rack and Val were still alive. Val had been off premises, making a run on behalf of the club. And Rack? Fucking Rack…

Shit. The entire infrastructure of his club was fucked up the ass, already in disarray before the shooting. Now…fuck. Interim elections would be held, just as they'd done immediately following Big Joe's…

Fuck that motherfucker and his fucking guilt.

Fuck. Him.

And fuck his fucking guilt.

Christopher didn't have time to think about that fucking drug addicted assfuck. He was right the fuck where he goddamn belonged. Fuck Boss. The club needed Christopher's attention. He needed to go into the rank and file, elect new officers, straighten this shit out and find the fucking weak link. What the fuck was he missing?

All roads pointed to Rack, but those roads were too straight and cleanly routed. Rack would be a stupid motherfucker to leave so much evidence if he was guilty. That left his boys, Val, Mort and Digger.

Christopher stiffened with tension. A chair scraped across the floor and he glanced in the direction of the sound. "You! Probate," he called, not bothering to figure out the assfuck's name until he became a full-fledged member.

Motherfucker jogged the short distance between the tables and the bar. "Prez?"

"Keep a eye on them screens. If a motherfucker ain't a member, turn him the fuck away. If my ass fuckin' find somefuckinbody ain't belongin' here…" He let the threat hang in the air and turned away.

"Um, Outlaw?"

He hadn't gotten two fucking feet before the assfuck called him back. "What?"

"That girl? Should she be here?"

Christopher didn't need to look at the screen to know what girl he meant. Only one girl never *ever* fucking listened to him. The blonde one with the gorgeous face and perfect little body. The bitch walking into the room, her hair damp, wearing the old fucking clothes good only for a garbage pile.

"Whatcha doin' out here?" he asked at the same time she demanded, "Where have you been all day?"

"Afuckinround," he snapped. "Ain'tcha fuckin' business." He jerked her behind him and pulled her down the hall. "I told you to fuckin' stay in my goddamn room and I meant it." He reached the room and pushed her into it.

Squeaking, she stumbled back, flailing her arms to keep her balance. She righted herself at the last minute and opened her mouth. He held up a hand to shut her up.

"You pushin' your fuckin' luck, Megan. Your lil' ass lucky you fuckin' with me instead of on the fuckin' streets. If you ain't listenin' to me, Ima putcha the fuck out and you fendin' for yourfuckinself."

Accusation turned to hurt. Her chin wobbled and her eyes filled with tears. With a frustrated curse, Christopher slammed the door shut and stalked to his office, his cock sending signals to his brain. His emotions toward her were going in a completely different direction. He wanted to fuck her as much as he wanted to kiss her.

After three in the morning, Christopher staggered back, nicely medicated with rum and beer. Both lamps and the bathroom light brightened his room. He stared sourly at the lump in his bed. He couldn't see much of anything besides her blonde hair. He drank from the bottle of rum he was determined to finish, cursing her and the lights as he walked around turning each one off before undressing and climbing into bed.

She tensed. She was awake, was she? Let her fucking sulk. He laid on his back and stared at the ceiling. She inched closer to the wall, the movement so minute he wanted to howl in laughter. Did she really believe a fucking wall would protect her if he wanted some ass from her?

Christopher turned toward her, simultaneously scooting closer and pulling her into his arms. She wore something big. Something belonging to him from the feel of it. He pressed his erection into her back and buried his nose in the soft golden cloud of her hair.

His hand traveled along the indentation of her small waist to the flare of her slim hip. A tremble passed through her. He nuzzled the tender skin on her neck and she drew in a sharp breath.

He guided her onto her back and met her mouth with his own. At first, she lay in his arms as straight and as unresponsive as a two-by-four. He coaxed her lips apart and slipped his tongue into her mouth, groaning at the sweetness of her. He plundered her mouth, took what she offered and also what he wanted, his tongue dancing with hers, sliding his body onto hers.

She pulled her mouth away, breathing like she'd run in a marathon. "Wh-what are you doing?"

Christopher leaned back and shoved his T-shirt over her waist. "Fuckin' you. Whatcha wanted all along. My dick in you."

She gasped and tried to wiggle away. "Not that way. You're being crude."

He thrust his face into hers and glared at her. "That's me, babe. Rude and crude. What the fuck you talkin' 'bout any-fuckin-way, Megan? Far as I know ain't no other way to fuck you without my dick involved. Only thing missin' is your mouth, ass, or pussy."

"You're disgusting."

"And you a goddamn fuckin' nuisance. I need to find somethin' to do with you. Fuckin' as good as anythin'."

"No, please," she started.

"You in my fuckin' bed."

"That doesn't mean I want to have sex with you!"

"Ain't said shit 'bout havin' sex with you. I said Ima *fuck* you. Say it. Say Outlaw gonna fuck me."

Her lips tightened. "No."

Her primness amused the shit out of him, and he barked a laugh. Why was she there? Why was he allowing her to stay there? Was his caring for her atonement for killing her bastard father? Maybe. But that wasn't the full reason. She wasn't a viable asset to him, yet he allowed her to stay. He knew why. His attraction to her was unreasonable and dangerous, partly because she was Boss's daughter and partly because he couldn't afford—and didn't want—emotional ties to a woman. He couldn't deny the pull to Megan Foy went beyond sexual, though. That didn't mean he didn't want her to give him her cherry.

Loosening his hold on her, he sighed. Deeply. And turned over, reaching for his bottle to take another swig. He decided to fuck with her. Since his conscience was interfering with the business of his cock, he needed some entertainment. He took another swallow and sidled a glance at her.

"Lemme get this fuckin' straight. If Ida said I wanna have sex with you…" He paused to chuckle because the words 'have sex' coming from his lips sounded fucking funny. He cleared his throat. "If I said I wanna have sex with you, you woulda give me some pussy?"

Her eyes shot daggers at him, but her cheeks turned cherry red. He took another swig then set the bottle aside. He pulled her against him and settled a hand on her breast, pinching her nipple and beading it. She pushed at his hand.

He nuzzled her neck and sucked on the tender skin there. "That's it, huh? Okay, baby. Let's have sex."

"Make love," she corrected in a small voice.

He stopped and raised his head. Unreasonable anger tore into him. This was the twenty-first fucking century. Bitches, even young bitches, couldn't be stupid enough to believe in all that romance bullshit? Even Cindafuckinrella here. She couldn't be *that* innocent not to recognize a man like him didn't "make love".

"You wanna make love?" he sneered.

Not innocent. Fucking moronic because she nodded and added, "with you."

Her fingers slipped through his hair and her touch jolted through him. He hissed in air, another entity he couldn't name entering the battle between his dick and his conscience. She licked her lips and he groaned, bending his head to slant his mouth over hers. He delved into her hot recesses and brushed his fingers through her pussy curls. Her legs parted, allowing him to thumb her clit, tease her slick slit.

He nipped her earlobe. "I ain't makin' love to you or no bitch, Megan," he breathed, inserting a finger into her tight pussy but going only so far. "You want me? Then we fuckin'. Ima eatcha pussy 'til you come. Getcha nice and wet." He tore open her shirt and licked her nipple. "Then Ima bury my dick in you. No condom. No nothin'. Ain't never had no virgin before. Ain't gonna ruin it with no cum catcher." She let out a sob but rolled her hips against his thumb and finger. He kissed her belly and continued to manipulate her. "When I come, Ima fill your pussy up." Jesus. God. The thought had him rock hard and his balls aching. He nosed her pussy, slid his tongue along her seam. "I put my kid in you—" He lapped her, digging his fingers into her hips. God, she was fucking delicious, sweet and musky. Her juices, a fountain of desire, was warm and wet, a temptation greater than Christopher had ever known. Her breath hitched and he tongued her faster. She grinded against his mouth, pulling at his hair, her legs trembling, her body jerking against him as she came hard.

He dragged himself up her body and kissed her again, driving his tongue into her mouth. Wrapping her in his arms, he rolled them until he lay on his back and she rested on top of him, her hair a golden curtain around them.

"You like the taste of your pussy on my mouth?" he asked when he pulled his mouth away from hers. She didn't answer and he drew her lips to his again, giving her another deep kiss. "Do you?" he growled when he ended the kiss.

"Yes," she whispered.

He palmed his cock. "Suck my dick," he ordered, pushing at her shoulders. "Ain't gonna take long. He already cocked and loaded."

Confusion dented her glazed passion. Instead of explaining, he urged her down. When her mouth wrapped around his dick head, Christopher moaned. "Suck," he breathed.

She started a soft sucking motion, and he twisted his hands in her hair. He pumped his hips, his muscles tightening. Cum exploded from him and into her mouth. He held her head in place, his entire body jerking with the force of his orgasm.

Wetness slid down his cock and pooled on his balls and pubic hair. Breathing hard, he lifted his head to see what the fuck was going on.

"*Swallow*, Megan," he growled, pulling his dick out of her mouth and frowning at the cum sliding down her chin.

She licked a bead of cum from her lips and Christopher's cock jumped. Her eyes were wide and bright, her features resembling someone who'd lost a best friend.

He wasn't going to regret this. He *wasn't*. She was just another bitch that he licked and then had her suck him off.

Tears slipped out of her eyes, silvery tracks in the moonlit room. Christopher knuckled them away. Fuck. What the fuck was he doing? Her step fuckhead had molested her and he, Christopher, was damn near raping her. But he wanted her so fucking bad and now, he'd had a taste of her sweetness. Only, her inexperienced mouth wasn't the part of her he wanted.

He shot out of bed and yanked his jeans on. Club problems, hours of drinking, sexual frustration combined with his dilemma over Megan. If he said anything more, it would come out all wrong. He didn't even know what the fuck he should say. Instead, he leveled a glare at her, grabbed his bottle, and sauntered out of the room.

Chapter Twenty-Two

Meggie

MEGGIE HADN'T SEEN CHRISTOPHER IN THREE DAYS. NOT since they'd made out in his bed and she'd waged a war between his words and his actions. Her body—his skill—had won out. Then he'd left without a word.

She told herself she was happy, that she didn't need to see him or *want* to see him for that matter. For the most part, she remained in the bedroom. She'd figured out how to work his stereo system even though the empty iPod dock made her long for the iPad she'd left behind. She tried to focus on the novels Christopher had bought for her, but every time she heard footsteps, she remembered hiding beneath the bed as the place was shot up. On the heels of waiting for gunfire to explode around her, she always expected Christopher to burst into the room. Or try to since she'd locked the door the morning after he was released from the hospital and left in such a snit.

Her small luxury was having a bathroom at her disposal. Being able to take showers and wash her hair. She couldn't stand wearing the same dirty clothes she'd had on since forever, so she rummaged through Christopher's drawers and found T-shirts to wear to bed and during the day, along with drawstring pants that she had to roll up a gazillion times. She used twine she found at the bottom of his closet to tie around the waist. As for bra and panties…she went without.

Yesterday, she'd gone out into the main room for dinner. At first, she'd gotten a few stares, but they left her alone. Feeling isolated, she'd gone to Christopher's office. Maybe, there, she could find peace, feel closer to her father—and Christopher. She decided to do the same thing today. Once she finished eating, though, she'd snoop a little and see what Christopher kept in the desk drawers. He had to have a record somewhere of her father's final resting place. She should've looked yesterday. But she'd worried someone would find her. That was still a possibility this evening, she knew, one she was willing to risk because she'd sat in Christopher's office for over an hour yesterday, just to feel close to him and her father.

Fixing a cheese sandwich and grabbing a soda, she mumbled greetings on her way toward the office. She noticed the light on and couldn't stop her goofy grin. Christopher had returned. He was the only one allowed to go into that office. She swore she'd confess that she'd gone into his office, knowing she wasn't supposed to.

Balancing her plate on top of the can, she pushed open the door. The food and drink slipped out of her hands and her greeting died on her lips, her stomach sinking to her toes. Christopher leaned over Kiera, bent over the desk, both of them naked. They looked up and Meggie stepped back, mute, frozen, her heart twisting in her chest.

Her gaze dropped to Christopher's erect penis. A condom covered him, but he was still huge, long and thick, and not nearly satisfied. He stared at her, his expression hard. Meggie's stomach turned and tears rushed to her eyes.

"Would you get out so he can finish doing me?" Kiera snapped, tweaking her nipples. She twisted around and kissed Christopher, the meeting of their tongues very visible.

Christopher chuckled and pulled away from her. "Wait a minute," he murmured. Unashamed in his nudity, he sauntered toward Meggie, sidestepping her lost supper. Grabbing her by the arms, he backed her out of the room and slammed the door in her face.

Meggie swiped at her tears then ran to Christopher's room. The time had come for her to leave and forget about the conversation she'd had with Digger.

Christopher

Christopher bought time with Kiera by cleaning up the mess Megan had made. What the fuck had she been doing in his office anyfuckingway? Just half an hour ago, he'd been ready to fuck Kiera into oblivion. Now? Not so much.

Kiera sidled up to him, reaching for his dick. He pushed her away, deciding his healing wounds had him fucking delirious. But he felt tangled inside, furious with Kiera for her accusations against Megan while he waged a war to do right by Megan. And doing right meant keeping his dick out of her. He pulled the condom off and discarded it. "Get dressed, babe."

Kiera's eyes widened and her mouth tightened. "Are you shitting me?"

"Nope." He grabbed his jeans and put them on. He'd lost most of his erection, but he still took care with the zipper.

She planted a kiss in the bridge of his shoulder. A tall girl, the top of her head reached his nose. She slipped her hands in his pants, gripping his cock. "Come on," she breathed, biting his nipple.

He pulled her hands out of his pants and shoved her away. "Get fuckin' dressed, Kiera."

"You have something going on with…with—" She jerked her head in the direction of his door, the place where Megan had stood frozen, hurt. Not that he gave a fuck. He just needed to smooth this over with her so she wouldn't be any trouble in the club. In spite of his threats, he'd hate to have to put her out.

"Ima give you two bitches a fuckin' choice," he snarled. "You be Megan's friend and look out for her or I'm barrin' you cunts from ever settin' foot in here again."

Christopher saw the wheels in Kiera's head turning. She stared at him through her lashes, scheming. He wasn't having it.

"If you acceptin' my offer and you backstab me, Ima bury you two."

She blinked at his harsh tone. He ignored it. He had to impress on them not to fuck with Megan. If he showed one bit of weakness in his stance, they'd take that as a fucking green light.

"Meetin's goin' on here tomorrow. Megan gotta leave for a while." He'd called Zoann but she'd help only if Christopher agreed to turn in his patch. He'd offered to drop Megan off and walk out of her life if Zoann allowed Megan to move in with her. Christopher had promised to pay Zoann's mortgage as long as Megan lived with her. He thought Zoann would be a good influence on her. He'd forgotten what a grudge-holding bitch she was. He'd hung up and decided to enlist Kiera and Ellen.

"Bar us? You don't mean that."

"The fuck I ain't meanin' it, Kiera. If you make Megan cry, hurt her pretendin' we more than we is, make her feel anythin' other than at ease and safe, you gonna be some sorry bitches."

"Ellen said you had your nose shoved up that girl's pussy. I guess she was right."

"Whatever the fuck I got with *that girl* ain'tcha fuckin' business."

She sucked in a breath. "You really like her, don't you?"

He shrugged and went to his safe. The safe Snake knew about but left untouched. Christopher counted out some bills and handed them to Kiera. "Get here bright and early tomorrow. Bring her to the mall. She need new clothes. Let her buy whatever the fuck she want. I'm thinkin' 'bout goin' to Long Beach. See my mother." But more importantly... "Get Megan the fuck away from here."

Kiera fisted her hand around the money, then kissed his lips and smiled at him. "Megan's a lucky girl. I just hope she can handle you."

Christopher laughed. "We gonna see, ain't we?"

Without speaking, Kiera began to dress, casting confused glances his way. Not only did she look bewildered, she also looked hurt. He wasn't about to deal with two emotional bitches, so he folded his arms and waited until she left before making his way to his room.

He turned the knob and found it locked. Scowling, he pounded on the door. "Open the fuckin' door, Megan."

She couldn't really think to lock him out of his own fucking room, could she? He lifted his fist to pound again when the door opened. While she stomped away, he stepped in and locked it behind him, staring at the books and magazines stacked on his bed. He recognized them as the ones he'd bought her the other night. Next to that was her backpack.

She swiped the back of her hand across each cheek. "I-I will be gone just as soon as I figure out what to d-do with my books and stuff." She sniffled.

"What was you doin' in my office?"

"I'm sick of being in here," she spat, her look shooting fiery daggers at him. "I sat in your office yesterday to eat. I-I didn't think there would be a problem doing the same thing today."

He stalked to her, pretending he didn't give a fuck seeing her things spread out. "Obviously, you was wrong."

Her lower lip trembled. "Obviously, I was," she whispered.

Her leaving was for the best. Right? "Where you goin'?"

She shrugged, then spun away from him. "I'll find someplace."

It was what he wanted, yeah?

Her little ass outlined his pants as she bent over. Cheeky little bitch, wearing his clothes without his permission. "Sit. Ima shower. Dontcha fuckin' move. If I gotta go lookin' for you, I think I'll beat you," he growled. He was angry he'd hurt her and angry he gave a fuck.

Twenty minutes later, a towel wrapped around his hips, he found Megan on the bed, arms crossed, glowering in his direction. Until she saw his state of undress. She turned red and lowered her lashes, but she didn't look away. Her gaze fastened to one particular part of him, and that part jumped. He dropped his towel and her eyes widened. She licked her lips.

A slow burn percolated in his balls and fanned out into every inch of his body. He'd warned her until he was blue as a fucking Smurf. Whatever starry-eyed shit swirling in her head made her not believe his words. Why, he didn't have a fucking clue. He knew who the fuck he was better than anybody.

He'd try one more fucking time. Pulling the last shreds of decency from his soul, he walked to her and crouched in front of her, his manner casual, when all he wanted to do was throw her down and fuck her for hours. He took her chin between his thumb and forefinger.

"I ain't a fuckin' gentleman, Megan. The closest my ass came is with you. Then you barge in my office in the middle of a down stroke. Runnin' away with those fuckin' blue eyes of yours filled with tears. All kinds of shit I ain't supposed to recognize but I'm doin' it anyway cuz I got fuckin' sisters." Even if he didn't, he'd still recognize Megan's hurt. She'd reached him that deeply. "Ain't ever recognized that shit on no other girl but them. And now you." He stroked her soft cheek, stained pink, warm beneath his caress. She sighed and leaned into his touch. "I ain't gonna say this shit but one fuckin' more time, so listen. You in my bed. If I sleep here, we fuckin'. Ain't no ifs or buts 'bout it. So think long 'bout that before you answer me. If I leave, I'm gonna go fuck Kiera and—" The name Ellen died on his lips. Megan didn't need to be subjected to shit that sordid. At the moment, Ellen just looked like a jealous bitch. "If I walk out, you ain't got shit to say 'bout who I fuck."

"Where have you been for the past three days?"

He frowned at her and dropped his hand. He'd been taking care of things, but he'd also gone to the cemetery and ordered a headstone for Boss. He didn't have a casket to put in the ground, but Megan needed a place to visit her daddy. If Christopher could give her nothing else, he could give her that. Not that she had to know anything until the headstone was placed. She *never* needed to know what it had cost him to get a headstone for an empty grave when everyone knew who he was. Who Joseph Foy had been. "My where'bouts the past three days ain'tcha business."

Her shoulders drooped. Fuck him, why did he have to notice every detail about her?

She cleared her throat. "So if we make lo—"

"Fuck," he corrected, wrestling with his need to keep some distance and his desire to make her happy.

She looked away, her eyes watering again, then nodded. "That's all we'll do? I-I mean I-I can't be your girlfriend?"

"Old lady," he amended. Confusion knit her brow and he sighed. He'd never worked so hard for pussy. But he wanted her pussy. No doubt about it. "Round here you ain't a girlfriend. You a old lady. Don't matter how old you is. It's a term of respect."

"Oh."

"And, no, you ain't gonna be my old lady."

She chewed on her lower lip. "What would I be?"

"Some ass, I guess."

His answers wasn't making her so happy. Tough shit. Her fucking questions wasn't making him happy. She wanted a relationship. Relationships meant obligations and obligations meant commitment.

She sucked in a breath and those damnable eyes of hers, the eyes that saw past his outer shell, clouded. "Th-that means anybody could do that with me?"

That's what it *should* mean. Ass was ass, passed around from one brother to the next, as the mood hit. The thought of another motherfucker touching Megan sent murderous fury through him. But he wouldn't tell that shit to her. "Not if you ain't wantin'. You gonna only be my ass 'til we straighten shit out."

"Would you still sleep with other ladies?"

Ladies, huh? "Probably." *Not.* Bitches were brutal. If he still dicked other chicks, they'd eat Megan alive and spit her out. She was too fucking naïve and they'd attack her like a feral wolf pack. As it was, he'd have to put the word out to more than just Kiera and Ellen. Megan was fucking off-limits to all that catty bullshit.

Christopher stood and her eyes rounded at his fully erect cock. He wondered what about his dick fascinated her so much. But, then, she reached out a trembling hand to touch it and he really didn't give a fuck.

She stroked him, light and unsure. His dick throbbed and her gaze flew to his, her little hand hovering just above his hardness. He grabbed her hand and wrapped it around his cock, reveling in her fluttery touches, needing to get inside of her. He wrapped an arm around her waist and moved her onto her back. All the while his mouth ravished hers and he was moving over her to cover her with his body.

He'd never tasted a mouth as fucking sweet as hers. He delved his tongue in, sipping from her, devouring her. His hand moved down, felt the tie around his pants covering her pretty little ass. He paused, glanced down at her clothes and shook his head. It wasn't as if she'd fucking need clothes for the rest of the night. Tomorrow, he'd get her some shit.

He untied her makeshift belt and inserted his hand into the waistband, finding her bare. He supposed she hadn't been able to find underwear. Easy access. All the better for him.

She froze when his finger caressed her slit.

"What?"

"He liked his hands there," she said quietly.

He being her fucking stepfather. He'd deal with that motherfucker. He rubbed her nose with his, using his forefinger to caress her with the barest touch.

He slid his finger over her again and she moaned.

"If you wantin' me to stop all you gotta do is tell me, baby." He thrust his tongue back into her mouth and feasted upon her lips for a minute before pulling away. His finger had found her cunt folds. He wanted to sing a chorus of hallelujahs at how ready for him he found her. Wet, hot, and tight, her pussy was his own personal Promised Land. He hoped like fuck she didn't halt him. But he'd do whatever she wanted. "Like now. You wantin' me to stop rubbin' your pussy, tell me." He twisted his thumb against her clit as he breathed those words against her ear.

She whimpered.

He laughed and kissed her again, speeding up his moving finger, adding a second when her hands went to his hair and combed through his locks. He bared the lower half of her body and shoved the shirt she wore above her breasts, laying his hand against the flatness of her belly, nearly covering her. In contrast to his big, tanned hand, her body was golden, perfect. He kissed around her belly button, her pubic bone, her soft, blonde pussy hair before going to the inside of her thigh and licking the tender skin there. Spreading her thighs wide, he bent his head, tonguing her pussy in one, long slow lick. She moaned. He lifted her up to him, settling her ass cheeks in his palms. He licked her, concentrating on her clit, wanting her to come to make his passage inside her easier. When he glanced up, he saw she'd lifted up on her elbows to watch him eat her. He guessed she saw his mouth consuming her sweet, pink flesh, his black hair dark against her champagne-colored skin, his jaw with five o'clock shadow rough looking next to her golden curls.

She trembled against his tongue and arched up, her nipples hard points. He licked her through her orgasm before kissing his way back up her body and removing the shirt she wore. His clothes had swallowed her, he thought as he took her mouth again, curling his tongue around hers, filling her mouth with her own sweet muskiness.

He rolled onto her, lost in the blueness of her eyes, determined to ignore the trust in them. He parted her thighs with his hips and settled himself between her legs, not losing the connection of their mouths. He pushed his cock into her, not yet reaching her cherry. He went deeper and found the barrier. He swallowed, realizing he didn't want to hurt her. Unfortunately, to fuck her, he *had* to hurt her this time. If the thought of another man having his cock in her didn't infuriate him, he'd get up now. But *he* had to be the one to do this. Couldn't imagine nobody else.

He spread her legs wider, kissed her deeper, and surged into her, burying himself fully inside of her. He caught her scream in his mouth, cursing to himself when her body stiffened beneath his. He groaned at the tight grip of her pussy around his dick.

He tore his mouth from hers, breathing hard. "You gotta relax, Megan," he whispered, threading his hands with hers. "It ain't gonna stop hurtin' if you stay so tense."

She whimpered.

"Relax, baby." He kissed her temple, her hairline, swiped her tears away. "Relax."

In slow degrees, her body loosened beneath his and her hands fluttered across his back, sending goose bumps along his skin. He began to move inside her, slow, deep strokes into her snug, little body. Stretched around him, wet and hot, she drove him to hard thrusts. He inserted his hand between them, found her clit and fingered her. His own release was near, but he wanted her to come first. She twisted against him, jerking her hips, and crying out.

He came hard, growling her name and shaking as his seed poured into her.

Breathing heavily, he turned over and drew her into his arms. He kissed the top of her head, not sure what to say, feeling the weight of Boss's murder more than ever.

Chapter Twenty-Three

Meggie

MEGGIE RESTED HER HEAD IN THE CROOK OF Christopher's arm. He'd been silent for the last half hour and, although she'd never admit it to him, twinges of shyness made topics of conversation difficult to think about. She knew he wasn't feeling shy at all. He'd done this many times before, so he wasn't awkward or sore or afraid. They were lovers. So now what?

Christopher made it clear he was making love to her because she slept in his bed. She shifted in his arm, turning on her side and facing away from him. She could just as well have been any other woman. Kiera, Ellen, or any of the other ladies who hung around. After what they'd just shared, the thought hurt her. She knew it shouldn't because he hadn't lied to her about anything.

She'd been drifting since she'd run away, the plans she'd made for her life a faraway dream. Instead of preparing for college, she'd been homeless. Instead of waiting for the man she'd spend her life with to take her virginity, she was now *some ass*.

What did that even mean? Christopher could have sex with her whenever he wanted? She didn't know. Neither did she know how long she'd stay around now that Christopher had made love to her. She wouldn't be able to stand watching him with other women. If she saw Kiera, Meggie would always believe she was there for Christopher.

"Now what?" she asked quietly since Christopher seemed content to say nothing.

Christopher's arms enveloped her, and he threw one of his legs over hers. He nuzzled her hair. "Now we fuck again," he said hoarsely, palming her breasts.

Meggie wiggled in his arms and turned to face him. A half grin curved his mouth, his eyes dark and heavy lidded. He knew her question meant more than his simple reply. Then, again, he'd already given his answer before they made love and he didn't intend to change his mind.

Christopher rolled onto her and settled his hand on her hip, his erection thick and hot between them. She sucked the skin on his uninjured shoulder, parted her thighs and sighed as he sank into her. "Okay."

When Meggie awakened the next morning, the sun streamed through the window. She sat up and realized she was alone in bed. She stood and winced, noticing dried blood combined with dried semen on her thighs and the bed sheet. Her stomach growled and she hurried through her shower before finding more of Christopher's clothes to wear and going in search of something to eat.

She didn't like turning the corner of the hallway and walking into the main room because she never knew what she'd find. It was always a surprise. This time when she appeared, Christopher was leaning against the bar, arms folded. One of the brothers watched the monitors. Rack chomped eggs and sausage, a beer in front of him. Other men, many of whom she didn't recognize but all wearing their cuts proclaiming them part of the Death Dwellers' organization, sat at the tables.

Kiera and Ellen occupied stools on each side of Christopher, commanding Meggie's attention. Jealousy swamped her and she glared at Christopher, ignoring how much attention focused on her.

Christopher narrowed his eyes and his mouth tightened. She wouldn't give him the satisfaction of making a scene. Throwing him a dirty look, she straightened her shoulders and started toward the kitchen. She reminded herself he wasn't her boyfriend. Not that she knew anything about boyfriends since she'd never had one. She only knew her feelings and what she wanted.

He moved quickly, blocking her way.

"Move," she ordered.

"Where you goin'?"

"I'm hungry. I'm going to find something to eat."

He grabbed her arm and dragged her in the direction of where he'd been standing.

She struggled against his hold, but he wouldn't let go and she *was* causing a scene, giving supreme satisfaction to the two women. Her emotions were all over the place this morning and she wanted to sob with all the hurt in her at the same time she wanted to howl with rage.

"Megan, give Kiera a chance." Christopher's deep voice rumbled the direction and Meggie swore she heard fondness when he spoke the woman's name. "Ellen, too."

Ellen barely acknowledged her, just lit a cigarette, gave her a small nod and turned her back. Kiera, however, stood next to Christopher and gave Meggie a slight smile. Though unfriendly, it wasn't as hostile as Ellen's.

Not speaking, Kiera glanced between her and Christopher.

"We got church," Christopher said. He and Kiera shared a meaningful look. He pulled out his billfold and pressed a wad of cash into Kiera's hands. "It's gonna be particularly intense, so women ain't allowed on the premises. Kiera and Ellen nicely agreein' to take you shoppin' today. I gave Kiera money last night and just now. She got 'nuff to let you buy whatever you want. Just ask."

Megan blinked, sure she'd misheard. He expected her to have a girl's day with his lover and her friend? And he hadn't even given *her* money? Instead, handing it to Kiera. Meggie had to *ask* for money to *let* Kiera allow her to buy things. She shoved him. "Jerk! I'm not going anywhere with them," she screeched. She pinched his arm—or tried to. He had no give anywhere, so she didn't do much damage. It didn't matter. She ran away as fast as her legs could carry her, reaching the hallway. Not even the Grim Reaper mural unsettled her just then.

Christopher pounded behind her, his boot falls loud against the concrete. His legs were longer than hers, so he caught up to her in a moment. He started dragging her back toward the way they'd come.

"I'm not going anywhere with your girlfriend," she said around a sob. He'd just taken her virginity last night. He could've given her a break and not shove other women in her face so soon. "I'll just stay in your room. Not come out for anything. Not even food."

"As if," Christopher said with a snort. "You ain't ever fuckin' listen. And I ain't givin' a fuck who you wanna be with. You go'n' with Kiera and gettin' the fuck outta here."

"You could've given me your truck and money. I would've preferred—"

"You ain't fuckin' knowin' where you goin'."

"I can follow directions," she shot back.

He thrust his face into hers. "You ain't fuckin' demonstratin' that yet. If you ain't followin' one type of direction, I ain't trustin' you to follow another type."

"I can follow geographical directions," she yelled. "And, maybe, I want to go to church. I need to pray. It doesn't matter how intense it gets."

Christopher burst out laughing and shook his head, wiping his eyes.

"It isn't funny," Meggie said in hurt tones. "Kiera has attended. I saw the way you two looked at one another."

His chuckles died down and he stared at her before taking her face between his big hands and kissing her lips with tenderness. "Church, Megan," he said between kisses, "a club meetin'. That was all our look was 'bout." He stepped back from her but didn't release her face. "Shit gonna be intense. After what the fuck happenin' when the club was hit and I got shot, we gotta elect new officers."

"And she knows what you're facing?"

"Yeah. She been 'round long enough."

"I don't want to go with them," she insisted. "I saw you two together yesterday and—"

"I ain't got time for your bullshit right now." He dug his wallet out and stuffed money into her hands. "Happy now? Your pockets fuckin' flushed with money, too."

No, she still wasn't happy. He'd given Kiera money as well, so what he did for Meggie wasn't because she was special to him. He just wanted her out of his way. She wouldn't budge him on how he felt about women and relationships. She nodded.

"Fine," she said in a small voice. "I'll get out of your way."

"Megan," Christopher called as she turned away.

She stopped and faced him but didn't respond. He walked closer to her. Sighing, he glanced away then looked at her again, fisting her hair.

"I ain't expect to tell you this." His hand twirled a curl. "Seein' as how shit been goin' this mornin'…I fucked Ellen, too. Most of the time—the exception bein' yesterday—*with* Kiera."

Meggie gasped before heat rose in her cheeks. Embarrassed, she shook her head. "A threesome?" she squeaked.

A muscle ticked in Christopher's jaw. He nodded.

"Why tell—"

"Kiera a nice chick."

Really?

"Ellen a bitch," he continued. "She'd open her fuckin' mouth to hurt you. I wanted you to hear it from me."

Speechless, she started to back away, but Christopher grabbed her and kissed her hard. She kept her spine stiff, despite how much she wanted to melt against him.

"Befuckinsides yesterday, I ain't fucked Kiera, Ellen, or no bitch since the night I met you. Hear what the fuck I'm sayin'?" He wrapped a hand around her neck and pulled her closer. "I been dealin' with club business. A motherfucker want me *dead*, Megan. Half my club officers fuckin' dead and we gotta put other motherfuckers in place. This serious shit." He shook her slightly and kissed her again. "Stop lettin' shit bother you. Especially them two. *You* in my fuckin' bed right now."

Right now, until he tired of her, and decided to return to his two girls.

"I gotta have your fuckin' cooperation today. Do that shit for my ass. Please?"

Put like that Meggie couldn't be a shrew and continue to nag him. She nodded.

He kissed her nose. "Good girl."

Kiera and Ellen kept a steady conversation between each other as they drove to the mall. They ignored Meggie, which was fine. Despite her cooperation, Christopher's audacity still chafed. She couldn't believe he was heartless enough to make her spend time with his lovers.

It took forty-five minutes to reach the Portland mall and, for half the day, Meggie roamed from shop to shop, listlessly going through the racks, not really seeing anything she wanted. Meanwhile, Ellen and Kiera were spending nonstop.

Around lunchtime, they went to the food court. Meggie watched while the two women pigged out on burgers, fries, and sodas.

"Hey!"

Meggie jumped as Kiera's voice penetrated her moroseness.

"C'mon. We're going to the van to save our purchases. Maybe, we can speed things up, huh, babe? Try to find some clothes when we get back in."

Outside, the sun had vanished and gray, drizzly skies promised a drop in temperature, which would bring the air from cool to cold. She trailed behind the two women. They hadn't warmed up to her, and Meggie doubted they ever would. She hated they knew more about Christopher than she did. He'd given *Kiera* money, only backtracking and giving Meggie money when she complained. They stopped in front of Ellen's pink utility van. Yes, *pink* and peeling. What a way to stand out. The aggravating woman would want something like that.

As she unlocked her door, Ellen blew smoke from her nostrils. They threw their packages in haphazardly, then shut and secured the van. Kiera sat on the bumper and took out a small mirror to apply lipstick.

"You planning on buying anything?" she asked.

"Yeah." Ellen put in around her cigarette. "You think we like this shit?"

"It seems so," Meggie sniffed, nodding to the cargo hold of the van overflowing with their purchases. "For someone who doesn't like this *shit,* you have no problem spending Christopher's money."

Ellen lifted a thin brow. "Christopher, huh?" She took another drag of her cigarette. "I have no problem sucking his dick while he eats my pussy. I should have no problem spending his fucking money."

Nausea churned in Meggie's stomach, and she looked away.

"Idiot!" Kiera chirped. "You know what Outlaw said, so shut up."

Ellen threw her cigarette on the ground and crushed it beneath her boot. She glared between Meggie and Kiera before grabbing her cigarettes again and lighting another one.

"Megan," Kiera began. Though her tone was clipped and her features tight, her body language was much friendlier than Ellen's. "This isn't easy. Okay? B-but he wants you to buy some clothes and he isn't going to be happy if you don't go back with new things." She shifted her weight. "He would've brought you himself, but he has…church."

Meggie glared at her. "I know what that means. He told me."

Kiera nodded. "So you know he has a lot of shit to worry about. He…he doesn't want you upset." She shrugged. "I don't know if that means he's keeping you. But I'd prefer not to upset you and still be allowed to be friends with Outlaw then him bar me from the club. You seem to be pretty nice, if a little young."

"I'm eighteen."

"Outlaw will be thirty-three in a few weeks," Ellen said around smoke and laughter. "Put jail fucking bait pussy on him and I guess his nose would open wide. Motherfuckers go crazy when you hit 'em with that young, tender flesh. Suddenly, women his own fucking age not good enough for him. Not when he has a sweet, tight pussy to fuck."

"Shut up, Ellen," Kiera warned, "or I'm telling on your crude fucking ass."

"Oh, shut the fuck up, Ki. You know what I'm saying is for fucking real. He never fucked either one of us on our own since he took us for himself. We always had to tag-team him. Suddenly, he's calling us to be her fucking babysitters."

Meggie processed Ellen's words and narrowed her eyes, thinking about yesterday. Unless Ellen had been hiding somewhere—which she knew she hadn't because Christopher had already told her—Kiera had been with Christopher on her own.

Oh.

Oh.

Her gaze flew to Kiera's and the other woman straightened. Kiera knew Meggie had guessed she'd crossed some line with Christopher that Ellen knew nothing about. But that was between them, and Meggie wouldn't pit one against the other just because Christopher had hurt her. She shrugged, a small, minute gesture she hoped conveyed the message to Kiera. At Kiera's flash of relief, Meggie lowered her eyes.

"So that's all I'm fucking saying."

Meggie frowned. Ellen had continued talking while she and Kiera had gone through their silent exchange.

"Oh fuck," Ellen snarled.

Meggie thought it was something else she wanted to argue about, but Ellen was glancing behind Meggie.

"Oh fuck," Kiera breathed, her eyes traveling in the direction of Ellen's attention.

Meggie decided she should turn around. When she did, her eyes widened. *Snake.* She hadn't seen his face, but she'd know those green and black reptilian boots anywhere. He halted next to Ellen, while five other guys, rigged out in Death Dweller cuts and leather, blocked their exit. Snake was a tall, intimidating figure and, when Meggie's perusal reached his face, she did a double take, her breath catching. She swore she was staring at her father. A tremble passed through her. Her mind had to be playing tricks on her. It just had to be.

Except...

He resembled Big Joe right down to one nostril being noticeably bigger than the other one. A ponytail queued his hair and his blue eyes held no warmth. Really, no anything. They were the eyes of a killer, cold and dead, as if his soul and conscience had been sucked away—if he'd ever had either.

Snake walked over—Boss's swagger—and Kiera and Ellen flanked her.

She knew why and she'd keep her mouth shut. She wanted to ask the identity of his father, even though his physical features screamed the answer. She should've lowered her lashes, looked away, and minimized attention. She couldn't, though. Her heart and her head hurt. She'd always believed she was her father's only child. And, she told herself, she still believed it. The only proof she had to any family connection with Snake were her eyes—and her instinct. He might've looked like Boss and walked like Boss, but he didn't have Boss's deceptively calm demeanor. One look at Snake and Meggie knew he had ice in his veins. She decided to keep quiet about her suspicions. She didn't know how these things worked, but it might cause deeper animosity between him and Christopher if he discovered she was Christopher's lover.

Something resembling a smile curved his mouth. "Who's the new bitch?"

Kiera and Ellen glanced at each other.

"I'm Meggie," Meggie responded, raising her chin, and folding her arms. She urged herself to proceed with caution, but her unhealthy curiosity wouldn't allow it. "Who are you?"

Ignoring her question, Snake stepped closer and bent to eye level with her. "You're the bitch, yeah?"

"I have no idea what you're talking about."

He grabbed her arms and shook her. "The bitch who survived. The bitch who fucking saved Outlaw."

Ellen jerked her out of his grasp and shoved Meggie behind the wall she and Kiera now created. "Fuck off, asswipe," she snapped. "If Outlaw knew you were handling his old lady like that, he'd carve your fucking heart out."

"Old lady?" Snake sneered, glaring at Meggie through the space between the two women's heads. "So this young bitch has joined you two fucking whores?"

"No. Of course not," Kiera said calmly, holding Ellen's hand down. "She's not used to how we do shit, so he's taking a break from us. She's his."

"And you know what the fuck that means, don't you, reptilian?" Ellen said with a smirk. She pulled out her cell phone and waved it in his face. "Outlaw is a phone call away."

Snake withdrew a blade from inside his jacket and held it to Ellen's throat. "Not gonna stop you from being any less dead by the time he reaches here."

"Fuck you. Kill me. As a matter of fact, why don't you fuck all three of us up?"

Meggie made a noise of protest in her throat. She didn't appreciate Ellen so casually offering up their lives.

"Just so you know, you'll be a dead ass walking," Ellen spat. "Outlaw wouldn't rest until he fucked you with a spiked pipe. So you can kill us and brag about it to Outlaw. Because you're such a dumb fuck, that's what you'd do. Or you can let us go about our day and have another day of your life to look forward to. Your choice, fuckhead."

"Sooner or later, Outlaw is gonna get his. I won't rest until he pays for what he did to my father," he swore.

Those words again. Snake swearing revenge for his father. A chill swept through her. She couldn't shake the sense of disaster, a hollow, bleak premonition of more blood and death.

"When I do," Snake continued, "you bitches going down with him."

"What would you have did?" Kiera asked.

"Shut the fuck up, Ki," Snake snarled, his icy fury on the verge of erupting. "You're in Outlaw's bed now. Not mine anymore. So you lost any power you thought your pussy had over me when you let him in your shit."

The image of Christopher and Kiera in his office rose in Meggie's head and she gritted her teeth against the jealous anger rising inside her. Needing air, she backed away from the other two women and spun on her heel, glimpsing a tall man with the look of a teddy bear and the heart of a demon, on the opposite side of their lane, staring at her. Thomas. She froze, her heart hammering.

Snake stepped in front of her and gripped her chin between his thumb and forefinger. He turned her head from side-to-side, ignoring Ellen's demands to leave Meggie alone.

He grinned. "I can see Outlaw wanting to fuck you," he breathed. "You're one gorgeous bitch. If you didn't have the look of Big Joe about you, I'd find a place for us to fuck."

Glaring, Meggie opened her mouth to speak.

"At least you're not that fucking perverted," Ellen snorted.

"Shut up," Kiera warned. "Snake, c'mon, baby. Leave her alone. She's innocent. A real good girl."

"Not so innocent if she's fucking Outlaw," he returned, still holding Meggie in his clutches. "Here's a message to the whore, the cunt, and the innocent. When I bring Outlaw down, you three bitches are going with him." He shoved Meggie away and she stumbled back.

One small comfort—Thomas was no longer anywhere in sight. Although she doubted it, Meggie could only hope he'd been a figment of her stressed out imagination.

Snake backed away. But he stared at Meggie, through her, bitter hatred in his eyes, before he and his boys turned and stalked off.

Ellen drew in a deep breath and sagged against the bumper, just then losing the color in her face. Meggie thought Snake had stabbed her after all, but when she heard Kiera soothing her, she realized it was fear setting in.

Meggie remembered glimpsing a bottle of water in a cup holder inside the van. Grabbing Ellen's keys from the bumper, she hurried and got the nearly empty bottle. There were no napkins available, so she tipped the water over her fingers, then went back to Ellen and rubbed her brow and cheeks, hoping the coolness calmed her.

Both Kiera and Ellen stilled and stared at her as if her caring gesture surprised them. Meggie sniffed, imagining it *would* surprise them. In their world, they'd just as soon stab her in the back and watch her bleed to death.

"This might help you to feel better," Meggie said impatiently.

Ellen stared at her a moment longer, then a hint of a smile crossed her features. "Are you okay, babe?"

Meggie's hands trembled. No, her entire body shook. She'd never met a viler man. She nodded, just wanting to get back to the club and lock herself in Christopher's room. But now, that might not be safe either. Snake might come after them. "I-I'm fine. You?"

Ellen nodded, then lit up another cigarette. "Yeah. Why don't we speed our day up? Don't give us no more shit. Pick out a fucking wardrobe, so we can get the fuck outta here."

"Shouldn't you call Christopher?" Meggie asked. "Warn him? I-I mean Snake might go and try to do him something."

"Take her, Ki. Let me alert Outlaw to what limp dick is up to."

"Come on, Meggie."

Meggie had even less inclination to shop now than she had before, but she wouldn't be difficult. Or stupid. She needed clothes. She spent less than half an hour in the first shop, where she picked out panties and bras, a robe, and several nightgowns. When she went to the second store, Kiera helped choose items from the racks. Still, they spent nearly an hour in that store and Meggie began to regret her lackluster shopping earlier. She hoped she liked her purchases as much later as she did now, viewing them under duress with two madmen circling about. The last shop they went to before they piled into Ellen's old, clunky utility van was a shoe store where Meggie bought two pairs of flats, a pair of pumps, and a pair of high, strappy sandals. On the way back to the club, they stopped at a drugstore, so Meggie could purchase her own soap, shampoo, new makeup, and feminine products. Although Christopher had brought her to a drugstore, he hadn't asked if she needed anything, and she hadn't bothered to mention it. At the time, his injury concerned her more. He'd just walked out of the hospital so buying items had been the last thing on her mind. Now, though, not only did she purchase her personal items, she also loaded up on Milky Way candy bars. They were her absolute favorite and she hadn't had one in weeks. She added chocolate milk to the basket.

"Hey, the price of this shit's fucking ridiculous here," Ellen pointed out, indicating the milk and candy with a nod. "We can stop at a grocery store and get that shit and any other food you'd like."

"We could? I-I thought…Christopher doesn't have a fridge in his room."

"And? Put your shit in the little kitchen. No one will fuck with it."

"In that case, we can go to the store." Meggie's stomach growled and she bit down on her lip. She really wanted a visit to the Pike Street Market. But it was in Seattle, and she was here, so she'd have to settle for whatever grocery store she could find.

"Shit," Ellen groaned with a scowl. "Fucking Outlaw is going to flip. You shoulda ate."

Meggie decided to buy the milk and dropped it in her basket. She wasn't sure where Kiera was, but Ellen trailed her as she roamed to the section with condoms. She stared at them, wondering if she should buy any. She couldn't help but remember the condom hanging from Christopher's penis when he'd been with Kiera. And, yet, he hadn't used any with her.

"He's out?" Ellen said with a knowing laugh.

"I-I think so," Meggie said quietly. She squirmed, feeling young and immature. But in her house, sex wasn't discussed. "We…he…we…"

"God, babe, spit it out. Your cheeks are as red as Rudolph's balls."

Meggie giggled and huffed out a breath. "He didn't use a condom last night," she said in a rush.

Instead of being shocked, Ellen just shrugged. "That's interesting. But, yeah, I can see why that might freak you out. Get some. Just make sure they're magnum."

"What the fuck you bitches doin' in a goddamn drugstore with that fuckin' motherfucker on the loose?"

Meggie jumped ten feet in the air at the sound of Christopher's growl. He was already shoving more money into Ellen's hands. "Pay for this shit. Kiera already on Traveler bike." He glared at Meggie. "You. Come with me. We waitin' for you outside, Ellen. And don't take fuckin' long." He looked down at Meggie, his green eyes bright with fury. "You okay?"

Meggie swallowed at the tenderness in his tone. "Fine, Christopher," she whispered, then braced herself for him to yell and holler about how she couldn't use his Christian name.

He grabbed her hand and guided her outside, where about a dozen bikers waited. It confused Meggie to see Kiera making out with another guy, whom she assumed was Traveler. Christopher glanced at them, and Meggie waited for a confrontation. Instead, he handed her a helmet.

"Does that hurt your feelings?"

He frowned in confusion. "What?"

"Kiera. Her and...and Traveler...? You know, Traveler was the name of General Lee's horse?"

Christopher grinned. "Up on Civil War history, yeah?"

She nodded. "I love *Gone With the Wind*. That's dorky, huh?"

"Nope."

She fell silent. He was avoiding her question and—

"'Bout Kiera—" He paused to light a cigarette and take a puff— "she fuck half the brothers in the club. Ellen fuck even more than that. They just like the other bitches that way."

"So I could fuck anyone in the club, too?" she teased.

All humor evaporated from Christopher. "You wanna fuck another motherfucker?"

"I was just joking."

"Don't fuckin' joke 'bout that," he growled. "My ass fuckin' clear?"

Meggie wrapped her arms around her waist and nodded.

"Yo, Outlaw," Val called. "Where the fuck is that slow bitch?"

"Right here, you fucking prick," Ellen said, hustling out of the door, loaded down with bags.

"Jesus, what the fuck you bought?" Christopher asked.

"Things," Meggie said. Her stomach chose that moment to growl.

"What? You ain't ate efuckinnuff today or something?"

"I wasn't hungry," she returned sulkily.

"What the fuck that mean?"

"It means she didn't fucking eat today," Ellen called.

Christopher glared at her, then turned and mounted his bike in one smooth motion. "Climb on," he ordered.

Meggie hurried to him and gingerly climbed behind him. The pipes of a dozen Harleys roared to life and she wrapped her arms around Christopher's waist, pressing her cheek against his middle patch, wanting to forget everything but him.

Chapter Twenty-Four
Christopher

CHRISTOPHER GROANED, HIS BODY SHUDDERING AS HE emptied his cum inside Megan. He refused to allow her to close those big, blue eyes of hers. He wanted her to see him while she came and watch him while he came. He wanted her to witness him at his most vulnerable—inside of her, surrounded by her gripping heat and spilling into her.

He collapsed on top of her, breathing heavily. He knew he couldn't keep his weight on her too long for fear of crushing or smothering her. She squirmed under him, and he felt himself growing hard again. She moaned, opening her legs wider. He sank deeper and raised himself up on his elbows, beginning a slow, steady rhythm.

She'd been quiet after they returned to the clubhouse, her thoughts far away. He thought maybe it had something to do with her run in with Snake. Even though she'd told him she hadn't eaten at the mall today, she merely picked over her food. Instead of socializing, Christopher announced he and Megan would retire early.

Behind closed doors, she'd uttered one, meaningful statement. "Snake is the spitting image of my father."

Christopher hadn't commented one way or the other. However, Megan was sharp, and it wasn't a stretch to believe her quietness *had* been due to her run in with Snake, but not for the reasons first suspected. Like fear. No doubt fear played a big part of it, but Christopher remembered Megan telling him Snake's claim of avenging his father. If she believed she and Snake was related, then she must've been thinking…speculating…concluding—about Boss's death and who was responsible.

Christopher had gone and taken a shower, his mind searching for plausible excuses if she confronted him. No matter the excuse, he doubted she'd ever forgive him if she knew he'd killed Boss. He'd washed away his alarm—quite a foreign feeling. As was his fear earlier when Ellen called and told him about the confrontation. Oh, he'd been livid, but the hard edges of his fury had been dulled by gut-wrenching fear. The moment the voting ended, he'd ordered his boys to prepare for a run. Instead of having to drive all the way out to the mall, he'd found her at the drugstore, studying *condoms*. Of all fucking things.

After his shower, he'd told her to take one.

Her smile had been sad. "I'd really love a hot bath, Christopher."

He'd shrugged, wanting to lash out at her for insisting on calling him *Christopher*. Ever since he'd heard his name in her sweet voice, he veered between thinking of himself as Outlaw and remembering he was also Christopher. Megan Foy was going to be the death of him. She drove him up a fucking wall. She wanted a bath instead of a shower? Fine. As long as he got her the fuck away from him for a little while. "Then take one."

"No, thank you. I don't like the mildew around the tub." She'd turned on her heel and locked herself in the bathroom.

If he had a soul, he would've sat her down and confessed to Boss's murder. Instead, soulless motherfucker he was, he'd unlocked the door and crashed to a halt. She'd been standing in the shower, her body pink from the hot water, her nipples a deeper shade. Her long hair plastered to her face, shoulders, and back. And lathered soap covered her blonde pussy hairs. She held her hands in front of her breasts and Christopher told himself to let her be. She looked so fucking young, his heart and his head hurt, and he'd felt as vile and evil as he ever had.

They'd stared at one another, then her gaze dropped to his dick, hard with want, almost touching his fucking navel. From that moment on, his cock had been in control, telling his legs to move as fast as fuck. His dick needed Megan's pussy, and it refused to let Christopher's conscience interfere.

He'd taken her in the shower before helping her to clean up. With a towel wrapped around her hair and one around her body, they'd gone back into the bedroom. Christopher had bent her over his desk and fucked her again. Her body was so fucking sensitive, responding to him the moment he touched her. She'd trembled when he'd leaned over her, his fingers gripping her hips, his dick pounding into her. He'd suckled the tender skin on her neck, and she'd cried out his name while she came.

Once he blew his load, he'd pulled out of her, using the damp towel from her hair to wipe the juices away from her pussy and her thighs. He'd sat her in the middle of the bed and then combed out her hair until it hung in waves around her. That had been an hour ago and he was fucking her yet again.

He slipped his tongue passed her lips, using it to fuck her mouth just as his dick fucked her pussy. Her eyelids closed and he wanted to demand she open them, but he decided not to press it. Instead, he slammed into her, and she whimpered.

They finished together and Christopher rolled off her, burying his head in the pillow while his breathing came under control.

"Snake is my brother."

Christopher tensed at the soft words. She wasn't questioning that fact, merely making a statement she wanted confirmed.

What the fuck had Snake been doing at that fucking mall anyfuckingway? The shopping-loving motherfucker haunted outlet stores. Assfuck liked shopping almost more than bitches.

Just because Snake somefuckinghow had his ass at the same place Megan was and made her so fucking suspicious infused Christopher with an extra dose of hatred. While he could appease her curiosity about her relationship to Snake, if she probed deeper she'd make the connection Snake was gunning for *Christopher* because *he'd* killed Big Joe. When she did, he was fucked.

Fuck.

And? He hadn't intended to keep her anyway. This wasn't no place for her to live. She mightn't have been a virgin no more, but she was still innocent. She didn't have blood on her hands and a head filled with murder, gunrunning, and drug shipments.

Fuck. "Yeah, he your brother. Three years younger than me."

She went silent, so Christopher turned his head toward her. She was staring at him, and he couldn't decipher her feelings. If she'd guessed her connection to Snake, then she had to have guessed what he'd did to Boss.

"My parents never told me I have a brother."

Momentary reprieve. He could answer honestly. "Your ma ain't know. Snake ain't knowin' 'bout you neither."

"How's that possible?" she asked tightly, sitting up to glare at him. "You knew about me."

Yeah, because Boss had talked to Christopher about his little girl, swearing him to secrecy, before he'd lost his fucking mind. "Yeah? I did?"

"Yes!" she hissed. "You didn't question me once when I came here looking for my daddy. You tried to search for my ID but didn't find it and just accepted I was who I said I was."

As he said, sharp as a tack.

"If I saw the resemblance between me and Snake, why won't he?"

"Motherfucker too self-absorbed."

Another long stretch of silence while she studied him. She hadn't factored in the missing link—*him.*

She trusted him. She believed in him so much that she couldn't make the connection that he'd killed Big Joe. The realization humbled him, made him yearn to have her at his side for the rest of eternity.

He could allow her to loop back to information about her father's death like a dickhead or he could steer the conversation in another direction. With Megan, it would be tricky. She'd recognize his tactics and find a way to get back on the subject.

Nope, not happening.

"I was thinkin' 'bout me and you visitin' my ma. I got a house in Long Beach, and she live in it." He'd been meaning to talk to her about this anyway. With Snake slithering about, getting her away was important to keep her safe. "We can stay with her through the New Year. Catch a fuckin' break from all this shit."

Megan frowned. "What about the club? I thought you needed to straighten things out."

"Yeah, I do," he admitted. "But I know the fuckin' holidays iimportant to you."

She smiled. "Okay," she breathed, sounding pleased and happy. "When do we leave?"

"The Saturday after Thanksgiving," he told her, unable to stop his satisfaction at her excitement. He couldn't wait until she actually saw his place.

Her red nipples begged him to lean over and lick them.

"The day after Black Friday?"

Christopher scowled. He was fantasizing about fucking her and she was dreaming about shopping. "I ain't gettin' up at no one o'clock in the fuckin' mornin' for some bullshit, Megan," he snapped, annoyed at how different they were thinking.

Lying next to him again, she nuzzled his neck and suckled his earlobe, pressing her breasts against his arm. His dick jumped, fire shooting through his entire body. She affected him like no other girl ever had. She licked the pulse point at the base of his neck.

"You don't have to go," she breathed. Skating her fingers across his stomach, she scooted up to rain kisses along his jaw. "I told you I know how to drive. I drove you to the hospital, didn't I?"

"Baby, in a minute, you gonna be drivin' your sweet lil' ass down my cock," Christopher murmured, dragging her closer and taking her mouth in a hard kiss.

She giggled when he pulled his lips away, her cheeks flushed and her eyes dark and needy. "So will you let me borrow your pickup?"

He paused midway pulling her onto him. "Ain't no fuckin' way you goin' by yourself." Holding one hand on her waist and using the other hand to guide his cock to her entrance, he sucked her nipple. She moaned and wiggled, assisting his invasion of her body. Her tight heat stretched around him, but she bounced up and he bit her shoulder. "Take me, Megan," he growled. He rubbed her clit, rewarded with the sexiest sound he'd ever heard, the one unique to her. He could spend the rest of his days listening to that soft whimper-sigh and watching her body, pink from their fucking.

She shimmied down his dick until he filled her completely and Christopher closed his eyes. She was wet and tight, the flames inside of her burning him and wrapping him in the wonder of all that was Megan. Her mouth touched his and he swore his heart melted.

Her fingers tangled in his hair, her lips soft and plump against his. "Look at me, Christopher," she whispered.

When he opened his eyes, he found her staring, searching for an entry to his soul. Gripping her hips, he drove up, taking control. "I love makin' love to you." Kissing her, he pulled her down and pushed up into her. "Tastin' you." Hearing her gasp, he curled his lip and repeated the hard motion. "Hearin' your voice." Her regard held him captive, spurring his deep drives, and not letting go even when she cried his name and came around him.

"Jesus. Fuck. God," he managed in a deep, rough voice he barely recognized as his own. He held her body still, a slave to her passion, and shattered inside her, her pussy walls throbbing while his cum simmered into her.

She fell against his sweaty chest, breathing as hard as he was. Closing his eyes, he rested his head against the headboard, still joined with her, where he wished he could remain forever. Locked in his bedroom, connected to her in the basest way, it was just them. No Snake or Boss. No reminders what was between them wasn't real. *Couldn't* be real. It was too pure, too sweet. Much like Megan.

He breathed in the scent of sex, her hair smelling of cherry blossoms, according to her shampoo and conditioner bottles.

He kissed the top of her head, remembering the conversation their lust had interrupted. He massaged her scalp. "I'll take you shoppin', Megan. But we leavin' at five and stayin' three hours tops."

She leaned back, her smile not quite hiding her wince. "If you insist," she murmured in her just-fucked voice.

Something in her tone alerted Christopher that he'd walked into her trap. "You lil' bitch, you played my ass." He couldn't help but admire how deftly she'd gotten her way. He pulled her off his dick and plopped her next to him. She must've had this shit planned before he ever mentioned going to visit his mother. Two could play her game. "You got money or credit cards, yeah?" he asked with a straight face, knowing fucking well she didn't.

Her face fell. "No," she said in a small voice.

"There gotta be a God! My ass off the hook."

"Yeah. Sure. Whatever, Christopher."

"You ain't believin' you gettin' me up so early *and* havin' me to foot the fuckin' bill, too."

Drawing her legs up to her chest, she rested her head on her knees, turning away from him. Christopher turned her face back to his and frowned at how her eyes were brimming. What the fuck?

"Megan—"

She swiped at an escaping tear. "It's okay. Really. I just thought you'd buy me things like you do them."

He didn't have to ask who *them* was. Anger flashed through him that she was stuck on shit he'd put behind him and all but forgotten about. "I ain't puttin' up with your jealous bullshit. Why the fuck I gotta take you shoppin' again, anyway, when you bought out the fuckin' mall with as much money as the three of you combined had for you to buy whatever the fuck you wanted?"

"Liar," she returned. "You didn't give them money just for me since they bought more than I did." She turned her furious gaze to him and scooted out of his reach, closer to the wall.

He wasn't sure what it was about that fucking wall, but whenever she was angry or afraid, she inched closer to it, like it could open the fuck up, yank her the fuck in, and shield her from whatever bullshit she faced.

"Anyway," she went on, talking *to* the wall since her back remained to him. She had perfect curves, a smooth back indenting to a tiny waist and flaring back out to a beautiful ass and nice hips. She was slim but curvy as a motherfucker.

She'd been yapping away while he was contemplating fucking her doggy-style.

He sighed. "Look, Megan. I ain't explainin' myself to nofuckinbody. You bought shit, so what the fuck it matter if *they* bought shit, too? It's my fuckin' money at the end of the day. So just drop it."

"I hate you," she said miserably. "Ellen said she deserves to spend your money because you eat her, and she sucks you."

Fuck. Him. He was going to fucking *kill* that bitch, in slow, painful degrees.

Megan jerked around and gave him the evil eye. "We do the same thing."

They sure the fuck did and Megan's pussy was the sweetest fucking pussy on earth. He reached for her, but she knocked his hand away. "Leave me alone. Don't touch me."

He sat up and dragged her closer, rolling on top of her and pinning her hands above her head when she tried to claw his eyes.

"You in my bed, so that mean we fuck. It mean I touch you whenever the fuck I wanna. *I'm* in control. *You* listen to *me*."

Her lips parted and her eyes darkened in that way she had whenever she wanted to fuck. The anger, desire, and tears glistening in those blue depths made his dick grow in response, pissing her off more. She squirmed beneath him, hissing like a little cat.

"Calm the fuck down, Megan. Now. I mean it."

She blinked at his dark tone but stilled.

"I know you upset and I gotta say I ain't meant for this shit to happen."

"You knew what would happen," she retorted. "You warned me about Ellen, didn't you? You told me about the th-threesome b-before she told me. It doesn't matter. You just hurt me because I'm in bed with you and naked and I have to realize you do for me what you do for them and nothing more. It doesn't matter, though," she repeated. "At the end, we reached a truce, the three of us."

Unfuckinglikely. He lessened his grip on her.

"Besides," she went on with a dull sniffle, "Ellen and Kiera stayed right by my side while Snake was there. If that was really Thomas I saw, he probably would've seen me—"

"Thomas? Your step fuckhead?" he snarled, unable to believe the pendulum of emotions between them. In thirty fucking minutes, there'd been a come so explosive he'd thought the top of his head would burst open when he blew his load; there'd been peace between them, happiness, jealousy, hurt, and anger. Now, there was nothing but bloodlust. "What the fuck fuckin' wrong with you? You *just* cluein' me 'bout that motherfucker...Fuck me." He sat up and gripped strands of his hair in pure frustration, then he shot out of bed and pulled on his jeans.

"Where are you going?"

Fuck him, the sound of her voice could bring him back from the dead. He drew in a deep breath. He had to take away the hurt so clear in her eyes. Oh fuck, yeah, he was going to teach that bitch, Ellen, a lesson. Bar her from the fucking club for three fucking months. He'd warned her not to fuck with Megan. Not to make her cry. Not only had she made her cry, but what he wanted to be a lighthearted moment between them was ruined because that bitch opened her fucking mouth and put ideas in Megan's head. "First, I was shittin' you 'bout money. Whatever the fuck you want, you got. You wanna go fuckin' shoppin' the day after Thanksgivin', we ride that mornin' to go shoppin'."

She was sitting up, listening closely, clutching the sheet to her chest and blocking her tits from his view.

"Second, Ima give Ellen a pass this fuckin' time." *Not.* He couldn't wait to get his hands on that fucking bitch. "Third, Kiera and Ellen…" Jesus, but he never had to explain his actions to nobody, especially a girl. "Look, yeah, I fucked both of them. For the past few months. I just chose them bitches at random. You know? Like the Quick Picks for the lottery. They been hangin' round the club for years. I bought Kiera and Ellen some boots. Fucked up when I bought you the same kind. But that was a mistake. I wasn't even thinkin'. I ain't never once sent them bitches shoppin'. If Ellen spent *my* fuckin' money before earlier today, then Ima go outside, and a rocket'll shoot from my ass to send me fuckin' flyin'." Over the years, he'd given Kiera and Ellen a few bills here and there as Dweller property. And, yeah, he had given *Kiera* his own money once or twice, but he'd never sent her shopping. His shoulders drooped. He was suddenly so fucking tired. Anything good in his life always went to shit. His…feelings…for Megan had to go because they didn't make any fucking sense. He'd put a stop to that, but first, he'd make something clear. "Finally, I ain't 'bout to tell you what I'm intendin' for your ma's husband. It ain't gonna be pretty."

"Don't say that. His death would be on your conscience."

Sad resignation filled him, and he gave her a half-smile. "My conscience left me a long fuckin' time ago, baby. Sorta like my soul. If I ever had either." Calmer, he walked back to the bed and sat next to her to brush a handful of hair behind the delicate shell of her ear.

"For you, though, riddin' the world of Thomas Nicholls would be worth another mark on my soul."

She hugged him. "Get him but bring him to jail. Promise. For me."

To lie or not to lie. Fuck it. "Sure, Megan. Ima spare his life." He refused to swear to a blatant fucking lie.

Her smile almost blinded him. She breathed in a sigh of relief, trusting that he'd answered honestly, even without a promise. "Thank you."

Usually, it was so fucking easy to say whatever the fuck girls wanted to hear, and not think twice about his truthfulness. Of course, the chicks normally in his bed never demanded shit from him. Nor did they ever pass their fucking opinions or require promises on how he handled motherfuckers. If he got the badges on his payroll involved, he'd have no choice *but* to keep his promise.

"You know," Megan started, her voice cracking, "I often wished for the courage to kill him. He hurt her all the time."

"Your ma?" he asked, not sure he wanted to hear whatever she might be thinking.

"Yes."

By the wounded expression on her face, he already knew pain and terror would fill her tale. All the fuck that would do was make him want to kill Thomas Nicholls with a fucking machete. Jab steel straws in his fucking body while Christopher watched as he slowly bled out.

Megan needed a motherfucker to listen, though.

"I don't want him dead, not by murder. Why ruin our souls because his is so black?"

Christopher held his tongue. His fucking soul was just as fucking black. It was only Megan that believed otherwise.

"Bringing him to jail is the right thing," she swore, with the innocence of a girl that still managed to see good in the world. "You'll see. It'll be a relief to you and I that he's off the streets, you had a hand in seeing justice done, and you didn't have to use violence at all."

"Megan—"

"I know you think you aren't good, but you are. I see your integrity and honor."

"Cuz you wanna fuckin' see it," he grunted.

"No, because it's there," she countered.

"So you tellin' my ass if the motherfucker comin' at me with a fuckin' gun, fuckin' duck, and disfuckinarm him?"

She frowned. "That's different. That would be self-defense."

Striking first, going on the offensive, was the best fucking defense in the world. Yet, for whatever fucking reason, he wouldn't fucking renege on the fucking agreement he'd given her. He just hoped that fucking decision wouldn't cause problems later. In his experience, once a motherfucker always a motherfucker, and the only remedy for a motherfucker to stop being a motherfucker was to fuck him up and drop tiny fucking pieces of him all over.

She crawled onto his lap and kissed his nose, his eyes, his cheeks. "Make love to me."

Make love to me. Words to put fear in his heart and stop his entire world. Love didn't, *DID NOT,* fucking exist in his life. He'd never had it, never given it. Actually, feared it. Despite how tangled Megan had him, he didn't want to give her false hope. Didn't want to leave himself vulnerable to any emotion.

Fuck. He couldn't even fuck another bitch because of Megan. No, this shit wouldn't fly. Though sweet, she was a prissy cupcake princess and he walked on the dark side of the moon.

"We ain't makin' love," he barked. "We fuck. Case fuckin' closed."

"That isn't true," she challenged, because when did she ever just shut the fuck up and accept what he fucking said.

"The fuck it ain't. My cock involved, so I fuckin' know what the motherfucker doin'."

"*You* said you love making love to me, not twenty minutes ago."

"My dick was in you?"

"Wh-what difference does that make?"

"Yeah or no?" he demanded, not interested in *her* questions.

She nodded.

"There you fuckin' answer. A motherfucker say anything when he balls deep in pussy."

She gasped and her shoulders sagged. "I see," she said on a swallow. "That means you say the same thing to...to...*every* woman you're with."

"The fuck I do. Ain't ever told one bitch befuckinfore you that I'm makin' love to her."

"You don't even remember saying it to me. How do you know you haven't said it to other ladies?"

Persistent lil' motherfucker. He forced himself to take a moment and really focus on what he'd said to her when he'd been fucking her. And, yeah, he'd been so fucking swept up in the blueness of her eyes and the tenderness between them, he'd told her he loved making love to her. It was hard to fucking explain to her how open he'd felt in that moment because he barely understood it himself.

Instead of trying to clarify, he decided to let her believe what she would.

He hardened himself against everything Megan. "When we get to my ma's house, Ima stay a day or two with you. Make sure safety precautions are in place."

Her face crumpled and her eyes widened. Not that he gave a fuck. "So you're taking me to your mother's so I can be safe?"

He shrugged. "A little of both. Safety and the holidays."

"Will you return for Christmas?" she asked, barely audible.

He. Did. *Not.* Give. A. Fuck. He really, really didn't. Too much bullshit stood in their way—their age difference, their backgrounds, the annoying fact he'd killed her father. He stared straight ahead, unable to stay firm under her scrutiny. "Ain't decided yet."

"Will you send Kiera and Ellen away, too?"

Jesus. The returning despair in her voice made him want to reassure her, but he'd use her words against her. She'd set herself up for the response he thought best. "No," he said, liking her jealousy but hating her sadness. "We need some kinda entertainment while we here."

She drew in a sharp breath, hurt tightening her features. "I hate you," she whispered in a wobbly voice.

His gut twisted. Somehow, he forced himself to continue. "You clued in 'bout the deal, princess. Just cuz we fuck don't mean I ain't fuckin' other women."

Tears rushed to her eyes, spilling onto her cheeks. Christopher clenched his jaw, a muscle ticking, feeling lower than dirt. She laid on the pillow and turned her back to him. Her shoulders shook, so he guessed she was crying.

"You let me pop your cherry and that shit a big deal with girls." And him, too. He'd never fucked a virgin before. Or no one like Megan. She was a dream come true and quickly growing to be his biggest weakness, as the past hour had proved. He scowled. "It mean you attached to me or something. In your head, any-fuckin-way. Not in mine, though. A fuck a fuck."

She scooted closer to that fucking wall Christopher was considering sending a wrecking ball through, but he didn't want to think anymore. He didn't want *her* to think. Or cry. Or dislike him.

He took off his jeans.

Knowing he added insult to injury by drawing closer, he pulled her body flush against his. His erection pressed into her back and she wriggled and jerked, trying to get away but he wouldn't have any of it.

"You know you want me to fill up your hot lil' pussy." Nuzzling her hair and not giving her a chance to answer, he caressed her pussy with two fingers. She was slick with her cream and his cum, growing wetter with his steady rhythm. He grunted in satisfaction when she groaned, the scent of her desire drugging him with need.

She rolled onto her back and parted her legs for him. He kissed her deep, his tongue pressing against hers. His fingers circled, dipped, tested and spread her juices around her clit.

"You play with your pussy, Megan?" He inserted a finger into her, still knuckling her clit. She lifted her hips and ground against his hand. "Answer me." He bit the lobe of her ear then sucked at the reddened skin. He increased the pressure on her pussy, coaxing more wetness from her. "You rub your pussy? Make yourself come?"

"Yes," she admitted, arching her back, her breathing shallow and quick.

He inserted another finger, stretching her, opening her for his cock. He bent his fingers inside her, found the spot he wanted, and massaged her gently, her wail of release satisfying him. Keeping one finger against her clit, he rolled onto her and thrust into her in a deep stroke. She screamed, her entire body shaking, her pussy convulsing around his cock.

Involuntarily, her muscles clenched his dick. She didn't yet know how to purposely use her body to give him pleasure. Sex was too new to her. Her movements sought rather than gave. She'd learn. Christopher would teach her. This was only her fifth time having a dick in her pussy. Still, she was sensitive to his touch, striving for release.

He pulled out of her and rose to his knees, his nostrils flaring. He lifted her hips and thrust into her, exploring her flat belly, his mouth watering at the beaded tips of her breasts. He held her hips in place to halt her wild movements, showing her without words the pace he wanted, the control he demanded. He drove into her, held her gaze, their eyes locked upon each other with invisible bonds.

A sheen of sweat coated her flushed skin. He released her, stretched out over her, and covered her mouth, wanting to absorb those little noises escaping her throat. She kissed him back, kept him locked in the cradle of her thighs.

She squeezed her muscles and he groaned in a pleasure he'd never known before. Megan looked startled, a fact Christopher noted because she seemed to test her body's control, clenching and releasing, studying his reactions. He curled his lip, slamming into her. Even if he wanted to hide how much she affected him, what her body did to his couldn't be tucked away. She followed his movements, angling up when he bore down. Hard and deep, he pounded into her.

"Come for me, Megan," he demanded. His balls were tingling. He wasn't going to last much longer. "C'mon, baby."

She whimpered and shifted, drawing his cum out.

"Fuck, your pussy good," he snarled, holding her rigid, her belly heaving against his, her nails digging into his back. He poured into her, and his entire body shook.

His ears ringing, he collapsed on top of her, breathing hard, surprised the top of his head was still attached to his skull. As he regained awareness, he felt the stroke of Megan's fingers through his damp hair. The caress of her hand along the bridge of his spine. The softness of her lips against his jawline.

Just as his pulse began to slow, it sped up all over again. His heart seemed to burst open and fill up with Megan.

She squeaked beneath him, and Christopher lifted himself on his elbows. Her awe and adoration were hard to miss and he swallowed, not fucking wanting this. Emotional entanglements hurt. They weakened. He still carried the scars of his grandfather's meanness; the agony of Boss's betrayal; the helplessness at his mother's sadness. He gave a fuck about those things, and he hurt because of them.

"Christopher?" Megan whispered, her voice hoarse and cracking after he'd fucked scream after scream out of her.

Fuck. Those eyes that seemed to see him so clearly probed into his soul now. On edge, he didn't want talking. He slid down her body, lowering his mouth to her pussy.

Megan snapped her legs together, trapping his head between her thighs, the viselike grip nearly decapitating him. Or, at the fucking least, smothering him.

"What are you doing?"

"I'm 'bout to eat your pussy," he muttered, pulling her legs apart and sniffing the musky aroma of her arousal combined with his cum.

"You can't possibly want to do that now."

She sounded horrified and embarrassed. He tipped his head back to look at her face. Her look matched her tone, and he chuckled. Keeping his gaze on her, he ran his nose along her slit.

"*What* are you doing?" she squealed in outrage.

"What the fuck you think? Smellin' your pussy."

She wriggled her body up, but he wrapped his arms around her thighs and pulled her down.

She covered her face with her hands. "Oh, God. Kill me now."

He laughed at her theatrics.

She raised up on her elbows. "I need a shower," she said with a prissy little sniff.

He licked the top of her mound and she shivered. "Don't wanna smell soap, Megan. I wanna smell your just fucked cunt filled with my cum."

"My God! Why?" she wailed, giving up her losing battle and plopping down on the mattress.

"Trust me, sweetheart," he said gruffly, taking pity on her. "I promise you, you ain't gonna give a fuck what condition your pussy in once I start lickin' you."

"Doubtful," she mumbled. She stayed focused on the ceiling. "Just get it over with."

Unable to stop his smile, Christopher pushed her legs open further and watched his cum drip out of her. He gathered the moisture up and worked it back inside her with his finger.

"Please, stop staring at that part of me."

"What part of you?"

"*There!*"

He laughed harder. "Where the fuck *there*, Megan?"

"My vagina," she snapped.

He laid his head against her hip and guffawed. "I guess my dick a penis to you, huh?" He didn't remember the last time he'd laughed so hard. "Ima give you lessons on the proper terms for our anatomy another day. Quick refresher. You got tits and a pussy or a cunt. I got a cock or a dick. Underfuckinstand? I ain't fuckin' *vaginas*. That shit borin'. *Hot vagina*. No. That shit sounds ridiculous. Hot pussy. *Hot pussy* much better."

She giggled and nodded, her tension easing.

"Now, Ima lick your hot pussy 'til you come for me."

She squirmed but whispered, "okay."

He spread her lips and swirled his tongue around her clit, sliding across her sensitive flesh. He licked the inside of her pussy lips, lapped at her juices. For all her fucking complaining, she pushed his head into her pussy and rested her feet on his shoulders, spreading herself for him like a porn star at a pussy contest. She rocked against his mouth, gripped his hair, and screamed his name before falling apart against his tongue. Her orgasm pushed more of his cum out of her pussy but Christopher had the remedy for that.

Before she came back to herself, he rose above her and buried himself inside her. He thrust his tongue into her mouth, the kiss wet and open-mouthed, a complete possession on his part and a total surrender on hers.

Christopher rode her hard and fast, swallowing her whimpers. She came around him, their mouths still fused together, her body open and vulnerable to his driving hips.

"I'm comin', Megan," he growled. "Take it, baby. Take all of it."

"Yes, Christopher," she whispered, her breath fanning his skin, the sound of her voice pushing him to another powerful release.

He collapsed next to her, panting. Not speaking, Megan curled against him. Once he got his breathing under control, he drew her into his arms and realized she'd already fallen asleep.

Christopher kissed the top of her head and smiled, truly contented for the first time in his life.

Chapter Twenty-Five

Meggie

CLOSE TO TEN THE NEXT MORNING, MEGGIE awakened to find Christopher's spot empty. He'd awakened her before the sun rose to make love to her again. Spooned against him, he'd widened her legs and then pushed into her. Though she'd been half-asleep, he'd coaxed an orgasm out of her right before she'd felt the warmth of his seed spurting deep inside her.

"Go the fuck back to fuckin' sleep, Megan," he whispered, kissing a spot behind her ear and withdrawing from her.

She'd groaned and swore she heard his bark of laughter as she drifted off.

Now, the sun shone through the window, sparkling on the sheets tangled about her body. Sex and musk and leather hung in the air, and her nipples responded to the smells. She wished Christopher was there with her to take her again, but he wasn't, and she didn't know his whereabouts. Maybe, he'd gone to Kiera and Ellen. Or one of the other girls she'd seen hanging around. She didn't know their names and they looked at her as if they'd gladly kill her, although Christopher never let her far out of his sight whenever they mingled with the others.

The thought of him with another woman sent panic through her and a wave of jealousy so intense she thought sure she wouldn't survive. This was Christopher's life, though, and he'd made it clear he wouldn't change. He'd made it clear they had nothing more than sex between them. He might've been taking her to his mother's house but then, he was coming back to Kiera and Ellen.

Meggie splayed her fingers on her belly. What was she thinking? Suppose she really did end up pregnant? Then what? She didn't have a job, hadn't even graduated from high school yet. She blinked at the ceiling, at loose ends. In Seattle, she had school and she had Farah and Lacey. She had homework. She knew her place, knew the fine line she walked between life and death when she was at home.

But here? What was she supposed to do? She wanted to help Christopher because she knew, without being told, he had a lot of responsibilities and a lot of people who presented themselves as friends, but Meggie suspected were really enemies. And this wasn't a frenemies type of thing. No, this was life-or-death, end-up-with-a-real-knife-in-the-back type of situation.

Rolling out of bed, she headed for the shower. After she dressed, she'd go to the main room and find someone to hopefully give her something to do with herself, if Christopher wasn't available.

An hour later, Meggie followed the low hum of voices. She'd checked Christopher's office, knocked on the door with the 'Board Room' placard on it, found the main room empty, and the parking lot cleared of almost all the motorcycles. Stepping back inside, she listened and then heard the voices and the clang of pots. The sounds took her through the small kitchen, where she kept her chocolate milk and supply of Milky Ways, through another door to a huge kitchen where she saw two Probates whose names she didn't know, another mountain of a man with a silver beard, a bald head, a hoop earring, and a patch over his left eye. His road name had to be Pirate, she decided. He looked like one. The only thing he needed was a peg leg and he'd be set.

Food was laid out on the counters and Pirate paused in chopping onions to direct one of the other guys to peel a mound of potatoes by thrusting his chin and pointing the huge knife he held. The kitchen had big appliances, almost like the ones behind the counter in the school cafeteria. There were double ovens and double sinks on each side of the room.

Just as Pirate looked up and saw Meggie, a revolving door swung open and a line of barely dressed girls walked in. Some of them carried bags filled with more food. Others carried the ingredients for cakes while a couple carried paper plates, plastic utensils, and stacks of Solo cups.

"Megan, right?" he asked her.

She nodded, disconcerted by the presence of the other women in broad daylight. Usually, she only had to contend with Ellen and Kiera during the day, not a dozen or so women who looked like centerfold girls and were more than happy to display their bodies even in the kitchen.

She forced her attention back to the man she'd named Pirate. "And you are?"

"K-P."

"Kitchen Pirate?" she blurted. Heat tore through her when the other women tittered, rolled their eyes, and curled their lips.

K-P hooted with laughter and elbowed the man next to him. "What do you think, Stretch? Think the bitch believes I look like a pirate?"

Stretch blushed as fiercely as Meggie, then raised a startling blue gaze to her. He was young but oh-so-handsome. She nodded and he smiled at her.

"Fuck with her, not only won't you get your patch, you'll lose your dick, boy," K-P growled, all humor gone. "Outlaw will rip it from your body." He turned his brown eye to her. "As for me, name's Kitchen Patrol."

"Yeah, as in Kitchen Bitch," Val commented, sauntering through the same door the other girls had come through.

"Fuck off, you little roach," K-P commented.

Flipping K-P the finger, Val walked to Stretch and slapped him upside his head. "Consider that a warning. I'm not telling Outlaw you were drooling over Megan's tits."

"How would you know what he was doing?" Meggie snapped. "You weren't even in here."

He pointed to the ceiling. "Eyes in the sky, babe."

"Cameras?"

Val nodded. "All over the place. In almost every room."

Just kill her now. She swallowed, deciding to act cool. "Which rooms aren't they in?" she squeaked.

Val and K-P exchanged glances, before the younger man laughed. "Gotcha, babe! No camera in Outlaw's bedroom."

She sniffed and shrugged. "I wasn't worried about that, Val," she lied.

As he snacked on some of the sliced, raw onions, K-P paused to direct the girls on what he needed them to do.

"What do you need, Megan?" Val asked when silence fell, only broken by the chopping of vegetables and seasoning or running water to wash utensils, food, and chopping boards. The girls were silent, eyeing her with curiosity, dislike, or hostility, depending on who was doing the staring. "Megan, ignore the Bobs."

She was almost afraid to ask if all these women's names were Bob, but K-P appeased her curiosity without her asking anything.

"If you suck cock, you bob your head up and down." He demonstrated using his finger and Meggie frowned, grossed out. "Anyway, babe, that's why they're called the Bobs. These bitches are expert dick suckers. If you don't have a Masters in Deep Throating, you need not apply."

She gasped in outrage. "So Christopher named them Bobs because they...he—"

Everyone but her laughed.

"You're precious, babe, I swear," K-P barked, chomping on more onions. "Outlaw isn't poetic enough to call these whores Bobs. That's my name for them. He just calls them Club Ass. The Bobs are exceptional, though, paraded out only on special occasions."

"I need something to do," she announced through tight lips. She wanted to ask where Christopher was but didn't want to look like she knew about as much—or less—than everyone else.

Val lit up a cigarette and took a few drags. "An emergency came up, so Outlaw had to ride, Megan." Holding his cigarette between two fingers, he twirled it to indicate the room. "This," he began, ashes floating in the air.

"Hey, asshole," K-P yelled. "Get the fuck out of my kitchen with that shit or I'm going to shovel whatever the fuck has ashes in it down your fucking throat."

Val glared at him and took another drag. "We're gonna have brothers from support chapters spending Thanksgiving with us. Some of them arrived earlier and we need food to feed everyone."

"Thanksgiving is weeks away," Meggie said, confused.

"Don't matter," Val responded. "Motherfuckers still need to eat."

"So you need girls to entertain everyone," Meggie said dryly, unable to help the comment.

Val smiled. "That, too. You were still sleeping, and Outlaw told us not to wake you up." He shrugged. "But shit needed to get going, so I rounded up some bitches to get started."

"Well, what can I do to help?"

"There's gonna be a party later. This'll be your first real taste of a club party, so just chill today. Okay? Call Kiera and Ellen. Go buy a pretty outfit. After today, this shit's yours to plan." He pointed to K-P, purposely allowing more ashes to fall from the tip of the cigarette. "This asshole is your kitchen bitch from here on out for parties and shit. What you tell him to do, he'll do." He thrust a thumb over his shoulder. "These bitches and any other bitch come through here has to follow what you tell them to do. They give you shit, you throw them the fuck out or have one of us do it." He shrugged. "If you like them, don't tell Outlaw if they fuck with you. Handle it yourself. Put them in their places. You tell him, whether you like them or not, he's either going to bar them from the club forever or take away their privileges for a few weeks. Either way, he'll forbid you to have contact with them. If you don't like them, tell him if they fuck with you."

"Umm—"

"What he's saying, babe," K-P called, popping more onions into his mouth and not looking up from his task, "is Christopher is president. That makes you the first bitch."

It was pointless to insist they not call her a bitch. They were going to do it anyway. She huffed out a breath. "You mean first lady?"

Val and K-P exchanged glances.

"Yeah, that, too," K-P agreed.

"Of the Death Dwellers?" she asked for clarification.

"Yeah, you got a problem with that?" K-P asked. His shoulders had tensed and it sounded as if he brought the blade down a little more forceful than necessary.

"Nope. Christopher loves this club," she said softly, thinking of another man who felt the same. "So did my daddy. It's an honor. I just hope I do them proud." She lowered her lashes, uncomfortable with the admiration in the gazes of Val, K-P, Stretch, and the other Probate whose name she still didn't know. She finally moved from the spot she'd stood in since she walked through the doors. "I don't have any money to go shopping. Besides, I went yesterday, and we're going Black Friday. I don't think Christopher would like it if I went shopping again today."

"Megan—"

"What I'd really like to do is cook Christopher a meal."

Val grinned. "Have at it in the smaller kitchen for now. I'm sure Outlaw would like that. But you can't do it today. He's not getting back until later. By then all this food will be ready." He threw the cigarette down and stepped on it to put it out. "Advice from a Valentine." He winked and grinned at her and, for the first time, she noticed his dimples. "There's gonna be a lot of bitches here. You're going to see shit you never seen before. Outlaw put the word out but vicious bitches out there. I'm gonna call Ellen and Kiera so they can take you back to the mall. Get an outfit…It's like this—better to have him jealous of you than you be jealous of him."

"That's totally up to Christopher," she snapped. "If he doesn't think enough about me not to make me jealous—"

"See them bitches in here? How little they have on? We're going to double that here tonight, all half-dressed, serving your man and all the other boys. Outlaw's a man, babe. He might not touch, but he's sure the fuck going to look at all that tits and ass."

"He'll look at them regardless if I'm showing *my* tits and ass, too."

"Just because he has eyes in his fucking head. He'll be looking but he won't be seeing if you're in here with some sexy little outfit, too."

She cocked her head to the side. "I'm getting a pervy vibe from you, Val," she pointed out, folding her arms.

"Aww shit, Megan. You're fucking gorgeous. Do I want to see you in some little dress with fuck-me-heels on? Fuck yeah. But I'm not the one whose attention you want. I'm telling you, babe, set the precedent now. So you don't have to worry about later."

Meggie allowed Val call Kiera, so she and Ellen could pick her up, but asked for at least two hours before they arrived. He agreed, slammed a wad of bills into her hands, and disappeared. She wanted to clean Christopher's bedroom and take care of the laundry piling up.

The laundry room was located off the west end of the building, right off the third hallway. Just like the kitchen, the laundry room was extreme with three commercial grade washers and dryers, minus the slots for coins. Along the back wall were four ironing stations. It surprised her they didn't have a commercial steam press. Whatever. At least she'd be able to get most of the wash done, including the bed sheets, comforter, towels, and a lot of their clothes.

In between runs to the laundry room, she scrubbed the washbasin, bathtub, and toilet, dusted the furniture in the bedroom, cleaned the mirrors then swept and mopped. Although she wouldn't have time to save their clothes, she made up the bed and placed the teddy bear Christopher had given to her for her birthday in the center on the mound of fluffed up pillows.

By that time, Val was calling for her because Kiera and Ellen were outside. It surprised her to see a late model silver Impala instead of Ellen's raggedy pink van. The passenger side door opened, and Kiera got out, wearing sweats and running shoes, her hair in a ponytail, looking like a regular girl. Reluctant, Meggie trudged to the car and slid into the back seat, returning Kiera's smile and scowling at Ellen's glare.

"Val said you need an outfit for tonight," Kiera began, strapping her seat belt on.

"Yeah," Meggie grumbled. She still preferred not to be around the two with Christopher's intentions to spend time with them over the holidays, but she'd either been at the club or in a hospital since she'd met Christopher, the exception being yesterday. It pissed her off, though, that he still wanted her to be around them. She settled against the leather seats, enjoying the new car smell, frowning at the growl of motorcycles. She glanced in both directions, startled to find bikes on either side of the car and another tailing when she looked out the rear glass.

"We have company." She remembered yesterday when Snake—her brother—and his goons surrounded them. "Are they trying to run us off the road?"

"No, babe," Kiera answered. "That's three of the Dwellers. Outlaw don't want you going nowhere without an escort."

"I'm not royalty or anything."

"No shit," Ellen spat.

She ignored that. "Why in the world would he order something like this?"

"Because of yesterday, I guess," Kiera answered. She met Meggie's gaze through the rearview mirror and shrugged. "That's why Val made us take this car. Everyone knows Ellen's van."

"I guess they would with its Pepto Bismal pink paint job decorated with patches of rust," Meggie said sweetly. She didn't appreciate the woman's jealousy when Christopher had made it so clear to her where he stood with them. Meggie sure hadn't demanded Christopher offer her this sort of protection and to her way of thinking having a three-bike escort brought more attention to her.

They fell into a tense silence until they turned into the parking lot of a strip mall with a ladies' boutique. Departing the vehicle, it surprised her to find Val there, although she realized he must've been left behind to babysit her. She wondered how he felt about that. The other two were Probates and she couldn't remember their names, either.

They escorted them to the door of the boutique, then backed out to stand aside. Meggie paused, her brow furrowing, not too sure about this place where everything from adult toys to hooker heels were on sale. Then, she thought about those other girls, the ones K-P called the Bobs, and hardened her resolve.

"Val gave me enough money for all of us to buy things," she began.

Ellen rounded on her. "You fucking kidding me, bitch?" she snarled. "You got my ass banned from the Club until the spring social and *now* you want to spend money on me? Or is it because it's *Val's* money and not Outlaw's?"

Meggie shoved her back, not appreciating Ellen getting in her face. "I didn't get you barred from anywhere, you evil witch."

A tall, dark-haired woman, with huge boobs walked over to them, cringing at Ellen's stare.

"Get the fuck out my face, Sapphire. This is between me and this backstabbing bitch."

"I'm not a bitch," Meggie shouted, anger rising in her.

Kiera elbowed Ellen. "Shut the fuck up. If Val hears you, he's gonna tell Outlaw, and you'll be banned for good."

"Fuck off, Kiera. Just because you wanna shove your tongue up this bitch's pussy doesn't mean I do."

Kiera rolled her eyes. "I never even thought of eating her pussy. *I* just want to be able to go to the Club, so I'm following Outlaw's orders."

"Bitch—"

"Would you stop calling everyone a bitch?" Meggie wouldn't bother to respond to any of their other crudeness. "Just because you have a degree in bitchiness, doesn't mean we do, Ellen. Now, leave me and Kiera alone or I *will* tell Christopher about how you're acting."

"Meggie, c'mon, babe, let's look around," Kiera pleaded. "Shopping'll cool you off."

"No. She jumped on me for no reason, and I want an answer. I've tried my best to cooperate with Christopher, so I don't deserve to have her attacking me for no reason."

"You want a fucking answer, *bitch?*" Ellen sneered, her eyes as rounded as a fish's. "You couldn't wait to open your fucking mouth to tell Outlaw what I said about spending his fucking money."

Christopher really, really, *LIKE REALLY,* should've shut up and not confronted Ellen. He'd promised he wouldn't, which would've been a huge favor to Meggie because she was having enough problems with Ellen and Kiera. He'd just made it worse. Unfortunately, if she cowered to Ellen now, the woman would use it to her advantage. She was a major bitch. "What I say to Christopher is none of your business," she snapped. "It wasn't my intention to get you banned. The issue we were discussing had nothing to do with you."

"Then how the fuck my name came up to make him forget whatever was being talked about that's not my goddamn business?"

"It was related."

Ellen snorted. "Doubtful."

"Whatever. I'll talk to Christopher," Meggie promised. "Ask him to let you come back."

Without answering, Ellen stomped past her and headed for a rack of skirts, Sapphire hot on her heels.

Meggie sighed and glanced at Kiera. "Why'd she come if she's so angry? Why'd Val call you two?"

"I suppose she came to light into you, and she figured this was her only chance for a while." Kiera rubbed her temples. "She loves the Club and the boys, and she's hurt Outlaw came down so hard on her. To be fair, he warned her not to upset you."

Meggie widened her eyes. "He did?"

Kiera nodded. "Yeah, babe. He did."

"Val said if Christopher bans anyone, I can't be around them because he'll forbid it."

"Meggie," Kiera said urgently, touching her arm, "if you like us, hang with us today. If Outlaw sees us getting along, he'll ease up on Ellen."

Meggie's nostrils flared. It would give her such satisfaction to make Ellen suffer because she'd been a thorn in her side from the first time they'd met. She'd disparaged her daddy and taunted Christopher's attention to Meggie. "I'll think about," she said, and glided away, just wanting this day over with.

Chapter Twenty-Six
ELLEN

"**I** FUCKING HATE THAT PISSY LITTLE BITCH."

At Ellen Cooper's announcement, her maybe best friend, until recently prime competition for Outlaw's attention, and sometimes lover, shook her head in disapproval.

Kiera slanted her dark eyes in the direction of the bathroom door. On the other side of that door, Megan Foy took a shower.

"You insist on antagonizing her," Ki said with a sigh. She shook her head in disapproval before turning on her heel, walking to her bed and sitting on the edge. "She's just going to run to Outlaw and then where will that leave us?"

Out in the fucking cold. It was bad enough the little cunt had opened her big fucking mouth already and gotten them banned. Well, technically only Ellen had gotten barred; Kiera stayed away in a show of solidarity.

"She's in the fucking shower, Kiera. All alone. We could stab her in the fucking back and dump her somewhere. Slit her fucking throat. I don't care."

Ellen didn't appreciate the horror on Kiera's face. The beautiful woman crossed her long legs, always so fucking poised. At one time, Ellen enjoyed spending time with Ki. She wasn't her maybe best friend, but her actual one. Then, Outlaw had taken Ellen to his bed. Once. Twice. Three times, and she'd felt so triumphant. He was the ultimate prize, simply because he held himself away from any entanglements.

He never claimed a bitch. Never pretended to care. That wasn't to say he wouldn't protect Ellen, Kiera, or any other woman, especially those belonging to the club. But even Mort and Val had had loose arrangements. Fuck, Johnnie left the club partially because of a woman.

Not Outlaw. Never Outlaw.

Until she'd gone to his bed. Back then, Ki had been a kid, so he hadn't wanted her. Then, a few months ago, he'd told Ellen she'd only fuck him. Almost immediately, he'd burst her joy and triumph by announcing he wanted both her and Kiera or neither one. He'd broken Ellen's fucking heart because she loved him so much. In her heart, they belonged together. She deserved to wear the 'Property of Outlaw' cut. She did anything the club asked of her. Her life was the Dwellers. She fucked. She sucked. She cooked. She cleaned.

She'd even brought Kiera to the club. How did that bitch repay her? By catching Outlaw's eye.

Out of the fucking blue, a few months ago, he'd chosen them as his. Never truly laying claim, though.

"Ellie, you aren't even listening to me," Kiera said with exasperation.

Bitterness swelled inside Ellen. Outlaw had regarded Kiera in a way he'd never looked at Ellen. Still, she'd been confident that she could win him for herself and make him love her.

The shower stopped and it took all her willpower not to get to her feet, rush into the bathroom, and kill Megan Foy.

"You touch that girl and Outlaw will bury us both," Kiera warned.

Perhaps, Ellen's expression had given her away.

"Besides, this is my fucking apartment. I don't allow murders to happen in it."

Despite herself, Ellen chuckled. "So what are we doing with her?" she asked, slanting a glance toward the closed door.

The apartment was small with only one bedroom, a living room, kitchen, and bathroom, but Ki kept it pin neat and smelling of potpourri. She made the world around her beautiful with fresh flowers and pretty décor.

"I don't know what Outlaw expects us to do with her," Kiera admitted, scrunching her brow. "When he texted me to keep her away from the club, he didn't say how to entertain her."

"We can fuck her."

Giggling, Kiera rolled her eyes. "As if that would go over any better than killing her. She's with him until he gets tired of her. We just have to wait him out."

Easy for her to say. Ellen could hear her biological clock ticking. Kiera still had a few years before the fear she'd never have a child set in.

The door to the bathroom opened and Megan Foy stuck her head out. Her skin was pink, and her hair plastered to her head. "Do you have a hair dryer?" she asked.

Kiera frowned. "Just braid your hair."

"I want to wear my hair loose at the party."

"What fucking party?" Ellen sneered.

Meggie opened the door and stepped into the bedroom, a towel wrapped around her body. "The party I bought the outfit for."

"Oh, that party," Ellen said with sarcasm. "The one Outlaw don't want you at."

Hurt flickered in those blue eyes too similar to Big Joe's. Then, she lifted her chin. "He can't stop me if I want to go."

"Joke's on you," Ellen clapped back. "He can stop you from doing any fucking thing he wants to. He gives the orders not you."

"Val said I could go. K-P was there, too, and he didn't say anything either. As a matter of fact, Val *told* me to attend."

"Well, Val's a fucking moron that don't have a goddamn thing to say," Ellen retorted. "Outlaw's word is final."

Meggie narrowed her eyes. "If Christopher doesn't want me there, then he'll have to toss me out, but I'm going with or without your help."

"We don't get to go. You don't get to go." Ellen gave her an ugly glare, but the annoying little cunt refused to fucking back down.

Mutiny lit the younger woman's eyes. Pissy little bitch.

"Give him one night to get pussy from other bitches." Ellen shrugged, changing tactics. "Maybe, you should go. He'll fuck with or without you there. At least, you can find another brother to get dick from."

Finally, Ellen's words chinked Meggie's armor, and her lower lip trembled. "I'm not going to the party," she said in a shaky voice, "but I *am* leaving here." With that, she backed into the bathroom and slammed the door shut.

"Are you out of your fucking mind?" Kiera cried, jumping to her feet. "If she walks out the fucking door, we're going to have to tell Outlaw she's gone. You want that?"

"It isn't like he'll beat us or anything. He'll cuss us out."

"And keep his cock from us. And bar us from ever setting foot on club grounds. And take away his protection. We won't belong to the Dwellers. Do you want that?" Kiera asked again.

Fuck. No. She didn't, and he'd be angry enough to do everything Kiera mentioned. Ellen huffed out a frustrated breath, just as the door opened and Meggie stormed out.

If she didn't love Outlaw herself, she'd leave him to the spoiled little bitch. She had the worst fucking temper of any bitch she'd ever met.

Holding her shoes, her hair tangled about her head, Meggie marched out of the room.

"Let's dress her up." Kiera threw those words over her shoulder as she hurried after Meggie.

Ellen wasn't quite sure what Ki meant, so she plopped in the chair and waited for the other woman to return, unsure if she wanted Meggie with Kiera or not. If things didn't go as planned, she would call Mortician's father, the Reverend Sharper Banks, and let the fucking chips fall wherever the fuck they landed.

Chapter Twenty-Seven

Kiera

"**M**EGGIE! STOP!"

The little blonde walked fast. Kiera had paused a split second to impart some words to Ellen, allowing Meggie the time to leave the apartment, make it to the landing, and rush down the concrete steps.

"Meggie!" Kiera cried because the girl ignored her first call, storming from the breezeway and into the parking lot. "Wait, please. I'll take you to the party. Just stop for a moment."

Finally, she listened and halted, allowing Kiera to catch up to her. When she did, she grabbed Meggie's hand and dragged her back to the passageway. She didn't try to mount the steps. She didn't want to lose her grip on Big Joe's girl.

"Where are you going?" she demanded.

"Anywhere that's not here," Meggie retorted, angry and hurt.

Kiera might've attempted to befriend Meggie if not for the threat she posed to her relationship with Outlaw. When Mort told her how Outlaw had changed the rules where Meggie was concerned, it had worried Kiera, but Outlaw hadn't taken Meggie to his bed yet. Kiera had thought once he tried her pussy, he'd be satisfied. But no. He *still* wasn't allowing any of the other brothers to have her, not even his close crew—Mort, Val, Digger, and Johnnie.

"You didn't even take the clothes and boots you bought today."

"You can have them," Meggie spat, her blue eyes flashing. "I bought them for the party. It seems as if I don't need them."

"I can't fit them, and you know it." Kiera was five feet ten inches in her bare feet. Next to Meggie, she felt like a giant. "Come upstairs and I'll do your hair and makeup. We have time. The party won't start for another couple hours. I'll order a pizza and drinks—"

"I don't drink," Meggie interrupted.

"Okay, I'll order apple juice for you."

Meggie narrowed her eyes. "You're very funny," she said coldly, so like Big Joe and Snake at that moment that Kiera blinked.

"Fine," she sniffed. "I'm sorry. I shouldn't have said that." Even if it was fucking true. "Would a Coke work?"

"I haven't agreed to your suggestion. Why should I? I don't trust you won't take so long, I won't go to the party anyway."

"I won't hold you up. I swear." A moment's shame went through Kiera at the ulterior motives she had in agreeing to help Meggie, but all was fair in love and war. Outlaw was so enamored of Megan Foy? Then he'd have to spend the night watching over her once Kiera finished with her. "You're a gorgeous chick. We don't have much to do, except sex you up."

"That's what Val said to do too," Meggie admitted, then bit her lip. "You're gorgeous too. I wish I could trust you. I wish we could be friends like Christopher seems to want, but every time I see you, I remember you and him together in his office—"

Every time Kiera saw Meggie, she remembered Outlaw pushing her away and leaving her in his office to rush after the blonde. Still, she owed Meggie for not opening her mouth to Ellen. "About that. I never got a chance to thank you for not telling Ellen what you saw. It would've caused such a shitstorm."

"I'm not here to make trouble," Meggie said quietly.

To Kiera's way of thinking, she'd started trouble the moment she came to the club. She got Outlaw's attention. At first, she'd thought it was because she belonged to Big Joe. Out of loyalty to the man, Outlaw wanted to look after his girl. But then…*then*…she began to see how he looked at Meggie. When the girl had been in the hospital, he hadn't fucked Kiera, Ellen, or any other chick.

All the Dweller boys, even *Johnnie,* were just smitten with Meggie. In truth, Kierra could see Johnnie and Meggie together. On the surface, he seemed so much more wholesome than Outlaw. Having Meggie went with the image he presented to the world. She was all innocence and beauty; he was good looks and charm.

To be fair, the brothers loved women, especially beautiful ones. That was one reason she and Ellen had always been so popular. That's why K-P's Bobs were such a hit. The guys also loved to share girls, so Meggie capturing such attention wasn't unusual. It was *Outlaw's* reaction to her that was.

Kiera cleared her throat. She hadn't meant for her thoughts to wander. "You came for Big Joe. But he's not here and you know he never will be again. He's dead, Meggie."

She went silent, her eyes watering and her nose reddening. Instead of shedding tears, she heaved in a breath. "So why am I still here, right?"

Even if that was her insinuation, she wouldn't admit it to Meggie. Maybe, if she played on her insecurities, the ones that every younger woman had when confronted with experienced women, she'd realize she'd never have what it took to handle Outlaw. "Did I ask you why you're still here?" she said innocently.

"You didn't have to," Meggie said evenly. "I heard that question in your tone. In your words. Sometimes, what you *don't* say is more obvious than what you do."

"You're here because Outlaw's fucking you," Kiera bit out, forgetting the rule he'd handed down about saying anything to upset Meggie. "You're addicted to his cock and having your pussy licked."

High color swept into Meggie's cheeks, but she didn't respond.

Jealousy burned into Kiera. She wanted to cry and kill. If she could get away with it, she would've spat in Meggie's voice. Except she wasn't a wilting flower. If provoked, Big Joe's daughter retaliated.

"I shouldn't have said what I did." Kiera swallowed, so torn. She wanted to break Meggie, send her away so shaken and scared she'd never return. Yet, she also risked alienating Outlaw while he was so smitten with Meggie. She had to play this game smarter. Play Meggie gentler. "He'll be so angry with me if he finds out. I asked you to talk to him on Ellen's behalf and I'm just pissing you off more."

"What happens if I do, and he lets her back in? Then I'll have both of you trying to force me away. I can't compete with your beauty and confidence or Ellen's…*whatever.*"

"Bitchiness?" Kiera supplied with a small smile, flattered by Meggie's compliments. Moreso, because the girl was unguarded and innocent. Honest. She wasn't blowing smoke up Kiera's ass.

"Yeah, that."

"Meggie, listen to me." When she tightened her fingers around Meggie's hand, it came to her she hadn't yet released her. She didn't then either. She didn't trust that Meggie wouldn't bolt. The girl had to leave *Outlaw,* not run while she was in Kiera and Ellen's care. That would defeat the purpose. He'd never want to see them again. "Outlaw don't want us right now. He's all about you. I'm not going to lie and say we aren't your competition. Fuck, Ellen's mine, too, but if you can't handle other girls trying to push you out…hell, if you can't handle other women period…then he's not the man for you and club life isn't for you."

Meggie's jaw clenched. After a moment, she snatched her hand away. "You're a bigger competitor than Ellen," she concluded. "He let you kiss him. He was with you in his office. He cares about you, Kiera, in a different way than he does Ellen."

Hope swelled in Kiera, but she pushed it aside, remembering her plan to get pregnant by whoever and proclaim Outlaw was the father. Mort still insisted the plan wasn't a good one; Outlaw wouldn't just believe her word, but Kiera was growing more and more desperate. Maybe, though, she did have a chance. If Meggie saw something between them, then… Fuck, who was she kidding? She was going by what Meggie believed? "You're eighteen years old, Megan," Kiera said sharply. "How the fuck do you know what a man like Outlaw feels for a woman?"

"I'm eighteen, not stupid." She started around her, going back toward the parking lot. "For instance, you're keeping me here and time's passing," she threw over her shoulder, stomping away.

Fuck, but Meggie was hard to handle. It would serve Outlaw right if he did something stupid like took her as his old lady. She'd run him fucking ragged. "I didn't want to try to get you upstairs," she called, the words stopping Meggie. "If you started struggling and I tried to force you, one of us might've fallen. We can go up now. I'll order the pizza while you put lotion on and polish your toenails. There's a dollar store nearby. Ellen can run there to get makeup for you."

Meggie turned. She lifted her chin and marched back to the steps, then went up without a word.

Relieved, Kiera followed behind her. Back in the apartment, she ordered the pizza, then showed Meggie the lotions and nail polish where she kept them in the small bathroom closet.

She needed to talk to Ellen, so she said to Meggie, "Why don't you take a quick rinse off in the shower. A little body wash to remove your adventure outside. Nothing long, just a couple of minutes before you lotion up."

"Fine," Meggie agreed.

The moment the shower started, Kiera told Ellen of her plan and asked her to go to the dollar store.

"You're fucking soft in the head if you're sending that cunt to Outlaw, dressed as his own personal fuck doll," Ellen spat.

"It's not going to work immediately," Kiera agreed. "We just have to wait it out, but it'll eventually dawn on him that she's more trouble than she's worth and he'll send her away or make her available to the other brothers. Please, Ellie? Besides, if we don't help her, not only won't she talk to him and ask him to remove his ban on you, she'll fucking leave anyway."

The shower stopped, and Kiera glanced uneasily toward the bathroom door.

"Fuck, fine," Ellen said grudgingly. "I still like my fucking plan better. Burying that little uppity bitch."

"Yeah, because you don't like living. I keep telling you to stop fucking around with the Dwellers. Snake, too."

Guilt crossed Ellen's face.

"Outlaw would fucking kill you if he knew you still fucked Snake."

"Outlaw don't fuck up bitches," Ellen reminded her again. "And I only started fucking Snake again after Outlaw released our pussies back to the fucking membership." She nodded to the bathroom door. "When she was in the fucking hospital."

"You're playing a dangerous fucking game," Kiera warned. She'd only dropped a helpful tip about which mall Snake could find them the day they took Meggie shopping. She'd thought Snake would take her. Fuck her. Kill her. Dump her. She hadn't really cared, despite the connection she knew Snake and Meggie shared. Until she'd actually seen the lunatic, and she'd realized she didn't want to subject Meggie to Snake's whims. He'd surprised Kiera and shown a small bit of morals seeing his resemblance to Meggie. Still, she had no intentions of fucking Snake, unlike Ellen. "I hope you know what you're doing."

"I know what the fuck I'm doing, but it seems that you don't, Kiera." Ellen walked out of the bedroom. A moment later, the front door slammed shut.

Sitting on the edge of her bed, Kiera released the breath she'd been holding. Elbows on her knees, she bent her head into her hands and thought over her years associating with the Dwellers.

Sharing was caring was an adage in the club that had existed since Ellen had first brought Kiera around. At that time, Boss was Prez and Outlaw was the enforcer. Kiera had barely been seventeen but pretended she was older. Still, Outlaw hadn't taken her to his bed. Somehow, he'd known she was much younger than she'd stated. He'd protected her by encouraging her to finish high school and keeping her away from most of the brothers. He'd allowed Mort, Val, and Digger access to her. Whether he knew it or not, Mort had been Kiera's first. Outlaw hadn't encouraged John Boy's attentions of her, but he hadn't interfered either. And Big Joe was Big Joe...*Boss...Prez.* He'd wanted her, so he'd had her.

None of the guys wanted Snake with her at that time, but it was Outlaw who'd implicitly stated the man couldn't even look at her.

Maybe, she'd fallen a little in love with Outlaw then. He'd been strangely honorable. Later, she'd learned that Outlaw had had that rule in place until he knew she'd turned eighteen. After that, he'd stepped back and let her decide for herself. That had disappointed her. She'd thought his end game was to have her for himself. But no.

When she and Ellen became official club property, they'd celebrated by fucking a bunch of brothers over a two-day period. Boss had started his decline. A lot of the members had begun to back away. Looking back, Kiera was grateful. Otherwise, her fuck count would've been much higher during that initiation.

Finally, a few months ago, her dream had come true. Outlaw had taken her as his. She'd hardly been able to contain her happiness and had had so many dreamy ideas building in her head. Questions had run amok—when would she get her '*Property of Outlaw*' cut; would he like to move into her apartment; what were his favorite foods; could she stop her shots so they could try for a baby. But then her bubble had been rudely burst when he'd brought Ellen in as well.

They took him together or not at all. Kiera had decided if he needed both her and Ellen to make him happy, then she'd accept his decision. He made Ellen happy too and Kiera couldn't begrudge two of the people she loved most a little slice of heaven. Outlaw had been suffering because of Big Joe's death. Rumors circulated that he'd killed the man. Suddenly, loyalties had split, some with Snake and others with Outlaw.

Snake had stopped coming around; a small faction aligned with Big Joe's son. Outlaw, as president, had threatened to kick them out of the club if they didn't adhere to the rules. Rack had protested, warning that Snake was grieving and he needed time. The club became even more fractured. Tempers flared and bitterness simmered.

Kiera knew it would only end one way—in death. But Outlaw was grieving too. Often, when he thought no one paid attention, Kiera saw the pain in his eyes. Deep down, she knew the rumors were true. He *had* killed Big Joe. Honestly, she was glad. The man who'd once been so no-nonsense...proud...strong had been reduced to little more than an abhorrent drug addict.

Kiera knew better than to share her suspicions with anyone. Even Outlaw. She could only be there for him when he needed her. If he needed Ellen too, well so be it.

Gradually, though, the rules had changed. Mainly because Ellen had. Kiera *knew* Ellen saw her as competition. She knew her best friend sought ways to push her out of their threesome. She always thought patience was the best tact. Ellen's mother and sister lived in Do-Do land. Peyton was a doctor, but the woman was *crazy*. Their mother, Audra...Kiera shivered. She didn't even want to think about her but having met those two made her better understand Ellen.

Then, Outlaw had been shot. Snake had finally struck. Kiera was sure it was Rack who'd let Big Joe's son onto club grounds. The rumor mill grinded on. She'd heard that footage had shown Snake entering from a forest trail. Kiera didn't know if that was true or not, but if it was then that meant Rack might really be innocent. So who was to blame?

She glanced toward the bathroom door. Meggie's appearance had come out of the blue. Kiera tried to make herself believe she'd been responsible for the raid, as much as she'd tried to convince Outlaw of Meggie's guilt. But Kiera now firmly believed in Meggie's innocence.

Outlaw wasn't a fool. Neither was Mort. None of them were. If she'd been out to get them, they would've figured out her game. Besides, she hadn't wanted to leave Outlaw's side when he'd been in the hospital. She'd also confronted Rack, and his anger had been very real. It wasn't until Johnnie reminded Rack of his woodchipper…

The bathroom door opened, and Meggie stepped into the bedroom, a towel wrapped around her, just as the doorbell rang.

"Pizza's here," Kiera said. She'd paid using her debit card, so once she accepted the pizza, she went to the kitchen. While she got plates and found Meggie's drink, then opened a bottle of red wine, Ellen returned with all sorts of makeup.

Tonight, Meggie would have Outlaw all to herself. In a few days, the club's Halloween party would happen. Kiera had stayed away from the club to support Ellen after her ban. If Meggie didn't convince Outlaw to change his mind, Kiera intended to attend that party. As usual, she and Ellen had helped plan it. More importantly, Kiera felt the clock ticking. This might be her last chance to get Outlaw.

Meggie

Eating proved an uncomfortable experience, and Meggie wished she was anywhere other than in Kiera's apartment, subjected to Ellen's hateful glares. Under different circumstances, Meggie felt she and Kiera might've been friends, but lines had been drawn. They were on one side, and she was on the other. Or, maybe, it wasn't that cut and dry, but rather like a triangle, where they each stood alone. For whatever reason, she didn't think Ellen was loyal to anyone, including Kiera. Maybe, that was unfair of Meggie to feel as she did. Yet, something about Ellen just gave Meggie a bad feeling.

"Let's start on your hair," Kiera said the minute they finished the pizza. She sipped her red wine. "You have a lot of it, so it's going to take forever."

"What are you going to do to it?" Meggie asked, standing from her seat at the small table.

"Come on. You'll see." Kiera got one of the chairs and carried it to her bedroom and placed it in front of her dresser so that Meggie faced the mirror, "Sit."

Meggie complied.

"Do you want the TV on or music?" Kiera asked. "Do you like Phoenix Rising?"

"Never heard of them," Meggie admitted.

Kiera's eyes widened. "They're only one of the biggest bands on earth. Their lead singer is so fucking hot, my panties get wet every time I see him on TV. Or anywhere."

The first vestiges of doubt crept into Meggie, so she didn't reply to Kiera's statement. "Christopher might get really angry that I'm there."

Standing in the doorway, Ellen folded her arms. "Too fucking late to back out. You wanted to go to the fucking party, so deal with the consequences."

Meggie glared at Ellen. "At least I have the option of going," she said sweetly. "Unlike you."

Kiera turning on the blow dryer drowned out Ellen's furious response, but anger settled in her face and never quite cleared. After the blow dryer stopped, Kiera and Ellen told Meggie of Christopher's involvement in selecting K-P's Bobs. Either they didn't see how much the information hurt her or they didn't care.

They laughed as they regaled Meggie with tales of past parties, and all the sexual antics that took place with myriad women always available. At some point, Ellen had disappeared. From the sounds Meggie heard, she knew the woman had escaped to the living room.

Once Meggie had dressed in her skimpy outfit, her hair tousled and wild, she stared at herself. Bright red painted her lips; mascara thickened and lengthened her lashes; a smoky cat-eye added drama to her look. She had a lot of exposed skin that glittered from the lotion she'd used.

It was as if she was staring at a different person, a woman oozing sensuality and out to seduce a man.

"Ellen, come see," Kiera called.

"Fuck," Ellen breathed the moment she walked into the bedroom.

Meggie smiled at Ellen's astonishment. She couldn't wait until Christopher saw her. This new side of her would impress him. She was sure of it. He might be so enamored he'd never want to let her go. Maybe, one or two of the other bikers would pay attention to her and Christopher would be so jealous, he wouldn't be able to focus on any other woman there. He might—

She gasped, catching Kiera's eye in the mirror. "You didn't dress me up to help me. You did it to distract *him*," she charged. "I'm the lesser of two evils, right? So young that I'm not much competition, whereas all those other women might be too many to overcome."

Glancing away, Kiera tightened her lips.

Meggie should've expected no less, but she couldn't care. All that mattered was she would get to the party and have Christopher see this sexy side of her.

Chapter Twenty-Eight
Christopher

K-P AND THE BOBS HAD DONE AN OUTSTANDING JOB WITH the food. Christopher knew K-P had a handpicked team of girls whom he called to assist him in the kitchen in times like these. After he'd started fucking Kiera and Ellen, they directed all the other preparations, but with Megan there and Christopher so pissed with Ellen, he'd left K-P in charge.

Christopher didn't trust the constant presence of the bitches wouldn't have upset Megan. But he'd had business to see to, some of it still undoing problems created by Big Joe. In the beginning, Boss had hidden the disappearing inventory by accusing rival clubs of intercepting and stealing shipments. Yeah, they'd been stealing the fucking shipments because fucking Boss had been tipping them off, playing them all, and getting paid in the drugs he'd come to depend on.

It had taken Christopher months to broker a deal with two of the clubs, which had happened only because the body count was rising in both clubs. The Dwellers had already begun to bring in support clubs to do their distribution, which made the situation even more fucked up because those clubs were also losing men thanks to Boss. The motherfucker was lucky he hadn't been put the fuck down then, but Christopher and Snake didn't want anything to happen to him. In turn, Val, Digger and Mortician had been loyal because of Christopher, and Rack thanks to Snake. They'd protected Boss.

Now, with a huge gun shipment being prepared for a Canadian buyer, Christopher had to get an extra escort for the run, and he needed some of those same clubs he'd worked so carefully with to undo all the damage that'd been done. Motherfuckers couldn't be trusted when they were dealing with two rocks. Though the club would give each of the five men twenty large and both clubs a quarter rock a piece, motherfuckers *couldn't* be trusted when his club would still make such a huge profit.

Christopher leaned back against the wall, watching the Bobs working the main room from where he sat at the corner table. Jesus. Fuck. Those bitches had their tits bouncing, only dressed in keyhole thongs and clear heels. They were doing his boys proud, serving drinks to the visiting brothers, and not hesitating to suck dick or give up some ass.

He hadn't been all that happy that Val had sent Megan off with Ellen, but he hadn't specifically said to only call Kiera. But, fuck, they were protecting Megan from this free-for-all, so all the better.

When he'd ordered Val back to the club then called Kiera with his instructions regarding Megan, she'd fucking agreed he needed a chance to enjoy himself with one of the Bobs. The question was did he want to? *Yes and no.* He didn't want Megan hurt if she found out he'd fucked one of these bitches. On the other hand, he was a fucking realist. They couldn't last.

Digger sauntered over, beer in hand. "John Boy on his way."

"Cool." Christopher hadn't hung out with his cousin in months. Because this was such a big deal, Johnnie was driving down to attend this party. If Megan was here, she'd definitely dampen their style. They had a friendly rivalry with bitches that usually ended up with both of them fucking the same bitch, together and separately.

"You sent Megan away so him and you could fuck some bitches, huh?"

Christopher shrugged. "At first, I ain't had no intention of tellin' Ki to keep Megan from here."

"You called right, Outlaw," Digger said. "Megan would've been so fucking out of place in jeans, a turtleneck, and nothing but clear lip gloss for makeup."

"You right," Christopher agreed on a sigh.

"Even after being in your fucking bed, she still just so fucking innocent. She probably wouldn't have wanted to stay out here and not wanted you to stay out here neither."

Another fucking fact Digger spoke.

"Ain't gotta worry, assfuck," Christopher growled, annoyed. "Megan ain't here." He beckoned a Bob over. She was rather plain with non-descript brown hair and unremarkable eyes. "Bring me a bottle, babe."

She smiled at him, her wide mouth sending lewd signals to Christopher's brain. Megan was so pure, so gorgeous. So fucking not for him.

"We not telling Megan about you sticking your cock in one of these bitches, so don't worry about it, Prez," Digger said. He must've noted something in Christopher's expression. "You deserve to have a couple bitches. 'Specially after what you did for her today. You let that motherfucker live."

Yeah, he'd let Thomas Nicholls live. After calling in a favor to the badges and providing the address where he lived with Meggie's ma, Christopher had him pulled over on his return to Seattle and escorted back to Hortensia. By involving law enforcement to get his hands on fuckhead, he couldn't leave a fucking body. They might look the other way while Christopher beat a personally delivered motherfucker to a pulp. Murdering the same fuckhead? Nope. Even officers on his payroll had their standards.

He hadn't had time to search high and fucking low for Thomas fucking Nicholls. *Truth.* Even if he had, he might've still gotten their assistance. Promise or not to Megan, Christopher wanted that fuckhead composting the landscape, instead of walking the fuck around. He didn't have fucking time for loose fucking ends. Just like he didn't have fucking time for torture. Unfinished business had a way of coming back to haunt a motherfucker. And torture was John Boy's thing.

Though Thomas fuckhead was a special case, deserving to have his cock sliced. Not fucking deep. Just efuckinnuff to cause agony before Christopher clipped in his hollows and emptied it in that motherfucker's head.

None of that shit happened, however.

Christopher had explained the details, though. Nicholls had been so helpful, carrying a photo of Megan. Once Mutt and Jeff had seen her and heard what he'd done, Christopher was sure he was due an ass whipping from them, too. If there was any justice, the injuries Christopher had delivered was severe enough that only a few more punches would end him. He'd just have to let it go that he wasn't the one who'd do it. Mutt was corrupt as a motherfucker and Jeff was meaner than a snake. Christopher didn't bother with their real names. Didn't give a fuck really. To him, they were Mutt and Jeff, doing favors for him when what needed doing couldn't get done without involving them. Like bringing a motherfucker in who Christopher didn't have time to find. He'd never tell Megan any of this. As far as she was concerned, he wouldn't know the fuckhead if the motherfucker walked up and bitch slapped Christopher.

The most important thing was he'd kept his fucking promise, lived up to the idealized version of himself that was only in *her* mind.

Fuck.

He scrubbed a hand over his face. He wouldn't fuck another bitch tonight. The mood to fucking party deserted him. As soon as he could, he'd hit the fucking road and get Megan.

Val walked up, his arm around a stacked, redheaded Bob. "Stretch just notified me Megan outside."

"What?" Christopher barked.

Neither Kiera or Ellen ever fucking disobeyed him. Even when they didn't fucking like what the fuck he said, they fucking listened. Only one little pain-in-the-ass-motherfucker never...*Fuck*.

Suddenly, he knew. *They* hadn't ignored his instructions. Megan had forced their hand in some way. He should be angry, but fuck if anticipation at seeing her didn't strike him. He could also use this as an opportunity to remind himself of how little she fit in. Once he saw her, dressed as a regular girl, sweet, innocent, and too motherfucking young for him, he'd remember she didn't belong in this fucked up life. "Tell Ki to come in." She was fucking there. She might as well come the fuck in.

As the redhead sidled away, Christopher noticed Val's unease. Suspicion rose in him. "Kiera dropped her off, yeah?"

"Kiera *and* Ellen," Val answered.

"Ellen?" Christopher snapped. "I thought I told that bitch—"

"I guess Meggie want her here, Prez," Val said. "Women funny like that."

"Ain't givin' a fuck. My word go, not nofuckinbody else. If Megan fuckin' clueless, them two bitches ain't."

"Megan must've made them think different, Outlaw," Digger said with a shake of his head, his tone just short of disgust.

"Ain't a fuckin' thing she coulda said. They know the fuckin' deal—"

"Do they?" Val challenged. "*We* don't know it. You made your cock off-limits to them because of Meggie. They been our property for fucking years. Long before you took them for yourself. Everything seemed fine until Meggie came, so maybe whatever the fuck she said to get them not to listen to *you*, because they don't know the fucking rules no more."

"Yeah, Prez, word on the curb we got to do whatever Meggie want," Digger said. "Remember? *You* put those instructions out."

Christopher scowled. "I ain't meant listenin' to her over me." He glared at Val. "Try catchin' up to Kiera and Ellen. Ima send Megan to the fucking room and clue all you motherfuckers in."

Val grinned. "Meggie punished, huh?"

"I ain't got time for no lil' fuckin' cupcake princess," he growled.

Digger grabbed his beer, tipped it back and took a long swallow. As he set the bottle down, his eyes widened, and the alcohol exploded from his mouth.

"What the fuck, asshole?" Christopher snarled, jumping to his feet, swiping at his wet cheek.

"*FUCK!*" Val managed, staring toward the doorway. He backed into a chair and plopped his ass down, his mouth hanging open.

"What—" Christopher choked as Megan strutted into view.

It took him a moment to realize his own fucking mouth was open and he snapped it shut. He gaped, his pulse pounding, his world turned upside down. The blue metallic halter top and matching belted miniskirt she wore drew the attention of every man there. Her golden hair, flowing down her back, had been curled and her exposed skin—too motherfucking much exposed skin—glittered.

K-P and Mortician stopped her, and she giggled at something they said. Christopher, however, continued to gawk, unable to do another motherfucking thing.

From the moment he'd met her, he'd recognized her stunning beauty. Thick, shiny, golden hair down to her ass. True blue eyes surrounded by thick lashes. A small nose, high cheekbones, and luscious lips. She was gorgeous. Case fucking closed. Along with that face and curvy little body was her fucking innocence. A trait that both lured and repelled Christopher.

She, in her all purity, saw him as worthy. She didn't fear or judge him like so many good girls would. Nor did she merely lust after him as experienced chicks did. Her virtuousness grounded him. Reminded him a dirty motherfucker like him had no future with an angel like her.

Except, tonight, she wasn't an angel. She was a fucking goddess.

She laid her little fingers on Mort's cut and he leaned down, whispering to her. Johnnie walked behind her, effectively wedging her between him and Mort and painting an image that infuriated Christopher.

Usually, Christopher was happy to see Johnnie. Not an hour ago, he'd been looking forward to seeing the motherfucker. Not now, though, when his cousin wrapped an arm around Megan's tiny waist and buried his nose in her hair, bending to murmur something in her ear. Even in her thigh-high, silver stiletto boots, she barely reached Johnnie to his chin. He pressed against her, and Christopher growled, balling his hands into fists.

Some assfuck he intended to mutilate worse than Johnnie strode to Megan, but she smiled that gorgeous smile—her red lipstick causing Christopher's heart to stutter—and pointed at him. Being surrounded by a bunch of motherfuckers didn't bother her in the fucking least. Whereas Christopher was about to fucking stroke out.

As she started in his direction, two Bobs attempted to block her way, but she gave them a look that could freeze Lucifer's dick and sauntered past them, throwing a response over her shoulder to their comment and tossing her hair in dismissal. Christopher would've loved to know what they'd said, then he didn't give a fuck about that either. Johnnie followed Megan, a smirk on his face, his eyes drifting down. To her ass, no doubt.

Finally at his table, she stopped and smiled. "Hey, Val," she greeted and waved at Digger. "Hey," she added.

The smell of her hair…the fragrance of her light floral perfume…reached Christopher nostrils, opening his nose wide and going straight to his head. He felt fucking lightheaded, broadsided with this new version of Megan.

"Meggie," Val responded, standing and not hiding his shameless inspection.

"Good evening, fuckers." Johnnie spared them a glance before his focus returned to Megan. "I ran across this beauty on my way in." He grinned at Christopher. "Decided to escort her to the table."

She smiled and looked up at his cousin. "Thank you, Johnnie. I appreciate your concern for my safety." His cut peeped out from underneath his leather jacket, and she fingered it in a way she'd never touched Christopher's. "I didn't know you were in the club."

Johnnie's heavy-lidded gaze endangered his fucking life. "Now you do," he murmured.

Always the fucking clown, Digger made a show of checking Megan out, while Mort, who'd also brought his ass to the fucking table, tried his fucking best not to look at her.

"Where the sweet Megan Foy?" Digger asked. "Where this new, hot bitch put her?"

"I'm still me, Digger," she said with a pretty smile and a lick of her lips.

She. *Licked.* Her. Fucking. Lips. Not at Christopher either. She hadn't even fucking *looked* at his ass.

"Do you want to play a game of pool, Mortician?" she asked, pinning him with blue eyes all the more brilliant because of the makeup she wore.

"I don't play pool unless there's money at stake," Mort lied smoothly, smiling to let her down easy.

Times like this made Christopher remember why Mort was such a good fucking friend.

"I'll play with you," Johnnie drawled, capturing Megan's attention.

In a sadistic way, seeing all her exposed skin flushing red pleased Christopher. But he still hadn't recovered from the shock of seeing her. Maybe, she wasn't real. The only way he'd find out was if he inspected her closely. Touched her.

Covered her.

"What do you say, sweetheart?" Johnnie pressed.

Before she responded or Christopher fucked up John Boy, K-P ambled to the table, took in Megan's outfit again, and scratched his bald head. "Didn't lie when I spoke to you a few minutes ago and said you are gorgeous, Meggie," he started. "But you're a little underdressed, don't you think?"

Megan's gaze fell on two Bobs standing at the bar. Big titties free for every motherfucker to see and pussy barely covered. The girl next to her had her back to them, displaying small waist and a lush, round ass. "I actually feel a little *overdressed,*" she grumbled.

"Your daddy—" K-P started, trying again.

"Isn't here," she snapped, glaring at Christopher then turning the look on K-P. "Don't be a hypocrite. Am I supposed to hide my body as Big Joe's daughter?"

No one else at the table said a motherfucking thing to that. Even K-P seemed at a loss and shoved his hands in his jeans, rocking on his heels.

They were all staring at her. Even Stretch was there now, joining the other assfucks. Blinking. Gaping. *Lusting.*

Christopher roamed from around the table and stepped toward her, not speaking, just circling her, taking it all in. The halter top shelving her breasts. The tiny skirt with the silver belt stopping just below her ass cheeks. The blue of the material that matched her eyes and made them gleam like jewels.

She was so fucking gorgeous, he couldn't even find fucking words.

Defiance entered her eyes, and she tossed her hair over her shoulders. Angry. Ready for all out fucking war. "May I have a drink or is this event only for your Bobs?"

Christopher's gaze flew to hers. "Where Kiera and Ellen?" It was their fault she was dressed like a slut.

"They left," she said coolly.

"I bet them bitches fuckin' did. Kiera shouldna took you here. I ain't wanted you here in the first fuckin' place."

Megan flinched at the words and her chin wobbled.

Mortician winced. "Prez," he said, a hint of censure in his tone.

Even if Megan hadn't recovered, she was currently trying to cleave Christopher in two by sheer fucking will. "Kiera had a choice," she said coldly.

"Neither of you bitches got a fucking choice when my ass sayin' what the fuck to do," Christopher snapped.

"Oh, yes, I do, moron," she snarled. "I can exercise it here just as easily as I did there. I left. She came and brought me back to the apartment. If she wouldn't have brought me here *tonight*, I wouldn't have been there *tomorrow*."

As he'd suspected, she'd forced their hand. Yet, his outrage they'd disobeyed him evaporated. Megan meant every fucking word she said. He saw it in her eyes. It was either bring her or lose her, and they'd chosen the lesser of two evils.

In silence, he watched as Mort got a business card from his cut, along with a pen, and wrote something, taking longer than expected. He handed Megan the card. "My cell number on there. I jotted K-P, Digger, and Val numbers on the back. Call one of us if you need to go somewhere, Megan."

"You can put mine down," Stretch volunteered.

"You're a fucking Probate, roach," K-P said. "Meggie's top priority, handled by only the most trustworthy brothers."

"Why didn't you put my number, Mortician?" Johnnie demanded.

"Trying to help keep your fucking cock attached to your body, motherfucker," Mort retorted.

Never a motherfucker to hide from the truth, Johnnie stared at Megan. She must've felt the intensity of his gaze because she looked at him, averting her eyes just as quickly and holding the card out to Mort.

"Thank you, but I don't have a cellphone. The numbers won't do me any good."

Just one more thing to darken Christopher's fucking mood. She *didn't* have a cellphone.

"K-P, get her on our plan," he instructed.

K-P nodded, then looked at Megan. "I'd like a word with you, Meggie," he said, sounding quite fucking fatherly.

She gave him a suspicious look, slightly uneasy but she squared her shoulders and nodded, following him to a spot still within Christopher's sight.

"Prez?" Digger said, staring at her as she listened intently to K-P. Just as they all were staring at her. "All that shit I said about Megan before she came? Throw it out the fucking window. Go back to the fucking drawing board."

She smiled and nodded. Christopher would've given anything to hear the conversation. But he was so fucking irritated, worsened by his aching balls.

"Johnnie, she not yours," Val said, drawing Christopher's attention away from her and K-P.

"Never said she was," Johnnie responded, still staring at Megan.

"Damn, bruh, you not acting like it," Digger said, shaking his head.

Johnnie snapped his attention to Digger and narrowed his eyes. "Is that so?" he asked coldly.

"Yeah, motherfucker," Mortician snapped. "It *is* fucking so. Prez always treated your fucking bitch with nothing but respect. She fucking beautiful, too, but he never disrespected your motherfucking ass by openly lusting after her then way you doing Megan."

"I'm not doing anymore than the rest of you motherfuckers are," Johnnie growled.

"Yeah, you is." Digger folded his arms. "Not a motherfucker here but you offered to *play* with her."

"We all fucking knew you wasn't talking about pool," Val said. "Even Meggie knew you was talking about her pussy."

Christopher frowned and would've warned Val to not *ever* fucking talk about Megan's pussy. Ever again. In his fucking life, if he wanted it to continue.

Johnnie's look challenged Christopher. "We've shared pussy before, Val, so why should I assume it'll be different with Megan?"

Fury layered Christopher's annoyance, but Megan sashaying into their midst, minus K-P, halted a response. All Christopher saw was Megan in the outfit that hadn't only given *him* a completely different perspective of her, but other motherfuckers too.

He glared over her head to Johnnie. "Gimme your fuckin' jacket, asshole."

Johnnie lifted a brow. "That should be her decision, Christopher."

"*Now!*" Christopher ordered, on the verge of really losing his shit.

She turned her head, offering a view of her perfect profile. "No. I'm fine just like this, Johnnie. Keep your jacket." She returned her challenging blue regard to Christopher. "I would like a drink, though."

They stared at one another, and he saw by her mutinous expression she wouldn't back down. "Ima spank your fuckin' ass for pullin' this fuckin' shit," he blurted without thinking.

She paled a little at his furious snarl and stepped back.

Johnnie whispered in her ear, and she nodded, glancing uneasily at Christopher.

In his anger, he'd forgotten about her history. Fuck, in her hot-as-fuck outfit, he couldn't even see the scars from the cuts she inflicted on herself. All he saw was *her*. On another chick, he would've appreciated the fuck out of the skimpy clothes. He scrubbed a hand over his eyes. He appreciated it on Megan, too, but not when every other motherfucker ogled her.

The bitch with the mousy brown hair sidled back with his bottle of tequila. She stopped in front of him, planting herself between him and Megan, and rubbing her tits against him. She could've rubbed her bare pussy on him; he wouldn't have given a fuck. But Megan saw what the Bob did and stepped back, her shoulders rigid with anger, her eyes filling with misery.

She turned, squeezing between Johnnie and Mortician, clear intentions to walk away and into the fucking crowd.

"Get fuckin' back here, Megan," Christopher snarled.

"Bite me," she tossed over her shoulder, not fucking listening. *Never* fucking listening.

Growling in frustration and grabbing the bottle, Christopher rushed to her and wrapped an arm around Megan's waist, then lifted her off her feet, not thinking, only acting.

When he reached his bedroom, which he noted was clean, he slammed the door shut, then set her on her feet.

He unzipped his jeans and pulled his cock out, forcing her to her knees. "You wanna look like a whore, then Ima treat you like one." He gripped her hair and twisted, thrusting his cock against her lips until she opened her mouth and allowed him to shove his dick in.

He should've expected the little bitch to bite him, but stupid motherfucker he was, he didn't. No bitch in their right mind had ever practiced violence on his person.

He yelped in pain and jerked away. Megan scrambled back and stumbled to her feet.

"Go back out there then," she yelled. "I don't care. I talked to them while I was dressing. They told me you're nice to the Bobs and they turn you on and they're dressed in less than I am."

"I ain't treatin' you no different than I treat those sluts."

"Liar. They told me how you buy your *Club Ass* drinks. How K-P *interviews* those girls and then sends the Bobs to you for a final *consultation*. They're handpicked based on how well they suck you off! I had a long conversation with them about all of it."

Fuming, Christopher grabbed her arm and yanked her to the bed, throwing her on it, then climbing over her. He was so fucking frustrated with *them*, knowing who *them* was.

"You fuckin' better than them. Ellen, Kiera, and the Bobs. Better than all us put together. You fuckin' better than this. Lettin' motherfuckers look at you almost naked. Eye fuck you. Imagine their dicks in you seven ways to fuckin' Sunday."

Only he was supposed to do that. Not his brothers. Not his cousin. Not the members of the support clubs. No one else but him.

"I didn't dress for them," she admitted, looking up at him. "I dressed for you."

He was about to have a fucking heart attack. That's the only reason it was beating like a jackhammer in his chest at her words and her earnest look. A weak fucking heart was the only reason her sweet response went straight through him and pierced all his defenses.

She pulled his head down and planted her mouth on his, opening for him, letting him take over once she touched her tongue to his. His hand slid under her skirt because he was dying to know what she wore underneath.

Thank fuck, she had a thong on. Her ass was bare, but her pussy was covered. Her kisses were wild, her body grinding like a whore's, her nipples hard, the sounds coming from her driving him insane.

Lifting her hips in invitation, she sucked his tongue and he groaned. Her heated skin singed his fingertips, his lips, his hands, and mouth.

"Megan, I gotta fuck you, baby, then we gotta go back out there." He tore her thong and pushed open her legs, thrusting into her hard. She arched against him, exposing her slender throat.

Christopher bit her. "You wanted dick, huh?"

"Yeah," she breathed. "Yours."

He closed his eyes and hammered her again and again until she came for him. This was a quick fuck, to appease his territorial rights over her and her insecurities. He grunted and trembled, filling her with his cum. Afterward, they lay wrapped around each other, breathing hard.

Christopher rested his chin on the crown of her head. "Put somethin' else on for me, baby. Please. I gotta keep my head on straight and I ain't gonna be able to if I gotta watch you." And fuck up any motherfucker who looked at her. He'd never thought of himself as the jealous type but with Megan, he'd kill anyone who touched her.

She kissed the spot where his neck and shoulder met. "What do you want me to wear?"

He pulled out of her and leaned back on his haunches. "A burka. A sari. A habit. You choose."

She lifted herself on her elbows. His dick hardened all over again at the sight she presented in that outfit, legs spread and revealing her reddened, engorged pussy, his cum leaking from her. Her curled hair was even wilder now, her lips were swollen, and her cheeks were flushed. He bent and suckled her clit and she shuddered. Her head lulled to the side. "I've never worn something so revealing."

"Coulda fooled me," he grumbled, dragging his mouth away from her and sitting up.

"It makes me feel naughty."

It made him feel murderous. "Feel naughty for my ass, Megan," he said, guiding her to a sitting position. Unable to stop himself, he buried his hand in her hair and pulled her against him to kiss her.

She drew to her knees and wrapped her arms around his neck.

"Christopher," she whispered.

With effort, he separated himself from her. "I gotta get the fuck back out there. See that everythin' goin' the way I ordered."

She wrapped her arms around her waist and nodded, her sadness returning. "When I arrived, there was a girl outside with two guys," she began quietly. "One had his penis in her mouth and the other one was having sex with her the normal way. They were on the ground out in the open." She cocked her head to the side. "Do things like that happen at all the gatherings?"

"Most of them," he admitted. "Unless old ladies 'round." He squeezed the bridge of his nose. "Fuck, baby, ain't none of us been havin' a old lady in a while. The brothers that do stopped hangin' round two years ago or so, unless there was church."

She lowered her lashes. "Did all those girls really perform oral sex on you?" she whispered.

"Whatcha think?" he asked with a sigh.

She drew in a shuddering breath. "Were you gonna let one of them do it tonight?"

He caressed her cheek, thinking about their conversation last night when he told her about leaving her with his ma to return to Kiera and Ellen. "I thought 'bout it."

Her lower lip trembled but she nodded. "Okay." She crawled past him and got to her feet. She looked so fucking hot standing there in that outfit. "Um, I'm tired, Christopher. I think I'm going to turn in. Why don't you go and enjoy yourself?"

Why did she do this to him? Any other bitch he'd let walk the fuck away. Instead, he scrambled after Megan and caught her shoulders. "I ain't said I was gonna do it. Fuck, Megan! Where you see us goin'? Huh?"

"Nowhere," she retorted. "Because you don't want us to go anywhere."

He did. More than he could ever explain. "Megan, I already told you we ain't ever gettin' married."

"Yeah, you just want me to have your baby."

That's not all he wanted from her. "My name, baby, ain't worth shit. *I* ain't wantin' the fuckin' name Caldwell. I'm shame of it. Why I want a beautiful angel like you havin' it?"

She blinked and her eyes glittered with fierceness. "Because it's part of you and there's nothing about you that I consider shameful."

Those words hung between them, and she challenged him with a look. But what the fuck could he say? When motherfuckers put him down or pissed him off, he knew how to respond. Her words, though? They were from her heart, expressing a belief in him no one ever had.

He took her in his arms and hugged her. "Come out with me, Megan. We ain't gonna be out there no more than another hour. I gotta make sure everybody seen to."

"You're sure?"

"Ain't never been surer of nothin' in my life."

She stepped back and smiled, scooting around him, and heading for the bureau where he'd given her a drawer for the clothes she'd

294 | Kathryn C. Kelly

purchased at the mall. Instead of getting another outfit, she pulled out another thong and put it on.

"Megan—"

"I wanted to talk to you about Ellen," she interrupted, heading for the door and opening it to step into the hallway.

Tuning her out, he gritted his teeth and followed behind her. His scent clung to her, so every motherfucker there knew she belonged to him. Besides, he wouldn't let her out of his sight or his reach.

Later, though, when Megan fell asleep, he was going to take the clothes she wore and burn those motherfuckers.

Chapter Twenty-Nine
Christopher

"I HEARD MEGGIE'S DRESSING AS MINNIE MOUSE," Kiera giggled, four days later, as she stood next to Christopher, so close to him that if he turned, his arm would brush her tit.

It was the club's annual Halloween party, the first time he'd seen Kiera since he added her to his ban after Megan showed up and nearly gave him a fucking heart attack. Somehow, she'd convinced him to let those two attend the party as usual.

They'd had a big hand in organizing the shit since plans had begun way before Megan arrived.

Ellen settled an arm around Mort's shoulders. "Maybe, she's telling you she wants to go to Disneyland, Outlaw."

"Fuck off," Christopher grumbled, swigging his bottle of rum.

"Maybe, her outfit the other night was a one-off," Digger said.

Kiera smiled. "It probably was. Without my guidance, she wouldn't have chosen something so daring."

"That shit ain't funny, Kiera," Christopher said, furious. "She got every motherfucker in here with a hard cock. She ain't never shoulda worn that if that ain't what the fuck she wantin' to fuckin' wear."

"Oh." Kiera swallowed. "Uh—"

"Ease off Ki, Outlaw," Ellen advised. "She didn't tell that little girl to buy the outfit. It was a stupid challenge. Since Meggie is so young, she fell for it and ended up dressed as she was."

"She not a lil' fuckin' girl."

"Next to us she is," Ellen said with a shrug. "Watch how she's going to be dressed without Kiera's influence. Wait until everyone sees her in her costume, when clothes at Dweller parties are optional at best. We all know what's going to happen, babe. She's going to be uncomfortable and quiet. I'll give her no more than sixty minutes before she asks to go back to the room."

"She really threatened to leave if she couldn't come?" Val asked before Christopher got the chance.

"Threatened?" Ellen snorted. "That bitch left."

"Your fuckin' ass wanna stay at this fuckin' party, stop callin' Megan out her fuckin' name."

"Why, Outlaw? I don't know where the fuck you see your relationship with the child going, but as long as she's here she needs to acclimate to *our* lifestyle. Not the other fucking way around. There's one of that bitch and a bunch of us motherfuckers."

Even though he wanted to blast Ellen, he couldn't refute her logic. *Still...* "I ain't givin' a good fuck if we outnumber her a thousand to fuckin' one. Her name Megan. You respectin' her or you gettin' the fuck."

"Well, genius, *Meggie's* a live one." Ellen smirked. "She doesn't fit here and she's going to run your fucking ass ragged trying to shape our world into what she thinks it should be. The sooner you accept you're too fucking old for her and too fucking raunchy, you'll get past your mid-life crisis, and we'll all be happier."

Since she was only speaking amongst them, Christopher didn't take offense. Despite the truth of her words, he found them funny and joined everyone else in laughter.

"Her name Megan. Or Meggie," he conceded when their amusement died. "Call her that. Or suffer the fuckin' consequences."

Ellen studied him. Seeing he was fucking serious, she nodded. "You can't make anybody respect or like her, Outlaw," she said. "She has to earn that. You've been around long enough to know that."

"Ain't givin' a fuck if you hate her fuckin' guts. If she the biggest fuckin' psycho cunt 'round this motherfucker. If you preferrin' to fuckin' piss on her then praise her…you *ain't* fuckin' callin' her out her fuckin' name. You ain't hurtin' her fuckin' feelins. You ain't makin' her feel unfuckinwelcome. As long as she in my fuckin' bed, you respectin' her." He caught and held her gaze. "Hear me?"

"Clearly," she said through tight lips. "My condolences when you lose your fucking dignity tonight. The moment they see her dressed as she will be that's what will happen. She's all alone dressing herself. We had to guide her every step of the way. Even after she got to Ki's house, she was unsure about her costume, so we told her to just put her regular clothes on. Like the young chick she is, she kept flip-flopping. She should've been happy that you didn't want her at the fucking party, instead of flipping her shit like she did. We had to give her pointers on how to act and how to walk in heels and—"

Ellen must've took him for a motherfucking assfuck. "You a lyin' fuckin' bitch, Ellen. Megan ain't had no fuckin' problem walkin' and she knew just how the fuck to act. Ain't no fuckin' way you fuckin' *taught* Megan none of the shit she fuckin' did. That shit just in her."

"If it was, she wouldn't be dressing as Minnie Mouse," Ellen retorted.

"Fuck." Digger scratched his chin. "Ellen right, Prez." He looked at Mort. "What you say, Mortician?"

"*I* say *I* ain't givin' a fuck what she wearin'," Christopher inserted, "so ain't none of you motherfuckers business neither."

"Ellie, back off," Kiera advised. "Outlaw's getting annoyed."

"It seems like I don't have a choice since nothing I'm saying is getting through to him," Ellen said.

"Know what that mean, huh, babe?" Val asked.

Ellen lifted a brow.

"Shut the fuck up," Christopher answered in Val's place. "That's what the fuck that mean."

Huffing, Ellen rolled her eyes, then changed the subject. "How do you like Ki's costume, Outlaw?"

At the words, Kiera backed away to a spot with more room, so she could turn and show her ass cheeks. The front of her outfit looked like a sheer French maid's costume with a low-cut top part and thin straps. He glimpsed her pussy through the see-through thong, but the back turned her into a fucking gift with the big bow that kept the outfit tight and drew immediate attention to her ass. Fishnet stockings covered her long legs.

She sailed back to him. "Do you like it, baby?"

He nodded. "Fuck yeah," he admitted as Johnnie walked to the table and took a seat. "You a fuckin' hot bitch," he told her.

"What about me?" Ellen said. "Do you like my outfit?"

"If Outlaw don't, I do," Digger said. "A see-through bodysuit with sparkles. Simple shit. Just tear the motherfucker off and get to fucking."

"You're so stupid," Ellen said, shaking her head and joining everyone else in laughter.

They were loud and rowdy, so Christopher backed his chair away, affording a small bit of privacy since Kiera was standing next to him, looking as if she needed a moment with him.

"Can we go to your office and talk?" Kiera whispered, her eyes pleading.

"No," he said, the word automatic.

"She's dressing as *Minnie Mouse*, Outlaw," she said. "While you're not even in costume. Minnie Mouse. Let that sink in. I'm a grown woman."

"She one, too."

Kiera shook her head. "I need to talk to you. It's urgent, baby."

Christopher shook his head. "You ain't hearin' me or some shit? No, Kiera. Fuck no."

"I have something to tell you."

Not liking the sound of that, Christopher stared at her. "What?"

She laid a hand on her belly. Smiled softly and lowered her lashes. Opened her mouth to speak.

Wrapping his hand around her wrist, he jerked her closer. "If you 'bout to tell me you got my kid in you, Ima warn you right fuckin' now, Kiera. Shit better be true. You lyin' in any fuckin' way to fuck with Megan, you gonna be so fuckin' sorry."

Kiera swallowed.

"My cock alfuckinways covered when we fuckin', but cock covers fuck up. Lemme clue you the fuck in 'bout this shit too. Since we was last tofuckingether you been with Traveler, Digger, Mortician, Val, Johnnie, Stretch, Shady, and K-P. Your pussy, your business. Motherfucker my business when you startin' to scheme." He released her. "Say what the fuck you gotta say."

She met his gaze. "Meggie already thinks we're a couple, Outlaw."

"Ain't my fuckin' fault. She ain't ever had cock befuckinfore, and the one she gettin' she saw in you. She ain't understandin' motherfuckers fuck just cuz, and it ain't got fuck to do with no fuckin' feelins."

"I don't want you with her and I don't want you with Ellen," she said. "I want you for me."

He had always watched out for Kiera, so maybe she'd mistaken his protection as romantic feelings.

"If Meggie hadn't arrived, I don't know how much longer I could've been in the threesome," she admitted. "I hated seeing you with Ellen. When I think about it, you always have treated me differently. Gentler."

Fuck, how the fuck he suddenly became some dreamy motherfucker bitches wanted to spend their fucking lives with?

Goddamnit, he was losing his fucking edge since Big Joe died more than he fucking imagined.

"My ass ain't everyfuckinthing, Ki," he told her gruffly. "You and Mort been tight. He feelin' you, babe."

She glanced in Mort's direction, then looked at Christopher again, her dark eyes vulnerable. "Why Meggie?" she whispered. "Is it because I'm just a whore in your eyes? I'm too old?"

Fuck him. Before Megan he wouldn't have fucking even entertained Kiera's need for a fucking explanation. But girls needed to know what motherfuckers were thinking, so they didn't jump to fucking conclusions.

He turned to her. Once, he would've pulled her onto his lap or rested his hands on her ass cheeks, but he didn't want to now.

"You ain't too old. Fuck, you the perfect fuckin' age. You a good girl, Ki. A motherfucker gonna be lucky to get you on the back of his fuckin' bike. Yeah, you a whore, but you ain't *just* one. You so fuckin' smart and pretty. You fun and you funny. If a motherfucker ever claim you, he gettin' a fuckin' prize."

"I want you to claim me," she said softly. "I want to be on the back of your bike. I'm loyal. You know I am."

He nodded. "Yeah, Ki. You is."

"I'm faithful and—"

"No," he said, shaking his head. "You pitch pussy *everyfuckinwhere.* Regular motherfuckers. Biker motherfuckers. Badges. Your fuckin' mail motherfucker. You fuckin' tag-teamed motherfuckers pickin' up your garbage. *You* told them fuckin' stories, Kiera."

"They were true," she said, and he hated the shame shadowing her eyes.

"Baby, ain't nothin' to sweat. You like fuckin'. Nothin' shameful 'bout that."

Kiera ignored the comment. "When you took me and Ellen for yourself, I stopped giving up my pussy like that. And you fuck everything you see, too. Is it so bad that either of us fuck different people?"

"When lil' babies get made, fuck yeah. 'Specially for girls. Shit might not be fair, but girls carry the babies. If they fuck a bunch of motherfuckers with no protection, sometimes in the *same* fuckin' day, how the fuck you pinnin' paternity on *one* motherfucker without a fuckin' DNA test?" His words might've been harsh, but it was the truth.

Since he'd turned away from Kiera and Ellen, they'd both taken to fucking whichever brother they wanted. Fine, as long as no bitch was trying to fucking trap him.

Or run Megan the fuck away.

"I'll keep my pussy to myself," Kiera swore, then gazed at him through the sweep of her lashes. "Meggie was a virgin."

Her change of subject, and the topic she chose, shocked him stupid. "Who the fuck—"

"Nobody had to tell me or Ellen. Guys don't see what women see, but we knew immediately."

He did, too.

"I'm right, huh?" she pressed. "She was, wasn't she?"

"Ain't fallin' for your fuckin' fishin'. What Megan was or wasn't aintcha fuckin' business. That shit our fuckin' private shit."

"Since when is who or how you fuck private?" she demanded. "We all exchange sexcapades. That's what we do. She got you thinking like her. Like she's too above us for you to talk about her pussy."

"That's cuz she is," he said flatly. "She above me, you, Ellen, Mort, Val, *all* us motherfuckers. And, yeah, what the fuck I do with her behind closed doors private."

"She can't know how to please you. And she'd be devastated if you fucked another chick. *I* know how to please you. And if you fuck other bitches, I won't care as long as you don't flaunt them in front of me." She shook her head. "Even if you did, I'd be hurt but I wouldn't cause trouble for you. She would. She'd be jealous. With her bad temper who knows what kind of revenge she'd seek."

"None," he said, catching her insinuation that Megan would bring in the badges. "Megan ain't like that. She might try and fuck *my* ass up, but she ain't gonna bring no fuckin' heat to the club to get her vengeance."

"How can you be so blind, baby?" Kiera said in frustration. "You and her can't be together, Outlaw. It's impossible. You like your cock sucked dry and your balls licked. She will *never* do that. Fuck, I can't even imagine her coming on your tongue. If she do, it won't be the same as when I do it. She'll just fucking lay there not appreciating your pussy licking."

Christopher scowled, which Kiera misinterpreted.

"It's finally sinking in, what I mean," she said softly. She didn't gloat, only showing relief.

Yet, Christopher's annoyance stemmed from all the images her words planted in his mind. Megan enjoyed her pussy being eaten as much as he loved licking her. He almost deserted the party then and there, to spend the rest of the night fucking Megan.

"Have you tried eating her pussy?" Kiera said, fucking fishing again.

"Aintcha fuckin' business, Ki."

"I think you have. All of us know Meggie is a spoiled little princess. If things don't go her way, she fucking flips out. Your life will be so fucking chaotic with her, and not in the way an audacious man like you needs. You'll make all the brothers bend to her will to keep her happy. They'll resent her and you."

He wasn't sure why he was still listening to Kiera. Maybe, it was because he wanted her to get all her worry and fear out of her system so she'd pay attention to his words. Or, maybe, it was because he saw how hurt she was. *Or*, he just fucking hated her desperation when she had no need to be.

"Kiera, I…you…" Fuck. What the fuck could he say? If he agreed that Megan *was* a spoiled little bitch, he'd be betraying her and talking about her behind her back. Worse, it would be to a chick he'd fucking forced on Megan, thinking they'd look out for her. As if *he* was a naïve dickhead that didn't know bitches. However, he never lied to Kiera. They had been friends years before they were lovers. But he couldn't—he just *couldn't*—betray Megan. "You gotta let me and her figure shit out, Ki."

Her lower lip trembled. "I understand you need more than one woman. I know you like to watch two bitches fuck. I can give you that. If you ordered me to find a different woman every week for you, I'd be hurt but I'd do it for you. You could fuck whoever and it wouldn't matter because I'd always be waiting for you with open arms."

"What kinda fuckin' life you willin' to have?" he asked gently. "Cuz that ain't one I fuckin' want. Why fuckin' bother involvin' yourfuckinself with one girl if she ain't givin' a fuck where you stick your cock?"

"Outlaw—"

"Ain't listenin' no more." They'd gotten way off the fucking track. There was no getting through to Kiera, though, so he was done. He returned to the original topic. "Look me in the fuckin' eye and say you expectin', and we gonna see if the kid mine, then go from fuckin' there. But if you lyin' in anyfuckinway, I ain't ever fuckin' forgivin' you."

"So you see a future with Meggie?"

No. He didn't. But that wasn't Kiera's fucking business either. "What my ass seein' with her, aintcha fuckin' business, Ki. I ain't expectin' this to happen with her." Whatever the fuck *it* was. "I ain't even understandin' *why* she fuckin' get to me like she fuckin' do. She just do, babe. She touch something deep in me I ain't able to understand. Cuz she young? Cuz she for Big Joe? Cuz she the most frustratin' lil' pain-in-the-ass motherfucker I ever fuckin' met and she never fuckin' listen to me? She hearin' what the fuck she wanna and fuck me if she ain't agreein'." Just thinking about her made his heart beat faster and tenderness burrow into him. "I ain't ever meant to hurt you, Kiera, and if my fuckin' ass did, I'm sorry. I just wantcha to fuckin' think befuckinfore you say shit cuz you panickin' thinkin' of ways to take me for yourfuckinself."

She nodded. "I'm sorry too," she responded. "I was desperate. I wasn't trying to hurt you."

"You woulda fuckin' hurt *her*, Ki, and that woulda hurt me and pissed me the fuck off. Ain't lyin' when I'm tellin' you you a hot bitch. You ain't gotta be desperate befuckinhind no motherfucker. You gorgeous and you smart and you loyal." He smirked at her. "And your pussy good. Motherfucker gonna be lucky to have you," he reiterated.

She pressed her lips together and her nostrils flared. He knew she was fighting back tears. When she leaned forward and pressed a kissed on his cheek, he laid his hand against her cheek and caressed it. She leaned into his touch. For a moment, he allowed her to, offering her a bit of comfort. He pulled his hand away and realized the other motherfuckers at his table had fallen silent.

"Ki, what are you and Outlaw whispering about?" Ellen demanded, as if on cue.

Kiera backed away from him. "I was asking if he'd remembered to order our favorite drinks."

Christopher slid close to the table again as Ellen got to her feet.

"Let's go and see. Maybe by then, Minnie Mouse will arrive."

With a last look at Christopher, Kiera scampered behind Ellen. He blew out a breath, hoping he hadn't made a fucking mistake by allowing the girls to attend the party. As it was, a fucking pallor hung over the club.

"Prez, Meggie girl really dressing as a fucking mouse?" Mort asked between sips of vodka.

Christopher shrugged, grateful for a new topic. "I ain't sure what the fuck she dressin' as, Mort. She ain't lemme see when she ordered the shit but accordin' to her she dressin' like that mouse." She'd tried to get him in a costume, but he'd held firm. He'd never fucking attended as nothing but the motherfucker he was. Just like the rest of the motherfuckers at his table. Which fucking reminded him. He looked at his cousin. "What the fuck bring you back four fuckin' days after you was fuckin' here, Johnnie?"

The motherfucker smirked at him. "This is Halloween. Snake's probably slithering about. I saw the guns on duty in the parking lot." He shrugged, playing off the fucking fact he was also here because he wanted his cock in Megan. "Even if I hadn't known about the extra security in advance, I would've come. Last year's celebration had been bullshit."

Big Joe had been fucking dead only for a few days and Christopher had been installed as interim that same night. The day before Halloween an emergency election had been held and he'd beat out Rack to stay president. There had been a lot of contention at last year's party, and it marked the last time Snake had come to the club with Christopher as president.

"It was important this party go on," Mortician agreed. He glanced around, a brief sadness crossing his face. Maybe, he was thinking about times past. Shit had been so fucking good then. "Show other motherfuckers we stand behind Outlaw."

Val swallowed tequila, nodded. "Show we solid."

Digger reached for an unopened chocolate peanut butter candy. "Remind motherfuckers we not backing down."

"It's a good showing," Johnnie agreed, taking in the room as if he searched for something or someone. Or, maybe, like Christopher, haunted by the ghosts of Halloweens past.

Unlike the other night, decorations had been hung, bowls of candy placed on each table and the bar. Celebrating Halloween was part of club tradition and had happened for as long as Christopher remembered. It marked the beginning of the holiday season, a mostly peaceful and happy time.

Tonight, he felt Big Joe's loss to his bones. It had always been fun and games. No girls scheming to get him anyway she could. No young bitches that drove him fucking crazy. Whatever fucking problems he thought he had back then was fucking nothing compared to now.

He tried to remember his hatred for the dirty motherfucker, but even that escaped him. When Big Joe had been alive and in his right mind, Christopher's ma attended some of the holiday events. Even that had had to stop because he didn't fucking trust Patricia not to be in danger, so he kept her from the club and, in turn, stayed far away from her.

He rubbed the back of his neck.

Johnnie caught Christopher's gaze. "Are you okay?" he asked, his concern hard to miss.

"I ain't too fuckin' sure," Christopher admitted. But Megan being there, amusing him, tempting him, caring for him, and challenging him, helped. She somehow soothed his inner turmoil, until he remembered he was the motherfucker that killed her father. He tasted his rum. "Rack bringin' his fuckin' table out, challengin' motherfuckers to get on that torture device for ten fuckin' minutes."

"Bruh." Digger released a noisy breath. "Boss let Rack keep it in that lean-to in the forest. Why he can't tell motherfuckers to go there if they want to try it? Fuck, it's the perfect setting. In a dark woods where Big Joe took motherfuckers alive and they came out unalive. *And* it's in the old building that used to be the club. It got to be haunted. Even the ghost of motherfucking Logan…er…"

"Shut the fuck up," Johnnie snarled.

Digger glanced at Mortician, then peeped at Val, Johnnie, and Christopher before bowing his head. "Sorry," he mumbled.

One day, those motherfuckers would confess the truth. Until then, Christopher wouldn't fucking sweat it. Wherever Logan was, and in hell didn't seem to be that fucking place, as long as he stayed the fuck away from Christopher, shit would be fine.

"Rack and his rack a Halloween tradition," Val said into the silence.

Just like that, motherfuckers got back on track.

Mort grimaced. "Big Joe shouldn't have never let him start that bullshit," he said in disgust.

"Boss shouldna never did a lot of fuckin' shit," Christopher snapped, heaving in a breath, grateful that Mort's words rekindled Christopher's hatred toward Big Joe. But it also brought to mind Kiera's vehemence that Megan wasn't fit for club life.

"What up, Prez?" Val asked, and they all looked at him.

"Shit gonna be intense with that fuckin' table," he responded.

"Meggie?" Val, Mort, and Digger chorused.

He nodded. "She a lil' hellcat, but this life…" Bleakness settled into him. "She a good, sweet girl. I was fuckin' livid at her lil' skimpy outfit the other night. But she went from a angel to a lil' fuckin' goddess. For a fuckin' moment, I ain't even thought…I ain't thought 'bout her *not* bein' able to handle us. *Me.* My fuckin' life."

"Prez, chicks fucking trip," Mortician told him. "Ellen would push Ki out the fucking door if it meant having you to herself. Looking at those two tonight, and listening to them, we all know the bullshit they was handing out. No fucking way Meggie girl could've been the sexy bitch that walked in the other night after one fucking day of instructions."

"But was she truly comfortable?" Johnnie inserted. "Was she just playing a role for your sake?"

"Meggie age don't bother you, Outlaw?" Digger asked and took a sip of his drink.

"Nope. She legal."

"Prez, for the years I've known you, you stay so fucking far away from young bitches," Mortician said. "Think about Hopper."

So named because she hopped from one motherfucker's bed to another.

"You was twenty-one and she was eighteen and you didn't want her."

Christopher rubbed his brow. "What the fuck my ass supposed to fuckin' say, Mort? I'm 'bout tired of hearin' 'bout her fuckin' age. One thing Megan givin' me that no bitch did is her trust and faith in me. She ain't seein' *Outlaw.* She seein' *Christopher.*"

"Unless you a split personality motherfucker, you know they the same, huh, Prez?" Digger asked curiously.

"Fuck off, assfuck," Christopher growled. "You know what the fuck my ass meanin'. Megan believe in me like nobody, motherfucker or bitch, ever done."

"She doesn't know the real—"

"Outlaw," Mortician interrupted Johnnie and glared at him, "if Meggie what you want *and* she withstand our life, we standing behind you, doing whatever you need. We'll keep her safe and we'll help you help her navigate this strange new world. If she make you happy that's all we can ask. And Ellen right. You can't make no motherfucker like Meggie or give her real respect. It's up to her. So far, she doing a fine fucking job."

"I concur," Johnnie said into the silence. "You deserve happiness. Megan…" His voice trailed off and he seemed to search for words.

"If you stick your cock in her, Ima fuckin' hack off your goddamn face with a spade."

Unperturbed, Johnnie grinned. "I'm not touching her unless you release her to us like usual."

If Mort anticipated that happening in the future, he kept his thoughts to himself. Unlike every other fucking assfuck at his table.

"We don't need a fucking cock war between you two paths," Digger grumbled.

"Paths?" Christopher echoed. "What the fuck that mean?"

"Psycho and Socio," Val volunteered.

"Kiss my motherfuckin' psycho ass," Christopher said around laughter.

"Megan's just a girl," Johnnie said with a shrug. "Like every other girl here. No more. No less."

"She forbidden fruit, John Boy," Mortician said.

Val drained his bottle and leaned back in his chair. "You forget we been knowing you a long time too, Johnnie."

"Yeah," Digger agreed. "Not only is you a stone-cold killer, you a fucking hunter. You thrive on the chase. That's why that bitch caught your attention and got you to leave the fucking club."

"And Megan not just a girl," Mortician said with a sigh, revealing what she'd said about her mother when Christopher had been in surgery. "She brave and she loyal. She's a fierce little motherfucker." Grief settled into his eyes and he swallowed. "Boss…Big Joe loved her so fucking much. I look at her sometimes and all I can fucking see is him. His head—" He closed his eyes. "Fuck, man."

"You ever hate a motherfucker but love him too?" Val asked, leaning his elbows on the table and staring at Christopher.

"Yeah, Val," he said quietly, the sorrow he tried so hard to ignore threatening to set in. Ruthlessly, he shoved it aside. "Big Joe deserve every fuckin' thing he got," he said flatly. "He almost destroyed all us motherfuckers."

They all nodded in agreement then fell into their fucking memories, looking away from each other.

"Fuck," Val groaned a minute later. He was still leaning back in his chair, able to have a partial view of the hallway. "Fuck everything Kiera and Ellen said. Meggie did it again and made them out to be fucking liars."

"What—"

Megan walking into the room stopped him.

"Fucking Meggie, man," Mortician grumbled, shrugging at Christopher's scowl.

"Fuck, I just got a new appreciation for Minnie Mouse," Johnnie breathed.

Mortician snickered as Christopher got to his feet.

Digger whistled. "Meggie in the house," he whooped, and she smiled at him.

She sure the fuck *was* in the fucking house. And…*fuck him.*

Megan's version of Minnie had her dressed in a pink and black polka dot outfit, belted at the waist, with an ass-length hemline one pussy bend from exposure. Her tits sat high, almost spilling out the fucking low-cut neckline. Black mouse ears fronted by a bow that matched the costume sat on her head. Knee-high stockings, each with a bow at the top, led to black, shiny pumps that had to be at least seven inches.

"What do you think?" she said, unknowingly mimicking Kiera's exact actions.

Where Ki had her hair in an updo, Megan's hair was wild and curly, streaming down her back.

"You so fuckin' gorgeous," he said, wondering why the fuck she wanted to waste herself on him.

She beamed a smile. "Thank you," she said happily, then turned to the table. "Hey, Johnnie." She waved at the other motherfuckers.

"Fuck," Ellen said, returning to the table with Kiera and glaring at Megan. "You said you were dressing as Minnie Mouse."

Hands on hips, Megan narrowed her eyes. "Happy Halloween," she said sweetly, too fucking sweet.

Kiera thumped Ellen's shoulder. "Hey, babe." She studied Megan, head-to-heel. Anger flared in her eyes and her mouth tightened before she pulled in a breath and pasted a smile on her face. "Where'd you get your costume? I'm obsessed."

Megan rolled her eyes at Kiera's blatant bullshit. It was fucking obvious neither her or Ellen was happy that Megan had managed to beat them at their own fucking game.

Returning to his seat and throwing Kiera and Ellen an unspoken warning, Christopher crooked his finger at Megan. When she reached him, he pulled her onto his lap.

"So, Megan," Ellen said, once she and Kiera had taken seats across from each other. Judging by the gleam in her eyes, she intended to fuck with Megan. "Do you like Halloween?"

"Christmas is my favorite holiday," Megan answered, seeming unaware of Ellen's intentions. "Didn't you tell me yours was Thanksgiving, Christopher?"

"Nope," Kiera put in. "You're wrong, Meggie. Outlaw's favorite holiday is Halloween."

Christopher exchanged an amused glance with Mortician. Right on cue, Megan shook her head.

"Noooo," she said. "Big Joe's favorite holiday is, er, *was* Halloween. *Christopher's* is Thanksgiving."

"Ha!" Ellen smirked. "Both you stupid bitches are wrong. Outlaw doesn't like any holidays."

"Uh, yeah, he do, Ellen" Mort said without heat. "Meggie right. Prez like Thanksgiving."

"Cuz that motherfucker get lost between Halloween and Christmas," Digger added.

"Outlaw felt sorry for Thanksgiving," Val said.

"Tell them," Kiera ordered, looking at Christopher. "Ellen must've forgotten and Meggie just doesn't know. What reason would you have to talk about your favorite holiday with her?"

"Ladies, this is getting out of hand," Johnnie said calmly, taking in every inch of Megan's face before finally looking at Kiera. "Ki, it isn't important what Christopher's favorite holiday is. We're here to party not argue."

"You're right, Johnnie," Megan agreed, sitting on his lap as stiff as a board and madder than a motherfucker but trying to wrestle her temper under control.

Ellen's eyes gleamed. "You're right, Ki. I did forget how much Outlaw loves Halloween." Smiling, she nudged Kiera. "Thanks for the reminder."

Megan drew in a deep breath, but Christopher had seen and heard enough.

He grabbed his bottle and drained it, energized by the feel of her hair brushing his arm and the scent of her.

"Megan right. Thanksgiving my favorite holiday," he said flatly.

Twisting in his lap, Megan kissed his jaw and he winked at her. The pleasure on her face made him grin like a fucking lunatic.

"Well, wow," Ellen conceded. "This is news to me. Did you know Outlaw's favorite holiday, Ki?"

Kiera shook her head. "No, I don't think he ever told us."

Ellen focused on Megan, her eyes turning to blue ice. She'd started off mildly but Outlaw knew Ellen's claws were fully unsheathed now.

"Megan insisted you two bitches come to the fuckin' party, Ellen," Christopher warned. He'd allowed the bitchy bullshit so he could assess just how much Megan could take from other girls. "If you turn into a fuckin' cunt, I ain't givin' a fuck what the fuck she say to my ass, you ain't ever gonna set foot in this motherfucker again. Hear me?"

"How do you usually spend Halloween, Meggie?" Val asked quickly.

Kiera swigged from Mort's vodka. "Trick or treating, probably," she giggled, laughing more when Ellen chuckled.

Christopher opened his mouth to speak, but Megan interrupted him.

"I like haunted houses," she said, unbothered by the bitchery. "I stopped trick or treating years ago. I stopped after twelve but then when I started a new school and met my two best friends, they convinced me to give it another try."

"That's adorable, babe," Kiera said.

"It's a happy memory," Megan told her, a smile in her voice. "One that I cherish. So I skipped the year I turned thirteen."

"Awww, that's sweet," Ellen cooed.

"You would've went if you were home?" Val asked, his eyes wide.

When Megan nodded, Mort winced. Johnnie lifted a brow and looked at Christopher. What the fuck could he say? He merely fucking shrugged.

"If you miss twick or tweeting too much, Meggie-Weggie, I can dwive you to a neighborhood."

Kiera made a face at Ellen. "Stop, dummy," she ordered.

"Yeah, fuckin—"

"It's fine," Megan interrupted him. "Ppreciate the offer," she said, and Christopher knew she was mimicking either Mort or Digger. "But I'm fine. No candy-wandy for Meggie-Weggie," she teased, standing and going to the bar, squeezing between Traveler and another motherfucker to talk to Bowlie, since Mort had taken the night off from bartending.

Christopher watched as Bowlie handed her another pint of rum, then followed her with a tray, containing everybody else's drink.

"You know little kids trick-or-treat?" Digger said with disapproval after Bowlie left. "That's some freaky sounding shit, Meggie, considering you here with us motherfuckers and fucking *that* motherfucker."

Megan chuckled, the words halting her from returning to Christopher's lap. "I know, right? I didn't go last Halloween," she admitted, a brief, haunted expression clouding her face. "But the first year I went with Farrah and Lacey, we went trick-or-treating through Farrah's neighborhood. At one particular house, there was a party going on. It was a frat house or something and the boys filled our bags with beer and wine coolers." She giggled. "Luckily, I was spending the weekend there."

"You drank?" Val asked.

"Yep," Megan answered. "One wine cooler and one beer and I was lit."

"Fuck, you're not supposed to mix that shit," Mortician chastised.

"Now you tell me," Megan said merrily. "Between that experience and the way Thomas gets…" Her voice trailed off and she swallowed. "Well, drinking alcohol isn't for me."

"Boring," Ellen chimed in.

Megan shrugged, seemingly still in a good mood because Christopher had backed her up.

"Well, fuck, that's not too bad," Digger conceded. "If that's what you did on Halloween."

"Aren't you bozos listening?" Ellen blared. "She said drinking wasn't for her, so the other times she hit the bricks for candy."

"The second year we did," Megan agreed. "In Lacey's neighborhood. We almost got arrested." She rocked on her heels. "*I* almost got us arrested. Lacey's girlfriend followed us. I don't know why the dummy wouldn't think Jacey wouldn't. She was so possessive—"

"Wait, hold on," Digger interrupted. "Lacey and Jacey."

Megan threw her hands up. "Exactly. Can you believe that's why they started dating? Because their names matched. Anyway, Jacey was the most beautiful girl in the entire school, so—"

"Then you must've gone to a different school than she did," Digger said.

Megan stared at him, then broke into peals of laughter. "Thank you," she said, laughing her fucking ass off.

"Fine, the shit lame," Digger said, chuckling. "But it's true."

"Thank you. Really," Megan said. "And I know you're not flirting. If you were—"

"You'd laugh in his fuckin' face and send him the fuck away," Christopher guessed.

She nodded. "Jacey was gorgeous, but she was really possessive and jealous. So she told Lacey she had something to do and the moron believed her and made a date with another girl. Luckily, Farrah and me saw Jacey before she discovered Lacey making out with that other girl…" Her voice trailed off and she thought a moment. "Well, making out is putting it mildly."

"How the fuck you almost gettin' arrested then?" Christopher asked, fascinated by her stories. It was giving him a little more insight into her. Despite everything they'd shared while they recovered from their separate ailments, she'd never discussed these particular times.

"Farrah told me to get Lacey, while she kept Jacey occupied. I barge in on them and…" She wrinkled her nose. "*Anyway*," she huffed, "I finally told Lacey she either leave with me *now* or all hell would break loose. She told me she'd met up with me and Farrah to be her decoys because she figured Jacey would show up. In other words, she'd used us as the morons. I told her she was on her own and left. By the time I leave the house, Jacey is in the yard and her cheeks are all scratched up. Farrah's lip is bleeding and she's crying. Those two are in front of me. Behind me, here comes Lacey and her hookup. Jacey grabs my hair, yanks me out of the way and shoves me to the ground. I was already furious. In that entire time, I still hand my bag of candy. So I used it like a mace and knocked Jacey out."

Mort's mouth fell open. "You didn't."

The way she cringed Christopher knew she fucking had.

"I did. The other girl started screaming that I killed her. It was awful. All these people ran to the house. Somebody called the police. As the light were getting closer, Farrah grabbed my hand and said we needed to run. We hid in the shadows of someone's house for an hour or more. I just knew I was going to jail." She glanced at the floor. "I called Daddy and told him what happened. He was at a party...probably here," she realized. "He couldn't talk long but he told me not to worry. I talked to him maybe two or three times after that and never heard from him again."

Tears shone in her eyes, but she plastered a smile on her face. She turned on her heel and went to the bar, whispering to Bowlie, that short little skirt and the glimpse of her ass cheeks turning Christopher's cock to stone.

Once Bowlie handed her a bottled Coke, she came back, fully in control again. "Anyway, Jacey had awakened by the time the cops made it through the crowd and nothing came of it."

Her mouth against the lip of the bottle made Christopher groan. She licked her lips.

"I told Lacey I was never going anywhere with her again. Omigod, Thomas would've killed me if I'd gotten arrested."

And just like that, Christopher's cock deflated. It wasn't the mention of Thomas but the thought of Megan being killed.

"Uh, that's two Halloweens," Kiera said quickly. She'd been staring at him and must've seen his rising anger.

Christopher knew she couldn't give less of a fuck about Megan's holidays.

"Yes! Year before last, when Farrah decided it would be a good idea for me to have sex and almost ruined my life." Megan rolled her eyes, tasted more of her Coke.

Rage slid into Christopher, even though he knew she'd been a virgin. A wave of possessiveness roared through him and left his ears ringing.

"They claimed they wanted me to go on my first date. Fine. Whatever. I couldn't blame them for their perception that I was a snob because I never told them why I never admitted to liking anyone."

"Thomas?" Mortician guessed.

"Yep," Megan said with a sigh.

"Our night started out like all the others. With us trooping past the parents. We were back at Farrah's house."

Realization dawned on Christopher. "Fuck me. You three lil' bitches ain't wanted to go trick-or-fuckin-treatin'. You said that shit to get the fuck outta the house."

Grinning, she nodded. "Exactly." She finished her Coke and sashayed to a trash can on the other side of the bar, pausing to talk to those who spoke to her.

"Fuck, man," Mort's grumble pulled Christopher's attention away from Megan as K-P walked in and Megan went and hugged him. "If I ever have a kid and she a girl, just fucking kill me.

"If you ever have a kid, just fucking kill *me*," Digger retorted. "Baby'll break my fucking bank in a month. Your stingy ass wouldn't want to buy it nothing."

Mort flipped Digger off as K-P guided Megan to the pool tables, so she could greet Stretch.

"Fuck," Johnnie said, staring at her.

"How does it feel not to be the club's celebrated beauty anymore, Ki?" Ellen demanding, the look she gave Johnnie filled with venom.

Kiera's high-pitched laugh covered her hurt. "It don't matter to me, Ellie, so shut up."

"Megan has done nothing to you, Ellen," Johnnie offered, still looking at Megan. "Nor has she sought anyone's attention, so set your sights on another target. What we're giving her is on us, not her."

"You can't tell me what to do, Johnnie."

"He fuckin' can't, but my ass can," Christopher told her. "Ima tell you one last fuckin' time. *Befuckinhave*. If youda shut the fuck up 'bout the goddamn holidays shit woulda died the fuck down."

"How is it my fault she's a pissy little attention seeker, Outlaw?" Ellen cried. "We didn't ask the little cunt to tell her life fucking story."

Christopher got to his feet, but Kiera rushed to him and laid her palms against his chest.

"She don't mean nothing," she said frantically. "Besides, Meggie want us here and Ellen is right. We don't want to hear about her stupid fucking stories."

He would've responded if he didn't see Megan floating toward him. She reached him and stared at Kiera until Ki backed away and Megan took her place.

"Hey," she said softly. "What's up?"

A whole barrel of bullshit. Instead of saying that, Christopher took her face between his hands and kissed her lips.

"Ain't nothin', baby," he said gruffly, her nearness, her *sweetness*, calming him.

"Meggie!" Cowboy called. "Betcha don't remember your old man favorite song."

Standing on her tiptoes, she tugged Christopher's head and brushed her lips over his, then turned. "Bet I do," she replied.

He nodded to the juke box. "Prove it," he said good naturedly.

"If he botherin' you, I can throw him the fuck out," Christopher said.

She turned to him and blinked, her look as incredulous as Mort's, Johnnie's Digger's, and Val's.

"I'm fine," she said, her look tender. "I can stay here if you want me to."

"You within eyesight," he told her. "So you can go."

Her brows snapped together. "I wasn't asking your permission to go. I was volunteering to stay with you." She placed her hands on her hips. "You are aware there's a difference?"

He scowled. "If I ain't wantin' you to fuckin' go, you ain't fuckin' goin'."

She turned. "You think?" she tossed over her shoulder.

If she had stomped away, he might've descended into anger but the way she fucking strutted, her hips swinging, her hair flirting with her nearly exposed ass cheeks took everything away but the need to fuck her.

She barely paused to snatch money from Cowboy before continuing to the jukebox.

A moment later, *Pour Some Sugar On Me* by Def Leopard started to play. Cowboy went to her and took her in his arms, dancing.

There was a good-sized crowd, but not many old ladies were there and no fucking Bobs. Christopher realized it was because motherfuckers weren't as at-easy as they pretended. Knowing Rack would bring his table *did* cast a pall over everything.

Ellen and Kiera went to the area where Megan was dancing and beckoned K-P and Shady.

"Prez?" Mortician called. "You okay?"

Christopher shrugged. Because he wasn't okay and hadn't been since he pulled that fucking trigger.

"You did what you had to do, Christopher," Johnnie said, raising his voice just enough to be heard over Big Joe's favorite song.

"The man Big Joe once was was gone, Outlaw," Val said.

"Ain't givin' a fuck 'bout that motherfucker," he insisted. "What the fuck that motherfucker was befuckinfore ain't matterin'. He was a girl killer." Christopher scraped his fingers over his scalp. "Not only grown ones neither. He was a fuckin' dog deservin' to be put fuckin' down."

He glanced in Megan's direction, taking in all the joy on her face as she danced with Cowboy. She'd loved Big Joe so fucking much. If she ever found out the truth, it wouldn't matter to her why Christopher killed her daddy.

"Prez, the only way you ever going to take control is to get fucking control," Mortician told him. "And until you forgive yourself, neither one of those things ever happening."

He could forgive himself all he fucking wanted to, but it was Megan's forgiveness that mattered to him. Something he knew he'd never get and didn't even deserve.

"Meggie a good girl, Outlaw, with a head on her shoulders." Mortician added. "She might be hurt and even angry, but once she hear the facts, she'll understand."

"What she thinkin' her business. Ain't got fuck all to do with my ass." Even as he said that, he felt as if he betrayed her.

"If you really feel that way, then give us a chance with her," Johnnie said, sparing him a brief look to impart that before looking at Megan again.

"If you fuckin' touch her, John Boy, Ima kill you," Christopher said viciously, meaning every word. He glared at each of his boys. "That shit go for all you motherfuckers."

Johnnie gave him a lazy look. "Even if she wants me to touch her?"

"Shut your fucking ass the fuck up, son," Mortician ordered. "I got on a new shirt and I don't want your fucking brain spatter ruining it."

"I know that fucking dollar you paid for it probably gave you nightmares," Digger quipped, "so we understand, bruh."

"Let's just drop this subject," Val suggested. "Once Rack and his fucking table come and go, we can all relax."

That shut them the fuck up.

"She did her old man proud, Outlaw," Cowboy said, escorting Megan back to the table, once the song ended.

"You said you were dressing as Minnie Mouse," Ellen said sharply, as she and Kiera returned to the table.

"I *am* dressed as Minnie Mouse, Ellen," Megan replied.

"No, you aren't," Ellen retorted. "You're dressed like a fuck doll."

"Umkay," Megan said. "And the problem with that is…?"

"What do you know about fucking?" Ellen demanded.

That was fucking it. Christopher buried his nose in Megan's hair and breathed in, her sweet scent intoxicating him. "Move. Lemme throw these two fuckin' bitches out."

"Why?" Ellen snapped. "We aren't doing anything to her."

"You fuckin' is," Christopher said, wrapping an arm around Megan's waist to move her.

"It's fine, Christopher," she insisted. "Truly."

"Megan—"

"I'm *fine*," she said again, this time with annoyance.

She was, but he fucking wasn't. Ellen was intent on stirring the fucking pot.

"I don't know a lot about sex," Megan admitted, then licked her lips and sent him a sexy look. She slid back onto his lap. "Yet."

The addition of that one word made Christopher's cock jump.

"As for the costume, the moment I saw it I fell in love with it. If I was at home, I wouldn't have been allowed to reveal so much of my body. Having the option to choose is freeing. That's why I know so much about makeup and was able to know exactly the look I wanted. Sometimes I had no choice in staying home and other times I just thought it best so I could be there if my mom needed anything. I think that was the real reason I stopped going trick-or-treating." She sighed and shifted, her little ass wiggling against his dick. He wondered if she even realized he was ready to bring her to their room and fuck her into oblivion. "We stopped giving out candy too. Halloween just wasn't the same anymore."

"What? You stopped getting gummy bears and animal crackers?" Kiera laughed. "Or your mama got tired of checking your candy for open wrappers and sharp objects?"

"You're hilarious, Ki," Ellen guffawed, despite the discomfort at the table. "That's it, huh, Meggie babe? Just so you don't despair this Halloween like it sounds like you did the previous one, I'll run out and buy you the gummy bears and animal crackers."

"Don't forget the punch and sippy cup, Ellie," Kiera added.

"You two are so lame. I spent last Halloween wondering if my ribs were broken after Thomas beat me because he heard I'd smiled at a boy at school." Megan laid a finger against her cheek, ignoring Christopher's anger turning to rage. "That was after I helped Momma clean her face of semen and tend to her cuts and bruises. How'd you spend yours?" she said sarcastically.

"Fuck, man," Mort grumbled.

"I never finished telling you about Halloween before last—"

"Shut the fuck up, Megan," Christopher snarled, "if you ain't wantin' me to ride the fuck out and gut that motherfucker."

"You can't go around killing people who've wronged you," Megan admonished.

The fuck he couldn't. He could—

She got to her feet and the thought fell away.

"I'm going to the room."

She sounded so sad, Christopher wanted to draw her into his arms and protect her from everything. She might've thought she could handle bitches and motherfuckers, but she was too fucking gentle and soft. Just as Ellen and Kiera said and wanted to prove with this conversation. The moment Megan left, he was throwing those two bitches off the fucking premises. His glare must've clued them the fuck in, because suddenly Ellen was on her feet and blocking Megan's escape.

"I'm sorry," she said quickly. "We like to joke. That's it."

"Meggie, don't go," Kiera said, throwing a nervous glance at Christopher. "Ellie's right. We joke around a lot. We don't mean any harm."

Shaking her head, Megan glanced up before closing her eyes. She heaved in a breath, then opened her eyes again and gazed between Ellen and Kiera. "I'm trying. I really, really am. Christopher tossed us together." She threw him the evil eye. "I know you both love the club, so I'm trying not to stand in your way of being here and I'm trying to get used to all the women around all the time. But you're not taking digs at me and you're not playing me for a fool. The *only* reason you want me to stay is because you know once I leave, *you* leave. I'm choosing to stay, but just leave me in peace. Stay. Go. Dance naked under the moon. I don't care." She turned to Christopher, her eyes frantic. "I need to call my mother. It's Halloween. Thomas has probably beaten her black and blue."

Fuck, Thomas wasn't able to do a motherfucking thing right now, but if Megan called her ma, Christopher might have some explaining to do.

"Megan, baby, only fuckin' thing'll happen if you fuckin' call your ma is you worryin' more cuz you ain't able to fuckin' be there," he said.

Jamming his cigarette in the corner of his mouth, Mort got to his feet. "You like dancing?" he asked her, then looked at Christopher, a question in his eyes.

Christopher nodded seeing the way her eyes lit up and some of the fucking fear and anguish left her face, so Mort took Megan's hand and led her to the empty space between the bar, entryway, and pool area. He bent and whispered, his hand gestures and finger twirls revealing he explained the dance to her.

Christopher intended to order Kiera and Ellen away, but he couldn't turn his attention away from Megan. As if she felt his gaze on her, she looked his way and blew him a kiss, not caring who saw how much she cared about him. Right now, she wasn't looking at him or any of them with lust. It was about friendship and affection.

Trust.

Finally, Mort's tutorial ended, and she nodded. He turned and summoned one of the club girls. A moment later, she headed to the jukebox.

"How much you want to fucking bet Mort putting on the *Electric Boogie?*" Digger said with disgust, a moment before the song started. "Fuck, Mort, that song fifty fucking years old."

Mort flipped him off, then beckoned him over. Digger got to his feet as others joined in, but Christopher couldn't take his eyes off Megan. At first, she didn't get the moves right, yet it didn't take her long to fall into line, those high fucking shoes not hampering her one bit.

When the dance ended, Megan pulled on Mort's hand, and he bent, listening to whatever she told him. Once he relayed her message, another song came on—*Achy Breaky Heart*. It was her turn to teach Mort and Digger. At the conclusion, she followed Mort back to the table. Christopher tugged her between the vee of his legs and settled his hands on her ass, stealing a few kisses from her.

"Do you want to dance, Christopher?" she asked.

"Not on your motherfuckin' life," he said with a grin. "My ass ain't a fuckin' dancer."

She sat on his lap. "Are any of you?" she asked the table at large.

Kiera raised a hand. "I am."

Megan nodded. "Wh-what's your favorite song?" she asked, her strained tone hard to miss.

Rack opening the door and directing four brothers to carry his fucking table in halted the conversation. All the noise in the club screeched to a fucking halt.

"Who wants to test their will against my table?" Rack called, after it had been put in the space where Megan had been dancing.

"What in God's name is that?" she squeaked.

"Come and see, Meggie," Rack said.

"That's the fuckin' reason motherfucker got the road name he do," Christopher confessed.

"That looks like a Medieval contraption," she responded, her brow creasing.

"It is, sweetheart," Johnnie answered.

"Big Joe always got a kick out of it," Rack added. "Especially at our Halloween parties." He met Christopher's gaze with a cold one of his own. "Remember those days, Outlaw? When Big Joe was alive?"

"Shut the fuck up," Christopher warned, glaring at Rack. The motherfucker didn't know for certain that Christopher had killed Boss, but he didn't need him opening his big fucking mouth to Megan.

"What about *you*, Meggie?" Rack continued. "Do you recall your old man being alive and vital?"

She slid to her feet, and Christopher got to his, starting forward.

"He baiting you, Outlaw," Mortician said, as some of the men aligned with Rack gathered around him.

"Christopher, don't," Johnnie warned. "This is what he wants."

"What 'bout what the fuck my ass want?"

"What the fuck is that?" Johnnie demanded, low. "Let *us* know, so we can deal with these stupid motherfuckers."

"Omigod, why do you all have parties, Rack?"

Megan's voice grabbed Christopher's attention. In the moment it took him to talk to Mortician and Johnnie, she had gone to Rack and stopped directly in front of him.

"What do you mean by that?" Rack asked. "I would think that's obvious. To fuck and drink and bring the brothers together. To remember old times." He nodded to the table that had leather foot and hand straps, spikes as a pillow, and pulleys to snap tendons and break bones. "To remind the brothers the type of entertainment Big Joe enjoyed."

Christopher went to the door, nodding to Rack as he passed him. "Take a fuckin' walk with me, motherfucker."

"Rack, why are you doing this?" Megan asked.

"Stay the fuck outta club business, Megan," Christopher ordered.

"I don't know what you mean, Meggie," Rack answered, blatantly ignoring Christopher's direct command.

"Come on, Meggie," Kiera said as Mort, Val, Digger, and Johnnie followed Christopher to where Rack stood. "Let's go to the room."

K-P and Stretch abandoned their places by the pool tables and joined the four already around Christopher.

"Yeah, babe," Ellen said, uneasy. "We don't have a place here right now."

"No."

"Megan—"

When she looked at him with a plea in her eyes, he snapped his mouth shut.

"I'm so sorry. I know I should leave. I don't mean to interfere, but I just have to say this."

"No interference, Meggie," Rack murmured. "Especially from you. You Big Joe girl. Whatever you have to say, we're duty-bound to hear. That works both ways, though."

"I don't want to start this off with contention," Megan said.

"You ain't startin' shit at fuckin' all. Get the fuck outta here."

"No, Christopher. I'm saying what I have to say to Rack *now* with you listening, my preference, or later whether you're with me or not."

He stiffened. She was fucking challenging his authority, making him look like a fucking dickhead and—

"Prez," Mort whispered next to him. "Let her get it off her chest. She'll be happy and we can deal with this motherfucker in peace."

"Me and you talkin' later, Megan," Christopher snarled, Kiera's words haunting him.

Megan nodded.

Rack grinned at her and Christopher hated him a little more. But this shit was his fault. The day he killed Big Joe was the day he lost control on the pulse of the club.

"What do you want to say, Meggie?" Rack taunted into the silence.

"I know I can't speak anytime, Rack," she said evenly. "Not even as Big Joe's daughter. I'm not a member of the club and I'm not a man."

Interest lit Rack's piggy eyes and he lit a smoke before he shrugged. "Say what you got to say."

She glanced at Christopher, the first sign of uneasiness entering her expression. But he was fucking annoyed with her, so he folded his arms and glared at her.

Megan tossed her hair and faced Rack again. "You say you're honoring Daddy," she started.

"I am," Rack said with a smirk, smoke curling around his head like the devil's spawn he was.

"You're a liar," Megan said, cold, precise, shocking the ever living fuck out of Christopher. He and his boys exchanged glances.

"Watch your fucking mouth, Meggie," Rack ordered.

"Bite me, moron," she retorted. "You beat me to a pulp. How is *that* honoring Boss?"

Rack seemed as taken aback by that question as every other motherfucker there.

"I don't know much of what Big Joe did, but I *do* know he loved me," Megan spat, giving Rack the once over as if she and that motherfucker was the same size. "Once I told you who I was, I saw it in your eyes that you'd heard about me. Big Joe...Big Joe would've...Before I left home, I wanted to find Big Joe so he'd make Thomas disappear. It was an abstract thought, thought of in fear and desperation. I didn't think he'd do it in the literal sense," she said softly. "I understand the truth now. And Daddy would've gotten rid of him."

"Your point?" Rack asked, sounding bored. He threw the cigarette to the ground and stomped it with his boot.

"You're in here with that stupid table—"

Fucked up table, Christopher supplied.

"And that stupid grin—"

Shit eating.

"And spouting your stupid words—"

Hypocritical.

"Because you're a big, mean rhinoceros."

Fat balled, fuckface motherfucker.

"You're trying to incite an argument when *you* seemed to have forgotten when my father was alive. You're disrespecting the club he loved and you're dishonoring *him*. *You*, not Christopher. Not any of the men here. You, Rack. And we both know—" She glanced around. "We *all* know if Big Joe was the father from my memory and he found out what you did to me, *you* would've disappeared."

"You stole from me."

"It was five dollars, jerk," she yelled.

"Big Joe would've understood," he replied.

"Oh no, he wouldn't have," Megan retorted. "Because I told you I was hungry. I hadn't eaten in two days. Most of all, I was his baby girl, so you say what you want, but your days would've been numbered just for that. And the club?" she snarled. "He never told me the truth about the type of club it was, but he loved this club. It was his everything. I have heard everything I was told about him the night I found out he'd never come back. You're overlooking the man he became to honor him? Remember him as he once was? Either way, your words are meaningless. You're either disrespecting Big Joe and everything this club meant to him or you're using him as mockery. Or both."

"You finished?" he demanded.

"Are you?" she shot back.

"I paid for what I did to you." Rack nodded to Christopher. "That motherfucker carved fucking words in my back."

"Oh, so sorry," she said sarcastically. "I hope you didn't cry too long."

"You're a little fucking bitch," he snarled.

"It takes a little bitch to know one," she retorted.

"Goddamn, girl," Ellen said with a shocked laugh.

"Come on, Megan," Christopher said, grabbing her arm, glad when she didn't resist and started to turn to him.

"I miss Big Joe, Meggie," Rack admitted, and she froze.

"We all do, Rack," she said, glancing at him. "That doesn't give you the license to make a mockery of a club celebration. Wasn't there enough violence when the club was shot up? You're doing the most. And for what? You and your friends are on that side? Christopher and his friends are on this side? And you have all these people in the middle. The *only* reason shots haven't been fired is because I'm talking to you. If I would've left, war would've broken out when you all escaped death only weeks ago."

"When you accused me of setting Outlaw up," Rack said, his anger returning.

"As if you're doing anything to make me believe otherwise," she said sharply.

Rack blinked at her and took a step but stopped at the warning Christopher threw him.

"Dinah wouldn't never think to confront me," Rack told her.

"You know my mother?" Megan blurted as surprised as Christopher.

"I've met her a couple times. Years ago. Before she was pregnant with you. She probably wouldn't remember me. I remember her because she was so sweet and shy." He looked her up and down. "Unlike *you*."

"I'm my father's daughter, and I don't suffer fools. I am, and always will be, a fighter. That makes me my mother's protector. Big Joe would expect no less from me. He would *expect* me to try and talk some sense into you."

"This club business, Meggie," Rack said.

Megan fucking *laughed*. "So it wasn't club business when I disrespected and disobeyed Christopher by refusing to leave but it is because you don't like what I'm saying?"

Rack grabbed onto her words and smirked. "You did both and made Outlaw a laughingstock amongst the brothers."

"No—"

"Yeah," he insisted. "You have. This not a stage play where a young cunt gives an inspiring speech and suddenly everything better. This is real life with real men and real issues."

Megan sighed and her shoulders slumped. Christopher wasn't sure what she'd expected and he hated to agree with Rack but the motherfucker was right. She'd just created more problems for Christopher and made him seem even weaker because he hadn't demanded she leave.

"Did you ever want to be president, Rack?" she asked.

"Megan, efuckinnuff," Christopher snapped, grabbing her arm to jerk her to him.

"Yeah, I did," Rack said, drawing the shit out to further humiliate Christopher. But the damage was done, so he released her without warning.

She squeaked and stumbled.

"Why do you ask?" Rack said before she could even look at Christopher.

"Why didn't you run for the position?" she pressed.

"I did." He jabbed a finger in Christopher's direction. "He won. He was Big Joe's VP, so of course he won. All that motherfucker ever did was look out for Outlaw for most of this motherfucker's life." Resentment underscored the words. "Look how he—"

"I don't think you should've told me any of this," she said, interrupting what Christopher knew he'd been about to say. "Club business," she said with a wave of her hand. "But I asked you a question and you being you blabbed it all. I didn't disobey you. I just turned you into a traitor." She cocked her head to the side. "Or did I reveal your true colors? We go places. That gate is the same one that's been up there from the night I met you. There's no earthly way those men got on premises unless someone let them in."

Fuck him. Megan was going to start the same fucking war she said she wanted to avoid.

"You accusing me of betraying my club when I just bared my soul and told you I miss your daddy?" Rack demanded in outrage.

"It doesn't land so good, does it?" Megan said. "Being labeled with some unfair name. You said Christopher is a laughingstock when he's actually being a gentleman. Unless he physically removed me and tied me up, I was determined to say everything I've just said. You're not a traitor anymore than he's weak. Furthermore, the members chose him. And if that wasn't enough, *my father* chose him. He chose him well before he turned into the man he became. He saw in him what we see in him, you included. Strength and honor and integrity." She looked at Christopher and offered him a small smile, the tears rushing to her eyes making them glisten like jewels. "We don't like each other, Rack." She swallowed and her nostrils flared, her nose reddening.

"But I don't begrudge your grief and I appreciate you allowing me to talk, no matter how dismissive you are of everything I've said."

She sniffled and swiped at a tear.

Christopher stepped behind her and wrapped his arms around her waist, laying his cheek on the top of her head.

"He's gone, Rack," she said in a tearful whisper. "Big Joe is *gone.* This isn't *his* club anymore. It's Christopher's. He's the president. Not you. Not Daddy. Not anyone else but Christopher." She rested her fingers on his arms. "You wish to truly honor Big Joe? Look at this club one last time as his and stop dividing it. Stop dividing *his* club." She pointed to the table. "That is singularly horrific and it has no place here in *Christopher's* club. It makes everyone uncomfortable. No one said anything about it and would've suffered through it because you're one of them. A member of the group."

"A full patch member," Christopher told her, lifting his head to stare at Rack. "He our brother."

Motherfucker glanced away.

"They let the table stay because you're their brother," Megan amended. "But you kept poking their tempers, leaving them no choice but to respond. Daddy liked it? Good. He's gone," she said on a small sob. "While we're here, picking up the pieces in the aftermath of his d-death, it's up to us to go on." She fell silent and broke away from Christopher's hold to give him an uneasy glance. For a moment, she lowered her gaze, then cocked her head to the side. "Unless you're trying to say something, Rack?"

Instead of looking at Christopher, Rack stared at K-P before offering Megan a small smile. "Not trying to say one fucking thing, Meggie."

She nodded, appeased.

"I hate your fucking censure, Kaleb-Paul," Rack grumbled.

"Don't give a fuck," K-P said mildly. "Never did so why the fuck would I start now?"

"Suppose you want me to drop it," Rack went on.

"Suppose you're right," K-P said.

"You knew about the fiver she stole from me, K-P?"

"Sure didn't," K-P answered. "Neither she or Outlaw clued me in."

Rack nodded. "Good, good." He cleared his throat. "Roxanne ever coming back to Hortensia?"

"Not if she can help it. Why?"

"I'd hate for her to give Meggie lessons on cutting motherfuckers," Rack said.

K-P chuckled, and Christopher remembered he'd mentioned her once before.

"I miss him, Kaleb. Every fucking day, I miss Joe," Rack said quietly. "You know how many years me and that motherfucker go back? I never thought...I always thought he'd come back to us."

Christopher pressed his lips together. There was no fucking love lost between him and Rack, but his deep well of grief was unmistakable, so clear because it was inside him too.

"I did, too, Wally," K-P said, and his voice cracked. "How do you think I feel? As long as I knew Joe. The world didn't seem right without him. Only time I ever cried before I found out he was gone was when Roxanne left. I loved that woman. And I loved Joe. We'd been through so much..." He glanced at the floor then met Rack's gaze. "He would've still been with us had he been in his right mind. We all thought he was asleep. Down for the count. We didn't know the trouble he'd find."

"He shouldn't have left club grounds," Rack said, in a tone that sounded torn between grief and suspicion. "They never would've gotten him."

"I agree," K-P said without missing a beat. "If there was anything any of us could've done, we would have. I would give up my other eye to have him back. I miss him everyday. But how do you think Outlaw feels? Joe was his guiding hand from the time he was ten. Johnnie had Logan. Outlaw had Joe. Now only me and you left. Some other old timers. Cowboy and Shady. Nothing changing our brotherhood. But you know what I mean. Outlaw been knowing you and me just as long. But it was *Joe* who was like a father to him. I'm here. Long as I got breath in my body I'm here for these little roaches. Except the type of connection I'm talking about happened between me and Mortician. He always been like a son to me. They're our young guns. Because of Joe, Outlaw was able to take Val under his wing. Mortician didn't need a motherfucker to tell him to watch over Digger."

"You talk good game. But what about Joey?" Rack demanded. "He lost somebody too. Big Joe was *his* old man, not Outlaw's."

That caught Megan's attention. Christopher wondered what she was thinking. Wondered if she remembered Snake saying he wanted to avenge his father.

"What about Joey?" K-P asked. "Boy's not right in the head, Rack. You and me both know it."

Rack snorted. "Still holding a grudge against a fucking kid because he put your eye out."

"Omigod," Megan gasped.

"A mild way to put it," K-P said without malice. "And he isn't a kid no more. He's almost thirty and was as remorseless as ever the last time I saw him."

"You beat him at wrestling," Rack snapped.

"Fair and square, motherfucker. He didn't like the fucking results and stabbed me in the fucking eye. You and me both know he wanted me dead, so fuck off."

Megan squeaked.

"It's okay, Meggie," K-P said kindly. "I recovered, so don't sweat it, babe."

Rack leaned against the table and thrust his fingers through his hair. "Joe sent him away to keep him safe while you recovered."

"I heard Roxanne went on the warpath," K-P said, chuckling.

"Joe said she likes knives but is a crack fucking shot."

K-P nodded. "She is. Taught her myself."

"Yeah, well, if she got her hands on Joey, he would've been fucked. I couldn't believe Joe didn't seem outraged that she was threatening his own kid, especially when all he ever fucking did was talk about Meggie to me. Fuck, from the time Dinah announced her pregnancy and, fuck, when he found out it was a girl—"

"He left the club," K-P supplied, not as lost in the conversation as Rack, because he gazed at Megan.

"Jesus Christ, he didn't even want Joey to know about her."

"Because Joey's a fucking mad dog, Rack," K-P said. "Joey tortured Outlaw but they were boys. Joe had a real fucking fear if Joey ever found out about Meggie, he'd find her and kill her."

"I know." Rack shifted his weight, folded his arms. "That fear was so deep, even when he was at his lowest and his brain had been fucking fried, he never once mentioned her to that boy."

"Joey is next level," K-P told him. "If he would've been elected, the club would've been destroyed. Joey is a fucking spendthrift. The boy loves to hit fucking shopping malls more than some bitches." He snorted in disgust. "The money, the businesses, the support clubs all would've been run into the ground. The club that Joe loved and that we still love would've crashed and burned by now."

"Don't mean I couldn't have run it," Rack protested. "After everything we all went through and survived, Joe didn't trust me enough to encourage the members to back me." He shook his head. "Or you, Kaleb-Paul. Don't that shit grate?"

"I joined because of Joe, but I never took to Logan. Not like Joe. Or you. Whereas you fucking jumped when Logan opened his fucking mouth, Joe called that crazy motherfucker out whenever he felt like it. You didn't deserve Joe's praise because you were never a leader. Not like Big Joe. And not like Outlaw."

"Club's falling the fuck apart," Rack said. "That's not the sign of a leader."

"How can he when you pulling your fucking stunts?" K-P said with disgust. "Bringing a fucking rack here. What the fuck is wrong with you? Every fucking thing Meggie said is true but let me explain in more eloquent terms. You're a motherfucker for dishonoring Joe the way you have been. You don't fucking like what's going on? Turn in your patch, you stupid motherfucker. Otherwise, back the fuck off. Joe kept this motherfucker running because he didn't get elected under the same circumstances. He came in and built a fucking respectable club with fucking grit and determination. It was also with the support of almost the entire membership. Up until the day he fucking died, motherfuckers who was still in the club stood behind him. Outlaw won the goddamn election, fuckhead. He stepped the fuck up…" He turned and pointed toward the archway. "Motherfucker stood behind the fucking podium right there, the same fucking night we found Joe, with a broken fucking heart. Shellshocked. But not once fucking hesitating to step in as interim president. He did his fucking duty as VP. How the fuck you and Joey and all the other stupid motherfuckers repaid him? By dividing the fucking club. By making us look like a bunch of weak pussies. Leaving us vulnerable to other motherfuckers. Instead of rallying behind him and uplifting him, we're acting like bitches in a fucking catfight."

Scratching his head, Rack shifted his weight.

"And look at this bullshit," K-P continued with gruff authority. "We've been the featured performance for I don't know how fucking long because you've decided to be a fucking dickhead, dickhead. I don't remember the last fucking time I expelled so much hot fucking air."

Rack gave a small smile. "Not since we all been together at the very least."

"We?" Christopher asked, curious.

"Just a bunch of old motherfuckers," K-P said. "Nobody none of you little runts would fucking know."

Christopher and his boys snickered.

K-P pulled Megan into his arms and hugged her before cradling her face and looking her in the eye. "You did good, Meggie. You can't interfere in club business, so don't make this a habit. Next time Outlaw tells you to leave, listen to him. Understand?"

She nodded.

"I don't want to give you ideas, so I hesitate to praise you anymore than I have." He released his hold on her and smiled. "You allowed cooler heads to prevail by meddling." He shook his head. "I must be going soft in my old age, spouting corny bullshit like that. I can't deny it's true, though. We were all ready to pull our fucking pieces. Where would that have gotten us except fucking dead. I personally got at least fifty more years left to live. I got shit I want to do, so thank you."

"You're welcome. I promise I won't do it again."

"That's all we can ask." K-P looked at Rack. "Anything you need to say?"

Rack looked at Christopher. "How about we call this a fucking draw, Outlaw? I take my shit and leave you to your bitch."

"He was just going to suggest that," K-P said. "Right, boy?"

"Yeah," Christopher said, heaving in a breath.

After Rack left, K-P clapped him on the back. "Come on, Meggie, babe. Want to show an old motherfucker like me some of your moves?"

She gave Christopher a tremulous smile as if she knew how shattered he was inside. Sometimes, he felt as if he struggled to breathe. He wondered if he *should* feel humiliation. Rack had defied him. Fuck, for that matter, so had Megan. Then, she'd spoken the words *he* should have.

The club no longer belonged to Big Joe. It was Christopher's to carry and guide, to lead. She sashayed to K-P, not caring that all eyes were on her, whispering low enough not to be overheard before she kissed his cheek and turned away to come to Christopher.

"Hey," she said softly, pressing her body into his and tipping her head up.

Bending, he grabbed her throat and jerked her to him, slanting his mouth over hers and kissing her deeply, almost brutally. She wrapped her arms around his neck and he lifted her off her feet, needing to fuck her.

He carried her to his room.

"Don't tear my costume," she said, dragging her mouth from his. He allowed her to remove her clothes, while he took his own off, then he carried her to bed, and laid her down gently.

She spread her thighs in welcome and he settled between them, groaning in pleasure when he sank into her and lost himself in her sweetness.

Chapter Thirty

Meggie

T HE WEEKS FLEW BY LIKE A DREAM FOR MEGGIE. Kiera and Ellen were still around but so were a lot of other women. Christopher's attention never strayed far from Meggie. Rack seemed to have calmed down. According to Christopher Snake had slithered back into his hole. If he had club business, he returned as soon as possible. He took her out for pizza. They went to the movie theater on two separate occasions. She even convinced him to go on a picnic near the creek where she'd lived for a month.

A few days after Halloween, Mortician celebrated his 29th birthday, and Christopher allowed her to use the small kitchen to bake a cake for the enforcer to serve at the barbeque thrown in his honor. Digger turned 26 only a couple of days later, so Meggie baked another cake, this one lemon flavored, because that's what he requested. Both parties had been organized by Kiera, Ellen, and some of the other club girls. A day later, K-P headed out to spend the next few weeks with his daughter.

Now, after riding on the back of Christopher's bike for two and a half hours, he turned onto a private access road. Meggie figured she'd walk funny. Maybe, bow-legged. He sped past a couple houses, situated several hundred yards apart, to the end of the road. She kept her cheek pressed against Christopher's back, her arms around his waist, breathing in his scent, the leather he wore, the tang of the ocean.

Memories of their shopping spree yesterday filled her with happiness, and she tightened her grip on him. True to his word given over a month ago, they'd braved the crowds of Black Friday, leaving at five o'clock in the morning to head across the Columbia to Pioneer Place in Portland, a more upscale mall. He didn't know until they arrived why she wanted to go shopping—to buy gifts for everyone. She'd received her last Christmas present, three years ago, from her daddy, a hand-blown glass Minnie Mouse. Thomas had taken one look at it, set it on the floor, and smashed it beneath his cowboy boots.

Dragging Christopher to the mall for other people and not herself hadn't sat well with him. He'd indulged her and allowed her the pleasure of buying gifts for whoever she wanted. She'd taken her time and chosen gifts for each person, based on what she knew about them. She'd mentally purchased her friends, Farah and Lacey, a couple things from Juicy Couture while she'd imagined giving her mom a Coach purse. She'd agonized over Christopher's gift and thought she wouldn't be able to purchase anything for him when he'd insisted he didn't get gifts, so "you ain't gotta had to worry 'bout me, 'specially since I gotta pay for it with my own fuckin' money".

"Well, put the money in my hands and give it to me. Then it'll be my money," she'd reasoned. "And once you give me money, it's mine to do with what I want."

He hadn't relented, until she'd given him the silent treatment and he'd stuffed money into her hands. Convincing him to leave her side for the time it would take to pick out and pay for his present hadn't been as easy.

"Ain't fuckin' happenin', Megan," he'd said through gritted teeth. "Not with that motherfucker on the loose."

"Christopher, Snake's not—"

"*No*. You dumb. I clue you in, you ain't dumb no more. But I ain't takin' stupid. Ain't a fuckin' lotta hope for stupid. And you bein' fuckin' stupid thinkin' that motherfucker won't take any opportunity to strike. Who the fuck said I was talkin' 'bout Snake anyfuckinway? You think I forgot 'bout your step fuckhead?"

Bull's eye. Meggie huffed in frustration. "Can't you just stand outside the store? You can monitor whoever's going in and out. If you see one of them, grab me and we can alert security."

He'd opened his mouth to say something, then snapped it shut and leaned his face into hers. "Like I said. Fuckin' stupid. I ain't got no clue how assfuck look, Megan."

They'd been standing in the middle of the mall, arguing like school kids. Pulling him to a bench, Meggie had described Thomas to him. He seemed uninterested and bored, almost as if he'd seen Thomas before.

Still, when she finished, he said, "Fine. Find the store you wanna buy my gift and Ima guard the entrance. You got thirty fuckin' minutes."

When she pointed out she didn't have a watch, he'd taken his off, being nice enough to set the timer once they'd reached the shop in question. By the time she finished, with three minutes to spare, they'd both been starving, so they'd gone to the lower level and gotten something to eat. Meggie was grateful for the rest, still exhausted from the club's Thanksgiving celebration where they'd feasted on all sorts of goodies and drank like there was no tomorrow. Well, Meggie hadn't but Christopher had and, if anyone had asked her, she'd have sworn he wouldn't have been able to move to take her shopping. He'd really fooled her.

After they'd eaten breakfast, she'd thought they would head back to his pickup. Instead, he'd taken *her* shopping. Like really, *really* shopping. As in Tiffany and Juicy Couture and Victoria's Secret and…yeah, *shopping*. When they'd returned to the clubhouse last night, they'd chatted with Val, Digger, and Mortician while the guys drank beer, then went to their room for their sex fest.

And, now, this morning…

Hedges interspersed with beach bindweed and lupine sat in the middle of the double entrance circular driveway. The large two-story house with a wrap-around porch and huge, wood case windows shocked Meggie. Christopher's body tensed as he glided to a stop and let the Harley idle. Spruce trees prevented Meggie from glimpsing the entire side of the house, but she heard the ebb and flow of the ocean and suspected the view was magnificent.

Christopher roused himself out of whatever world he'd gone off into and, before long, Meggie was rising from her seat, wincing at her sore butt. His scent clung to her body. Before leaving that morning, she'd taken a nice, long shower. Little good that had done. When they finished breakfast, Christopher made love to her again. She was a disgrace because, as many times as he'd been inside her in the last eighteen hours, she wanted to feel him inside her again.

"Megan!"

Meggie jerked at Patricia's call. She hurried down the wide steps in a blur of motion, squeezing Christopher's arm and heading for Meggie.

"Are you all right? You seem awfully pale."

The two women stared at one another and Meggie's heart beat fast. They'd met in passing when Christopher was in the hospital but hadn't had a chance for any real conversation. Now, she wanted to make a good impression on this woman whose son Meggie had become so attached to.

Patricia grabbed Meggie in a hug, and Meggie sagged against her. She didn't want to be a baby, but she missed her mother's affection. In all honesty, she'd missed Dinah's motherly touches for some years now. Hesitant, Meggie returned Patricia's hug, warmed by the cinnamon scent of her. Patricia was a small-framed woman and it almost seemed impossible she'd given birth to a strapping man like Christopher. Her unlined face worked well with her black hair that showed no sign of graying. Unless she colored it.

"I'm fine." Stepping back, Meggie looked at her toes, flushing beneath the weight of the woman's continued study.

She lifted Meggie's chin and frowned. "Are you sure?"

"She fine, Ma," Christopher answered with an innocent grin. He sauntered to Meggie and held her waist. "Want some more dick?" he whispered with a silky laugh.

Yes. "No," she snapped, jerking away from him, mortified he'd ask her such a thing within earshot of his mother.

"Shameless boy," Patricia chirped, shaking her head.

"Pervert." Meggie threw the word out of the side of her mouth. She hoped her grin masked the movement of her lips, even as she prayed for the ground to swallow her.

"Shit all good, Megan," Christopher promised. He kissed the tip of her nose before stepping around her and lifting his mother off her feet, displaying more emotion than Meggie had ever seen. He kissed Patricia, a loud smack on her cheek, before setting her on solid ground again. "How my favorite girl?"

It was then, in that moment, Meggie lost her heart to Christopher. Her feelings for him went beyond mere friendship, attachment, and lust. Some people were meant to rise up and shine, glittering as brilliantly as the stars in the night sky. They reached pinnacles of fame and fortune, leaving behind bright memories long after they were gone. In Christopher's case, it was more like infamy. Few knew him beyond the fringe world he lived in. And yet those who knew him, *really* knew him, loved him. As Meggie loved him. As Patricia, Johnnie, Val, Digger, and Mortician. They all loved him in different ways, but he was still their shining star; they wanted him happy and safe and at peace. Whatever he wanted, they wanted for him.

Overwhelmed with her new discovery, Meggie backed away, allowing Christopher and his mother private space. Patricia's hand lay against her son's cheek and he was bending a little so she could reach him. Tears glinted in her eyes, but couldn't hide the reverence and awe.

Patricia stepped back and Christopher raised his head. Seeing Meggie wasn't near, he turned and beckoned her closer. The moment Meggie drew near, he enveloped them in a bear hug.

"I'm so sorry I hurt you, Ma. But I been dealin' with serious shit. It's been fuckin'—"

"Enough foul language, son," Patricia chastised. "I can only take so much."

Christopher's face flushed and Meggie's mouth fell open. Was he...No, he couldn't be..._blushing?_ He was. Unable to stop it, peals of laughter broke from her. He tried to shut her up with the stink eye. That didn't stop her, so he just let her and his mother go and scowled.

"Ma," he growled after a moment, "this Megan Foy."

All humor gone, Megan blushed herself at the tenderness in his voice and in his look.

"Megan, this my beautiful ma, Patricia Donovan."

He acted as if they hadn't met, but his formal introduction showed how much respect he gave to his mother.

"I've met her when you were in the hospital, Christopher."

Megan nodded. "Is there anything I can help you..." Her voice trailed off and she frowned when a Navigator pulled to a stop behind Christopher's motorcycle. Johnnie emerged and headed straight for her.

"Megs!" he greeted cheerfully, ignoring Christopher's narrowed gaze to kiss her cheek.

Her blush deepened. "Hi, Johnnie," she mumbled.

Johnnie's grin widened.

"Ma," Christopher snarled, "take Megan inside. Show her to our room."

Patricia nodded and indicated they go inside. Without a word, Meggie followed.

All the way upstairs and into the bedroom, Patricia spoke about the plans she had for the holidays, culminating in a big family dinner on Christmas day with all of Christopher's sisters and nieces.

Meggie gaped around the huge room. It had dark hardwood floors, a high ceiling with exposed beams, a wall of floor-to-ceiling windows with a glass door leading to a private balcony with a magnificent view. The windy day sent white capped waves foaming onto the sand.

Patricia cleared her throat.

"I'm sorry for letting my mind wander," Meggie blurted. It wasn't as if she hadn't ever seen such raw beauty and elegant luxury before. Farah was wealthy, after all. But she couldn't reconcile the man she knew Christopher to be with *this house*. Besides, Patricia's attitude made her distinctly uncomfortable. "Your house is beautiful."

She smiled and nodded. "Thank you."

Another awkward silence fell between them, and Meggie shifted her weight. She thought of ideas to jumpstart the conversation, but she didn't want to say the wrong thing and make the disapproval she detected turn into dislike.

She thrust her chin toward the windows. "The view is magnificent." Safe topic. When in doubt, discuss the scenery. The woman who'd greeted her outside was so different from the woman now facing her.

"You're very young, Megan."

Not this again. She'd gone through the same thing with Ellen and Kiera. Maybe, she should just paint the number 18 on her forehead, so everyone would stop speculating.

Patricia lifted an eyebrow and Meggie gritted her teeth, knowing she had no choice but to answer the silent question.

"I'm eighteen," she said firmly. She wished Patricia would leave. Meggie needed a bath and a nap. She was sure she'd see things from a different perspective then.

Instead of leaving, the woman began pacing. "You're Big Joe's girl?"

Another question she was sick to death of. Still, she nodded.

Patricia paused in front of Meggie and took her hands in her own. "Christopher has never introduced me to a girl he's dating."

Meggie smiled, still hesitant with this woman, but warmed by her words.

"I don't want you hurt," she went on. "I adore my son. I have from the moment I held him in my arms. But, my Christopher, he...does things. Mean, vile things."

Meggie pulled her hands free and shook her head in denial. "Please," she whispered. "I-I don't want to hear it." She'd already been exposed to Christopher's dark world and still had nightmares from the retaliation he received because of it. Dead, bloodied men would haunt her dreams for the rest of her life.

"You have to listen to me," Patricia snapped, turning away and crossing the room. "Are you prepared to stand by my son no matter what? Suppose you find out something even more horrible than what you already know?"

An unspoken message lay in those sharp words, but Meggie couldn't fathom what it was. Patricia stared at her, almost through her. The worry and sorrow in her eyes frightened Meggie. "Wh-what are you trying to say?"

Patricia swallowed. "Answer me."

Meggie knew she'd get answers from Christopher if she told him about this odd conversation, but, then he'd either get angry with her for being annoyed with his mother, or he'd get angry with his mother and then Meggie would be responsible for a rift between them. She'd answer the woman, and then, keep her eyes and ears open to solve this riddle Patricia challenged her with.

She raised her chin. "For as long as he wants me, I'll be at his side. Whatever he needs, I'll be there for him."

"Your family—"

"Christopher *is* my family," she interrupted.

Patricia's brown eyes never wavered from Meggie's face. "He does things. He's done things." She huffed out a breath. "If they're discovered, it will affect everyone." Tears filled her eyes and she hugged herself. "You say he's your family but this life isn't for everyone. You must be a strong man to face the decisions my son has faced and lived to tell. He's happier than I've ever seen him. You're good for him. Just promise me, you'll stand by his side no matter what."

Though unsettled by Patricia's fierceness, Megan nodded, sure in the knowledge she'd never turn her back on Christopher.

Patricia headed for the door. Hand on knob, she asked, "do you cook?"

Finally, a decent topic. "Yes."

"Well, you're on vacation."

"I know," she said timidly. "But I-I'd like to cook a meal for Christopher. And you, of course," she added when Patricia bristled.

"My son is very particular about his food, Megan. About as particular as I am about my kitchen. I have your vow to stand by Christopher and you know where we stand with the cooking and my kitchen, dear. We'll get along fine as long as you remember this discussion."

Giving Meggie no chance to respond, Momzilla walked out of the room and closed the door quietly behind her.

Christopher

Christopher watched his ma lead Megan into the house, a breath away from choking the shit out of Johnnie. For no reason other than the fact Megan *liked* him, and his cousin was the type of college-educated, intelligent assfuck she should have.

He turned to his bike to busy his hands with removing her backpack from one of the saddlebags. "How Iona?" he asked, to remind Johnnie *he* had a bitch, so he needed to back the fuck off from Christopher's.

"Married and pregnant," Johnnie answered on a sigh.

The news startled Christopher out of his jealousy. "Not to you or by you."

"Nope. To some nerdy fuck." Johnnie shrugged. "If that's what she wants, I'm happy for her."

His cousin had turned Nomad three years ago to please his girlfriend, a bitch that turned Johnnie's head the moment he'd met her. She hadn't wanted him in the club, so he'd limited his time there, backing away completely with Boss's shenanigans. Though it worked out in the long run—Johnnie now managed the legitimate business they used to launder money—he still hadn't gotten the girl he'd wanted.

He gripped the strap of the backpack and faced Johnnie. "Stay away from Megan."

A slow grin spread across Johnnie's features. He pulled out a pack of cigarettes, offered one to Christopher then lit both. "Aunt Patricia invited me over for dinner," he explained on a whiff of smoke that the ocean breeze caught and carried away. "Since you were coming to town, and I haven't seen you since the Halloween party."

"You and me, we always been close," Christopher began, gesturing with the hand that held the cigarette between two fingers. "We cool long as you ain't fuckin' with Megan."

Unruffled, Johnnie clapped Christopher on the back. "Relax. Megs—"

"Stop fuckin' callin' her Megs, motherfucker!"

He laughed and Christopher knew Johnnie was yanking his chains.

"Come on, assfuck. Time to go inside," Christopher ordered, not bothering to see if Johnnie followed.

When he walked into the house, sunlight streamed in all directions from the numerous windows in the open floor plan. The hardwood floors gleamed, and everything smelled fresh and clean. Across the room, Christopher saw the dunes beyond the deck, the foamy Pacific crashing onto the sand.

If anyone, he had Boss to thank for this house. He'd gone along with Christopher's idea to begin the hydrogrow operation. Instead of moving herb, they grew it inside one of the warehouses on club property. That first year had surpassed everyone's expectations and Christopher immediately purchased the medical lab. He needed a legitimate front to make major purchases. Fucking cops might've looked the other fucking way thanks to payoffs, but the Feds wouldn't be so easy. Boss hadn't complained. He knew how much Christopher wanted a house of his own. He knew, too, that Christopher wouldn't shirk his duties to the club or forget about the Dwellers' collaborative interests and other businesses they worked at to "earn" money.

If it hadn't been for Big Joe's mentoring and his support behind Christopher...he didn't finish and, instead, wanted to throw up. He rubbed a hand over his eyes.

"Outlaw," Johnnie called. He held out a beer. "Go see about your woman. Aunt Patricia said she went to take a bath. Maybe, she needs her back scrubbed or something."

Grabbing the beer, Christopher forced his thoughts away and nodded, glad Megan remained upstairs. He was pretty sure she needed *something* and that something was already rising in his pants.

Just as he started upstairs, his mother was starting down.

"Megan is getting settled, son," she said briskly, pushing her sleeves above her elbows. "Give her a chance to do what girls do after they've ridden on the back of a bike for hours."

Christopher gripped his beer tighter. "C'mon, Ma. Megan won't mind if I'm in there."

She squeezed past him. "Follow me. I need to talk to you."

Speechless, he stared at his ma's retreating back and emptied the bottle of beer in one, long swig. His very own ma was cock-blocking. Stomping through the great room, past a very amused Johnnie—whom Christopher flipped off—he allowed his ma to lead him to the sunroom. Enclosed in glass, the yellow and white décor reminded him of Patricia. He disposed of the bottle in the wicker trash can and stuffed his hands in his pockets, gazing at the three-tiered shelf of pictures. She had photos of her parents, the girls' father, him and his sisters as well as his nieces, Big Joe, Johnnie, Val, Mortician, and Digger. He'd need to add Megan's photo to the collection. Speaking of Megan, she'd probably like this room, too. Beach grass broke out from the high rise of the dunes. On a quiet day, the roar of the ocean slipped through the glass, filling the room with the sounds of nature.

Shadows haunted his ma's eyes. "Big Joe's daughter."

Those three words fell like stones between them, and Christopher's eyes widened. "Ma, what—"

"You killed him. *You killed her father.* How long do you think she'll stick around when she discovers his blood on your hands?"

No. No. *NO!* Christopher wasn't prepared for this. The anger and condemnation in his ma's eyes almost killed him. This was why he'd stayed away. He hadn't been able to face her, knowing what he'd done to Joseph Foy. In a life filled with hurting the people who meant the most to him just by being conceived, he hadn't been able to face Patricia with Boss's blood on his hands. He'd grieved for the man well before he'd had to make that fateful decision. Now, that grief came back, worse, almost bringing him to his knees. The pain of what had been was nothing compared to the pain of what could've been, what would never be because he'd killed Megan's father.

He held out his hands. "It was me or him." His throat worked and he willed his ma to believe him. He didn't know how she'd found out. She didn't know anyone from the club, other than Boss, Johnnie, Val, Digger and Mortician, and they all knew the truth. At least, the live motherfuckers. Boss knew, too, but the motherfucker was dead so he couldn't fucking open his goddamn mouth.

Had one of his boys blabbed to his ma?

Christopher had moved her out of her house in Hortensia to his house here to keep her safe when things had gotten bad with Boss and the rival clubs.

She came and squeezed her arms around him, almost like she never wanted to let him go, and sobbed against his chest. Christopher just stood there, not returning her hug, staring straight ahead, until she settled down and got control of herself again.

She roamed away from him, faced the windows. "Megan's young. She doesn't know about your world. Boss's world."

He hadn't thought his mother knew about "his" world, either. Not as much as she sounded like she did. Yeah, her old man founded the Dwellers, so she'd grown up on the fringes of the club, but Christopher had always thought she held herself above the goings-on.

"She'll hate you," she continued.

All the joy he'd felt these past weeks vanished. Even that shopping bullshit with Megan felt good because of the smile it put on her face. She was happy so he was happy. Now, that was gone, and he didn't think he'd ever get it back again.

"So whatcha wantin' my ass to do, Ma?" he demanded. "Goddamn it, you been made it clear you ain't wantin' to meet no club bitch if Ida ever took one as my old lady."

"Those club women are sluts," she sneered. "I'm not a saint unless you compare me to one of them. They spread their legs for any man who wants them. They're dirty and filthy. You couldn't know if any babies they popped out belonged to you."

"You ain't heard of DNA testin?" he asked with biting sarcasm. "How the fuck you placin' me afuckinbove them bitches when I stick my cock in everyfuckinthing, too?"

She gasped, spun from her spot at the windows, marched to him, and slapped the fuck out of his cheek.

Her hit was so fucking hard, his ears rang. She slapped his fucking jaw sideways. Turning away, she stomped back to the window and looked outside.

Christopher rubbed his fingers over his jaw. Fuck, she hadn't hit him in years. Sometimes, after Logan beat the shit out of him and her, she'd find the strength to whip Christopher as well. He'd been a fucking punching bag.

"They are all sluts." Her shrill voice cut into his thoughts. "I'm sure there are ways to falsify DNA tests."

"Science, science, Ma," he said. "Ain't no fuckin' changin' results."

"You're a fool if you believe that. I can't stop you from entering a relationship with whatever woman you want, son. You are always welcomed here—"

"Yeah, cuz this motherfucker my fuckin' house," he grumbled, angry and frustrated.

She threw a warning glare over her shoulder and he snapped his mouth shut. Offering a small smile, she faced forward again, focusing on whatever the fuck was so interesting.

"Mother of your child or not, I wouldn't allow any club girl to cross the sill of my door. That includes this house. You own it, but you've allowed me to live here. Unless you intend to physically remove me, you wouldn't force me off the premises if I didn't want to leave."

She was right, so he shut the fuck up. Reminders and threats were worthless because he'd never back them up.

"I couldn't stop you from bringing your child here," she continued sharply, "but I'd want nothing to do with it, not if its mother was a Jezebel."

Christopher drew in a breath. He couldn't please her. She wouldn't want him with Kiera, but neither did she approve of him being with Megan. Which reminded him.

"Carissa wasn't no club girl and she wasn't no young bitch. She was a year older than my ass and she think you ain't like her neither."

At first she didn't answer, but her shoulders tensed, so Christopher knew his ma knew who he was talking about. "I don't remember a Carissa," she said tightly.

He glared at the back of her head. "Yeah, you do. I hear it in your voice."

"She never knew her father!" she spat. "She was the first to graduate college and wouldn't have done that if Joe hadn't paid out of pocket."

"What the fuck you talkin' 'bout?" Christopher said, truly bewildered. "My ass ain't even graduate high school."

"My father wouldn't have wanted her in the family."

"Motherfucker ain't want Mort and Digger in the fuckin' club, but I thought you was above all that, Ma."

"Do *not* call Daddy out of his name."

"I call that motherfucker what the fuck ever I fuckin' want. I fuckin' earned that fuckin' right from every fuckin' punch, kick, and insult I'm sufferin' at his hands, so fuck him. I hope he burnin' in fuckin' hell." Or living a hell on earth if, by some chance, he was still alive.

Christopher hadn't ever seen a body. He'd gone on a run and, when he'd returned Big Joe, Johnnie, Mort, Val, K-P, Rack and Snake said he'd bit the fucking dust. Shit hadn't felt right then and it still didn't years later.

"I *love* you, Christopher," Ma told him briskly. "It is my duty as your mother. Despite the shame and humiliation your existence caused me."

The pain of those words washed over him, and he stood stock still, mortification stinging him.

"Joe took you under his wing because he was a good man and he loved you. I wish he could've whipped you into shape so you'd rise to Johnnie's level." She shrugged. "Considering everything, I suppose club life was your only way."

That offended Christopher, more or as much as every other shit she'd handed him. "You makin' it sound like bein' a Dweller a last option. For me and a lotta other motherfuckers, it's the fuckin' first. Ain't nothin' like the freedom or the fuckin' acceptance. I ain't gotta worry 'bout no peripheral bullshit like what society expectin'. More than anyfuckinthing, I love ridin'."

"And killing," she sneered.

"Ma, what—"

"I love you because I *have* to love you. Joe had a good heart and felt sorry for you I suppose. And look how you repaid him. K-P cares about you, but he's all about Mortician. For whatever reason, Johnnie has always admired you. But no one will ever truly love you beyond me. A fitting punishment for the way you betrayed Joe."

Christopher didn't say anything, the words cutting him to his core.

"I was told Megan went to the club searching for her father."

Although that wasn't a secret, whoever was passing information on to his ma had been fucking thorough. "Yeah. So what?"

"Her stepfather abuses her. Basically, she's homeless."

Christopher drew in a sharp breath, his stupid dream of having Megan by his side in the future already fucked. Fury settled into him, and he was so fucking sorry he'd driven to this motherfucker. He wanted to kick something. "She ain't homeless," he snapped. "She livin' at the club with me."

His mother faced him and drew herself up. "Do you think she's with you because she *wants* to be with you?" she asked quietly, sniffling. "Or because she has nowhere else to go? Why would this young girl, with her entire life ahead of her, fall in love with a man who lives on the fringe elements of society, son?"

"Whatcha tryna do here?" Christopher shouted, her words hitting him right in the fucking gut. All his life, he hadn't believed he was worthy of anybody's love. All his life, his mother had sworn he deserved love as much as anybody. Now that he'd gotten the closest he ever had to finding it, she pointed out what he'd known all along. "You ain't got a fu...damn right to question her. Or me. We both adults, Ma. We do what the fuck we want. If she usin' me cuz I ain't worthy to love that's my fuckin' business if I want her to use me." His lip curled in a sneer. "As if I give a fuck. I got more bitches, club ass, than I know what to do with." Turning, he stalked to the door and slammed it behind him. By the time he reached the great room, Johnnie had left.

He only hoped Megan had remained upstairs while he and his mother had gotten into their argument.

Instead of the happy occasion Christopher imagined, tension hung over dinner, later that evening, preventing any conversation. He couldn't take this fucking shit. Tomorrow couldn't arrive soon enough. At sunrise, he was hitting the road, going back to the club. He wouldn't even tell Megan—he didn't owe her any explanation. His mother was right. Once she discovered the truth, she'd hate him.

However, as much as he wanted to ignore Megan, he couldn't. Not when she was observing him through her lashes and sneaking glances at Johnnie. A muscle ticked in Christopher's jaw, and he felt as if he'd explode any moment. He'd stormed upstairs earlier and found Meggie asleep, so he'd taken a walk along the dunes, watching the ocean, wishing the water could cleanse the dirtiness of his life.

A spoon clanked and Christopher glared in his mother's direction. She was usually so friendly and warm. Understandable, she wouldn't be so loving toward him, the blight on everyone's lives, but why not chat with Megan? Even Johnnie, always so ready with a joke, kept silent.

Heaving a sigh, looking as miserable as Christopher felt, Megan moved a piece of baked fish around her plate. She'd barely eaten anything. Concerned that maybe she'd heard something, he leaned over and tipped her chin up.

"I ain't knowin' you to be so quiet, babe. What's runnin' through your head?"

Megan faked a smile and stabbed a piece of fish then shoved it into her mouth. "Nothing."

"She's probably still tired," Ma offered with a sigh.

Instead of acknowledging his mother, Megan stiffened.

Fuck him, his mother had said something to piss Megan off with *her*, not him.

"Tell us a little about yourself," she continued with a weak smile. "What high school did you graduate from? What are your career plans?"

Megan threw his mother the evil eye. "I didn't graduate," she mumbled.

"What the fuck you mean?" Christopher asked, surprised.

Megan shrugged. "I was supposed to graduate in the spring."

Shit. What could he say? Any words he spoke would be hypocritical, since he hadn't graduated from high school, either.

Ma glanced between them. "You're welcomed to stay here with me, Megan. I know Zoann made a similar offer and you refused because she wanted you and Christopher to sever contact." She turned pleading eyes to Christopher before focusing on Megan again. "Don't hate me, but my condition is the same. I think it's for the best."

High color rose in Megan's cheeks, and she narrowed her eyes at his mother. "Thank you, Ms. Donovan, but I have to decline. If you—or Zoann—really wanted to help me, you wouldn't ask me to stay away from Christopher in exchange for your help."

"Megan, maybe, we gotta talk 'bout this," Christopher said. "You too smart not to graduate from high school and go to college. Big Joe…" His voice trailed off when his ma raised her eyebrows. He cleared his throat. "Big Joe said you wanna be a meteorologist. You need college for that. Don't let me or no man stop your dreams." *Especially* him. He rubbed a hand over his face at the bleak thought.

Megan slid her chair back and jumped to her feet, leveling him with her own glare. She shook with anger and Christopher knew it wasn't only this conversation. No, Megan had a bad fucking little temper, and if his mother pissed her off earlier, and she hadn't said anything, this was like a ripple effect.

"I'll go back to school. Either online for my GED or to the school in Hortensia. As for college, I'll decide that next summer. But this isn't a conversation that's anyone's business but yours and mine." If looks could kill, he'd be so fucked. "I thought this would be a happy visit. Family. Food. Getting to know one another. If it's going to be like this"—She spun her finger around. No one needed to ask what *this* was because *this* was shit. "—then I want to go back to the clubhouse."

"Megan—" Ma began, her eyes wide.

Megan raised her hands. "No, ma'am. Please save whatever you have to say. I didn't come here seeking your approval to be with Christopher or your judgment because I haven't finished school." Folding her arms, she stiffened her spine and raised her chin, staring directly into Ma's eyes. "Being his lover is my decision, not yours. I'm sorry the visit has turned out like this. I was really looking forward to getting to know you." She stomped toward the door. "Goodnight," she flung over her shoulder.

"That went well," Ma muttered.

"You've had five girls, Aunt Patricia," Johnnie said, after he finished watching Megan's little ass wiggling in her skinny pants, her long, golden hair fluttering behind her. "Sex, men, and advice don't necessarily mix with young women."

Ma's lashes lowered and she looked tired and drawn, much older than her forty-eight years. "Do you think she'll listen to me?"

"She probably ain't if you gonna repeat your offer, Ma. I think Megan should finish school, too, but if she pushed against a wall, she fight back."

She leaned and rubbed his cheek. "I was out of line, Christopher," she whispered. "For everything. Forgive me?"

He bared his teeth in a semblance of a smile, the words from earlier still replaying in his head. But Patricia was his mother and, despite how much their conversation hurt him, he loved her. "Anytime, Ma," he said gruffly. "Always."

Chapter Thirty-One
Christopher

AFTER TWO IN THE MORNING, CHRISTOPHER shuffled the tiles in the boneyard, the smoke from his and Johnnie's cigarettes resting in the ashtray rising between them. He hadn't seen Megan since she'd stormed from the dinner table. It'd been a long day, but he was restless, angry, and frustrated. He could imagine Megan upstairs in his bed, waiting to take him into that tight pussy of hers, wanting his mouth on her. Needing to talk to him about his mother's attitude. But he stayed down here, hiding from her, like he'd hidden from his mother for a year.

A fucking lot of good that'd done him. She'd still found out he'd killed Boss.

Christopher scowled, threw back his shot of tequila, then chased it with a long swig of beer. His restlessness wasn't the usual sort. He wasn't longing for different pussy. Megan liked fucking and was willing to try whatever he wanted. Her body was his to do with as he saw fit. On the other side of that, his body was hers to explore, touch, learn, and use.

Yeah, he missed the club. But he missed the way it had been when everyone had each other's backs. When friend was friend and foe was foe.

"You planning on drawing your tiles, bro? Or are you gonna fucking stare off in space all night?"

Christopher glowered at Johnnie. "Fuck off," he barked. He drew his allotted number of dominoes and reached for the tequila.

Johnnie leaned back, his bare chest annoying as fuck. It didn't have as much evidence of their lifestyle as Christopher's bare chest. He was only glad Megan was asleep. Johnnie, the sly fucker, sensed Megan's...what the fuck ever...with him, so he'd drank enough where he'd had no choice but to sleep over. Lying motherfucker. He lived right up the road. He could've walked the fuck home.

The thought of Johnnie touching Megan drove Christopher fucking insane. But his mother had made a very valid point. Megan had nowhere else to go. She gave him pussy because she knew that's what he expected from her to continue to sleep in his bed. The little bitch didn't know shit about fucking working at a job. She *needed* him rather than wanted him. But with Johnnie...with Johnnie she had a choice. Even when he'd been a full member in the club, Johnnie was smoother than Christopher. Johnnie, with his light blond hair and light gray eyes, could pass for your ordinary, everyday angel. Christopher, on the other hand, had blue-black hair and green eyes, a devil among men.

He chugged the tequila and laid down a 5-4.

"Talk to me, Christopher."

"Whatcha want me to say?"

"What has you so upset and distracted?"

Christopher scrubbed a hand over his eyes. Another idea came to him. "Think I should turn in my patch?"

Johnnie didn't laugh or judge him or even seem surprised. He cocked his head to the side. "Because of Megs?"

Unless Christopher knocked Johnnie's teeth out, the assfuck wouldn't stop calling Megan "Megs".

"Yeah."

"She know?"

Christopher shook his head.

"So this wasn't her request?"

"Nope. She ain't fuckin' Iona."

"No, she isn't," Johnnie said evenly, the only indication Christopher hit a nerve.

"She deserve better than me. She should have this." He made an elaborate arc to indicate the room, the house.

"This is your fucking house. She has you, she has this."

"You know what the fuck I mean. She should have this and the type of man…" He sighed. "I wonder if she turnin' beet fuckin' red when she look at you cuz you such a preppy lookin' motherfucker. So clean-cut and shit."

Johnnie's wide smile told Christopher the fuckhead knew how Megan looked at him. He had the good sense not to comment, though.

He shrugged instead. "My look goes with the territory. Remember, I'm the manager/owner of a lab company. I can't walk the fuck around in my cut."

"I don't have nothin' I'm good at, John Boy. Nothin' legitimate, I mean."

"If she means that much to you, you need to make sure the feelings are reciprocated. For what it's worth, I think they are. Which leads me to ask you: would she allow you to do it? Would she recognize what you're willing to give up for her?"

"Havin' a man new to her."

"Having an old lady is new to you."

"She wanna be my girlfriend."

"I'm sure. It's those subtle nuances you have to work through. Of course, since having a man is new to her—"

"If you touch her, Ima fuckin' kill you."

"You're a goddamn barbarian, asshole," Johnnie grumbled, cigarette hanging from his mouth.

"What are you two doing?" Megan's sweet voice stopped the conversation and Christopher's cock perked immediately.

She stood in the doorway, a thick robe swallowing her.

"Playin' dominoes," Christopher answered, harsher than he intended.

Johnnie winked at her. "Want to make it a threesome, Megs?"

Megan sniffed and crossed her arms, her lips thinning into a straight line.

"Ima castrate you yet, John Boy." Christopher turned to Megan and cleared his throat to interrupt the staring contest going on between her and his cousin. He'd leave in the morning, clear his head, which he couldn't do as long as she was anywhere near him. If Megan was just in his bed because she needed to survive, then she could have at Johnnie. And if she was with him because she had real feelings for him? Then he'd deal with that, too. *Somehow.* "Go the fuck back to sleep, Megan."

Megan swung her gaze to him. "I wasn't sleeping. I was playing a game on my new iPad, then I downloaded a few Christmas songs. Would you like to hear them?"

"Fuck, Megan. I ain't in the mood to hear 'bout some nuts roastin' over a fuckin' fireplace."

A frown creased her brow and she shifted her weight. "Do you—" she paused and licked her lips, staring into his eyes. She did that a lot when she was nervous, like she could draw courage and strength from him, just by gazing into his eyes. Christopher searched his brain to recall a time when she'd looked at Johnnie with such shy tenderness and couldn't come up with anything.

"Stay with us, Megs. A little Christmas music would liven up the early morning."

"Ignore his dumb ass. What was you about to say, baby?"

"I was wondering if you wanted to come to bed," she said in a small voice, her cheeks red.

Christopher smirked at Johnnie, pleased to see his cousin's scowl. He rose to his feet, already hard for her. Her eyes danced between his face and his dick, sparing a small glance at his chest, which reminded him he needed a new tat to cover his most recent bullet wound. Reaching her, he grabbed her neck and pulled her closer, kissing her hard. He wanted to make it clear who she belonged to. To her, himself, and Johnnie.

Johnnie brushed past them. "I'm going to bed," he said, his disgust evident.

Christopher wanted to beat his cousin to the ground, but the way he saw it, Megan did as much flirting with Johnnie as he did with her. Johnnie was dangling bullshit coupled with the idea of a few, hard fucks, baiting Megan with the words Christopher wouldn't use. It wasn't him. But, fuck, didn't girls need a few dicks in them to know how good the dick they ended up with was?

He'd trust Johnnie with her. They'd shared girls forever. Why not let Megan test Johnnie's dick, just so she could compare? He'd even be nice enough to have enough of Johnnie's body left over to have a proper burial once Christopher fucked him up for fucking Megan.

He listened for Johnnie closing the door to the guestroom, right down the hall. His cousin liked that one because the waves were louder on that side.

Christopher untied the belt at Megan's waist and slid the robe off her shoulders, revealing one of the short nighties he'd purchased for her. He lifted her off her feet and she wrapped her legs around his waist.

"Not here," Megan breathed, already kissing his jaw. "Someone might catch us."

Ignoring her, Christopher shut her up with another kiss and pulled his cock out of his pajama bottoms, guiding it to her burning pussy. He slid into her and grunted in satisfaction. She felt so fucking good, her fingers clutching his shoulders, her body wet and tight around him. He slammed into her, angry at his weakness for her, his strokes bordering on vicious. She whimpered.

"You like Johnnie, yeah?" A pound into her body stressed each word.

"Christopher—"

"Shut the fuck up, you lil' hypocrite. Bitchin' cuz I was fuckin' Kiera all the while dreamin' of fuckin' Johnnie."

"I would never sleep with him," she swore on a gasp. "I love you."

If only those words were the truth, but he knew better. "You fuckin' liar. How the fuck you know you love me? Girls need more than one dick to know the difference between love and lust." He hammered into her and she sucked in a breath.

"Please. You're hurting me."

Christopher heard a growl from down the hallway, his anger intensifying at Johnnie's blatant eavesdropping, furious at Megan's inexperience and immaturity. Some whores were made and others were born. Megan was well on her way to being turned into one with the way she liked fucking. As long as she was *his* whore, he had no problem. That meant, only *he* knew how she fucked.

"You fuckin' drive me insane, you fuckin bitch." Her eyes rounded at his words and he grunted. "I want to walk the fuck away but thinkin' 'bout nobody but me in this pussy make me wanna fuckin' kill."

She sucked in another ragged breath and slipped her fingers through his hair. "Shh," she soothed.

"Aww fuck." He gripped Megan's ass, losing all control, pumping into her without mercy. His lips turned as bruising as his thrusts and he expanded inside of her, tasted blood on her lips when he bit her after realizing she didn't deny his claim she liked his cousin.

One final time, he buried himself inside her and filled her with his cum. Their breaths heaving in and out of their mouths, he set her on her feet. Yeah, he was acting like a maniac but he couldn't seem to stop himself. It was in his genes to hurt those he loved. Fuck waiting 'til the morning. He was leaving tonight. He didn't need her, didn't need this fucking shit.

Megan's fingers caressed her swollen clit and Christopher slapped her hand away, then dropped to his knees and threw her leg over his shoulder, plastering his mouth on her cunt. She'd gotten used to having her pussy licked after sex, and now just rolled with the movements of his tongue, making those sexy noises that drove him fucking insane. He suckled her clit, bringing her over the edge, and she groaned, rocking her pussy against his mouth, her legs shaking with the force of her climax, her little fingers gripping his hair.

Panting against her core, Christopher kissed the top of her mound, her pussy hair tickling his lips and nose. He trailed his way up her body until he reached her lips where he pulled away and took in her features, caressing his thumb over her lip and wiping away the blood.

Christopher gave her a half-hearted smile and helped her back into her robe. "Yo, John Boy," he called, moving away from her and sticking his cock back in his pajama bottoms.

He had to give his cousin credit for making a production of rattling the doorknob like he was just opening it. Megan glanced at him uneasily. When Johnnie stopped in the doorway, her gaze traveled between the two of them.

Christopher looked at Johnnie. "Ima head back to the club."

"Wh-what?" Megan asked. Her lips were red and swollen, her eyes dark, her voice low and sexy. She looked and sounded thoroughly fucked. "We're leaving now? It's the middle of the night. Can't we go tomorrow?"

"Ain't said shit 'bout *we*," he pointed out. "*You* stayin'. *I'm* leavin'."

He could do without the disapproval in Johnnie's eyes. He, more than anybody, should understand the situation. Anyway, the separation would do him and Megan good. Since he'd started fucking her, they'd been glued to each other's sides. Really, since she'd arrived. Here and there, he'd put himself out of her reach, but he'd never been very far.

"Ma'll give you a real good Christmas, Megan." He waited for her to ask him to stay, tell him she wanted him to be a part of the celebrations, that she wanted *him*.

She lowered her lashes. "What about the Christmas tree?"

The Christmas tree he'd promised to help pick out. Jesus. He hadn't even been able to drive Megan here in his pickup to use that death wagon to store a Christmas tree. He'd thought about the hidden compartments that had transported drugs, guns—bodies. How could he use it to store a Christmas tree? Bad enough he'd taken Megan shopping in it.

"Johnnie'll take you to get one."

Johnnie narrowed his eyes and thinned his lips but remained silent.

Christopher kissed her forehead. "So, yeah, see you soon. Gimme a chance to grab my things, Megan." Before she could protest, he turned on his heel and hurried toward the staircase.

Meggie

Meggie listened to the rumble of Christopher's bike in stunned silence. She recalled him saying he'd leave her there after a day or so. But, besides that night, he hadn't mentioned it again and, after the way Meggie and Patricia had started off, she didn't think he'd just leave her. And, in the middle of the night, no less.

She jumped as arms encircled her and she stiffened, recognizing Johnnie's cologne. He urged her head to his chest. Tired, Meggie relaxed against him and let out a gut-wrenching sob. She sobbed because of her mixture of emotions toward Christopher. She sobbed because she felt so alone and abandoned with no one in the world. And she sobbed for Big Joe. Really, truly mourned him for the first time since learning of his death.

"Shh, Megs. It'll be fine. I promise," Johnnie finally whispered, twisting strands of her hair around his finger.

She didn't want to stay here without Christopher. But he'd never intended to keep her, and he'd never pretended he would. She'd built something up in her head that wasn't there. She'd fallen in love with him. Not the other way around. Now, he was gone, and, without him, she was completely alone.

Included in all their plans was a visit to the boardwalk and going to see one, if not both, of the lighthouses.

What could've happened between those plans and Christopher's decision to just leave?

Chapter Thirty-Two

Meggie

"I want to hear your Christmas carols."

At the sound of Johnnie's voice, Meggie looked up from her game of Angry Birds. Exhaustion clung to her. She hadn't slept in the seventeen hours since Christopher stormed out. She'd left Johnnie and returned to the room she'd looked forward to sharing with Christopher, doing nothing but staring out the window where the darkness swallowed any view, going over scenario after scenario about what sent him running from her in the middle of the night. She'd called him five times already, but he never answered. She'd called the clubhouse twice and both times she'd been told he wasn't available. Her heart seemed to break into a thousand pieces, the pain of his sudden departure cutting her deep. The only way she'd feel better was to talk to him.

"Megs?"

Heat rose to her cheeks at Johnnie's husky tone. She didn't know why she blushed when she looked at him, what fueled her need to stare at him. Her actions were conspicuous because Christopher had taken note. But that couldn't be the reason he left. Could it? He was protective of her, but not jealous.

Blond hair falling carelessly over his forehead, Johnnie strolled forward and sat next to her. She was sitting in the room that served as both a media room and a game room. Meggie decided to call it the playroom because it had a pool table, pinball machine, the biggest television she'd ever seen and a stereo system she loved. It also had a bar and a sectional in front of the TV, which was where she sat.

Her fingers shook under Johnnie's scrutiny. Though she pretended to ignore him, she was quite aware of his hard, honed body next to hers.

"I can sit here all night until you decide to acknowledge me."

Insufferable jerk.

She really wanted to start dinner but dared not since Patricia had made it so clear the kitchen was off-limits. She hadn't seen her at all today, which, really, was fine.

"We can go tree hunting," Johnnie offered.

Out of the corner of her eye, she saw him lean back, hands behind his head, legs spread, making her all the more determined to ignore him. Besides, she didn't want to go Christmas tree shopping with *him*. She and Christopher had planned on doing that, then pulling out whatever decorations Patricia had stored away.

"You want to go for a walk on the dunes, Megs?"

She concentrated harder on the game, the oinking of the victorious pigs more annoying with Johnnie there.

"Megs—"

"Stop calling me Megs," she hissed.

He leaned closer to her, his mouth near her ear. "No," he whispered, his breath fanning her skin, the smell of alcohol sending her heart plummeting.

Edging out of his grasp, she drew in a sharp breath, suddenly aware of how very alone they were. She didn't really know Johnnie, other than the fact that he was Christopher's cousin. She sat her iPad on the small table next to the sectional, her hands shaking, every confidence she'd gained away from Thomas and his intimidation caving. She rose to her feet. Johnnie didn't lunge, an encouragement and a relief.

Silver-gray eyes narrowed. "I'm not going to hurt you," he said harshly, coming to his feet.

She backed away and he stilled, staring at her in shock. Embarrassed at her fear and paranoia, she lowered her lashes and studied her bare feet, her breath escaping in frantic pants.

"You're afraid of me."

She flinched at the disbelief in his tone. "Don't take it personal."

"I take it quite fucking personal."

Not responding, she waited for an insult, a snide remark, a painful grip.

Instead, he put more distance between them and cursed when she visibly relaxed.

"If we ever fuck, it's because you want me. My cock could be sliding into you and, if you change your mind and tell me you don't want to fuck me, I'd stop."

"Would you shut up?" she demanded, her body and her head at odds with one another.

Johnnie laughed, some of the tension easing from his broad shoulders. "Are my words making you hot? You're getting wet for me?"

Her cheeks flamed. "No."

"Liar." Cautiously, he stepped closer to her again. "You want some cock, don't you, sweetheart?"

"I want Christopher."

"Fair enough." He shrugged. "But he's not here. I don't have to put my cock in you. There's always another way."

Meggie tightened her jaw, refusing to allow his low tone to lure her.

"I can taste you, Megs," he whispered. "Lick your clit. Make you come on my tongue."

This wasn't Christopher. Her belly shouldn't be clenching, and her panties shouldn't be soaked. But, along with both of those things, her breath hitched, and her heart pounded.

"C'mon, Megan. Nothing more but me eating your pussy. No harm done and you'd feel good. Not look so lost."

"Go away."

"You're too young to attach yourself to one man. The fact that you want in my bed proves that."

"You're so conceited," she snapped.

"That so?" Johnnie asked, grabbing her hand and guiding her back to the sofa. "Want to test that theory?"

Meggie huffed. "I'm sorry I've given you the wrong impression. You seem like a very nice man. Sexy and so very handsome."

He smirked at her.

"But the way you make me feel and the way Christopher makes me feel is completely different." She licked her lips and met his gaze. "If I slept with you, it would be wrong because neither of us has any real emotion for the other." She ventured closer to him. "Please, stop flirting with me. Stop staring at me like…like…"

"I'm undressing you with my eyes?"

She nodded, a jerky movement.

"Even if I am? Even if I'm imagining how you taste? How you feel?"

Her nipples hardened and heat shot through her body. "Stop."

He caressed her cheek, her ear, brushing her hair over her shoulder and resting his hand on the back of her neck to pull her closer. He slanted his mouth over hers, his hand holding her head in place, as he pillaged her depths, his tongue touching hers, tickling the roof of her mouth. He tasted like scotch and man and sin. She scraped her fingers through his hair, and he groaned, guiding her back and stretching out over her, grinding his erection into her belly. His skin burned against her, spurring her frantic kisses.

The realization doused her desire like a bucket of cold water. She squirmed beneath him and tore her mouth from his. He was breathing as hard as she, his mouth moist, his eyes a well of dark need. They stared at one another.

"Get up," she said softly.

He closed his eyes and leaned his forehead against hers, his erection throbbing between them.

"This is wrong. On so many levels. Christopher's your cousin. He's my…" Nothing. He wasn't her anything. He hadn't even believed her when she said she loved him.

Sighing, Johnnie dragged his body from hers. "I probably shouldn't tell you this, but we've shared girls in the past." He shrugged. "He left you here with me. He's not stupid. He knows we're attracted to each other—"

"Shut up," Meggie cried. She sat up and hugged herself, ashamed of her body, even more so than when she made those marks on herself and needed to feel the sting and release of pressure. "I-I can't stop you from coming here but I-I don't want to s-see you anymore."

He squeezed the bridge of his nose and reached for her, but she pushed his hands away. "Megs…Megan," he amended when she glared at him. "I'm sorry. I want to be your friend."

"No, you want to have sex with me," she said flatly.

"What I want right now doesn't matter. What you need is more important."

"I need to talk to Christopher and hear his voice. That's what I need. Can you give me that?"

"No. Only Christopher can," he responded, his expression grave.

She asked the question eating at her, hoping he had the answer since it seemed as if Christopher didn't intend to talk to her again. "Why did he leave?"

"He's going through a lot. He needed space to think."

"He needed to get away from me," she guessed, whispering.

He shrugged, allowing her to reach her own conclusions without a denial or a confirmation.

"I'm going to leave for tonight. But let me come back—"

"I can't stop you—"

He placed a finger over her lips to silence her. "If you're going to be uncomfortable around me, I won't visit. If you don't want to see me, then I'll stay away."

"Okay."

He stood, his hard penis imprinted against his jeans, eye level with Meggie because she still sat. "Okay, what? Stay away?"

She shook her head.

"Then get some rest and I'll see you tomorrow." With that, he walked out, leaving Meggie alone.

Not ten minutes had gone by before Patricia found her still sitting where Johnnie had left her. Now that Christopher was gone, she could only imagine how Patricia would treat her. Wanting to ignore her, exhausted to her soul, she reached for her iPad again and unlocked it. Maybe, she'd investigate online GED courses. She really did want to get her diploma, but some things couldn't be helped. A GED was better than nothing, and she'd still be able to get into college eventually.

"Are you hungry, Megan?"

Patricia's gentle voice froze Meggie, but she shook her head, unable to get any words past her throat, her emotions all jumbled up.

"Have you eaten anything today?"

"No."

A sigh greeted the monosyllable and she walked into Meggie's line of vision. Self-conscious all of a sudden, Meggie bowed her head. Johnnie had thoroughly kissed her, and she hadn't quite recovered from it.

"He'll come back. Christopher. He'll come back."

The woman hadn't asked about Christopher, so she'd walked in with the knowledge he'd left Meggie there. Maybe, Johnnie had called her or, maybe, she'd heard Christopher speed away early this morning on his Harley.

Not that it mattered. Meggie shrugged and Patricia seemed like she wanted to speak, then thought better of it. She began to back away but paused and sat on the other end of the sectional.

"I've gone about everything all wrong. We had words, me and Christopher, and he left."

Meggie bristled. "What did you tell him?"

"Things…" Her voice trailed off and weariness pulled down Patricia's features. "Things I didn't mean and should never have said. I spoke out of grief and anger."

Patricia's confession didn't relieve Meggie's anger on Christopher's behalf. "You're his mother, Patricia. It doesn't matter what else is going on in his life, he should always be able to turn to you without wondering if he'll face censure."

"You don't even know what I said to him."

"It doesn't matter," Meggie retorted. "The way he was treated his entire life, singled out, has shaped the man he's become. He came here to enjoy his holidays and you hurt him." Although Meggie knew that didn't mean anything regarding her, she hated the thought he'd left because of wounds his mother opened. He tried so hard to ignore his hurt, but it was there, festering inside of him like a slow working poison.

"He'll be back," Patricia repeated quietly. "He has you here."

"I'm sure he won't come back until I'm not here," Meggie replied, her belly hurting at the mere thought. Yes, she needed him, but she wanted him, too. She loved the way his eyes lit up on the rare occasions he laughed. He stood head and shoulders above all the others and drew attention wherever he went. Beneath the big, bad biker, he was human and vulnerable, so many things wrapped in one package, some bad, some good, but all him. "As soon as I can find somewhere to go, I'll be out of here."

"He needs you. I shouldn't have said anything to either of you. It's just when Rack called—"

"*Rack?* Rack calls here?"

"Yes. Every now and then. He…lets me know—"

"It doesn't matter what he lets you know," Meggie interrupted, everything else forgotten. "Rack beat the crap out of me and—" She stopped to draw in a deep breath and calm her racing nerves. Despite the shock on Patricia's face, she explained everything, including about the day of Christopher's shooting and her confrontation with Rack. "So you really shouldn't talk to that idiot. Christopher will be furious."

Patricia covered her face with her hands and shook her head, seeming dazed by all that Meggie had explained to her.

"Don't tell my son. Please?" she whispered. "I knew none of this."

"Of course not. Because Rack is a mean rhinoceros and wouldn't tell you the entire story. What did he say for you to have words with your own son?"

"It's complicated. More than you'll ever know. Most of it I know nothing of. Club business."

"Well, what do you know? What was so bad you confronted Christopher?"

Patricia gazed off into the distance and Meggie thought she wouldn't answer, then she said in a voice so low, Meggie strained to hear. "I loved my girls' father. He was killed. Left me with a houseful of young children. I never thought I'd love anyone again. Then…then I met someone. A man among men. That's what everyone always said about him and, once I got to know him, I couldn't have agreed more. He *was* a man among men." She shook her head as if forcing herself out of a trance. "Then he…he left…and my h-heart has been broken ever since. Rack was friends with this man—"

"If Rack knew him, then Christopher must have, too. If you need to talk about your grief, talk to Christopher. Talk to the moon. *Talk to Jesus.* Just *do not, DO NOT,* talk to Rack."

Laughter bubbled from Patricia and Meggie chuckled, too. "Talk to Jesus, Megan?" she said with raised eyebrows.

"You get the point, Patricia," Megan retorted, still smiling.

"I do. But Christopher doesn't know…about me…and this man. Only Rack." She stared at her hands, spread her fingers. "I'm hurting, deep in my heart. I'm hurting. I just want to hear this man's voice one last time. Tell him how much I love him."

Meggie popped to her feet and ran to where Patricia sat, looking so lost and alone. Her heart broke for her. She wrapped her arms around Patricia, cradling her against her breast and rubbing her hair, blocking out images of her and Dinah in a similar pose. After a minute, Patricia returned Meggie's hug, and they remained that way for long moments before Patricia pulled back and Meggie did, too.

"Promise me, you won't ever tell Christopher about this. It'll hurt him for a lot of reasons."

Megan nodded. "Would you promise me you won't talk to Rack? He's bad news."

Patricia smiled sadly. "I'm sorry, child. That I can't do. He's the only link I have to the man I lost." She drew herself up. "Rack's loyal to a fault, to the Club especially. As his president, he'll be loyal to Christopher. I'd stake my life on it."

Chapter Thirty-Three

Meggie

"**I**S CHRISTOPHER...OUTLAW AVAILABLE?"

"No, he not."

Meggie wasn't sure who was on the other end, but music and laughter roared in the background. She swore she even heard Christopher, too. He didn't want to talk to her, however.

"C-can you tell him that Meggie called?"

"Yeah."

"Ask him to call—"

The line disconnected. Meggie held her cell phone to her ear, unable to move it away, her hand trembling. She hoped he would've returned by now. Or contacted her in some way.

Upon awakening this morning, she'd sent him a text. By noon, when he hadn't answered, she'd called him. It went to voicemail. Now, it was early evening, Patricia had left to go to a movie with a friend, and Meggie had tried to find something to do to keep her mind off Christopher's departure.

"Megan?"

She started at the sound of her name and glanced in the direction of the doorway, already knowing it wasn't Christopher. His tone was rougher, more commanding. In comparison, the man who addressed her had a polished quality to his voice.

Dressed in trousers and a dress shirt, his tie undone and hanging around his neck, Johnnie stood, his silver-gray eyes touching on every detail of her face. She'd never seen him in anything other than jeans and his cut.

Slowly, she lowered the hand holding her phone and rested it on her lap, watching him walk toward her. He dropped down next to her, so close his thigh touched hers, but she didn't care.

He took her phone and sat it next to him. "What would you like to do this evening?"

She shook her head, swallowed.

"Sweetheart," he said softly, and her lips trembled. "Don't," he whispered, close to her ear.

She didn't know what to say. For the entire day, she'd held out hope she'd hear from Christopher. When she decided to call the club, she'd believed he'd come to the phone.

Johnnie's fingers touched her jaw. Gently, he turned her head toward him. "What have you done today?"

"Patricia didn't want my help with anything. I've waited for Christopher."

"He's going to come back, Megan," Johnnie said, "but it's only been a day. You've got to give him a chance."

Nausea rolled through her, and, for a moment, she felt lightheaded at the ideas Johnnie's words conjured. "To sleep with Kiera?"

"To miss you," he answered simply, tipping her chin up to better stare into her eyes.

"I can't compete with her."

"You don't have to. I promise you, sweetheart. She's never been a threat to you because she was never his girlfriend. It's only you who insists that she was."

"He cares about her." The image of him and Kiera together in his office rose in her head. Meggie couldn't hold in her tears any longer. "I saw them," she got out. "It was always supposed to be Ellen and Kiera together with him, but I saw *them*, Christopher and Kiera in his office having s-s-sex."

Johnnie took her face between his hands, the look on his face and in his eyes fierce. "When?" he demanded.

"Three or four days after he was released from the hospital," she said hoarsely.

"That was weeks ago," he said. "You can't torture yourself with thoughts of what he may or may not be doing now. Confront him when he returns. If he's been fucking other women and you can't accept that once you hear his side, then leave."

Unable to stand his scrutiny, she lowered her lashes.

"In the meantime, you've got to pull yourself together, sweetheart. When he returns and finds you moping, he'll appreciate it for a while. But unless you show him that you can have a life beyond him, he won't learn his lesson and he'll walk away over and over again."

"If he loves me, he won't. If he loves me, he wouldn't want to know I'm moping or hurting in any way."

Instead of commenting, Johnnie drew her face closer, within inches of his. He gazed at her lips and, for a moment, Meggie thought he meant to kiss her again. She hoped he wouldn't and respected the boundaries she'd set.

Releasing her, he got to his feet. "Have you eaten?"

She shook her head. "No."

He held out his hand to her. "Come, Megs. I'm starving myself. Let's find food."

Placing her hand in his, she allowed him to pull her to her feet. "I'm not too hungry."

"I hate eating alone," he countered. "You don't have to eat but join me while I do."

"Patricia might—"

"I'll text Aunt Patricia," Johnnie interrupted.

Out of arguments, Meggie nodded. "Okay."

Smiling at her, he guided her out of the playroom and down the hallway, to the huge room surrounded by windows that showed the magnificent view. He led her to the front door. Outside, he dug in his trouser pocket and pulled out keys, then locked Patricia's door.

The tang of the ocean drifted over Meggie's senses, the setting sun casting a golden pink hue over the evening. From the place they stood on the wraparound porch, the spruce trees hid views of the beach, but she heard the crash of the waves.

"Come on, sweetheart," he said gruffly, even though he hadn't released her hand, so she had no choice but to follow him down the steps. The circular driveway was empty, and she frowned.

"Where's your Navigator?" she asked, appreciating how he adjusted his pace to her shorter legs.

"At my house," he answered, nodding in the direction they'd began to walk, bypassing the hedges, beach bindweed, and lupine. "Where I'm going to eat."

Drawing her brows together, Meggie worried her bottom lip. He'd said he was hungry. "Do you cook?"

"Some," he said, vague.

She tried again. "Do you want *me* to cook?"

"Do you want to cook?" he threw back at her.

Glaring at him, she huffed out a breath. "Why are we going to your house if you're hungry?"

"Because I haven't had a chance to shower."

"*What?*" She dug her heels in, forcing him to halt. "You can't shower while I'm there alone with you."

"Unless you intend to join me in my bedroom, I certainly can, Megs." He grinned at her, his eyes smoldering. "But my house is big enough where I'll be well out of your view."

She hesitated, thinking of Thomas. Christopher trusted Johnnie enough that he'd left Meggie with him.

"If you want to go back to Aunt Patricia's, I understand," he said softly. "I won't hurt you, sweetheart. Whatever happens between us will be with your full consent. If you tell me to stop, even if I'm buried inside of you, I will stop."

When she'd ordered him to stop kissing her, he had. Pretending she hadn't heard his last statement, Meggie started walking again. He easily fell into step beside her.

"I can cook, while you shower," she offered.

"Nothing's defrosted. You can order food. When we get inside, I'll give you my credit card."

"What do you feel like eating?"

He smirked at her and heat rose to her cheeks. Despite herself, she laughed. "Food," she said primly.

"Whatever you have a taste for," he said with an overdramatic sigh that made her poke him.

"Behave," she said severely.

"Always, Megan, although I'll tell you a secret."

"Omigod. Do I really want to know?"

"I'd say you do."

"I know I'm going to regret this," she retorted, "but what's your secret?"

"Bad behavior brings out my best. I can assure you I've had no complaints."

"You're incorrigible."

"But truthful."

"Enough about your prowess in bed," she ordered.

His carefree laughter further eased Meggie's discomfort, but it also took away some of her misery.

Though just a short walk from Patricia's, by the time Meggie followed Johnnie into his house, darkness had fallen. After flipping a light switch just inside the entryway that lit several rooms, he led her to the living room. The place didn't have an open floor plan like his aunt's. Nor did it have a bank of windows offering a magnificent view, but it was bright, filled with Johnnie's warmth and cheer. One of the walls had a panel that probably controlled the air and heating systems.

"Make yourself comfortable," he told her. "I don't have a TV, but I have a sound system if you care to listen to music."

"I love music."

He smiled. "I know."

Her stomach growled, the first time today she'd even hungered for a meal.

"Ahhh," he said with satisfaction. "Someone's hungry."

"I am," she agreed. "Where are the menus? Give them to me, then take your shower, while I choose food."

Without speaking, he walked away, returning in moments with a stack of menus. He handed them to her.

"When was the last time you had a homecooked meal before yesterday?" Meggie demanded, slightly outraged that he seemed to only eat out.

"Two or three weeks ago," he admitted. "Whenever Aunt Patricia last cooked for me." He gave her a hangdog expression. "I could benefit from having a woman lovingly prepare meals for me and awaiting my arrival home, wearing nothing but heels and a smile."

Meggie pointed her finger toward a doorway that she presumed led to the bedrooms. "Go," she ordered.

The scoundrel winked at her, then turned and strolled away.

There were so much variety to choose from, Meggie wasn't sure what she wanted to eat. Once hunger set it, it overwhelmed her, and that same nausea she'd felt a little earlier returned. After narrowing down her choices to three, she finally settled on Thai. She almost waited until Johnnie reappeared to order, but decided against it, since he'd put her in charge.

The restaurant was busy, so there was a seventy-minute wait. She doubted she could wait that long, though she'd try her best. With nothing to do, she sat on the sofa, the sound of the shower finally settling into her head.

Christopher's image rose in her mind. What little peace she'd managed in the last forty minutes disintegrated. She would've called him again if she hadn't left her phone at Patricia's. Her phone wasn't with her. Panic set in, and she got to her feet. Maybe, he'd be ready to talk to her. He hadn't called because he believed she was angry with him. She had to let him know she understood. Or she had to *tell* him she understood, though she truly didn't. She'd leave Johnnie a note, explain something had come up.

"Megs, have you—"

Their gazes met, collided. Meggie hadn't realized she'd moved until she saw Johnnie in the doorway, near where she stood.

Dampness darkened his hair. His five o'clock shadow seemed more prominent now, his eyes more silver than gray. He wore only sweats, leaving his upper body bare to her gaze. He was tanned, with a flat abdomen defined by abs, and muscles cording his arms.

She'd never noted his tattoos before, but they jumped out at her now. A lethal looking dagger on his upper right arm. The blade pointed to his forearm, with an hourglass tattoo with gilded detail on each end. At the bottom, the upper portion of a skull looked lonely. To Meggie, it was a grim reminder that the passage of time ended only one way.

Shoving the thought away, she looked at his left arm. On the upper arm he had a scary green face with a samurai helmet topped with a skull, surrounded by flames and flowers. A snake sliding out of an eye socket and another out of the open mouth of a devil's head covered his chest.

"Are you going somewhere?" he asked, breaking their silence.

"I forgot my phone at Patricia's," she said, embarrassed that she was noticing anything about Johnnie or that memories of their heated kiss were seeping into her thoughts. "Christopher might've called."

"He'll call back," he told her flatly. "Let him wonder where you're at as he's making you guess his whereabouts."

"You're making it sound like a game when it isn't."

"It is," he responded. "Make it too easy for him and you'll lose, sweetheart."

One of them was always imparting advice to her about how to handle Christopher. Maybe, if she did it her way, things would work out better for her.

"Did you order the food?"

She nodded. "Thai. Spicy garlic chicken, papaya salad, and spring rolls."

Johnnie stared at her a moment longer, then turned and disappeared the way he'd come, allowing Meggie a glimpse of his back piece—a replica of the club's mural, with the words *Death Dwellers MC* above it. He returned within minutes, phone in hand and walked to her. Staring into her eyes, he took her hand in his and placed the phone in her palm, then wrapped her fingers around it and released her.

"Call him if it'll put your mind at ease but expect the same results. You'll be happily surprised if the outcome's different and not devastated if it isn't."

"Thank you," she said, grateful. She didn't hesitate to dial the club. "May I speak to Outlaw?" she said upon hearing a gruff 'hello' that she strained to hear because of the noise.

"Fuck you, Mort."

That was clearly Christopher's voice in the background. He was close to the phone or it was near him.

"Hello?" the man who'd answered repeated.

"Didn't mean it like that, Prez," Mortician responded.

"Is Outlaw available?" Meggie asked, louder.

"Nope," he responded as Christopher laughed.

"Tell him to call Meggie."

"You got it." The line disconnected.

Johnnie snatched the phone from her and drew her into his arms, allowing her to cry against his chest, all the while crooning to her. The ringing doorbell made her step back. His erection brushed against her belly.

"Food's here," Johnnie said on a sigh, turning away from her.

Meggie stumbled back to the couch and sat, staring into space but not focusing on anything. Johnnie returned with two bags and two plates, topped with flatware and cloth napkins. Setting everything on the coffee table, he sat next to her and began doling out the food.

"I'm not hungry anymore," Meggie said when he held out a plate to her.

He put her plate next to the empty containers and dug into his own food. Halfway through, he held up his fork, a piece of chicken dangling from it. "One bite," he coaxed.

"I'm nauseated."

"Because you haven't eaten."

She didn't have it in her to argue any longer, so she opened her mouth, allowing him to feed her the chicken. At first, she thought her stomach would reject the food, but it actually turned out to be delicious.

"Plate's right there," Johnnie said around a mouthful of food, nodding to her forgotten plate. "Do you want a glass of wine?"

"I don't drink," she answered, picking up her plate and starting to eat.

"You don't drink or you've never drunk?" he challenged.

Meggie shoved more food into her mouth. "Momma kept me on a tight leash. I was barely allowed to visit my friends. And my stepfather was even meaner when he had alcohol."

"Your stepfather sounds like he needs a date with my woodchipper," Johnnie said casually.

She gasped. "I can't...no! No!" she got out. "No. That's not...a woodchipper? You can't fit a body into a woodchipper." She lost her appetite and set her plate on the table. "Thomas isn't worth it, even if you could. He deserves jail, not a stain on your soul."

Johnnie snatched her plate. Half her food remained. "My soul's stained already, sweetheart," he said, shoveling chicken and noodles into his mouth. "Chop a fucking body into pieces and feed it to the woodchipper and it works fine."

She blinked at him.

"You can't interfere in our natural instinct, Megs. If you've told Christopher not to bury your stepfather, then you've just given him another reason why he shouldn't be with you."

"Because I don't want him to be a murderer?"

"Because you don't want him to be who he is. On the fringe of society. A man who knows about vengeance, retaliation, and betrayal. A criminal in the eyes of civilians."

Glaring at Johnnie, she jumped to her feet. "That's how *you* see him, but he isn't that. My daddy said his club was just a bunch of men who loved Harleys..." Her words trailed off at Johnnie's raised eyebrows.

"You know that's bullshit. The club was shot up. Men died. *Christopher* almost died. You confronted Rack."

She swallowed.

"And I'm not calling Christopher what I'm not. I'm a killer, too," he said without a shred of remorse.

"Why are you telling me this? When Christopher was in the hospital, Val danced around the subject. He was worried about whether I'd run to the police. Even if that had been my intention, does he really think I would've told him?"

"Why?"

"Why?" she asked with incredulity.

"Because your sense of survival kicked in," he answered because his question had been rhetorical. "Because you'd realized who we really were."

She averted her gaze, unable to withstand his scrutiny. He took her hand and guided her to the panel on the wall. He entered a code. Suddenly, what she believed was a wall slid partially open, revealing a room on the other side. Keeping her hand in his, he leaned into the room and flipped on a light, then led Meggie down a stone step.

It wasn't a regular room, she realized, but a garage with a big Harley, trimmed in a gleaming deep blue. The garage door faced the direction of the ocean, instead of the street. She glanced around, peeked over her shoulder into the house, studied the bike, then considered the garage door again.

"A secret escape route or something?" she guessed.

He nodded, and she could see she'd impressed him by the appreciation in his eyes.

"To the beach?"

"Why do you think that?"

"It faces that direction."

"I can get to Aunt Patricia's or ride down the beach about a half-mile to get to a barely used road."

"Why are you telling me all this? Revealing club secrets? Are you going to kill me?"

"No. You've proven you're not a danger, so you don't need to die."

"Did you ever think I did?"

He shrugged.

Meggie snatched her hand and backed away from him. "Did Christopher?"

"No." He cocked his head to the side. "It was a shock that he trusted you so completely, so quickly. That's it right there, Megan. He's fighting to do right by you because you've always showed him that same courtesy. But if and when he comes back to you, you have to see him, accept him, for who he really is. A flawed man who's made mistakes, yet still fair and loyal. A man who wields the same sword that has been used against him too many times to count. None of us will ever ask you to give up the good you see in the world, least of all Christopher, but you have to respect the ugly in his life as well as how he deals with it."

"Thomas?" she asked quietly.

"Yes, sweetheart. If the motherfucker deserves to fucking die, you have to step out of the way and don't get in Christopher's head."

"Is that why he left?" she asked miserably.

"Stop torturing yourself with that question. If it makes you feel better to call the club every day and ask to talk to him, do it. But use this time to search your heart and soul to decide if this is the life *you* want."

"Okay," she said softly.

"I'm going to walk you back to Aunt Patricia's. I'll pick you up about nine tomorrow morning, so get a good night's sleep."

"Don't you have to work?"

"I'm the fucking boss, so I set my own hours."

Meggie opened her mouth to tell him she'd think about his offer.

"I'm not taking no for an answer, Megs. You don't need to stay in the fucking house and wait for him to call."

He was right. Besides, she could still call and text Christopher. Maybe convince him to return. "Okay. Nine o'clock it is."

"Come on, Megs, dance with me," Johnnie said, two days later, as he pulled her into his arms and smiled down at her.

A classical song blasted from the wireless speakers in the playroom at Patricia's house. She'd left early this morning for a trip to Seattle, saying she'd be back in a day or two. While Meggie was out with Johnnie, she decided to invite him to dinner.

Yesterday, he kept her out for hours, mainly running errands. Picking up dry-cleaning, going to the post office, stopping in at his office to grab files, buying alcohol. Mundane tasks that kept her out of the house. She did try to reach Christopher and got the same result. When Johnnie dropped her off last night, she'd been exhausted and went to the bedroom, took a quick shower, and climbed into bed.

"Relax, sweetheart," Johnnie murmured now after dining on her meal of baked chicken, roasted potatoes, and steamed carrots.

He sounded amused but his intense expression made Meggie lower her lashes. He pulled her closer, pressing her against the hard planes of his body. His erection throbbed between them. She pretended not to notice.

"What's the name of this?"

"*Claire de Lune*," he responded. "Debussy."

"It's pretty."

"You're still as stiff as a board, Megs."

"I've never danced this way before," she admitted.

He swung her around, then lowered her into a dip. She giggled as he lifted her and drew her close to him.

"My own special touch that you anticipated perfectly."

"You're so modest, Johnnie Donovan."

"My name's John Paul Donovan," he corrected as the song ended and silence fell around them.

She didn't respond, her emotions running amok. Maybe, she should leave. It had been enough to endure when Patricia was in residence. Now, she would be gone for a day or two, and Meggie would have to be alone in a house she'd never truly felt welcomed at.

"What's going through your head?" Johnnie asked.

"Being alone in this house," she answered, wrinkling her nose. Another thought came to her. "It's the holiday season." She made a point of looking around. "There are no decorations. There's not even a tree."

"We'll get a tree. I'm sure Aunt Patricia has decorations around here somewhere. We'll find them and hang them as soon as she returns. If she doesn't have any, we'll buy some."

"We'll see."

"I'll sleep here tonight and tomorrow. However long my aunt's away."

She chanced a glance in his direction, not sure why she blushed as her gaze fell on him. Maybe because insinuation filled the rumble in his voice. "In one of the guest rooms," she said, not wanting him to expect anything else.

He winked at her but nodded. "If you're too frightened, we can sleep in the same bed. I'll stay on my side." He raised his right hand. "Scout's honor."

"Separate beds are fine," she said primly.

He picked up his phone and looked at the screen. "One more dance with me. This time, relax. Lay your head on my shoulder." He swept his gaze over her. "My chest," he amended. His eyes twinkled. "My stomach."

She threw him a dirty look. "I'm not that short and if you go any lower, I'm going to punch you."

He laughed, pressed the screen on his phone, and took her in his arms again as *Everything I Do I Do It For You* by Bryan Adams began to play.

"Johnnie—"

"Shhh. Relax, Megan. Just trust me and dance with me. It's nothing but a brief respite from reality to give your brain a rest."

Sighing, she nodded and didn't resist when he rested his hand on the back of her head and urged her against his chest. He smelled of mint and cigarettes. She tried to appreciate him and the way he was taking care of her, but the words to the song sunk into her, opening a new wound inside her at Christopher's treatment. She couldn't stop her sob or her deep, raw longing that could only be soothed by Christopher.

Johnnie placed tender kisses along her hairline, over her wet cheeks, along her jaw. When he tried to cover her mouth, she turned her head. He backed away. At his intake of breath, her shoulders slumped. Then he pulled her close again and wrapped his arms around her.

"Cry, sweetheart," he told her. "If that makes you feel better and I'll do nothing but comfort you and be the friend you are so in need of right now. You're hurt and overwhelmed, but Christopher must go through a process before he accepts he's worth your love. There's a lot…" Johnnie sighed. "Give him the space he needs."

"I have no choice," she sniffled. "He won't take my calls."

"He will."

"How many more times are you going to say that?"

"Until my words prove correct or until you accept what you can't change, Megan. Whichever one happens first doesn't matter to me, as long as you're not so broken."

She wasn't sure how long she stood in his embrace, but she gradually felt better, a fact he sensed because his hold loosened by degrees, until he finally released her.

"Walk to my house with me, so I can pick up pajamas and a change of clothes. We'll come back and watch movies all night."

The idea appealed to her. "I'll be fine here. While you're getting your stuff, I'll scrounge up snacks for us."

"What type of movies do you like?" Johnnie asked.

"Horror," she answered without hesitation. "The scarier, the better."

He gave her a wolfish grin. "I'll bring blankets for us to cuddle under. I'm a big wimp, so you'll have to comfort me and ease my fears."

"We can watch another kind of movie if you prefer."

"I'm joking, Megs," he said, laughing. "I just wanted to hold you under a fucking blanket." He shook his head. "You really need to be educated on the ways of motherfuckers."

She pursed her lips. "Are men so complicated?"

"We're hunters. We home in on what we want and plan our strategy to achieve the goal. Suppose you were on a date and a fucker was strategizing on how to convince you to give him a shot. He might say something along the lines of, I'll put just the tip in, so—"

"The tip of what?" Meggie interrupted. "And where?"

He gazed at her for long moments, before guffawing so hard he had to wipe the tears from his eyes.

"I'm glad you find my confusion so funny," she grouched.

"The tip of his cock, Megan," Johnnie said, on the verge of exploding again, and ignoring her annoyance.

"You said give him a shot. I thought you meant to date me."

"Apologies," he said, around more laughter. "Come on. Walk with me. The moment I leave you alone, you're going to start thinking about Christopher again."

Since he was right, she didn't protest and instead, followed his suggestion.

Chapter Thirty-Four

Meggie

FOR THE NEXT TWO WEEKS, JOHNNIE WAS Meggie's constant companion. They picked out a Christmas tree and decorated it with Patricia's help. He took her to the lighthouses, drove her around to different shops and stores. When she protested because Christopher had already taken her shopping, he insisted, pointing out the need for stocking stuffers and gifts beneath the tree here since she'd only brought along the gifts she'd purchased for Christopher and Patricia.

She tried to put her heart into it, but she missed Christopher more with each passing day. It hurt that he hadn't called her once. After the first week, she stopped calling him, too, because it was clear he wouldn't return her calls or answer at the time she called. Nor, it seemed, would he dial her number unbidden, just to check on her. He'd dropped her off and forgotten about her as if he couldn't get rid of her fast enough. She and Patricia reached a turning point, although sometimes she'd catch the woman staring at her and Meggie would glimpse undecipherable emotions. Then, her face would clear, and all would be well again.

Ten days before Christmas, Johnnie convinced her to go to the movies and dinner with him. Now, she sat across from him in a quiet corner in the restaurant. Festive décor gave the place an enchanted feel, the individual lamps and cordoned off spot lending a sense of romance.

She pushed her salad greens around on her plate and listened half-heartedly to Johnnie's conversation. It took her a moment to realize he'd stopped talking. She raised her gaze to his.

"The elves won't leave you anything. They want good cheer, Megs."

Meggie sighed and laid her fork aside. "I'm sorry I'm not good company. You've been so kind, too."

He smiled. "I get that you're lonely," he said quietly. "There's no remedy for a broken heart except time. I really thought he'd realize what he was doing and stay away a couple days, a week at most." He thrust his fingers through his hair, agitated. "But his leaving...there are things...he's trying to protect you."

"He never promised me anything, so I'm fine. I've survived worse." She blinked away tears, the truth bitter in her throat. He hadn't even promised they'd spend Christmas together. Judging by all the plans they'd made, she'd just assumed they would.

They fell into silence as the rest of the meal was served. Meggie declined dessert, grateful that Johnnie did the same. She kept her head turned toward the window on the drive back to Patricia's house. However, she swiveled her gaze to Johnnie when, after turning on the private road, he stopped at the second house instead of continuing to the end.

"Spend the night with me," he urged softly.

In the dark night, shadows hid Johnnie's expressions, although desire hummed in his low tone.

"Just because Christopher is sleeping with other women doesn't mean I have to do the same."

A flash of white, the showing of his teeth, as he smiled. "No," he murmured. "And you wouldn't be doing the same. The last time I checked I'm a man, not a woman."

Meggie scowled. "You know what I mean!"

"I do, Megs," he said with a sigh, all humor gone.

Meggie studied her clasped hands where they rested on her lap. She liked Johnnie and she was more aware of him than she should've been. But the thought of getting naked in front of him, while allowing him the liberties to do all the things to her body Christopher had done, disconcerted her. Though Johnnie had been nothing but sweet and kind, an utter gentleman, a shoulder to lean on, a friend to confide in, she still felt a certain loyalty to Christopher. In the dark of night, she'd touch herself, hearing the deep rumble of Christopher's voice in her head as he made love to her, imagine the feel of his big hands all over her body, his work-roughened fingers and palms caressing her sensitive skin. She'd come, always with the thought of Christopher, never of his sexy cousin. That had to say something. She shook her head. "I can't."

"Do you think Outlaw is alone?" he asked. His voice held no malice, just curiosity.

She shook her head, the implication cutting through her. "No. I-I guess he's with Kiera. And Ellen," she added after a brief pause.

He unhooked his seatbelt and caressed her cheek. "Outlaw...Christopher," he amended, "has a deep-seated sense of decency toward the innocent, Megan."

Before she responded, he got out of the car and came around to her side, opening her door for her and holding his hand out. She accepted it and stepped down. The night was clear and mild, the sky black velvet with glittering stars.

He bent his head and took a slow, leisurely kiss from her. His lips were gentle and coaxing, sipping from her mouth when his tongue found hers, completely different from their first kiss. He tasted of wine and smelled faintly of aftershave. Meggie stood on her tiptoes and leaned further into the kiss. He drew her closer and pressed his throbbing erection into her belly.

She pulled her mouth away and turned her head.

"Megs," he murmured huskily, then nipped her ear. "I want you. I swear Christopher will never know if you two work things out. I'm lonely. You're lonely. Why shouldn't we make love and find comfort in each other?"

"Because there should be real feelings involved," she blurted. She stilled, wishing she could kick herself since they both knew Christopher didn't have real feelings for her. Bracing herself for Johnnie's mockery, she tensed. "Besides, I'm not one of the club girls to sleep with whoever wants me at any particular moment."

"Of course you aren't," he snapped. "None of us see you that way."

"It doesn't matter how you all see me, but it matters how I see myself."

"Megan—"

"Anyway, I'm not on any sort of birth control," she admitted in a small voice. She was beginning to fear Christopher had left his baby inside of her.

Johnnie paused and she felt the weight of his gaze on her. "Condoms work."

Meggie refused to say anything more. "I can walk to Patricia's house." She ducked under his arm and around his body, refusing to acknowledge her achy nipples and wet sex.

He caught up to her, but she didn't slow her stride. He adjusted his steps to her shorter pace. "Why are you lonely?" she asked after a few minutes of walking in silence.

"My girlfriend decided to marry someone else."

"I'm sorry," she said, meaning it. "That must've been devastating."

"It was," he agreed. "But I wanted her happy. I left the club to make her happy. In the long run, we weren't right for each other."

"It's hard to imagine you not being right for someone."

His teeth flashed again. "That so?" he asked, smug. "That means I'm right for you?"

"I walked right into that, didn't I?" She chuckled.

"I'm afraid you did."

A few moments later, they reached the porch. She opened the door since Patricia didn't believe in locking anything and turned to Johnnie. With the porch light on, she saw his beautiful eyes, more silver than gray just then, and handsome face. He kissed her again.

"Invite me in. There are other ways to give each other pleasure. I don't have to penetrate you."

Patricia had already retired, and the house was quiet. Emptiness loomed and the temptation to give in to Johnnie almost overwhelmed Meggie. He wanted to use his tongue on her, and Christopher had taught her how to enjoy that. What would it hurt?

"Licking your pussy isn't the same as putting my dick in you," he said, nuzzling her neck.

Meggie pressed her hand to her belly. If Christopher's baby grew inside of her, she couldn't give herself to anyone else. They'd become lovers about a month ago and she was growing more and more anxious waiting for her period.

Johnnie licked her ear and Meggie gasped. "You smell so fucking good," he rumbled. "And I want you so fucking bad, Megan."

"Y-you promised," she murmured in an unsteady voice.

"I know but you're so fucking gorgeous and, tonight, fuck…tonight, Megan. In that little red lace dress."

He looked like temptation himself wearing a tan Henley, camouflage chinos, and black leather jacket, left casually open.

"Baby, I swear," he said, clasping her waist, "I swear, I'll make you come so many times." His thumb flickered over her sensitive nipple. "Let me come to your room." He kissed her throat. "Lay you on your bed." A lick to the pulse point at her neck. "Shove your dress above your waist." He brushed her lips with his mouth, teased her nipple again. "Spread your pussy open." He sucked her bottom lip and she moaned. "Taste your clit with the tip of my tongue." Covering her nipple with his mouth, he suckled, hard, the wet heat of his tongue sparking fire in her, even though her dress still covered her breast. He bit the hardened tip and Meggie cried out, stars exploding behind her eyes, her body weaker than her intentions.

One arm around her waist, he kissed her deeper and Meggie kissed him back, allowing him to guide her hand to his penis. She caressed the slippery head, spreading his moisture, then fisted him, doing everything Christopher taught her. His hand slipped into her panties, and he tore his mouth from hers.

"You're fucking soaked. For me," he growled, caressing her clit and slipping two fingers inside her. Her pulls and strokes on his penis grew harder while the in and out motion of his fingers sent shivers through her, and she cried out against his mouth.

His grunts lowered and harshened with each thrust into her hand. Meggie could hold off no longer and shudders racked her body, his fingers massaging her slippery inner walls, his thumb circling her clit. He swallowed her soft cries, her orgasm tipping him over the edge and hot semen gushed from him, raining onto her fingertips and his Henley.

Slowly, he backed away from her and she stood there, trembling from the aftershocks of her orgasm and his overwhelming passion. Their heavy breathing punctuated the silence, but Meggie didn't know what to say. He used his shirt to clean her fingers, then tipped her chin up.

"Christopher is one lucky fucker." He sighed. "I'd fight an army to have you, Megan, but you don't want me. You want him."

Unable to dispute that, she whispered, "I've never lied to you. But it doesn't matter. He doesn't want me."

"If Christopher doesn't come back soon, I won't rub your pussy while you jerk me off standing on a fucking porch. We'll be in my bed. You'll be fair game."

"It seems like I was fair game, anyway."

He smiled and knuckled her lips. "Not really. Besides, you're underestimating my cousin."

"What if I am? I've just betrayed him. Christopher doesn't know who to trust because whoever he trusts always seem to let him down." She lowered her lashes. "Like this. Me. Us. He deserves better than what I've done with you tonight."

Johnnie hugged her and sighed. "I know, Megan. Being in the club, though, we always shared girls."

"I've heard and seen more than I care to in the club," she admitted, then shifted her weight. "Do you really think I've underestimated him? That he'll return?"

He patted her hair. "Yes. Sooner or later. I can't guarantee what he'll say to you or want from you. Just remember—if you two end up together, this is our secret."

It wasn't as if she'd advertise she and Johnnie had masturbated each other to orgasm. Nor was it likely Christopher would care even if she did advertise it. Johnnie would only defend Christopher, so she nodded.

"I'm serious, Megs. If you like my pretty face attached to my head, you won't ever mention this to anyone."

She snorted and rolled her eyes. "Now, you're being dramatic."

"And now, you're underestimating not only Christopher but his wrath, too. He'd fucking kill me if he knew I seduced you."

Meggie shrugged, not believing the sentiment. "It's our secret. Besides, you didn't seduce me without my participation." She only wished the orgasm she'd had had taken away the agony of Christopher's continued absence.

"All right, Megs," he said and gave her a soft kiss on her lips. "I'll see you tomorrow." With that, he backed away, went down the steps and soon disappeared into the darkness, leaving Meggie to dwell on her life until this point and wondering what her next move should be.

Chapter Thirty-Five
Christopher

CHRISTOPHER LEANED HIS BACK AGAINST THE headboard of his bed in his room at the clubhouse, drinking a beer and listening to *Apologize* by OneRepublic. That song, along with one of Megan's favorites, *When I Was Your Man* by Bruno Mars, and *Meant* by Elizaveta—a favorite of Mortician—played on repeat. Regret rode him hard. He wished he'd never left Megan at his ma's house. Several times, he thought of rejoining her. Then, he remembered his predicament caught him between a partial truth and the murder of her father, and he didn't have good answers for either, so he stayed at the club. It was time well-spent. He checked inventory and double-checked the books. He sent "gifts" to the police chief and extra money to the hospital for their pediatric ward for the kids to have an extra special holiday.

Business went on as usual. But he missed Megan and regretted not being with her to carry through on all they'd talked about. Everything at the club was the same, except she wasn't there with him, and everything felt different without her.

The first week after he'd left her, she'd called constantly. He'd gotten all her messages. Sometimes, he'd been standing at the bar, waiting for the phone to ring. Once, when a Probate had answered and said, 'hello', Christopher had snatched the phone just to hear her voice.

He'd almost given in and talked to her, then he'd shoved the receiver back to the Probate and stormed away. Knowing she continued to call eased his aching need and gave him comfort. As long as she tried to reach him, she still wanted him.

Gradually, her calls lessened, until they stopped completely. That, more than anything, tortured him. Each day, he remained in Hortensia, and she stayed in Long Beach without even attempting to talk to him, he missed her a little more. He wondered what she was doing and if she still wanted him.

Always, his mother's words came back to him and changed his mind about hitting the road and riding back to claim Megan. Sooner or later, he'd have to face her. If he kept delaying, he'd return and there would be no chance of ever having her. If he persisted in resisting, he'd lose her forever.

All around him, Ellen, Kiera, and some of the other bitches were decorating, planning a big meal but without Megan included, as she had been for Thanksgiving. It wasn't as if there were old ladies around, who the boys had to hide the whores from. If it wasn't for the bitches who hung around, it'd just be a bunch of dicks there for the holidays. When Christopher saw the Christmas tree in the main room, he winced, remembering what he'd promised Megan. He'd left her in Johnnie's hands, but, as the days passed, he realized he'd made a mistake and hoped Johnnie hadn't seduced her yet. Megan was a light in Christopher's life, the shining star he was doing his best to extinguish.

A knock sounded on his door.

"Come in," he called, grabbing his smokes from the table and lighting one as Kiera pushed the door open.

He blew out smoke through his nostrils and eyed her long legs, tiny, frilled skirt and cropped tee. It was obvious she wore no bra.

She leaned against the closed door. "I figured since Meggie's gone, we could fuck."

Silent, Christopher took a drag of his cigarette, then gulped some beer. Kiera wouldn't move without him urging her forward. He could fuck her, just like he swore to Megan he would. It's just that he couldn't really. He didn't want twenty-five-year-old pussy anymore. He wanted eighteen-year-old pussy and not just any eighteen-year-old pussy, but the one belonging to a beautiful little bitch who skirted the edges of bratdom.

"Ain't interested," he said.

Kiera's eyes widened. "Is she coming back?"

He shrugged, wanting to be with Megan more than anything. He prayed to God she'd somehow come back. It didn't matter that he no longer believed *in* God. Megan was important to Christopher. Innocent. Sweet. Untouched by any man but him. He prayed to God Johnnie hadn't touched her. After warning Johnnie to keep his hands to himself, he'd pushed her right into his cousin's arms. "We gonna see. I ain't sure right now."

"Then—"

He squashed his cigarette. "Then, nothin'. I ain't gonna have her walkin' round here with you smilin' in her face, knowin' you fucked me and *would* fuck me whenever she gone."

She wrinkled her nose. "Isn't that what usually happens with old ladies?" she asked, sounding genuinely confused.

"Yeah. Don't make me no difference. It ain't happenin' to *my* old lady." No matter if Megan thought that was exactly what would happen. "Just go, Ki. I got shit to work out in my head."

"I like Meggie," she said quietly. "We might've underestimated her a lot, but she still don't seem like she's cut out to be an old lady, though. Especially your old lady. She's a real good girl."

"She tougher than you think," he snapped, her words getting to the heart of the matter and playing on all his fears just as they had during the Halloween party. Some of the same fears his mother had played on. They all knew Megan tried to be tough, but the life he led was fucking brutal.

"You love her?"

He glowered at her, refusing to even entertain the notion. "Go."

She left. Thank fuck.

For the next three days, Christopher took care of club business, disappearing two of the fuckers who'd been with Snake that day at the mall when Megan had gone with Ellen and Kiera. He had his boys see to a shipment while he collected the money. He met with the president of the club from the next town over, assuring the man's allegiance against Snake and the other dissenters. Except for smoking Snake out of his pit, he'd gotten shit done, making it relatively safe to get Megan back.

The wind whispered through the trees edging the cemetery, the breeze cool against Christopher's face. An arc of colors—magenta, orange, purple, red—painted the evening sky, but a lone ray of sunlight burst through the coming dusk and glimmered off the black marble he faced.

He stared at the gold lettering. **"Big Joe" Joseph "Boss" Foy. A man among men.**

Before he brought Megan, Christopher wanted to make sure everything would suit the man she'd loved. He'd never expected *his* emotions to well up, unfeeling motherfucker that he was. He'd thought he'd want to piss on the monument, not fall to his knees and howl with rage at the same time he begged forgiveness.

Heaving in a ragged breath, he traced the inscription. The date of Boss's birth. The date of the man's death.

"You motherfucker," he snarled. "Why? *Why you make me fuckin' do that to you?*" A sob escaped him, and everything knotted up inside of him. He hated Boss so much, but he loved him, too. Despite everything, the vileness of his last months, the jeopardy he'd put the club in, the way he'd let down Megan, Christopher loved Boss. He leaned his head against the headstone. No, not a headstone. Nothing so simple for Big Joe. Christopher had insisted he wanted to impress Megan, so he'd ordered an obelisk erected with a leaf top carving. It stood alone on a small rise, toward the back of the cemetery. But, standing there, he knew he believed, somewhere deep inside himself, Boss deserved such a tribute. Or the man he'd once been deserved it.

Angry tears. Bitter tears. Tears of grief and guilt, sorrow, and anguish. The water leaking from Christopher's eyes and raining down his cheeks contained so much welled-up feelings, he thought he might go mad, his insides as hollow as the empty grave the obelisk rose above.

"Goddamn you. You hear me, Joseph Fuckin' Foy? God fuckin' damn you. You turned into a fuckin', goddamn monster. You deserved puttin' down like a fuckin' dirty dog. But why me? Why you gotta make *me* do it? *YOU HEAR ME, MOTHERFUCKER?*"

His yell echoed in the eerie silence, where only the trees, the sky, and the souls of all those buried there absorbed it. He drew in ragged breaths to calm himself, relieved as fuck he hadn't seen this for the first time when he brought Megan. Right now, Christopher couldn't be sure when he'd let her see this. She needed closure, needed to grieve, but, fuck, *this* brought his grief on.

He was such a selfish fuck, trash, like Zoann said. He'd gotten this to show Megan. To win brownie points with her, he guessed, hoping she'd somehow overlook the fact *he'd* killed her daddy. As if she'd ever forgive him if she found out. He couldn't stay away from her, though, needing her now more than ever.

"Megan here," he blurted, not having the strength to be ashamed of his pussy-like behavior. He sniffled. "She everythin' you always said and more. You'd be so fuckin' proud of your beautiful baby girl. I know you said she wasn't for me. Long time ago. Remember, Prez? When I asked you her name? You said don't worry about it cuz she ain't for you, asshole." Christopher laughed through his tears and thrust his fingers through his hair, agitated. "I tried to leave her alone. I swear I did. I even left her with John Boy. He better than I can ever be for her. Motherfucker got a heart and a soul. But, Prez, I ain't lettin' her go. I just ain't. And she want me, too. She think I'm worth somethin'. Ain't knowin' why cuz she smart as fuck, but the way she look at me…Prez, Ima take good care of your baby girl. As long as she want me, Ima lay the world at her feet. I'd kill for her and I'd die for her."

Christopher blinked away the last of his tears. He'd bring Megan here. One day. Now, he'd let this remain his secret. He'd forget this place to enjoy the rest of the holidays. With only ten days left to Christmas, he had one more order of business to see to in the morning, then he'd ride out, back to Megan, away from *this*. As he hurried to his Harley, he hoped Boss found the peace in death that had escaped him in life.

When Christopher walked into the boardroom the next morning, he sat at the head of the table, anxious to get this behind him. Digger, Mortician, and Val sat close to him as they discussed their plan of action. Christopher had decided Val would hang with Rack. He'd stick to that motherfucker like a leech and Rack would let him, too, because everyone was going to think Val had gone over to Rack's side. In turn, Christopher hoped the ruse would get them closer to Snake.

At least, that was the plan. Patricia's words ate at him, and he missed Megan with a fierceness he hadn't expected.

Mortician leaned back and folded his arms. "You hanging round for Christmas, Prez?"

"Nope. Promised Megan we spendin' Christmas together."

The door swung open, and Rack sauntered in, helmet held under his arms. He nodded to everyone and set the helmet on the table.

"Showtime," Val mumbled.

Christopher acknowledged the word with a thinning of his lips. Val was one of his best friends, but to pull this shit off, he'd have to focus on the here and now, not anticipate seeing Megan again.

Rack's perpetual smirk deepened as he shoved his chair back and dropped into the seat at the end of the table.

Christopher didn't have to pretend to glare at Rack. He disliked the motherfucker more and more with each passing day. When he buried him, he'd burn his fucking cut, patches still attached. He didn't want nobody tainted by Rack's stink.

"Yo, Outlaw."

Christopher nodded. "Rack, I been needin' to talk to you 'bout Boss—"

Right on cue, Val snorted. "Like you been fucking talking about him for months, Prez? We all know you put Boss to ground, and it was to save your own fucking ass."

Mortician and Digger frowned, shifted in their seats. Real discomfort hung in the room. Anything to do with Boss was a tough fucking topic. But this was the heart of the fucking matter. Rack, Snake, and their faction suspected Christopher had killed Big Joe, though they didn't have proof to confirm it.

"I ain't kill Big Joe," Christopher barked, glaring at Val. After the elaborate cover-up they'd done to keep that secret and all the blow-up on Halloween, the stupid motherfucker was opening his fucking mouth about *this*? This was nothing they'd rehearsed. "You know that a rival club did that."

Confusion flashed in Val's face. Real, true fucking confusion, like the motherfucker was suffering amnesia. "You don't have to admit it, Outlaw. It's an open secret."

Rack smiled nastily and nodded to Val. "Be sure you around when that little bitch he's fucking find out the real story. That Outlaw was at the club with her daddy the day he died."

Just as predicted, Rack couldn't resist the jab if it had to do with Boss.

Val sniggered. "I feel sorry for him to be honest. He's too pussy-whipped to get in her face and tell that bitch he killed her father."

Christopher gritted his teeth, reminding himself of the long-term goal and ignoring the nerve Val hit.

"Val, shut your fucking mouth before Outlaw shove his foot up your ass," Digger warned with a grimace.

"Outlaw?" Val echoed, eyes wide. "Who's Outlaw?"

Rack barked with laughter. "Spot on, Val. He ain't no fucking Outlaw no more."

Val smiled. "Sure isn't. Nowadays, he's *Christopher.*"

A muscle ticked in Christopher's jaw. This ad-libbing shit was about to get a head fucking busted. Yeah, Val was goading him, but he was going too fucking far, first with Big Joe and now by bringing Megan into this and enjoying himself too fucking much at her expense.

Rack leaned back, pulled out a smoke, and lit it. Christopher got his anger under control. He had a fucking goal to accomplish. Val had to goad him enough to cause a big—seemingly—irreconcilable fight. As friends, Christopher had to overlook Val's taunts for the time being. If he flew off the handle too fucking quick, Rack would never believe it.

He glared at Rack and Val, reminding himself he couldn't see Megan for the first time in almost three weeks with bruised knuckles.

"You two through bein' fuckin' comedians? We got some serious shit to discuss, so shut the fuck up so I can get to it."

Presumably, Rack wouldn't be interested in hearing about Boss. Everyone knew he resented Christopher for how things had gone down. But the man was silent, appearing to be waiting for Christopher to continue.

Val cleared his throat. "Before we get to that, I have a favor to ask you, Prez?"

Christopher tapped his fingers on the table, noticing a flicker of remorse in Val's face before the assfuck smiled.

"You left her there with John Boy, so you know he's fucking her by now."

"Aww man," Mortician complained, "you actually fucking went there."

Yeah, this motherfucker actually fucking went there. Red spots flirted on the edges of Christopher's vision, matching the steam of fury rising in him.

"Can I have some pussy from her, too? I assume since you letting Johnnie get some ass from her, we can, too. We all dying to tap that."

"Fuck you," Digger snarled. "I ain't dying to tap nothing on Meggie body. Your dumb ass not about to get me fucking killed."

"Outlaw understands, brother," Val went on. "I want to find out if her ass is as hot as it looks. That bitch is one hot piece."

The room fell silent. Not a peep. No one moved a muscle, waiting for Christopher's reaction. Thing was, if Christopher reacted, he'd pull his nine and blow Val the fuck away. And he really didn't want to do that.

Val, the fucking moron, must've thought Christopher stayed silent because he was "pretending" to consider Val's request. Had to be the reason he opened his fucking trap again.

"Rack, I ever tell you about the time we walked in on Megan naked?" He indicated himself, Digger, and Mortician with a finger point.

"Fuck off," Mortician ordered. "Don't put me in the middle of your I-want-a-bullet-in-my-dick speech."

"Shut up, Mort," Rack growled. "I wanna hear this. I wanna know if her pussy is shaved or if—"

"Nope, her pussy hairs are blo—"

That was fucking it. Christopher couldn't take it anymore. He moved fast, backhanding Val out of his seat and pounding his face. "I'm gonna fuckin' kill you," he snarled, wrapping his hands around Val's neck.

"Outlaw! Prez!" Mortician yelled at the same time he and Digger started trying to pry his fingers from Val's throat before dragging him off the man.

Christopher struggled against the hold of the two brothers while Val was looking at him as if he'd never seen Christopher before. He didn't know if Val's fury was an act or not. Christopher's rage sure the fuck wasn't.

"Nobody...*nofuckinbody*," he repeated through clenched teeth, "ever talk 'bout Megan like that. Nobody ever think 'bout touchin' her. You crossed the fuckin' line, motherfucker." He jerked out of Mortician and Digger's grasps and pounded Val again. "I owed you that from the night in question, fuckhead."

"See what your bitch ass done?" Digger snapped, glaring at Val when Christopher swung his gaze to him and Mortician. Digger knew what was coming since they'd seen Megan naked, too.

Christopher didn't waste any time, everything combining and ending up right here and now. He punched the two brothers, then indicated the door. "All you, get the fuck outta my face. Meetin' canceled due to a fuckin' epidemic of assfucks. And, Val, if you know what the fuck fuckin' good for you, stay the fuck outta my face."

As Val led the way, limping out, Digger smacked the back of Val's head.

Alone, Christopher kicked the chair Val had sat in and sent it crashing against the wall. Val had fucked up by bringing up Megan, and Christopher had fucked up by losing his shit and forgetting the greater goal of bagging Rack and Snake.

Damn fucking Megan.

Because of her Christopher had gone from badass, pussy-loving biker to one pussy-whipped motherfucker.

Later that evening, he pulled to a stop in front of his mother's house. The road had cleared his head of the rage, leaving only anticipation of seeing Megan. When he saw Johnnie's Navigator parked in his driveway, however, he balled his fists. Fuck him, he was going to garrote that motherfucker. He hit as many bitches as possible, then cut them loose. Not that Christopher cared, anyfuckingway. The motherfucker could've been a one-woman man and he'd still fuck him up if Christopher found Johnnie too close to Meggie.

He paused at the front door, wondering what he'd find inside. He and Johnnie had shared more bitches over the years than Christopher wanted to admit. He couldn't identify most of them in a photo lineup if they'd had fingers pointing at them and signs hanging on their asses proclaiming *I fucked Christopher and Johnnie.*

Bracing himself, Christopher walked inside, realizing how cool the overcast day was when the warmth of the house hit him. Faint music came from the direction of the media room. As he drew closer, he heard Megan talking, no *singing.* Johnnie's guffaws mixed with Megan's caterwauling and the song?

Santa's A Fat Bitch.

What the fuck? Megan was listening to Insane Clown Posse? Since fucking when? The song ended but Johnnie whooped and clapped while Megan giggled and offered Johnnie a grand bow. She wore one of Christopher's button-down shirts, a pair of her own pajama pants and socks, her hair blanketing her shoulders and back.

She didn't even notice him while she was preening for Johnnie, too focused on him, Christopher thought sourly. His cousin noticed him first. Christopher's jaw clenched. She followed the line of Johnnie's attention and her smile faded.

She looked at him with accusation and hurt. And guilt. A whole fucking shitload of guilt.

He glared at Megan. "Interruptin' some shit?"

Johnnie stood. "Christopher."

"John Boy."

Megan yawned. "I'm tired," she announced, attempting to scoot past him, "so I'm going to turn in."

Christopher grabbed her and shook her, his fury exploding. "You fucked him."

"I did not!"

He shook her again. "I might not be a fuckin' genius but I ain't fuckin' stupid."

Johnnie came up and pushed Christopher back. "Back the fuck off, Christopher."

His fist connected with Johnnie's jaw, sending his cousin on his ass. Megan screeched and started toward Johnnie. "If you wantin' that motherfucker to continue breathin', get the fuck away from him, Megan."

She was staring at him, her eyes wide and frightened. Johnnie got to his feet, holding his jaw.

"What the fuck is your problem, dude?" he snarled.

"You, fuckhead, and you know that. You ain't touchin' her now, but I ain't been here in almost three fuckin' weeks. I'm sure you touched her durin' that time."

"You're seriously fucked in the head." Johnnie started for Megan but stopped at Christopher's growl. "I'll talk to you later, Megs."

"The fuck you will," Christopher shouted as Johnnie stormed passed, slamming the door behind him.

"I'm not staying here with you. You're nothing but a bully," Megan cried, running toward the stairway as Patricia came rushing into the room.

"Megan?" she called but Megan kept going. "What's going on in here, son?"

Christopher rubbed his face, then glared at his mother. "I ain't believin' that motherfucker. Movin' in on *my* Megan."

"Is she? You left her behind to go frolic with your…" She waved her hands in the air. "Biker girls."

"Yeah, she *my* Megan, and, if Johnnie got her in his bed, Ima fuckin' choke him with…" He caught the words *his own dick* before they fell from his lips. He was talking to his ma. He huffed out a breath. "I did what needed doin' after you and me talked. I had to tell her somethin'."

Patricia gave him a sad look. She reached up and gripped his cheeks between her hands. "I'm so sorry, my beautiful boy. I never should've said anything to you. I not only hurt you, but Megan got hurt. I just hope you can undo all the damage."

"Me, too."

The murder of Boss aside, Christopher had never practiced monogamy a day in his life and had no desire to. Girls threw themselves at him, like he was a fucking rock star or some shit. He got as much pussy as possible from as many women as possible. He also practiced safe sex. With Megan, however, he wanted to own her in every way possible. He wanted to fill her with his kid and give her a reason to stay at his side. And the thought of Megan laying with another man almost fucking killed him. That was some hypocritical bullshit, but it was what it was and he couldn't deny it.

"Do you love her?"

"Ma, c'mon. What kinda question is that?"

"A legitimate one."

Love failed motherfuckers all the time. Love broke your heart and crippled you with grief. He'd seen it with his mother, and he'd seen it with his sisters when their loser boyfriends fucked over them.

He clenched his jaw. "Nope. I don't," he insisted.

"Then you're going to lose her. She's young. She has the idea of the fairytale in her head."

He frowned. "You mean like Cinderella or some shit? How that gotta do with anythin' 'bout love?"

"*Christopher!*" his mother snapped in exasperation. "It's metaphorical. Stop pulling straws. You get the gist of what I'm saying."

He did, he thought sourly. That didn't mean he had to like it. "What I'm supposed to do with her? I ain't exactly date material."

"You are, Christopher," his mother insisted as mothers do. "Johnnie ate dinner with her and watched movies with her and took her out to eat—"

"You ain't helpin' his cause, Ma. I need to kick his ass right now."

"You told him to watch over her. Or have you forgotten?"

"No, but—"

"Spend this time with her to show her she's more important than that club."

"Ain't nothin' more important than my club," he growled, then regretted his stout conviction at the hurt in his ma's eyes. "See what I mean? I ain't son material, so I really ain't date material."

"To me you are," a sweet little voice murmured.

Christopher sucked in a breath and ignored his mother's satisfied smile. He glanced in the doorway where Megan stood, clutching her bag in front of her like a Medieval shield. She'd changed and now wore a pink shirt and a form hugging skirt that reached her knees. Did she really think she was leaving? To go fucking where? A rush of color stained her cheeks, and a combustible mix of emotions brightened her beautiful eyes. He was vaguely aware of his mother excusing herself.

He moved toward Megan with singular purpose, although he couldn't imagine the mutual embarrassment they'd endure if Patricia returned while he drove into Megan. But fuck him if he could convince his dick of that.

He reached her and lifted her into his arms, wrapping her legs around his waist. He shoved her skirt up and pushed aside the seat of her panties. He unfastened his fly and shoved his cock into her, capturing her small cry in his mouth. He grunted, her delicate flesh stretching to accommodate his thick dick. She whimpered, such a soft sound compared to his harsh groan. It made him harder, more frantic.

His eyes bored into hers. "Johnnie fuck you?" He braced her against the wall and slammed into her. She was vulnerable now, her body filled with him, quivering around him. He curled his lip, thrust harder. "Did he?"

"No," she said with a gasp, gripping his biceps, not dropping her gaze.

"I'm the only one who fucked this sweet pussy?"

"Yes," she breathed, coating his dick with her juices, his rough talk exciting her.

"Keep it that way, Megan. Don't make me kill some poor motherfucker cuz you givin' him pussy."

Another whimper and she threw her head back. Unable to resist, he sucked the tender skin of her neck, sinking his teeth in, then blowing on the bite once he had left his mark. He twisted his hips and she shivered. Once, twice, three more times and he brought her to release, coming a moment later.

He held her in his arms, still encased in her, and kissed her damp forehead, then leaned his own on the wall above her head. They stood silent for long moments, then he pulled out of her and set her back on her feet. She stared up at him, her beautiful face flushed and glistening with sweat, her lips red and swollen. Passion still clouded her eyes, and he felt his dick hardening all over again.

He'd missed her like a motherfucker and intended to fuck her for hours to make up for their days apart.

Chapter Thirty-Six

Meggie

THIS WAS THE FIRST CHRISTMAS MEGGIE HAD EVER spent without her mother. It shouldn't have bothered her so much. She was a woman now—Christopher had seen to that—and she had her own life. She couldn't be Christopher's old lady and her mother's little girl. She knew that. But she also knew how wasted Thomas got. On holidays, his drinking increased exponentially, and his violence went off-the-charts.

Not only that but she'd been so used to Christmas gifts until he put a stop to that, too. Now, she barely had a roof over her head, not sleeping on the streets because of Christopher. While she might've worried about her place in his life at the clubhouse, at his mother's house, he was a different person. Gentler and kinder. He seemed more worried about family, his real, true family, not the men he called brothers.

Meggie had learned bikers lived by a strict code, one that demanded loyalty and respect. They were as much a family as the people related by blood. Yet, it was still a violent, dangerous world, and she wasn't sure if she could ever get used to it.

Tomorrow was Christmas Eve and, despite everything that stood between them, Meggie couldn't wait. She'd begged and pleaded for Christopher to have Val, Digger, and Mortician join them, until he'd relented. She needed the presents she'd purchased Black Friday, anyway. When she suggested also calling and inviting Kiera and Ellen, he drew the line.

"Ain't havin' them two club whores in this house, Megan. You can bat your pussy at me all the fuck you wanna, I don't want them here."

"How do you bat a pussy, Christopher?" Megan had asked, laughing.

He'd chuckled. "You know what the fuck I mean." They'd been in the bedroom, enjoying the late afternoon after they'd stayed out until the early morning hours, visiting the boardwalk before returning home and starting a bonfire on the dunes while the ocean roared, and the wind blew.

Meggie had started to rise, but Christopher pulled her back.

"Listen up, Megan, and I ain't bullshittin'. As long as you here with me, all them other motherfuckers can go fuck themselves." A sheepish expression came over his face. "Except Ma."

Meggie had thumped his shoulder. "Christopher Caldwell, you're soooo bad."

He'd tensed and bleakness stole their light moment. "I wish I coulda had Donovan for my last name. I hate my fuckin' name cuz I hate the prick it belong to."

"Christopher—"

"No, Megan. My grandfather insisted Ma use Caldwell on my birth certificate. Worse thing, the fucker that raped her there to sign it. She ain't had no choice and I ain't had no choice."

"Your name doesn't make you. You're loyal and protective and funny. You rose above—"

"Did I?" he scoffed. "I fuckin' dropped outta school in 9ᵗʰ grade. If risin' above livin' in the dirty fuckin' world I live in, then I hate to see what I woulda done if I woulda stayed mired in shit."

"*You chose to live in this world,*" *she pointed out, surprised at the derision in his voice. "No one forced you to stay in.*"

"*Once you in, you in for life.*"

"*Johnnie isn't.*"

He glowered at her, a distinct chill added to the austerity. "Yeah, what the fuckever. Johnnie a fuckin' saint. I get that. He got everythin' a girl could ever want," *he said with bitterness. "A college education. A good job. A pretty face. A big dick even if his shit ain't bigger than mine.*"

Meggie squeaked and, try as she might, she couldn't stop the heat of embarrassment spreading through her entire body. She bit her lip, not knowing what to say, and Christopher blew out a noisy breath, more vulnerable than she'd ever seen him. He was opening up to her, showing her a side few, if any, knew about.

"*You fucked him, huh, Megan?*"

She couldn't look at him because he'd know for sure something had happened between them, so she just shook her head.

"*I think you did, but you afraid to tell me cuz you know Ima cut his fuckin' dick off.*"

Then why ask? *She wouldn't say that aloud, though. It would only alert him to the fact that something* had *gone on. As long as he wondered about it, he couldn't castrate Johnnie. And, from his tone, she believed he would do it without hesitating.*

"*You are who you are,*" *she said instead. "The choices you made might not be the perfect ones, but they were the ones you needed for the place you were at in your life.*"

She peeked at him through the fringes of her lashes, hoping she'd diverted the conversation back to a safer topic.

He remained quiet for a long while, then he sighed and nodded. "I left you here, Megan. I know I hurt you. I know I said you needin' to test different dicks. Whatever happen between you and John Boy—" *He inhaled a deep breath and relaxed for the first time since they'd began talking. He pulled her into his arms and tangled her hair around his hand. Then he spoke again. "It happened. That's between you and him.*"

She thought about the fact that, in all likelihood, she was pregnant. If he believed she'd slept with his cousin, he might not believe the baby was his. "Christopher, I didn't have sex with him." She skated her fingers across his chest. She loved touching him, feeling the ripple of his muscles beneath her fingertips, learning where each scar was, the most recent the ones to his shoulder and thigh. "I didn't."

"So you ain't knowin' what his cock look like?"

"No." Honest answer. She hadn't seen *Johnnie's penis. She'd just felt it and caressed it.*

Silence. "And you ain't knowin' how it feels."

Omigod. If she didn't answer, he'd know but he'd get the wrong idea, too. If she did answer, she'd have to lie to him and, really, the last thing she wanted to do was lie to him. He might've hurt her for a bunch of reasons, but never because he'd lied to her.

"Motherfucker," he growled, rolling onto her to pin her arms above her head.

"It isn't what you think," she whispered, desperation creeping into her.

"It's a fuckin' yes or no answer, bitch. You felt his dick in you or what?"

"I already told you no. I never felt him inside me!" she flared, squirming beneath him, and glaring at him. "Why are you giving me the third degree? Would it matter so much if I had?"

He clenched his jaw, a muscle ticking, hurt and hopelessness in his green eyes.

"Johnnie and I are friends," she said quietly. "He kept me company while you were gone. Took me places." She wouldn't point out he'd taken her places Christopher had promised to bring her. He didn't need her censure right now. He needed her understanding and reassurance. "But I missed you. I wanted you." She swallowed, hoping he understood her next words. "I thought about making love to him. We kissed, Christopher," she admitted, opening her legs to cradle him between her thighs. She caressed his jawline. "He wasn't you, though. I couldn't imagine doing all the things with him, I do with you."

He nuzzled her neck, and she threw her head back to give him better access. He sank into her, and all thoughts of Johnnie had been set aside.

Now, after ten at night, Christopher sauntered into the room, a towel wrapped around his waist, the tats on his arms and chest glistening with water, his swagger unlike any man's she'd ever seen.

His earlier vulnerability had vanished as if she'd imagined it. He saw her standing there and smiled, the light in his eyes one she was becoming quite familiar with. He crooked his finger at her, and her heart rate increased. With just a flick of his hand, her body responded to his and obeyed him without thought.

When she reached him, she rubbed her palms over the hard expanse of his chest, the rigid pole of his penis raising the towel. He settled his hand on her neck and pulled her to him, kissing her hard and rough, leaving her breathless.

She stood on her tiptoes and circled his neck with her arms, giggling when he swept her off her feet. He took a few steps, and they reached the bed, falling together onto it. He landed on top of her and shoved her nightgown above her waist, entering her with a deep thrust. She closed her eyes, the sheer bliss of him driving into her making her sigh and groan. His fingers tightened on her chin, and she opened her eyes, knowing his signal.

He held her gaze and slammed into her, over and over again. She whimpered and he threw his head back, the muscles in his strong neck straining, his shoulders flexing. He worked his body inside of her. Meggie dug her nails into his back, nosing his throat and smelling the spice of his aftershave.

"Megan."

Wet heat surged through her, tightening her core, at his harsh groan of her name.

"Christopher," she breathed, sucking the skin on his neck.

He kissed her again, his wild, rough lovemaking throwing her into a tumult and stoking the flames of her growing hunger. He sucked her lower lip and pinned her arms above her head.

"What am I doin' to you?"

Her body was on sensory overload, nearing orgasm, soaking her center, and making the tips of her nipples ache. Tiny explosions were bursting through her, starting in her womb, and spreading out over her entire being.

He opened her legs wider and pounded into her, deeper than he'd ever gone. Meggie gasped, his rough movements bordering on pain. She fisted her hands, still above her head, and he tightened his grip on her wrists.

"What I'm doin' to you, huh? Fuckin' you, yeah?"

She nodded, pleasure exploding through her, a soft cry falling from her lips. She arched against him and canted her hips. "Yeah," she said. "You're"—She swallowed— "fucking me."

He growled at her confession, the intensity of his stare and his grinding hips bringing another orgasm on. She screamed.

"I'm gonna put my baby inside you, Megan, yeah?"

"Yes," she gasped, wanting to confirm he'd already done just that before she mentioned anything. Hearing his demands, though, turned her on, and she doubted she would've told him right then even if she was already one hundred percent sure she carried his child.

"You want my baby?"

Her breath came in short pants and her brain could barely process his words. She'd agree to anything, do anything he wanted, as long as he stayed inside of her. "Yes."

"Say it, Megan. Tell me you want my baby."

His baby. He *still* wanted to give her his baby. He truly would be happy when she told him of her pregnancy.

"Tell me," he demanded, leaning over and licking the shell of her ear.

She arched against him, shivering when he sucked her neck. She gripped his firm butt cheeks and dug her heels into the mattress. "I want your baby, Christopher."

"*Fuck*," he growled, his big body stiffening and pouring his warmth into her, then collapsing on top of her.

He rested his weight on her, drawing in deep drafts of air. After a moment, he lifted himself up on his elbows and stared down into her face. He passed a thumb over her lips and smiled down at her, his look so tender Meggie's heart turned over. She blinked, another world opening up to her, the moment one of blinding clarity. It was as if she was seeing him for the first time, his powerful beauty, his Olympian-like build. Those brilliant green eyes that missed nothing and spoke volumes.

Christopher withdrew from her and turned over on his side. "Face me."

She mirrored his position and faced him. They remained like that, not saying a word, only staring into one another's eyes. Once in a while, they smiled or kissed. But they were drinking in each other's nearness, lost to the outside world, only seeing, knowing, feeling, each other.

Meggie's eyes drooped closed, popping open when Christopher pulled her closer.

"Sleep, Meggie," he whispered.

That was the first time Christopher had ever called her Meggie. She smiled and closed her eyes, contented.

Chapter Thirty-Seven
Christopher

S ITTING IN THE GREAT ROOM ON CHRISTMAS DAY, Christopher sighed with contentment, a foreign feeling to him. Even his five sisters couldn't kill the mood, although Zoann continued with her self-righteous bitchiness and still harassed him for not keeping in contact with Patricia. As far as Christopher was concerned that was old news. Zoann didn't understand, so that was *her* fucking problem. They didn't understand staying away from them had kept them safe, which was also how he wanted to keep Megan. He refused to own up to his true feelings about her. If she found out how much she meant to him, that she'd become his heart and soul, she'd somehow get him to agree to put a ring on her finger.

Then, she'd have that hated fucking name, *Caldwell,* attached to her for the rest of her life. He wanted to give her her own cut, proclaiming her the *Property of Outlaw*. Even that would give her too much leverage. Megan had a fucking way about her and the next thing he knew he was agreeing to shit.

Inviting his three brothers to spend Christmas with them, for instance. Buying gifts for those same motherfuckers. Convincing them to bring those same gifts, wrapped with stupid fucking shiny paper and stupider fucking twirly bows. Making Digger and Mortician—and him—shift their weight restlessly when she'd asked why Val hadn't come.

No one had answered, but Christopher didn't think she noticed because Johnnie had walked in and swept her in a hug. Since Johnnie had saved him from coming up with an excuse for Val's absence, he'd let the greeting pass. Besides, Megan's Christmas Eve present had him nice and mellow. While he'd been in the shower, she'd been hookering herself up and greeted him in a tiny red thong lined with white fur, a Santa cap, and six-inch shiny red heels. Her hair had been wild, her lips stained red. He'd gotten a dick stand the moment he'd seen her, posed on the bed. Instead of allowing him to touch her, she'd given him a lap dance to *Love In An Elevator* and a blowjob that curled his toes just thinking about it.

When they'd finally fucked, his dick had been as raw from her sucking him as her pussy had been from him eating her.

Just as the thought crossed his mind, Megan scampered from the kitchen, the gingerbread apron she wore longer than the fucking dress it covered. The black dress had a plunging neckline that ended with a rhinestone. On her feet, she wore some kind of booties with metal ankle cuffs.

While he shot the shit with Johnnie, Digger, and Mortician, Megan was everywhere, and helping in the kitchen, checking on his nieces, and keeping their glasses filled. This time, though, she didn't stop but headed for the door.

"Hey! Where the fuck you goin'?" he growled, not missing the way Johnnie was eye-fucking her. The other two were doing their best *not* to look at her, but she was fucking hard to ignore. She was one hot little bitch.

"With me, Christopher," Ophelia said, appearing around the column to head toward Megan. "We're going to get some fresh air."

At twenty-two, Ophelia was the youngest of the family. Her hair was about two inches long and spiked. She was in some school for film production and sang in a band on the weekends. He knew she had a boyfriend, but she'd never introduced him.

"Girl talk," Megan announced, opening the door, and stepping out into the overcast day. Every now and then, sunshine gleamed through, but, for the most part, it was dull and cool.

Ophelia paused and threw her arms around him. "She's great, Christopher. I love her. Bev, Nia, and Avery are busy with their girls and Zoann offers advice when I don't even ask her. When we saw Meggie at the hospital after you were shot, we didn't even introduce ourselves. We were so worried about you." She shrugged. "We also thought she was just one of the many women in your life. I'm so glad that isn't the case and you brought her here. Meggie is the best gift you could've given me." She kissed his cheek and hurried after Megan.

Through the window, he saw Megan climbing onto the banister and sitting on the edge. Fuck, but he had to grit his teeth to keep from yelling at her to get the fuck down. She laughed, looking young and carefree and at ease. Without warning, she slid to her feet again and started hopping before stopping and talking, her hands moving with each word. She was telling his sister a story, he realized.

"Uh, Prez, we over here," Digger called.

Christopher dragged his gaze away from Megan. Before he could answer, Zoann came in, carrying a bottle of red wine. She held it up.

"Anybody want a refill?"

"Yeah, but not that shit," Mortician grumbled.

"Call Megs. She knows what we're drinking," Johnnie said, tipping his glass back and emptying it.

Zoann rolled her eyes and sat the bottle on the table. She sat near Christopher. Patricia and his other three sisters, along with his three nieces, trooped out of the kitchen.

"Where's Meggie?" Sasha, his youngest niece, asked, craning her neck.

"On the porch with Aunt Ophelia," Christopher answered, looking at the other two little girls, who seemed like they weren't sure if they wanted to stare at him or run away from him. Shit, he knew they were young, but it'd only been a year since he'd seen them.

Sasha didn't wait for any more conversation. She barreled to the door with all the determination of a four-year-old and struggled to open the heavy wood. Once she succeeded, she hurried out and headed right to Megan. Megan ruffled her hair and lifted her into her arms. She was born to have a family, he thought, barely aware of his other sisters and their mother filling wine glasses and joining him. The other little girls stuck to their mother's sides. Fuck him, he'd have to remember their names. Or ask Megan. He had enough names to remember with his sisters.

Wine in hand, Patricia announced, "The turkey still has a few minutes to go."

"Sound good to me, Ma," Christopher said. He swept his sisters with a warning. "But I ain't answerin' no questions 'bout nothin'."

Nia, the oldest girl, sniffed. "Why? You got something to hide?" she challenged.

"I ain't in your shit, stay the fuck outta mine."

"Today is Christmas, so watch your language," Patricia warned. "Besides, we have guests." She smiled at Digger and Mortician just as Megan walked in, still carrying Sasha, with Ophelia trailing behind her.

"They ain't guests, Ma," Christopher growled. "They my brothers."

"We don't want to show Megan a bad side of us," Patricia tried again, gulping her wine.

"Don't mind me," Megan said, setting Sasha on her feet and walking to him, her hips swinging. She went to sit next to him but he pulled her on his lap. She scowled at him and sat ramrod straight.

"But, Megan—"

"No, Patricia, really. I know how siblings are. My two best friends were always fighting with theirs. I only wish I had a sister or brother—" She snapped her mouth shut and frowned, probably remembering she did have a brother.

A giant, diseased asshole, but a brother all the same.

Arm around her waist, Christopher leaned forward to pull his jacket from behind him to settle it around Megan's legs before dragging her higher on his lap. Perfect. Her hot pussy nestled against his growing dick.

"We'll be your sisters," Bev called, craning her neck to see exactly where Megan sat.

Like she didn't know.

Christopher shifted beneath her and Megan folded her arms, but not before Christopher saw her hardening nipples.

"Er, I-I'm flattered, um…" She glanced at his sister. "Bev." She drew in a sharp breath and ground against him, giving him an innocent smile when he hissed. "You know your family better than I do, Christopher," she purred. "Should I accept Bev's offer?"

She moved again and Christopher let out a low groan. "Suit yourself. Just cuz I ain't gettin' along with them, ain't meanin' you ain't."

"Maybe, we'll stop badgering you, if it'll help you get along with us," Avery announced.

"A fuckin' deal I can live with. You stay outta my shi…outta my business and I ain't givin' a fuck 'bout yours."

Megan slapped his shoulder and burst out laughing. To his surprise, the others joined her, even his mother. In spite of himself, he laughed, too, this moment so rare, it frightened him. He'd never gotten along with all his sisters at the same time. Never. He contributed it all to Megan.

Megan, who'd come like a whirlwind into his disordered life.

"You're impossible," Patricia said with mock exasperation.

"See, Christopher?" Zoann began and he tensed. "This could be your life. If you stopped your criminal behavior. Tell him, Megan. You're not going to hang around a man who society fears."

"Not now, Zoann," Patricia started.

"He doesn't even have normal friends, Mama," she snapped. "He has criminals around your granddaughters. He's only comfortable with criminals."

"You're one to talk, Zoann," Megan retorted. "As I recall, you were *flirting* with one of his criminals."

Zoann's mouth fell open and Christopher lifted a brow. He'd warned all his brothers away from his sisters, but the entire club could fuck Zoann for all he cared. She was a fucking mean bitch.

"Stay out of it," Zoann warned, coming to her feet.

"Girls…" Patricia began when Megan shot to her feet, too.

Christopher grabbed her wrist to pull her back. "Zoann, get the fuck outta here."

Megan jerked her hand away. "You brought me in it when you called my name and when you talked about Christopher, Zoann."

"Christopher, huh?" she sneered. "Outlaw. He's *Outlaw*. It should be assassin, murderer, man-whore, pig."

"Wow," Ophelia muttered, "tell him how you really feel."

"It's Christmas," his mother tried again.

Avery ushered the little girls down the hall, toward the media room.

"I knew you ain't able to fuckin' keep your fuckin' mouth shut," Christopher snarled to Zoann.

"Why should I? You have her here, glowing with happiness and living in a fantasy world. You're never going to do anything but bring her down to your level. If you had any decency, you'd let her go. Because this isn't the real you. This—" She gestured to him in his black slacks, white shirt, and cut. "You can't even dress up without letting everyone know you don't belong here."

Christopher stepped forward but Megan placed her body in front of his.

"If you'd pull your head out of your butt, you'd realize there's more to Christopher than just his club," she said fiercely. "You asked me to tell you, Zoann? I'll tell you. You see what you want to see because of your own narrow mind. I'll never ask Christopher to leave his club. It's a part of who he is."

"Then you're a fool. They aren't faithful. They aren't nice. The world knows it. All you have to do is look at them—"

"Man, fuck this shit," Digger barked, starting for the door.

"No," Megan called. "Wait, please."

His hands fisted at his sides, he paused but remained standing, ready to bolt.

Megan walked closer to Zoann, stopping directly in front of her. Christopher contemplated following her. He didn't trust the two of them not to throw down.

Megan put her hands on her hips and rocked back on her fuck-me-heels. "There's a man named Thomas Nicholls," she began, ruining Christopher's day a little more just mentioning that fuckhead's name. She raised her chin and stiffened her spine. "You look at him and you see a model citizen. In private, he's mean and he's violent and he's abusive. He takes pleasure in hurting people. If you want a man like that, a man the world approves of, because you don't have the backbone to go with who your heart leads you to, then you're the fool. Christopher and Digger and Mortician take better care of a woman than Thomas *ever* would. You're out of line talking to them like that and you don't deserve to have Christopher as a brother if you can't appreciate him for the man he is."

Zoann and Megan faced off in silence. Christopher swallowed. No one had ever stood up for him like Megan had and he wanted to kiss the ground she walked on. He wanted to hug her and love her and fuck her. And, he knew Digger and Mortician liked her before, and would watch out for her because he'd expect it of them, but she'd just gained servants for life with her defense of them.

Megan huffed out a breath. "There's nothing in this world worse than having a family member whom you want to be in your life but

426 | K a t h r y n C. K e l l y

they're just out of reach because of something. You can either be his sister or you can walk away with all this anger in you. The choice is yours, Zoann," she added, gliding around his sister and heading toward the kitchen without another word.

Zoann glared at him and pursed her lips. "I guess you want me to leave?"

"You owe everyone an apology, Zoann," Patricia said tightly, angrier than Christopher had seen his mother in a long time. "We were having a wonderful day, but you had to open your mouth and ruin it."

"*They* ruined mine."

"Maybe, you mean *he*," Bev offered. "Megan said—"

Zoann hunched her shoulders and flattened her hand on her belly. "It doesn't matter. I just hope Megan gets out before she finds herself pregnant and without the baby's father. Have more sense than I did."

Christopher didn't even give a fuck she'd just announced her pregnancy after guzzling half a fucking wine distillery. She'd given up on him way before she'd fucked whoever she'd fucked and gotten knocked up. If she'd come to him, instead of coming at him, he would've been willing to do something for her.

"I suppose you want me to leave," she repeated quietly.

He looked at Digger and Mortician. "You mind if she hang around?"

Her eyes widened in surprise and Christopher glowered at her. "Ain't doin' it for you. Ain't even doin' it for Ma. I figure Megan still wantcha fuckin' bitchy ass here. She sayin' what she gotta say and it's over. But you the most two-faced cunt I ever fuckin' met."

"Christopher!" his mother gasped.

Zoann's lips quivered, and Bev's mouth dropped open.

"Don't Christopher me, Ma. Why dontcha Zoann her? This bitch been up in my ass for fuckin' ever cuz of my club, then she spreadin' her pussy for one of my brothers and insultin' everyfuckinbody cuz the motherfucker ain't callin' her. What the fuck she expect? We murderers and manwhores, remember? That's what the fuck we do. Fuck a bitch, knock her up, and walk the fuck away."

A noise caught his attention, and, through his rage, he saw Megan, just behind his mother, chalk white and wide-eyed. She backed a little away.

"Don't, Megan," he warned. "Today Christmas. Don't let all these fuckin' emotions fuck with your head. You know exactly what the fuck I'm sayin' and you know this ain't got shit to do with you."

She studied him and he could see her mind turning, the hurt churning and he damned the anger that made him yell loud enough to be heard down the road.

She nodded and gave him a small smile. "Yes, you were making a point." She left it at that and turned to his mother. "Patricia," she said softly, "I think the turkey is ready."

His mother nodded but it wasn't as if anyone felt like eating. Zoann's bullshit had ruined it.

"Bev, can you help me set the table? Zoann, I need you to fill the water and wine glasses. Ophelia, you get the butter, salad dressing, and salt and pepper in the proper dishes."

Like a drill sergeant, Megan called her troops to action, and they obeyed. Christopher thought dinner was shot to shit, but surprisingly it wasn't. The little girls, Megan, Ophelia, and Patricia kept conversation flowing and laid back. Slowly, they pulled the rest of them in, including Zoann, and it seemed as if the big blow-up between them had been just a glitch in a perfect day.

While the women cleaned up and Avery got the kids ready for bed, him, Johnnie, Digger and Mortician brought a couple bottles outside and started a small bonfire.

"Is this the life you want, Outlaw?" Mortician asked, passing the tequila to him.

Christopher took a swig, searching his heart. As much as he wanted to be able to do this day in and day out for Megan, he couldn't. This wasn't him. It wasn't his life and hadn't ever been. He'd always been on the fringes of his family, just as he now lived on the fringes of society.

The ocean roared behind them, the glow of the fire lighting the sand, the sky filled with stars.

"No. I wish it could be. This where Megan belongs."

"As if where you're at matters to Megan," Johnnie jeered. He snatched the bottle from Christopher and took his turn before wiping his hand across his mouth and thrusting the booze to Digger.

"Hey," Megan interrupted, dropping into Christopher's lap and curling against him. "What are you guys talking about?"

She'd approached so silently, they hadn't heard her come up, and Christopher wondered just what she'd overheard.

"I got a question for you, Meggie," Digger called.

She leaned her head over and looked at him upside down. Christopher realized she was in her bare feet, even though she wore his jacket.

"What?"

"What you did back there, saving the dinner, when it was really going down the shitter. How you did that? I mean I might need to get a bitch that know how to calm shit down like that and make dinner seem like shit never happened."

Meggie straightened on Christopher's lap and rotated to face Digger. "Welllll, some people have it and some people don't."

But, later, when they were alone, after Christopher had taken her to their room, he repeated Digger's question, knowing there was more to it than her breezy answer.

"Although your sister's words were hurtful, they were nothing compared to getting punched, watching your mother get punched, and then being ordered to talk because it was Christmas, and we could act happy." Her smile was sad. "According to him, we didn't want to be happy. Nothing he did made us happy, he said. You learn to adjust to any situation if you want to survive. It's something you never forget."

Christopher tightened his hold on her, but she went on.

"After a while, I was the one who kept my mom encouraged. I cleaned her up after Thomas beat her to a pulp or f-forced her to have sex," she whispered. She shrugged again and kissed his naked chest. "I love being here and getting to know your mom, but when are we leaving to go home, Christopher? I sorta miss the club. You're there and the new friends I've made, and I just feel so close to my daddy."

So many fucking lies and deceptions with Megan. He gripped her hip and squeezed. "That's my life, babe; it ain't yours."

"Huh?"

"If not for Thomas Nicholls, you woulda never met me. You woulda been in school, lookin' forward to graduation shit, thinkin' 'bout college to be that meteorologist."

"You're right," she said softly. "But that didn't happen, and my life went a different way. The only way to survive is to take the punches and bounce back. Otherwise, life just beats you to a pulp until you're too bruised to get up and fight back."

"You sure you ain't older?"

She smiled. "When I was little, I always wanted to get married and have four or five kids. I saw how my mom exhausted herself working away from home and then working *in* our home to take care of me. I had chores from early on. To me, it always seemed like Mom had two jobs, you know? But the one at home never ended. I always talked about my wedding and my children. One day, Mom asked me what about a job. I told her my family would be my job. She grounded me and took all my Barbie dolls away. She said I'd set women back two centuries by my stupidity."

"Your ma sayin' that to you?" Christopher already didn't like the stupid bitch for not getting her little girl out of the clutches of her husband.

"Yeah. She was different, then. Stronger. A real tough woman. Seeing her brought so low is even harder because of that." She moved against him, restless. "By the time the weekend was over, and I went back to school and Farah and Lacey asked what had I done, I was determined to find a career. I liked science and I liked everything about the weather. It fascinated me, so I chose that and stuck to it." She laughed, low. "But I always thought I lived in the United States of America. You know? The country with a Constitution and the Declaration of Independence that gave me the freedom to choose what I want to do. I didn't realize because *I* exercised *my* right to choose what *I* wanted to do with *my* life, I would be kicked out of the sisterhood."

Christopher bit back his laughter because, although she was fuck on with her observation, she had a fucking way with words, and she didn't hold back on her opinions. He could only imagine how well that went over with Thomas Nicholls.

"You right," he said. "You ever tell your old man?"

She nodded. "Daddy said he'd set aside money for me so I could have my own bank account and not have to depend on my husband if things would go bad or something, like it did with him and Momma. He also said he'd make sure the man I married had life insurance because things happened, and I couldn't be too protected that way."

Christopher could imagine Boss saying that, although Megan didn't seem to realize that had been a veiled promise. If her marriage ended, no doubt Megan would've become a very wealthy widow because Big Joe would've fucked any man up who fucked over his baby girl.

He realized his memories of Boss were getting easier, some of the better times breaking through all his bitterness.

Christopher couldn't remember when he'd enjoyed being in his mother's company more. Or, maybe, because Megan was with him and not his aggravating-assed, bratty sisters and nieces, once they'd departed and stayed the fuck away. Long Beach was a good escape when Megan needed a break and the illusion of normalcy. He knew they'd visit at Christmas, if at no other time.

Christopher couldn't deny he was looking forward to getting back to the place he felt most comfortable. His mother asked to go to the club for the annual New Year's celebration. It seemed so important to her, and Megan looked excited, so he agreed. Besides, he'd turned thirty-three on January fourth, and he hadn't celebrated a birthday with his ma in fucking years.

Two days ago, his fucking evening had been ruined when Rack walked the fuck into Ma's house like he owned the place. Christopher had been left fucking speechless when he discovered Ma and Rack were friends. Even after that motherfucker left, Ma hadn't wanted to hear Christopher's objections. Later, Megan revealed she and Patricia had had a similar conversation over Rack.

"Are you mad at me?" Megan had asked.

"Cuz you ain't told me 'bout Rack and Ma?"

She'd nodded.

"I wish you woulda, butcha gave Ma your word you ain't tellin'. A motherfucker only good as his or her word, baby, so fuck no, I ain't mad."

Smiling at the memory, he leaned over and brushed his lips over hers.

No one had heard from Val since the confrontation in the boardroom and Christopher blamed himself. He allowed his personal feelings to interfere with club business, which was inexcusable.

However, he refused to have his mother stay at the clubhouse, so he had some of the Probates clean her old house, where he'd grown up, and air it out. Until she returned to Long Beach, he and Megan were staying with her. Besides, as he told both of them, he wanted Patricia watching over Megan.

He'd hoped by the time Ma left, he would've made contact with Val. So far, he hadn't succeeded.

Fuck!

He hadn't heard from Val, could no longer find Rack, and still didn't know where Snake hid. It was already the second week in January and Patricia would be leaving in two days. He'd just have to keep Megan guarded, twenty-four/seven.

Now, as he watched her sleep, he thought about everything he and Megan had talked about, the baby he'd asked her for. He supposed men had asked women to have their babies since forever. And, women, sweet, pleasing creatures that they were, opened their bodies and allowed men to give them said babies.

He pressed his hand against Megan's flat belly. He'd come enough inside of her to give her five babies. Call him looped out of his head, but he wanted to bind her to him in some kind of way. He wanted her to have his child, continue his legacy if worse came to worse and he ended up dead.

Christopher's thoughts idled for a minute before gunfire shattered the stillness. He bolted upright, rushing to the dresser for his gun. Megan sat up, too, and blinked, clutching the covers to her naked breasts.

His ma screamed before he could tell Megan to find clothes. Fuck, before *he* could find clothes. Another burst of gunfire.

"Christopher!"

He ignored Megan's frightened cry and burst into the hallway. He'd apologize to his mother for his nudity later. Right now…he stopped in his tracks, a roar of pain and fury escaping him at the sight of his mother's body on the ground.

Without heed, he opened fire, not bothering to closely identify the gunman, only wanting the fucker dead. Only—

"Christopher?"

He squeezed the trigger, not responding to Megan, tears running down his cheeks. He emptied his magazine in the fucker, splattered him to hell.

"Outlaw."

Snake. That voice was behind him, too, and he held a fucking gun without ammo. Useless. Christopher turned, trembling because the body of his mother lay behind him. In front of him, Megan stood, her naked body as white as a sheet, her lips trembling. Snake pointed a sawed-off shotgun toward them.

Christopher shoved Megan behind him, hoping she didn't see his mother, hoping she stayed quiet. He had to keep his shit together, so she wouldn't end up dead like… "My ma. You killed my ma."

"My father," Snake snarled. "Your mother."

"Megan ain't my ma."

Snake smiled coldly. "No, she's not. She's my sister, though, a whore like your mother. Fucking my father because my sister's fucking mother married a fucking prick and broke my father's heart."

Megan squeaked while an eerie calm settled over Christopher. Somehow, he'd survive and torture Snake when he got his hands on him. He had to survive and get Megan the fuck away. Boss *wasn't* fucking his ma. He couldn't have been. Patricia hadn't once let on, hadn't once…Fuck him, that's why she'd confronted him about killing Big Joe. They'd been lovers.

"You *knew* about me all along?" Megan asked, not commenting on anything else.

Christopher had to stay focused, stay in the present situation. Megan's life depended on it. He had to get her to shut the fuck up. The less she said, the better for her. As long as she lived, he'd deal with everything else later. At least, she remained behind him, protected from Snake.

"Didn't know about you 'til Rack told me. How the fuck you think I knew where the fuck to find you tonight? Rack's such a loyal brother. Always keeping in touch, checking on her. She was grieving so bad for my father."

Christopher intended to chop Rack into little pieces. He'd used his mother to get intel from her and pass it on to Snake.

"Now, move, fucker. I want that little bitch you've been fucking."

Megan laid her head against Christopher's back, her arms around his waist, holding on for dear life.

"I swear to fuck, if you don't move, I'm gonna blow you the fuck away now rather than later."

"Then blow my ass afuckinway cuz as long as my ass livin', you ain't gettin' my girl." And she was his girl. She'd been from the moment she'd come searching for Boss, needing the man's protection.

Christopher tensed and felt another presence behind him, heard a gun clip snapping into place.

"You don't move, Megan's head gonna be gone," Rack explained, the words as mild as if he was talking about the fucking clouds.

Snake smiled. "Your head or hers?"

He glared at Snake. "Drop your gun, motherfucker, and Ima pull Megan next to me." He'd keep her against the wall, keep his hand on her shoulder. If bullets started flying, he prayed he could shove her down and, by some miracle, she'd make it.

Once he had her situated, Snake let his gaze roam over her naked body and Christopher wanted to cover her from her brother's perversion. Snake rubbed the barrel of the gun against her cheek and Christopher's heart all but stopped. One wrong move and she'd be dead at his feet.

"You gonna off your own flesh and blood?"

"You killed my father, fucker. He was like your flesh and blood, and you fucking killed him." Snake's blue eyes were wide and wild, crazed. Christopher didn't care. What he did care about was Megan's horror as Snake's words sank in. He took a step toward her. Snake shook the gun against Megan's head. "Stay!"

"She ain't in this life," Christopher hollered. "She a innocent girl."

"Bullshit. She's your bitch. Fucking the asswipe who murdered our father."

Megan shook her head, heedless of the gun pressing into her cheek, staring at Christopher, a silent plea to tell her Snake lied. The hope and denial in her eyes ebbed away in painful clarity, in a way he'd never forget, when Christopher nodded ever so slightly. She cried out, swaying on her feet.

"*She ain't know,*" Christopher gritted. "Let her go. Deal with my ass."

What did he have to live for now, anyway? If he had to go by the look on her face, Megan hated him, and his mother was dead. If he got Megan out of the way, he'd lunge for Snake and let the asshole shoot him. Put himself out of his misery.

"I knew. It don't matter if she knew. She's the bitch who got you out that day. She's loyal to you, not her family."

"*I* killed Boss," he finally confirmed. "She ain't. You think I wanted to kill him? A man like a father to me?"

The gun shook. "Whether you did or not—"

"I went to get that girl outta his bed!"

"If a bitch wanted in his bed—"

"She was fourteen. Fourteen, Snake. A fuckin' kid! Despite that. Despite Boss sellin' us out to that other club and almost ruinin' us...despite his shootin' up and snortin' afuckinway inventory...I ain't plan on killin' him. He pulled his fuckin' piece first. And, fuck me, I ain't no monument of goodness, but, choosin' befuckintween my life and that piece of shit, I pick me any fuckin' day."

Snake pulled the gun an inch away from Megan's cheek and studied Christopher. He pumped the barrel. Megan's eyes widened as Christopher lunged. Grabbing Snake's arm, he forced him to turn the gun. The shotgun blasted off, pellets flying into the dark room behind them. Christopher jumped on Snake and buried his fist into the man's face. Blood spurted from his nose. When he slammed his fist into Snake's mouth, teeth flew out.

Christopher didn't need a gun. He was going to beat the asshole to death.

Something slammed against the side of Christopher's head. He grabbed his face at the stinging pain, the warmth of his blood seeping down his skin. The last face he saw was Snake's before he toppled over, and darkness overcame him.

Chapter Thirty-Eight

Meggie

MEGGIE SCREAMED UNTIL SHE LOST HER VOICE, reducing her to pitiful moans. She didn't know her location, but it was dark, damp, and cold. They'd left her naked and shivers wracked her. Stretched out on Rack's table from Halloween, her arms were chained above her head and her feet tied up. She tried to keep her back arched, but her neck and spine were hurting. Every time she went lax, pins pricked her skin from the small spikes poking through the table. Her throat was raw and swollen and her only company were competing images of Christopher on the floor of his mother's house, bleeding from a head wound, and that of his mother. Dead.

A sob escaped her again, remembering Snake's hateful words. That Christopher killed her—their—father. Christopher *had* killed her daddy.

She moaned, pain and betrayal cutting her deeply. Christopher was one of them, a violent biker, a man who lived on the fringes of society and allowed nothing to get in his way. Because of that, his mother was dead, she was going to be killed, and…and *he'd* lost his life, too.

Another wretched sob fell from her lips. They were all dead. Her father, Patricia and Christopher. Meggie twisted again and tried to scream at the agony in her body.

No, he wasn't dead. He couldn't be.

She had to get to him. He had to be okay. She needed to know what type of vile man would kill her father. She had to tell him about the baby. The one he'd wanted her to have for him. He'd said he couldn't ask for a better man than Big Joe's genes to be in his offspring when, all along, he'd known he killed him.

"God! Oh God!"

Sudden light hurt her eyes and Meggie heard footsteps, but she didn't care, too worn out to focus on who was walking in. She wished they'd killed her the way they'd finished the others.

Snake came into her line of sight, his long blond hair and blue eyes giving him an almost angelic look, despite his battered face. She shivered, dizzy with fear. What would they do to her before they killed her? She had an innocent baby inside of her but they wouldn't care. Her innocent little baby would die before it got a chance to take its first breath outside her body. Inside her, it was supposed to be safe.

One by one, an army of men surrounded her, like specters from hell, all staring at her naked body, leering at her. Even Snake, her brother. And…and *Val*. Oh God! Did honor exist anywhere? Christopher considered Val one of his best friends. And he'd betrayed him. Betrayed the club.

To avenge Boss. This war had started because Christopher had killed Big Joe.

Nausea roiled in her belly and she twisted against her restraints. The men were still, not making a move or a sound.

"Please," she croaked, the word a bare whisper, pushed out from her dry mouth.

"Megan."

She closed her eyes at the sound of Rack's smug voice. She hadn't noticed him, too busy reeling from Val's presence, too busy considering whose side she should be on. Not that it mattered. She was in Christopher's bed, so they considered her a traitor to her daddy. To them. Rack cupped her feminine mound. He squeezed and she moaned like a wounded animal. Because her feet were tied together, she didn't have a lot of room to open her thighs, but he managed to dig his thick fingers into her.

He gestured to the other men and a couple of them stepped forward, groping her breasts and pinching her nipples. She'd begun to hallucinate because, for the briefest second, she'd imagine seeing black fury on Val's face. She thought his fists had balled and he'd stepped toward Rack. But, no, her vision was wavering and her mind disconnecting, so his almost interception had just been an illusion. She let out a soundless scream and her arms felt as if they were going to pop from their joints. Rack pushed his fingers further into her and she thought she just might die from the pain.

Through her dizziness, she prayed for all of them. Everything she felt for Christopher—had felt for him—grew inside her. If any of them had an inkling of her pregnancy, they'd beat the baby out of her.

"Enough."

Meggie never thought she'd welcome the sound of her brother's voice, but his hard command was the best word she'd ever heard. She turned her head toward Snake, sending him a silent plea. He stared at her, hard and intense, a range of emotions crossing his face.

"Bring in the other two," he ordered, turning his back on her.

If Meggie could've made any sound, she would've screamed her head off again when Kiera and Ellen were marched in, naked and bloodied, their hair in tangles. They were jerked to the foot of the contraption Meggie was strapped to. The fear in their eyes increased hers.

Snake came to her, gun in hand. "Pity we didn't meet under different circumstances. I think we could've been friends. But seeing as how your lover killed my father, I'd just as soon piss on you." He leaned closer. "That shit Outlaw said? About Dad's problems? They were all true. But Dad trusted him more than he trusted me. He wouldn't have threatened Outlaw's life. That was a crock of shit."

Meggie shook her head wildly.

Snake waved his gun. "You get to choose, Megan." He tipped the gun toward Kiera and Ellen. "Which bitch lives and which one dies."

Her breath came in short pants, her stomach churning, this nightmare growing in horror.

"Who, Megan? 'Cause if you don't choose one, then both of them die."

Who was she to be judge and jury and make such a decision? Besides regular female cattiness, these women never did anything to her. "Don't. Please. Don't hurt either one of them. They've never done anything to me." She let out a desperate sob. "Please."

Rack slapped her across her cheek and her ears rang, her head snapping back.

"I'm losing patience," Snake snarled, pressing the barrel into Ellen's temple.

"I'll see you shortly in hell, fuckers," Ellen snarled. "No way you're gonna fucking continue breathing and doing this to Outlaw's girl."

"Ellen, no!" Meggie said. "Don't provoke them."

Ellen turned resigned eyes to Meggie, a small nod matching the weary smile. And Meggie knew. It didn't matter who she chose. Either way, they'd all die.

Ellen spat in Snake's face. "Nothing she says is gonna save us, so fuck you."

Before Meggie blinked, Snake pulled the trigger. Terror crossed Kiera's features before Snake shot her, too.

"No!" In her mind, Meggie screamed the word. In reality, it was mouthed, drowned out by the gunfire, two quick shots. Blood and bone fragment sprayed everywhere as Kiera and Ellen dropped, dead before they hit the ground.

Meggie turned her head, the bile bubbling up and gurgling from her mouth. Snake leaned over her and freed her hands.

He smiled, unperturbed by the gruesome evidence of his kills on his clothes, skin, and hair. "I have one more present for you, little sister. You get to watch Outlaw breathe his last." He snickered. "If he hasn't already."

Christopher

Christopher awoke to darkness, the smell of wood and dirt suffusing him with every breath he took. He tried to turn to the side but couldn't. He tried to sit up, but his hand felt wood. His lungs tightened in the heavy, moldy air.

He couldn't get his bearings, the lack of light disorienting. He rifled through his mind in a frantic search and memories barreled back. His mother was dead. All he'd done to protect her and keep her out of harm's way was for nothing. He'd brought it to her door, and she'd paid the ultimate price.

With a roar of anguish, he punched out blindly. The wood splintered and a patch of dirt rained onto him.

Dirt?

Dirt. Fucking dirt. No. *No.*

He slid his fingers along the top since it was almost impossible to move his arms at his sides. He stretched out a foot, encountered more wood. And he knew. He fucking *knew*. He was buried. Jesus. Fucking. God.

Jesus. If anyone knew of his unreasonable fear of being buried alive, it was Snake.

Sweat popped out on Christopher and he drew in sharp breaths, growing lightheaded. The air shrunk and his lungs burned. He would've preferred Rack's torture table in the fucking shed at the compound. They could've stretched him until they pulled him apart. They could've cut little pieces out of him until he bled to death. Fuck, they could've hacked *big* chunks from his body.

But buried alive?

He had no chance of survival. He'd used up half his fucking air panicking like a pussy. At most, he had ninety minutes of oxygen and he had no idea how long he'd been in this death pit.

Megan's gorgeous face came to him, and he closed his eyes, drawing in a deep breath and holding it as long as possible. He wondered if she'd been thrown in another hole and, if so, had she been alive. He couldn't imagine his sweet, innocent Megan facing such a horrible end. Just the thought made him want to hurl.

He shivered, cold inside and out, naked as the day he'd made his entrance into this cruel, vicious world. What a curse that day had been. His mother had given birth to her killer. He hadn't pulled the trigger, but he might as well had. He'd stayed away from her to protect her, but Megan made him think of family, gave him a conscience. Now, they were both dead.

"Godfuckindammit!" he exploded.

Something banged against the lid and Christopher stilled, listening intently, sucking back his grief and rage. He counted to sixty, heard the noise again. Digging?

He heard voices, so he was nearly disinterred. They mustn't have buried him very deeply. So fucking what? He didn't give a fuck any longer. His mother was gone and so was Megan, a girl he'd come closer to loving than he'd had any other woman. A girl who'd been so full of life, so full of promise. So full of love.

The lid opened and Christopher was yanked out. A flashlight shone in his face, and he squinted, off-balance and stiff. Just as suddenly, the light was pulled away, flickering on four faces, one of whom almost made him drop to his knees.

Megan.

She was trembling, her hair matted to her, blood and gore spattered on her.

He pulled his gaze away, unable to see anything but fear. Not hate or relief or love. He curled his lip at Rack, wishing he had a weapon on him.

Finally, Snake stood close to him, gloating, triumphant. Christopher was going to die but not without attempting to save his Megan. He knew their pieces were a flicker away. Taking a deep breath, he crashed into Snake, screaming, "Run, Megan!"

He didn't have time to see if she listened as he and her brother landed hard on the ground. Christopher smashed his fists into Snake's face, again and again, taking out his rage and grief, satisfied at the crack of the man's nose and the cloud of blood. He grabbed his head and bashed it into the ground...once, twice, three times before Snake stilled.

Turning and expecting to have to fight off Rack, he took a moment to take in Val holding a gun to Rack's head. He nodded to Val, giving him the go ahead to blow Rack away. He pulled Snake's gun from his waistband, stood over him and pumped all but two into his head. He hadn't heard any other gunfire, which meant he might still have to shoot Val's ass off along with Rack's. He turned, the gun pointed at Val. He hadn't heard from the motherfucker in weeks. For all he knew, he was with them.

"I figured you'd want to do him," the man said quietly. "He had his fingers all in your old lady's pussy."

"Tight, dry little—"

Rack didn't finish his words. Christopher shut him up with a bullet between the eyes. He only dropped his weapon when Val walked forward and handed Christopher the gun, butt first.

"Call in Mortician and Digger," he instructed. "Ima find Megan."

"You have nothing on."

Christopher scowled, his head pounding from the blow he'd taken earlier. "You think I ain't fuckin' knowin' my dick swingin' in the wind?"

"She ran to the truck." Val nodded in that direction. "Go wait there until Mortician and Digger get here with the equipment."

Christopher clenched his jaw and started forward.

"Yo, Outlaw?"

"Yeah?"

"Kiera and Ellen, man…Snake popped 'em right in front your girl."

Later. He'd break down later. There'd been too much collateral damage tonight and all innocent women. He gave Snake's corpse a vicious kick.

"Your young bitch. Go see about her. We have to wait 'til the boys come here."

Without a word, Christopher brushed past Val and headed to Megan, wondering what he'd find. A locked door wasn't what he expected, although he should have. He leaned against the glass and saw her sitting in the backseat, staring into space, and trembling, hugging her arms around her stomach.

"Open the door, Megan."

She didn't move, didn't even blink. Christopher banged on the glass.

"MEGAN! It's me. Christopher."

She turned her face toward him, her expression so pitiful he had to grit his teeth to keep from howling like an animal. But she was alive, unlike…no, he'd think about…about—

He swallowed. Megan was alive. He needed to hold her, be inside of her to feel her warmth, have her heartbeat vibrating through him.

"Open the door, Megan."

She reached out, her fingers trembling, but then she paused, and stared at him.

"Please?" he coaxed. "I ain't gonna hurt you."

She studied him a moment longer before unlocking the door. The roar of Harleys could be heard in the distance. He'd let Val deal with them. He closed the door behind him, and she launched herself into his arms, pounding on his chest and sobbing into his neck.

A "good" man handled grief and fury different than a woman. A man like him didn't want to handle tears. Tears reminded him of all that was sweet and fragile in life, represented all that he wasn't. He didn't want conversation. Her licks he could handle. He'd just beaten Snake to death, hadn't he? But he didn't even want that. He didn't want to understand her feelings or have any sympathy.

Guilt washed through him, and he grabbed her hands, pinning them to her sides, and ravishing her mouth. She gasped against his lips, but he ignored her, bypassing the stiffening of her limbs, and guiding her back. He refused to remove his mouth from hers. He didn't want to hear her blame and hate. The salt of her tears was a bitter pill best ignored. Still kissing her, he cupped her cunt and massaged her clit. He just needed her aroused enough not to hurt her when he entered her.

Just as her body began to soften and melt, the door opened, and Megan tried to shove him away.

"Oh, sorry, Outlaw," Val said, sitting in the driver's seat and slamming his door closed.

"You, stay," he ordered, pointing at Megan. He lifted up and cracked Val across the back of his head.

"OW!" he whined. "What the—"

"Get the fuck outta here, asswipe," he growled and whopped Val again. "That's for not givin' Megan your fuckin' jacket to cover her up. I'm gonna letcha slide on the fact you saw her naked again. Stress and duress, underfuckinstand? That don't mean Ima forget that fuckup." He slapped him again simply because Megan was lifting herself and he had to grab her waist and hold her against him. "But, unless you a brain-dead motherfucker, ain't no fuckin' reason for you to sit your dumb ass in this cage when you saw me with Megan.

Interruptin' my shit cuz you upset her. Go take a smoke or a piss and wait 'til I call you back here."

Val hustled outside, so fast Christopher would've smiled if Megan wasn't struggling against him now. It took him a minute to get her under control and back in position. When she lay beneath him, he pushed two fingers into her. She croaked a sound.

"It's okay, Megan," he promised her, nuzzling her neck, and gentling his touch in her pussy. "It's just me. I'm so sorry, baby. I ain't protected you." He closed his eyes. "Or Kiera and Ellen. Or—" He couldn't. He just couldn't finish the last. "I deserve whatever I got," he whispered, his voice breaking. He leaned his forehead against hers, replaced his fingers with the tip of his dick. "But none of you did." He drew in a deep breath and exhaled a sob. She stayed still for half a second before she lifted her hand and thumbed his tears away. She thrust her hips up, allowing him to sink into her.

He groaned, not saying a word, just moving inside of her, accepting her soft caresses on his back and tiny kisses on his chest. He wanted to bring her over the edge with him, but everything was topsy-turvy. He wasn't sure if anything would ever be right again. He emptied deep inside of her, shouting her name. As soon as he could, he withdrew and sat up. She curled up, turning her head away, making it clear she had offered him the comfort of her body, but she really didn't want anything to do with him.

"Fine, Megan." He scrubbed a hand over his face, smelling her pussy on his fingers. "Have it your way." Opening the door, he ordered Val back in the car. The man handed him clothes, then started the engine.

"Digger thought you might need those."

"Smart fuckin' man," he grumbled, pulling on jeans. "Before you cut out, lemme jump in the front with you."

"You don't want to…er, okay," Val finished when Christopher glared at him.

He glanced at Megan again. Her eyes were closed. He didn't know if she was really asleep or if she was just blocking him out. It didn't matter. He got the message.

Once the car got on the road, he realized they were close to the compound. Although Val offered to drop Megan off there, Christopher declined. He'd put her up in a hotel and allow her to stay there as long as she wanted. She didn't ever have to see him again if she didn't want to. And he imagined she didn't.

He ignored how the thought of never seeing her again—of having her hate him—made him feel.

He remained in the car with her while Val took care of reservations. It wasn't the Ritz, but it was the best he could do at the moment. Weary and tired, he wished she'd say something, *anything*, but her silence hurt him worse than a thousand accusations. And she wasn't asleep. He looked back at her more than he wanted and, except for the first time, found her eyes wide fucking open.

Finally, he was opening the scratched up gray room door and urging her in. He flipped on all the lights. A girl like her would probably think the place was a dump. No matter. He was going above and beyond already.

She stared at him, silvery tracks of tears sliding down her face. He pulled her into his arms and kissed the top of her head.

"Val gonna bring your stuff and some bills, Megan. Stay here as long as you wanna. I'll keep the room paid up."

She didn't hug him back. Turning away from him, she walked to the bathroom and shut the door behind her.

Chapter Thirty-Nine
Christopher

"I
T'S YOUR FAULT!" ZOANN SCREAMED FLYING at Christopher the moment he stepped out of the rain and walked into the living room of her house, three days later, where all his sisters and nieces were. "It should've been you! You're nothing! Nothing. I'll never forgive you. You're a thug and you should be put down, like the dog you are."

Christopher had no response because, for once, he agreed with Zoann. His mother had been undeserving of going like she had, and she'd gone like that because of him. But he needed comfort, too. She'd been his mother, whom he loved as much as he could love, and she'd loved him, as unworthy as he was of it. He thought of going to Megan, but she hated him, too, so he'd done the next best thing. Sought out his sisters.

Nothing hurt so bad as the wrath of your family. His family. His sisters and their kids all pointed fingers at him. Didn't they know he'd have given his life to protect Patricia?

Yeah. It should've been him killed, but it wasn't. They'd just have to deal with it. *He* had to. For the rest of his life, he'd live with the knowledge he'd caused his mother's death.

Christopher swallowed tightly. "Can't change what happen, Zoann. It is what it is." He fought to keep his tears at bay, wishing he had the right words, knowing what he'd said just made him sound like an unfeeling assfuck. But he didn't need his sisters labeling him. He knew what and who he was and so had his mother. So had Megan. And they'd loved him anyway, faults and all.

He'd loved them, too. But had he ever said it? Did his mother know he loved her? Did Megan?

"Why are you here?" Avery sneered. Sitting on the sofa, she had her arms around Zoann. "You've done enough."

"She was my ma, too. I wanna be part of the plannin' for her..." He couldn't finish.

"*Funeral! FUNERAL!*" Bev wailed in a strangled voice.

Christopher sniffled, unable to summon the man inside him to hold back the tears. He'd just reconnected with Patricia, but, at least, in the year he'd stayed away from her, he'd known she was alive. Angrily, he swiped at another goddamn tear, vowing this would be the last time these self-righteous bitches saw him cry. He pierced Zoann with a furious look.

"Put your anger and disgust aside and tell me how my ass able to help."

Sasha scampered to him and leaned her head against his thigh. "I still love you, Uncle Chris." She smiled up at him again. "Where's Meggie?"

Despite what he said, he felt like crying all over again. Fuck him, he was turning into a pussy and, proven by the size of his dick, no one could call him that. He crouched down and kissed Sasha's cheek. "I love you, too," he got out.

"As if you know the meaning," Nia managed through her tears. "Get out of here, Sasha. Your uncle and I have to discuss Nana. Go outside and play with your cousins."

"Okay, Momma." Sasha scampered to the door and disappeared outside.

"At least she don't think I'm a monster," he muttered. Though he was.

"She doesn't know you like we do. Neither do the other two." Ophelia spoke for the first time since he'd walked in.

Though he'd barely taken note of her presence, he thought she'd remained silent because she understood his pain. But no. "Right. I'm sure you bitches gonna fix how those innocent lil' girls feel 'bout me."

"They have eyes, and they have ears. They'll learn soon enough for themselves," Zoann said.

Ophelia sighed. "I don't want to argue with you. Mom wouldn't want that."

"Nope. She wouldna," Christopher agreed, not wanting to put too much into Ophelia's words.

Bev and Avery helped Zoann to her feet, leaving them alone without another word.

"They want me to talk to you. They thought maybe you might stop over, so they chose me."

"They can't stand the sight of my ass, huh?"

"They're stricken with grief and anger," Ophelia whispered. "Can you blame them?"

No, he wanted to say. He deserved their scorn. But not their hatred. Families stuck together, no matter what, even for death. *Especially* for death. Couldn't they see he was grieving, too?

He drew in a broken sigh, experiencing emotions he didn't know he possessed. He couldn't handle grief. Anger, scorn, and hatred was his comfort zone.

"What, Fee? What you bitches conjurin' up for my punishment?"

"You can certainly be dramatic when you want," Ophelia scoffed. "We're not punishing you. We can't do to you what it's obvious you're already doing to yourself."

"So, what they wantcha to talk to me 'bout?"

"None of us can forgive you for what's happened."

"Then don't," Christopher snapped, fed up. "That it?"

"No. We don't want you sitting with us at the services. We don't want to hear from you after the funeral."

"Anythin' else?" he asked icily, ready to get the fuck out of there. The curtains were drawn, and he suddenly felt like he was suffocating, like he was still buried in that dirt, fighting for air.

She wrung her hands in her lap and squirmed, unable to meet his eye.

"Lemme guess," he snarled sarcastically. "Money. You want me to fuckin' pay for...for Ma's funeral." His voice cracked through the word.

Ophelia nodded. "It's the least you can do."

"Fine," Christopher spat, stalking to the door. "Ima pay, then fuck all you bitches. I ain't needin' none of you."

Pausing long enough to say goodbye to Sasha and the other two, he got on his bike and sped away.

Chapter Forty

Meggie

A WEEK LATER, MEGGIE CLUTCHED HER COAT around her, the cold drizzle adding misery to an already grief-stricken day. Christopher stood on the other side of the cemetery, his brothers and their old ladies behind him. It shocked her to see him in a suit. She didn't know bikers owned suits. Her daddy hadn't.

Her nostrils flared at the thought of her father, and she pushed the pain aside, studying the man she couldn't stop thinking of. In contrast to his club members, his blood relatives—his five sisters and three nieces—stood away from him. Meggie had witnessed their snub of their brother at the church. They hadn't even reserved space for him delegated for Patricia's family.

All too soon, the minister spoke a few final words and then mourners were placing white flowers on the elaborate casket. His brothers patted his back, touched his arm, or nodded and kept moving toward their bikes. Christopher barely took note, instead following the progression of his sisters and nieces.

Meggie covered her mouth with the back of her hand, terribly confused. She hadn't slept much this past week, haunted by nightmares of all that had happened. Every time she closed her eyes, she saw blood and the dead faces of Patricia, Ellen, and Kiera. She heard Snake's sneering words when he told her Christopher had killed her father.

She was exhausted, sick to her stomach, and heart sore. All the plans she'd had were pushed aside to run to her daddy. She hadn't thought, beyond escaping Thomas, about what else she'd do. Now that Big Joe wasn't there—he wasn't even alive—she had absolutely no direction.

Returning to her mother would defeat the purpose of all that had happened in the nearly five months she'd been gone. Thomas would be merciless. He didn't like to be bested and Meggie had run away, thereby thwarting his intentions for her.

She felt Christopher's gaze on her and looked at him. He wore dark glasses. That, coupled with his black suit and black hair, made him look like an A-List movie star.

"Go to him, Megan," Johnnie whispered, his hand on her shoulder.

She glanced up at Christopher's cousin. He was the one who'd called her and offered her an invitation to Patricia's funeral. She insisted to him, and herself, she'd only attend out of respect of a woman she'd liked. But, deep down, she knew she wanted to see Christopher. She'd never asked how Johnnie got the location of her whereabouts, but she supposed Christopher had told him.

Johnnie squeezed her shoulder and she saw Christopher ball his hands into fists, his body growing even more rigid. If such a thing was possible.

"He needs you," Johnnie insisted. "Judging by the way he's debating on if he should storm over here and beat me to the ground, I'd say he wants you, too."

"Johnnie—"

"Go. Please. You don't have to leave with him. Just go to him. Offer your sympathy. His sisters have spurned him—"

That was all the impetus Meggie needed. Pressing her hand against her belly, she made her way through the damp grass. She stopped an inch away from him and he looked down at her, silent. A muscle ticked in his clenched jaw. Meggie noted the Death Dwellers preparing to hop onto their bikes, the chrome on the heavy machines shining like beacons in the dull day.

She brushed off the lapel of his coat. "I'm so sorry, Christopher," she whispered.

He sandwiched her face between his hands and bent to kiss her. "Me, too, Megan." He kissed the top of her head and pulled away, striding toward his bike without a backward glance.

After all twenty bikes had roared away, Johnnie walked up to Meggie.

"Did you tell him?" he asked, twisting her hair around his fingers.

Meggie frowned, staring into the distance until only smoke from the exhaust pipes remained. "Tell him what?"

"About the baby."

Her gaze flew to his and she flattened her palm on her belly, something she did a lot of lately since confirming her pregnancy, three days ago. She'd only taken three or four—maybe, five—home pregnancy tests, but all of them were positive. She shook her head.

"Are you going to?"

"I-I don't know."

"Fair enough. But he's going to find out, sooner or later. You stay here and your belly starts growing, he's going to figure it out."

"He hardly comes to the area where I'm staying."

Johnnie raised a brow. "That doesn't mean he's unaware of what's going on. He has one of the boys watching over you constantly. They have rotating shifts. So if he doesn't see with his own eyes, they will, and he'll find out."

"He has people following me?"

"Protecting you."

"Spying on me."

"Does it matter?" Johnnie snapped in frustration. He shrugged his shoulders. "Of course, we can make everybody think the baby's mine."

"I-I'll let you know," she promised.

He smiled. "Do that. Let's get you out of this weather."

JOHNNIE

"Do you need anything, Megan?" Johnnie asked, twenty minutes later, standing outside her motel room.

The drizzle that had begun at the cemetery turned into a downpour on the drive over. The rain had let up again, but the rolling thunder and flashes of lightning hinted that more storms were on the way. Temperatures were also dropping, so it wouldn't surprise him if snow ended up falling.

"I'm fine," Megan answered, her face drawn and dark circles ringing her eyes.

He hated that she was in so much pain.

"It looks like another downpour is coming." She stepped aside. "Would you like to wait it out in here?"

Thunder boomed again and lightning briefly illuminated everything. Electricity charged the atmosphere in more ways than one.

He examined her face, searching for any signs that her invitation had an underlying meaning. But he found nothing. He looked at her hand—the one resting on her belly, where Christopher's baby grew in her womb.

"Johnnie?"

He met her gaze. Sadness dampened her usual sparkle. Her heart was broken because she loved Christopher. She was vulnerable right now. More so than when they'd spent so much time together in Long Beach. Then, she hadn't known Christopher killed Big Joe. Now, she did, and it devastated her. She was also grieving. Not only for her father but Patricia and probably even Kiera and Ellen.

If Johnnie accepted Megan's offer, he could make love to her. Judging by her innocent expression, her suggestion had no ulterior motives. Yet, she'd still issued it after he'd made his offer to allow everyone to believe she carried *his* baby.

What the fuck was he thinking? He couldn't take advantage of her. She meant too much to him for such an underhanded move.

He shook his head. "No, sweetheart. I have to hit the road."

She nodded. "Be careful."

"I always am."

"Okay."

Unable to stop himself, he drew her into his arms and hugged her. She didn't resist, laying her head against his chest and encircling his waist in an embrace. He didn't want to let her go, but she allowed him his moment and waited until he released her.

She smiled softly. "See you, Johnnie."

"Megan," he said, a goodbye.

She closed the door. In spite of the renewed downpour, Johnnie stood in place and flattened his palm against the door, willing her to open it again. If she did and invited him in, he'd accept.

She didn't.

By the time he reached his Navigator, he was soaked and chilled to the bone. Although he started the SUV and turned on the heat, he didn't drive away.

Somehow, Megan had gotten under his skin like no other woman ever had. He'd already been attracted to her when Christopher left her in Johnnie's care. Then, he'd spent every waking moment with her for almost three solid weeks. Knowing in advance that fucking wouldn't be included in their time together, Johnnie had just gotten to know her and enjoy her company.

He would've preferred it if she'd just been tolerable, instead of the intelligent, passionate, loyal girl she turned out to be. She had moments of immaturity and a fucking bad temper, but it didn't turn him off.

Fuck, it didn't matter. She wanted Christopher.

Maybe, Johnnie's sins were coming home to roost. All the coverups and fucking lies doomed him to fall for a girl who saw in Christopher what Johnnie had always seen in him. Worthiness. Humanity. Steadfastness. Logic. Christopher deserved happiness. He deserved love and devotion.

But, *fuck*…Why did it have to be from the same girl Johnnie wanted?

He grimaced. Sooner or later, it was bound to happen. They always fucked the same women—Iona being the exception. Johnnie had always taken it as a friendly rivalry. Now he knew Christopher had never competed for any woman. He just hadn't given a fuck.

Johnnie looked at Megan's motel door again, shocked that the rain had stopped. She was young and confused, alone in her room. All he had to do was go to her. Take her in his arms.

Hold her. Kiss her.

A fucking bed would be right there…

Deep down, he knew this might be his best chance, his *last chance*, to claim her as his. He could make her reciprocate his feelings and fall in love with him.

His sentiments for her began the first time he met her. No, *saw* her. Her beauty had nothing to do with it. Of course, he noticed it. Only a blind motherfucker wouldn't. However, it was her actions that enthralled him: confronting motherfucking Rack.

Admittedly, it had been quite fucking stupid on her part. She was aware Rack's propensity for violence since he'd already laid hands on her. To protect Christopher, Rack's past assault hadn't mattered to Megan. She'd been her father's daughter. Not the fucking irresponsible, murdering, backstabbing fuckhead who Johnnie despised and took particular pleasure in disemboweling, beheading, and dismembering.

She'd been like the Big Joe Johnnie remembered from his childhood. Tough. Steely. Fearless. Boss had been big, blond, and charismatic. Motherfucker once had the ability to make anyone think he was a friend, even those he was moments away from fucking up.

His daughter was petite, blonde, and charismatic. She had the best of her father. Even if she didn't drink or curse like he had, she was nurturing, had a helluva sense of humor and loved to have fun.

Her beauty made Johnnie want to fuck her. Her personality made him love her.

A knock on his passenger window startled him. Seeing Mortician, he unlocked the door. When the man opened it, cold, damp air blasted in.

Mort slid onto the seat. "What your ass doing here, John Boy?" he demanded, slamming the door shut.

Johnnie scowled. "I dropped off Megan."

"Fifteen fucking minutes ago," Mortician snapped. "Just my fucking luck you pull your ass up when I'm on my own. Digger rolled out to fuck some chick and pick up food for me on his way back. Almost soon as he blazed out, here your ass come with Meggie. I was fucking praying you not going in that fucking room."

"What's it to you, fucker?" Johnnie demanded. "We're both single and we're both consenting adults."

"*You* fucking single. *She* belong to Outlaw."

"Then why the fuck is she here and he's at the club?"

Mortician gave him a dark look. "I don't need to answer that, fuckhead. You been knowing Prez longer than me, so you already know the goddamn reason."

"You've been in the club longer than me, so I call bullshit."

"I don't give a fuck if you call dog shit. Your ass didn't join sooner 'cause of Lowman."

To keep his temper in check, Johnnie changed the subject. "Where the fuck were you earlier? I would've thought you would've attended Aunt Patricia's services to show support for Christopher."

"Prez know I'm here for him, Johnnie," Mort said with a sigh. "Always. But, fuck, Ki dead." He shook his head. "Kiera gone, Johnnie. I went to her services. Fuck, man. We just starting to feel normal again after Outlaw fucked up Big Joe 'cause Big Joe was fucked up."

Johnnie snickered. "He's where he belongs."

"Yeah, but we fucking here, left to pick up the pieces."

"Are you really grieving for him?" Johnnie asked, surprised.

"You not?" Mort waved a hand. "Scratch that. You Logan kin, cold to the fucking bone. A fucking psychopath. Prez got the way he is 'cause of his upbringing. Your ass just born this fucking way." He shifted in the seat. "I guess you not even sorry about Kiera and Ellen."

"I *am* sorry they're dead, Mortician. Am I grieving over them? No. I'm not."

"I really liked Kiera."

Mortician's misery surprised Johnnie. "You wanted her for your woman?"

"She always been a cool chick. Love to have fun. Love to fuck." Mortician smiled sadly. "I don't think I would've ever claimed Ki. First off, she wanted Outlaw. She loved him and I didn't want to compete. Besides, if Prez and Meggie work shit out and he keep her for a little while, Kiera and Ellen couldn't have kept coming around. They would've got up to all kinds of fuckery because they wouldn't have given up their places in the club without a fucking fight. And Meggie don't fucking back down. Fuck, man. If she wasn't the size of a fucking elf, shit would be a little better—"

"Santa Claus was the size of a grown man and he was an elf."

"I can't believe your bitch-ass said that. Besides, Clement C. Moore put that in his poem. There was no fucking factual evidence to back that shit up."

"Oh, *I'm* the bitch-ass and you're discussing the Jolly Old Elf like there's a possibility he was real?"

"Fuck off."

"And *you* know about the fucking children's poem," Johnnie added, ignoring Mortician's order.

"I wasn't always the sexy motherfucker I am today, Johnnie. I was a kid once. Rev hosted performances about the nativity at the church. My mother hired motherfuckers to act out that fucking poem at the crib. It's one of the few fucking things I remember about her."

Huffing out a breath, Mort glanced at the window, then looked at Johnnie again. "That's the fucking past. In the here and now, I'm not up for a fucking bitch war. If Meggie around and Kiera and Ellen was still…if Snake hadn't gotten them, that's what we would've fucking had."

"If that scenario came to fruition, Christopher would've straightened all three of them out."

"You on something," Mortician said with a snort. "Prez protective of Meggie and jealous as a motherfucker behind her. He was just interviewing her—"

"Feeling her out," Johnnie supplied.

Mortician side-eyed him but went on as if he hadn't been interrupted. "He wanted to see how she handled shit. He was also living in fear she found out what he did. All that is out in the open, so if she come back, shit changing and every motherfucker around better not upset her."

"How do you feel about that? No, how do you feel about her now?"

"When Snake and his motherfuckers came in that warehouse the day Prez got shot, I was ready to blow Meggie the fuck away. Then I walked in the clubhouse and I'd just gotten to the bar when Outlaw marched Kit out. I was so relieved he was alive, I forgot all about

Meggie. Of course, Prez don't have no fucking patience. He shot the fuck out of Kit and just added to the fucking gore."

"Damn," Johnnie said, disappointed. "I wish I would've arrived in time. It's been a while since I've spent any time in the meatshack."

"Rack and Snake fucked up now. Why don't you become full patch again?"

"I'm thinking about it. Now answer my fucking question."

"What? About Meggie? I like her. After I saw her in the hospital while Outlaw was in surgery, I started to change my opinion. She was all alone, so I had every chance to lure her away and shoot her if I thought she was a threat. When Val grilled her about what happened and felt confidant she wouldn't talk, he decided against slitting her throat, too. I said all that to say I don't want to kill her anymore. Neither does Digger or Val."

"Neither do I."

"Did your ass ever?"

"I suppose we've started killing women now," Johnnie answered instead of responding to Mortician's question. Because, yes, if she'd been a danger to Christopher, he would've killed her.

"No, Johnnie, we don't kill chicks."

"Unless you know something I don't, Megan has a pussy." A hairy one that Johnnie wanted to see and taste.

"Fuck, don't bring up her pussy." Mortician covered his face. "Just don't fucking remind me. There are brothers who have their old ladies and don't share. Fine. That's not the way it work between us. Me, you, Digger, Val, and Prez."

Even Snake, Rack, K-P, and Big Joe had been in that loop at one time.

"A gorgeous, sexy broad walk in the club and want to party, none of us barring her from the other. So it's taken Roscoe a minute to catch up to Prez rules for Meggie."

"Who the fuck is Roscoe?"

"My cock. He special like that."

Johnnie guffawed. "You named your cock?"

"Old news, motherfucker, so shut the fuck up."

"Well, I never got the newsflash," he said, still laughing his ass off. "Anyway," he continued, wiping the tears from his eyes, "we've gotten way off topic. What were we talking about?"

"Meggie."

"As well as Ellen and Ki."

"We'd moved on from them," Mortician said quickly.

"They belonged to all of us, Mort."

Mortician nodded. "Yeah, I know."

"Megan doesn't."

"She belong to Prez."

She was also carrying his child. And she loved him. Maybe, she was hurt and angry over Big Joe but her feelings hadn't changed for Christopher.

"I'm sorry you lost her, Johnnie, but back off. In the current situation, she might not be able to resist a move you made on her this time."

"What the fuck do you mean *this time*?"

"Did I stutter, fuckhead? Just what the fuck I said. I know you and I know girls fall all over your ass. You don't even have to fucking work to get pussy."

"You do?"

"At least I *pretend* to. Fuck, man. I think Meggie got a crush on you, but she love Prez, Johnnie, so you might've tried to get pussy from her but she shot you down."

"All speculation on your part."

"You fucking want Meggie. You not just going to hold her fucking hand and skip to my fucking lou. Give Prez the fucking respect he always show you and stand down. At least for now."

"What does that mean?"

"I don't know. Fuck, I've been thinking about how this shit not going to cause bloodshed between you and Outlaw. If he knock her up, then take her somewhere and fuck her if she let you. Or have a blowup doll specially made to look like her. *Something.* Just give him his chance at happiness, Johnnie. We did a lot of shit to protect him. Now, step aside for him. If Meggie take him back, that mean she forgive him. If *she* forgive him and Big Joe was her daddy, Prez can finally forgive himself and be the motherfucker the club need. He can be Outlaw again."

"He's still Outlaw."

"No. Prez drifting. He so fucking lost. She'll anchor him, in a different way than Big Joe. He got nobody anymore. The only two sisters he gave a fuck about turned their fucking back on him. His mama dead—"

"He has us."

"That's fucking different. You live with the knowledge of Lowman love and devotion to your ass. I got my little brother and K-P. Kitchen Bitch got relatives in New Orleans."

"What about Val? Who does he have?"

"Prez, Johnnie," Mortician conceded. "But Val been without his fucking family for years. Stop making fucking justifications to take Meggie from Outlaw, motherfucker. Step the fuck back. When I get the fuck out this cage, you ride the fuck away. If you try to fuck with Meggie, you going through me, fuckhead."

"Is that a threat?" Johnnie demanded, his anger rising in spite of his best efforts.

Mortician opened the door. "Take it however the fuck you want. A threat, a promise, or just real fucking talk. But you not fucking with Meggie until her and Prez figure shit out. I couldn't even go to the repass for Kiera 'cause Digger wanted to fuck and Prez want one of us watching over Meggie. She here and where the fuck he at? At the fucking clubhouse with nothing but fucking thoughts. He got you? Then why the fuck your ass sniffing after his girl instead of being there with him?"

With one last glare, Mortician got out of the Navigator and stalked away.

For long moments, Johnnie sat in stunned silence, until he realized what he had to do. He glanced at Megan's door one last time.

He loved her and he loved Christopher, so he'd go to the club and explain what would happen if Christopher didn't claim her soon.

Either he would heed Johnnie's words, or he wouldn't. In that case, Johnnie could claim her with a clear conscience.

Chapter Forty-One
Christopher

CHRISTOPHER CHECKED THE AMMUNITION IN HIS gun, the tequila boiling in his blood but not blotting out the hatred in his sisters' eyes or the fact that his ma had to have a closed casket. He couldn't forget the unreadable expression in Megan's eyes when she'd come to him, urged on by his cousin. Not because she gave a shit about her father's killer. She was just a good girl with good manners.

She had absolutely no place in his world, and he had no place in hers. When their two worlds collided, death and destruction happened. He didn't have a kind heart. Nor a forgiving one. Once he made examples of the rebels, he'd never return out of the darkness.

The four men who'd deserted with Snake and the eight who'd been assisting Rack stood handcuffed, blindfolded, and gagged. They were moments away from joining the three fucks in the corner whom

Christopher had killed in the meatshack with a more personal touch. The ones daring to touch Megan and humiliate her. According to Val the ones that caused her to scream until she lost her fucking voice.

Christopher held his semi-automatic up and glared at his brothers all gathered at the edges of club property inside the old building. "This what happen to motherfuckers betrayin' me."

Remorseless, he opened fire, pumping bullets into the men who'd had no second thought of planning his demise. It was over in a matter of minutes. He stared at the carnage.

This was his life. Megan Foy had absolutely no place in it.

Two hours later, he stood at the bar in the clubhouse, holding a bottle of gin. The club would never be the same. *He* would never be the same. Sighing, he seated himself and swigged from the bottle. Emptiness ate at him. He half expected the door to open so Kiera and Ellen could walk in. Fuck. Never again. They were gone forever.

Treachery and other bullshit aside, knowing Kiera would never return hurt. She'd been a part of his life for years. He'd liked her a lot. No, fuck, he'd cared for her and was so fucking sorry about the way she'd been killed. That she'd died at all. These past days, he hadn't had a lot of time to reflect. There'd been bodies to dispose of and motherfuckers to hunt down. Now, though, with Ma buried and assfucks fucked up, he felt so fucking empty. He missed her.

Maybe, eventually, he would've claimed her as his old lady in the wake of Ma's death. If she'd wanted him, given the fact that he would always belong to Megan. He was in love with Megan. Fuck, it wouldn't have mattered to Kiera. As long as she had him and he let the world know she was his, she wouldn't have cared. Ellen wouldn't have been able to stay around. Maybe, not even in town. Or, fuck, within a hundred-mile radius of Ki.

Bleakness settled into him.

Ellen might've been a messy bitch, but she'd fought for the place she'd earned in the club. Not quite an old lady, yet so much more than club ass, even if she had pitched her pussy around. Him and her had a lot of fun times together, something forever lost to him. Like Ki, Ellen was gone, too.

His sisters came to mind, specifically Ophelia and Zoann. They fucking hated him. All five of his sisters, but those other three cunts could go fuck themselves. They never really liked him. If they ever needed him, he'd be there, but he wasn't seeking them out just for a fucking 'hello'. Maybe, his little niece, Sasha.

Zoann and Ophelia didn't know Ma kept in contact with Rack. Fuck, he wouldn't have known if the dead motherfucker hadn't brought his ass to the house for dinner a couple days before her death.

Christopher hadn't liked it, but Ma had insisted he had nothing to worry about because Rack was a fine man. He'd never thought Ma needed fucking eyeglasses cuz motherfucking Rack had never been fine. Not to look at and not to trust. One look at that beady-eyed, fat-balled assfuck, and you saw how much of a fuckhead he was. He just fucking wore contempt and hostility.

Bitsy…Zoann…or Fee hadn't known Ma told Rack they were still in Hortensia at the house they'd grown up in. All they fucking saw and knew was she was dead, caught up in a war because of Christopher's involvement with the club. All the three of them had ever wanted was for him to walk away.

Club life was all he knew, though. What the fuck else did he have? Who else wanted him?

Ma, yeah. Mostly. She'd had her own life, however, one that had her involved in the club, too. And fuck it all, she had fucking grown up around this motherfucker, thanks to Logan. Ma hadn't even wanted Christopher to have a relationship with a club bitch. She'd placed him above them. Even a girl as sweet as Kiera didn't meet her approval.

Ma made a show of support toward Megan, but Christopher knew she wasn't happy he was with Big Joe's girl.

Regret twisted inside him. He'd ignored Ma's feelings about Megan when he'd used them as an excuse to keep Kiera at bay. Fuck, maybe, he was a fucking hypocrite. He just hadn't been able to get past how many men she'd fucked. Besides, he just had never felt for Kiera what he felt for Megan.

Yeah, he liked how Megan needed him. She wanted him, too, though. Or she had. She'd also expected things from him. First and foremost was faithfulness. Despite having nofuckingwhere to go, she would've walked the fuck away if he'd touched Kiera again or any other bitch. On the other hand, Kiera wanted to be his old lady, but would've looked the other way if he decided to sink into another girl's pussy. She would've excused it as being part of club life. Megan didn't give a fuck. She expected better from him, *despite* club life.

But beyond her expectations, she'd trusted him. She'd trusted he respected her and their relationship enough that he wouldn't betray her. And she'd believed in him. She'd looked at him and saw a man. Not a biker. Or a club president. Nor a high-school dropout or a killer.

She'd seen him. Christopher. And it was Christopher she'd believed in and felt was a motherfucker worthy of her love.

Who the fuck had ever given him that? Maybe, Big Joe.

What about Zoann? With all her bitter hatred and fucking finger-pointing? Once upon a time, she had loved and admired Christopher, then she'd turned into a fucking wicked bitch. He'd made a run and come home to find out Logan was kicking up his cock, six feet under, and Zoann had turned into a fucking shrew. Worse than one of those bitches. At first, he'd thought she was fucking grieving. He'd had a thought or two about Logan maybe not being dead and wondered if he should tell her. But, fuck, she wouldn't even take his fucking calls for him to tell her anyfuckingthing. When he went to visit, she'd storm off. For a solid fucking year, he'd begged to see her. He'd sent her letters and cards and money and gifts. She always sent his gifts back with notes that she burned the letters and cards. The fucking final straw had been when she wrote him and said she wished it had been him she'd watched turned to ashes. The hurt he'd lived with over her treatment had turned into anger. Eventually, the love he'd once had for her was a hollow pit, filled with nothing.

Except, somewhere inside him, there was something. She still mattered to him. If she didn't, the blame she'd laid at his feet for Ma's death wouldn't have affected him so much. Yet, she didn't hate the MC life that fucking much. She was pregnant for a motherfucker in the club. Obviously, she was fucking involved in it.

The only one who wasn't a fucking hypocrite was Ophelia. Club life wasn't her thing and she rarely visited.

Fuck, in the end, it didn't matter how Rack had found out they were still in town or if Zoann and Ophelia knew. Their mother, Ma, was still gone.

Dead.

Buried.

He couldn't believe it had just been this morning he'd been at the cemetery, telling her goodbye and hearing Megan's sweet voice offering her sympathies.

Fuck. Yeah, the shit had been this morning. When he'd hung his cut in his closet and worn a suit for the first time in fucking years. Big Joe would take them oversees every summer. There, it had been sometimes necessary to wear ties and shit.

That time was gone, and this morning was, too.

Megan didn't want him. Zoann and Ophelia hated him. Ma, Kiera, and Ellen was dead. Case fucking closed.

He needed to move the fuck on. It was all over and done with. That's why he wore a pair of jeans, debating on whether he'd take one of the bitches to his room and have his dick sucked.

Mortician and Digger were on guard duty at the motel. More than likely, that's where Christopher would end up. He wouldn't send the other two away. If he did, he'd do something stupid like go to her door and knock on it, when he was no good for her. She had her whole life ahead of her and didn't need a motherfucker like him tying her down.

No, he'd just join Mort and Digger in watching over her to keep her safe, until she decided what she wanted to do with herself. She was carefree and unattached, and Christopher would see to it that she had bank.

It was the least he could do for her.

"Yo, John Boy," Val called from his spot at the table they usually sat at.

Since he hadn't felt like socializing, Christopher had sat at the bar. Now, he scowled, tipping back the bottle to swallow more booze.

What the fuck was his cousin doing here? He'd fuck him up if he was coming to lay blame at his feet over Patricia's death. He'd heard enough shit from his sisters.

"Give me a beer, Bowlie," Johnnie said.

Christopher's eyes widened. His cousin wore his leathers and his cut. "What up?"

Johnnie shrugged as Bowlie sat a beer on the countertop. "Not much. I figured I needed to see what was going on. Been awhile."

"Yeah. Since Boss started his road to fuckin' hell."

Johnnie swigged his beer. "Yep."

"You back in all the fuckin' way?"

"Dunno. That depends."

He had a feeling what it depended on, but he wouldn't discuss her. He'd done what he thought right by calling his cousin and asking him to invite Megan to Patricia's services. He refused to give his verbal blessing for the motherfucker to have her as his old lady.

"Ain't nothin' but a thing. Don't matter," Christopher added.

Johnnie stared at him. "Don't," he said quietly. "You need her."

"Yeah?"

"Yes."

"And what the fuck Ima do with her? Kiss her goodbye and tell her have a good fuckin' day while I go work? Only my job dangerous as fuck. The kind that can get me killed or locked up." Or her killed.

"You don't care if you see her at functions, on the back of my bike, knowing she's just come out of my bed?"

"Shut the fuck up."

"And what about if she ends up pregnant? Maybe, I could use a condom, but I want to feel her cunt—"

Christopher jumped off his stool, knocking it over and grabbing Johnnie's jacket. "Shut the fuck up before I rip your fuckin' dick off."

Johnnie smiled calmly, stared into his eyes. "Lucky me, you already took care of that."

"I fuckin' said—" Christopher's thoughts whooshed out of his mind like a vacuum cleaner had sucked them away. "She havin' my kid?"

"Ummmhmmm."

"Well—"

"If you hadn't been licking your wounds, you would've noticed how her hand kept pressing against her belly. She'd gaze at you and look lost and forlorn and flushed. But she's young, scared, and confused. And you're not helping by trying to push her into my arms."

"She said that?"

"No. I'm saying it. I'm not a girl who's only had one lover and ended up pregnant."

"Johnnie—"

"I'm giving you one chance. I'd like to come back to the club. But I don't want to risk having a bullet in my ass because she's in my bed. You piss this chance away, she's fair game, Christopher. And I won't stop until she's mine."

Christopher studied him for a moment, searched his mind about how he'd feel if he didn't try for Megan. No ifs, ands, or buts about it. He'd kill Johnnie, especially if his cousin had the nerve to make a play for her while she was still pregnant with Christopher's baby.

He'd get dressed and go reclaim his girl.

Chapter Forty-Two

Meggie

MEGGIE SAT ALONE IN HER MOTEL ROOM. SHE'D cried so much, she suspected she was dehydrated. She had to get past this crippling grief, though. She had to stay focused for her baby. Christopher's baby. She needed to be strong, but she'd been suffering with morning sickness since Christopher had brought her there and forgotten about her. She knew her overwhelming sadness only added to her sickness.

Big Joe had been killed by the man she loved, the father of her unborn baby. In turn, her own brother killed Christopher's mother and then, Christopher had killed her brother. It was all so surreal.

She stumbled to the dingy window. Lightning streaked across the sky, followed by a loud rumble of thunder. Staring at the darkened skies, she tried to get her head straight and figure out why so many people had to die.

She knew why. Because her father was cut from the same cloth as her brother. They were corrupt, evil personified. Maybe, with therapy they could've been saved. She'd never really known her dad, just seeing the best of him when he decided to visit. And she'd never get to acquaint herself with the brother she hadn't known about until a few weeks ago.

She shuffled back to the bed and sat, flinching at the thunder, and pressing her hand against her belly.

While she was wallowing in grief and anger, Christopher was…what? He'd lost his mother and Meggie knew how much he'd loved Patricia. But he'd be Meggie's big, bad biker and hide his grief.

She curled into a little ball, no longer able to deny how much she still loved him and how much she wanted to be there for him. She wanted him to be the father to their baby that her father hadn't been to her.

She screamed into the pillow. So what if her father and brother were dead? And Patricia. So what if Meggie would never get to know her better and really become her friend? Or introduce her to Christopher's baby? *So what?* People died every day.

But not people she knew. Not her own flesh and blood and three women who hadn't deserved to die. Because, in all her current grief and anger, somewhere inside of her the thought of Kiera and Ellen crept in from time to time.

She screamed again and pounded the bed, wondering if she was losing her mind. The rain started falling in sheets, beating against the roof and the windowpane. She sat up, hungry and weak. She needed to get to the minimart when the rain let up. She wanted a Milky Way and some chocolate milk. She wanted…what?

Swallowing, she made her way to the bathroom and turned on the tap, splashing her face with cold water. Her mirrored reflection revealed the mess of her red, swollen eyes, puffy face, and hair hanging like limp noodles.

Pulling a strip of toilet paper from the roll, she blew her nose, then dried her face with a towel from the rack. She drew in a deep breath. At one time, her mother had loved Big Joe, too. Maybe, Dinah could be a comfort to her. Meggie would never tell her mom everything, but she'd have someone to grieve with her where she wouldn't feel guilty because she *was* grieving.

She pushed her tears aside and walked out of the bathroom. Sitting on the side of the bed, she dialed her home number. It was safe since Christopher had one of the boys watching over her. They wouldn't let Thomas get anywhere near her if, by any chance, he saw the motel number on Caller ID and traced the address.

"Hello?"

"Daddy's dead." Meggie sniffled around the words, the moment her mother picked up. Her hand trembled as she held the receiver. Silence. "Did you hear me, Momma?"

"Yes," Dinah whispered. A hiccupped sob escaped her. "Are you all right, baby?"

Meggie bit her lip. She wanted so badly to have her mother with her, especially now. She knew she couldn't and wouldn't. Dinah was too afraid to leave Thomas and Meggie could never return to live with them. As much as she wanted to protect her mother, she had *her* baby to think of now. She swallowed, tears slipping down her cheeks. "I can't believe he's gone!" she cried. "I just wish I'd gotten to talk to him one last time like you did."

"So that's why you left," Dinah said dully. "You heard what I said to Thomas."

"Yes. And I thought Daddy could protect me and rescue you. He would've."

"Oh Meggie. My sweet Meggie. He…I…he never said anything. I never spoke to him," she admitted. "I just wanted Thomas to leave you alone. If he thought Big Joe was coming…"

Her mother's voice trailed off.

"I hurt him, Meggie. I never should have stopped him…he loved you so much. Seeing you kept him focused and I took that away from him. I ruined his life."

"No, of course, you didn't," Meggie soothed. "You—"

"I was angry," Dinah confessed. "I couldn't stand…I hated his lifestyle. I detested the fact that he had another child."

"You knew?" Meggie squeaked. "About his son?"

Silence met the shocked question, then Dinah sighed. "Yes. And…"

"And?" Meggie prompted when Dinah's voice trailed off.

"I wanted to have a son for him, too. I didn't think he'd have any place in his life for a daughter. But I was wrong. He loved you with everything in him. There were always so many women around. I was afraid to leave him around them and I refused to have anything to do with the MC."

"It's okay, Momma. We all make mistakes that we end up regretting. Only, at the time, we think it's the right thing to do. None of us have a crystal ball to know if our decisions are the right ones. Even if we did, I think it would be pretty boring to get everything right. We'd never learn. We'd never love, for that matter."

"Yes. You're right." Dinah cleared her throat. "When are you coming back home?"

How could she ask that? "I'm having a baby," Meggie admitted softly.

"Oh, dear God! Thomas got to you, didn't he? That's why you ran away."

"Thomas never—" *Touched me.* The lie died on her lips because Thomas *had* touched her. He just hadn't penetrated her. "We never had sex." She shored up her courage, knowing this had to be said. "He fondled me. But that's all."

"I wish he'd die!" Dinah spat vehemently.

Meggie did, too. Since that wouldn't happen anytime soon, another approach was necessary. "Do you have your passport?"

"My…? Yes. Why?"

"Why don't you go to Europe? Start over."

"Alone?"

"Um…"

"I went straight from my parents' house to living with your father. Then I had you and I haven't been alone since."

"Don't worry about me," Meggie said. "You need to leave to save your life. Get away from the monster you married."

"No! I just can't. I…you have to understand."

She didn't. Hearing Dinah's determination to remain with Thomas brought Meggie's mood down further. She realized she hadn't called Dinah in the months she'd been away not only because she was afraid Thomas might trace her whereabouts but also because she knew Dinah wouldn't change her mind about leaving her husband.

She didn't have the energy to fight Dinah just then.

"Thomas has been in and out since you left. He was gone for several weeks in late October. He said he'd gotten beat up and had to recover. I was wondering if Big Joe somehow got his hands on Thomas."

No, not Big Joe, but Meggie knew who had. A smile ghosted across her face.

"He's out of town. He had a conference in Vancouver."

"V-Vancouver?" Meggie stuttered. That wasn't far from Hortensia.

"British Columbia," Dinah verified. "The house is so silent with both of you gone. Please think about coming home. I've been so lost without you."

"Momma—"

"It's okay," Dinah gulped. "You have your own life and have no place in it for me."

"That's not true," Meggie said quietly.

"I love you, Meggie," Dinah said, not addressing Meggie's denial.

"I know. I love you, too."

"Meg—"

A knock at the door pulled Meggie away from her mother's voice. She frowned, wondering if Johnnie was visiting to continue the discussion they'd begun earlier today. Hopefully, if it was his, he wouldn't bring it up again. She liked Johnnie, maybe a little too much, but she just didn't feel about him the way she felt about Christopher.

"I'm coming," she called when the knock sounded again. "Someone's at the door. I'll call you tomorrow."

"All right."

"Think about what I said," Meggie urged before saying goodbye and rushing to the door, throwing it open. "Christopher!"

He scowled. "You alfuckinways open a fuckin' door without askin' who the fuck there?"

Meggie rolled her eyes. "Since I have my own personal bodyguards, I figure they wouldn't allow anyone to harm me," she sniffed.

He brushed past her without waiting for an invitation. "We gotta talk."

Slamming the door, Meggie stomped to him. "About?"

He narrowed his eyes. "How 'bout we start with my baby?"

Meggie gasped and opened her mouth to speak.

"Ain't no use tryna deny it," he growled, untying the belt on her robe, and revealing her nightshirt. "Johnnie ain't gonna lie 'bout that kinda shit."

"He had no right to tell you," she huffed, the feel of Christopher's hands roaming over her breasts and belly burning through her. She closed her eyes when he thumbed her nipples. Her breasts were so sensitive and so much fuller. "It was my news to share." She gasped as his fingers found her center, already wet and empty feeling.

Christopher bent his head and covered her mouth, sucking on her tongue, destroying her thoughts of anything else. She stood on her tiptoes and wrapped her arms around his neck, loving the taste and scent of him. His hard body pressed against hers and he back-walked her the few steps to the bed. He stopped a moment to remove her nightshirt before he sat on the bed and pulled her between his legs.

Meggie knew she should stop him so they could talk. But she'd missed him so much. Death had been all around them. He needed to feel life. He'd put life inside her belly. She clutched his shoulders, opened her mouth in submission, whimpering when he massaged between her legs. Arms around her waist, he laid back and pulled her on top of him before rolling over. He lifted himself up and stared into her eyes. She raised her hips, urging him to bury himself inside her.

"We gotta talk, Megan," he whispered, caressing her cheeks, gliding his fingers through her hair. He kissed her again. "I love you. Stubborn, cheeky lil' bitch that you is."

She glared at him.

Christopher sighed and rearranged them on the bed. He held her in the crook of his arm, wrapped tight against his body. "Girls that to me. If I ain't sayin' it with no heat, I ain't meanin' nothin' by it."

"Oh."

"Jesus. See what the fuck I mean." He scraped his fingers through his hair. "You ain't belongin' in my world. And I thought long and hard 'bout this. 'Bout leavin' the MC. And, fuck, Megan. I ain't able to. That shit what the fuck I know. Who I am. I'm in too deep. I got my own ma killed."

His voice broke just as Meggie swore her heart was breaking, too. "Christopher, it wasn't your fault."

"Then fuck it ain't. I got her involved."

"By bringing me to her. You must hate me. If you hadn't sought to protect me—"

"No. Don't even think that bullshit. I ain't ever hatin' you," he swore. "I just wish...fuck, my life ain't got no place for wishes. Dontcha see? Ain't no way we ever able to be together. When you look at me, you always gonna see the motherfucker that killed your pops."

Meggie considered Christopher's words. The past four and a half months since she'd runaway had taught her a lot about herself and her father. And the last ten days had shown her how precious and fragile life is. Living under Thomas's brutality, she'd always believed it in the back of her mind.

"Ima always take care of my kid. Just don't shut my ass outta the lil' motherfucker life. Ima buy you a house wherever you wanna go. Send you to fuckin' school so you can do that weather girl shit."

"I loved—love," she corrected on a swallow, "my father. He put you in the position of having to choose his life or your own. He should never have done that. Knowing my dad, he would've done the same thing if the situation was reversed. No, he probably would've done it the moment he realized you'd started using the, um…" She frowned. "Merchandise."

"Fuck. Boss was a tough motherfucker. He ain't fuck 'round. He probably woulda cut my fuckin' fingers off first."

It was the first time Meggie heard Christopher mention her father with such reverence.

Christopher scooted down and pressed his forehead to hers. "I came here to getcha back. I fucked 'nuff chicks to know I don't need to keep fuckin' no random bitches."

Meggie growled. He laughed.

"You a jealous lil' bitch, huh?"

"Would you stop?"

"This ain't the life for you, Megan. Ain't matterin' how much my ass wantcha with me. How many babies I wanna give you."

"B-but I love you, Christopher," she said softly, drawing her fingers along the angle of his jaw. "Do I want to live at the clubhouse? No. Not full-time. I saw you at your mother's house. How much you enjoyed the normalcy." She swallowed, scared he'd turn her down. Besides her father, she'd never met anyone so willing to put actions behind the words to protect her. He believed she deserved better. What exactly was his idea of better? It was the height of irony that society would view Thomas as the *better* man. Thomas was a child molester, an alcoholic, and a wife beater. The scum of the earth cloaked in middle-class respectability. "Can't we be together? I don't want anyone else but you."

"Megan, no. I thought Johnnie better for you, but ain't no way now. He wanna patch back in and—"

Meggie lifted herself up and glared at him. "Did you ever consider who I wanted? I like Johnnie. A lot—"

"He fuckin' kissed you."

Scrambling out of bed, Meggie stalked to the dresser and snatched open a drawer. She pulled on her panties before finding a pair of leggings and a sweatshirt.

Christopher pulled himself up on his elbows. "What the fuck you doin'?"

"I'm going to buy myself a Milky Way," she muttered, slipping her feet into her shoes.

"No, the fuck you ain't. It's been rainin' fuckin' buckets. It stopped now but for how fuckin' long?" He got to his feet and pulled out his cell phone. "Lemme call Digger. He can make the run for you."

"No," she snarled. "*No!* You have my entire life planned out. Never mind asking me what I wanted." Hurt and angry, Meggie stomped around the room, grabbing her wallet for some money. Money Christopher supplied her with. She stuffed a ten in her shirt pocket. "I'm too young to know. I wasn't too young to get pregnant. No. Not at all. You *wanted* your baby in me. But I can't make my own decisions beyond that," she fumed.

A knock sounded at the door. Christopher sauntered past her and opened it. Seeing Digger, Meggie screamed in pure frustration.

Digger frowned. "What's wrong with your bitch?"

Tears rushing to her eyes, Meggie shoved Digger aside. "If either of you follow me, I'm going to kill you both," she yelled. She spun. "Just leave me alone."

"Megan—"

Her glare silenced Christopher and he ran his fingers through his hair. "Awright, you stubborn fuckin' bit…brat. You ain't back in half hour, Ima find you myfuckinself and I swear, if I gotta do that, Ima putcha over my knee. You wanna act like a child, Ima treat you like one." He indicated the room. "Get the fuck in here, Digger. Half hour, Megan," he warned and slammed the door the moment Digger walked inside.

"Asshole," she muttered, turning on her heel and heading toward the minimart, sidestepping puddles of water. Her mood lightened at the thought of having something she'd been craving all day. If she were honest, she'd been too down to make the trek, between the breaks in the rain, no matter how much her body begged her to sate its desire for the candy. She'd wanted Christopher. She'd just had to work everything out in her head. Him showing up helped speed up her foregone conclusion, but she would've made the same decision without his arrival. She gave herself two days tops before she'd have given in.

Someone grabbed her around her waist. The hand slamming over her mouth and nose cut off her air and caught her scream. "You've led me on a merry chase, Megan," Thomas whispered against her ear, shaking her. "But I've got you now and you're never leaving my sight again."

Megan elbowed Thomas, struggling against his hold.

"Keep fucking still!"

No. Never. He loosened his grip slightly and Meggie's elbow came down harder. He grunted but her action momentarily shocked him, and he let her go. Meggie screamed at the top of her lungs, kicking his groin.

"You little bitch." He used his favorite technique—a backhand— and Meggie fell to the ground.

He dragged her to her feet, and she struggled more. She couldn't allow Thomas to take her anywhere.

"Your bitch of a ma always loved you more than she loved me," Thomas breathed. "Always wanting you around. And your fucking man should've killed me when he had the chance if he wanted to keep me away from you."

Meggie had the briefest glint of the blade arcing toward her chest and thrusting. She screamed, a burning pain slicing through her. "My baby," she cried, falling to her knees.

"Megan!"

Mortician called her, she thought dizzily. A gunshot. Thomas hollered.

Gripping the handle of the knife, blackness swirling around her, Meggie pulled. Blood dripped from the blade, and she let out a sob, feeling her life draining away.

Meggie shoved it toward the wavering mass of her stepfather. "That's for my mother." She wanted to spit the words. Instead, she gasped them.

She heard another gunshot, another scream from her stepfather, before the darkness claimed her, and she heard no more.

Chapter Forty-Three
Christopher

CHRISTOPHER COMPARED HIS WATCH WITH THE digital clock on the nightstand. Megan had been gone 28 minutes if he wanted to go by those red numbers. He didn't. According to his watch, she'd been gone 29 minutes and 34.13 seconds. If she wasn't back in 25.47 seconds, he intended to ride to that minifuckinmart and drag her ass back to the room.

He paced, his gut telling him something wasn't right. He knew her. She might do her best to test him, but she never purposely worried him. She knew motherfuckers got hurt that way, and she did her absolute best to keep him calm so there would be no unnecessary blood spilled.

"Time fuckin' up," he growled. "You wait here, Digger. If I miss her some kinda way and she come back without me, tell her I ain't happy."

"Slack up, bruh," Digger said with a laugh. "She was pissed. Let 'er cool off."

"Megan ain't supposed to be out there alone."

"She lived on the street a whole month alone and we took care of Thomas Nicholls."

"We left him breathin'," Christopher muttered. "I ain't fuckin' considerin' that takin' care of him."

"He can't be that much of a stupid motherfucker," Digger reasoned. "And if you notice Meggie not frightened—"

"Why the fuck she scared when she know she got protection?"

"She can take care of herself, so what you sweating her for? I never seen you act like this behind no bitch."

Christopher drew in a deep breath. Digger was right, but, shit, he ain't never felt like this about no bitch. "She pregnant."

"For you?"

Christopher slapped him on the side of the head. "Yeah, asswipe. Who the fuck you think for?"

"Damn, man. All I'm saying is I thought you always kept your shit covered. Didn't think I'd ever see a little you running round."

Christopher glared at him.

"I understand your worry," Digger said with a laugh, raising his hands. "If I was you, I'd get a better handle on my old lady. Feel me, bro?"

"Megan fine just how she fuckin' is. Don't wanna change one hair on her head."

"That must mean you going to keep her."

That's what Megan wanted. Fuck. That's what *he* wanted. She gave him all sorts of ideas. He'd buy a house near the club or even build one for her. He intended to sell the house in Long Beach. Though it was *his*, everything about it reminded him of his ma. That shit wouldn't fly.

House or not, Megan could come to the club whenever she wanted. He'd never bar her. They could even keep a crib there for the baby. Shit could work out. No, shit *would* work out. He didn't have his mother anymore, but he had Megan and she loved him for him.

Whatever she wanted was hers. Whatever.

His heart twisted. Except leaving the club. Call him a selfish fuck, but this was his life, and he couldn't give it up.

Someone banged on the door, hard enough to shake the shitty frame. That same awful feeling came back in his gut.

"Who is it?" Digger called.

"It's Johnnie and Mortician," Johnnie called, the trembling words making Christopher's heart drop. "Open the fucking door."

By the time Johnnie had the words out, Digger had already swung it open. It took a moment for Christopher to process the blood on Mortician, a moment longer for him to realize *where* the blood was coming from. Megan. Limp and pale in Johnnie's arms. No, limp, pale, and bloody.

No. Not that either. Limp, pale, bloody, and pregnant for Christopher.

Bile rose to Christopher's throat, and he staggered back.

Johnnie shoved her into Christopher's arms. "We have an ambulance coming for her. I hope they make it in time," he rasped. "We have the fucker. None of the usual suspects. Big fuck. Never seen him in my life."

Even now, the blare of sirens cut through the night. Within moments, EMTs and police officers were swarming the small room, pulling his beautiful Megan out of his arms, and laying her limp body onto a stretcher.

"Go with her," Mortician ordered. "We got this covered."

Christopher didn't argue. He just nodded and followed behind as Megan was hustled into the back of an ambulance.

"We can finish fuckhead," Val swore, two hours later.

They were all crowded in the waiting room at the hospital. Johnnie had called everyone to report what was going on and they'd come running to support Christopher. Megan was in surgery, hanging on by a thread. The doctors hadn't mentioned the baby, but he couldn't help but wonder if her blood loss had somehow affected it.

Christopher was losing his fucking mind with each passing minute. If he didn't get the fuck away, he was going to fuck something up. He pulled out his smokes and lit one up, the nicotine not calming him at all. He released the smoke through his nose, daring one of them nurse bitches to say anything. The security guards had teamed up, two standing nearby. They must've called in backup because, every five minutes, two other dickheads marched by, hands on their weapons, glaring at all of them.

Pacing, Christopher drew in another drag, staring down the fuckheads as more smoke poured from his nostrils.

Zoann was also on duty. Instead of offering him any type of comfort because his girl lay close to fucking death with his baby inside her, his sister had just stared at him, the look on her face taunting him with the knowledge he ruined everything he touched. Cunt.

"You stay with Megs. Val's right. We got this."

Christopher shook his head at his cousin. "He mine," he swore.

"He won't last much longer," Johnnie said with a shrug. "If he's still alive now. He has two slugs in him along with the superficial wound Megs gave him."

"Megan fuckin' *what?*" Christopher asked, shocked.

"She jerked that motherfucker's knife out of her chest and stuck him in his fat belly." Mortician laughed. "She said *this is for my mother.*"

"Motherfucker," Christopher snarled, the pieces falling into place. "Her fuckin' stepfather."

"Shit," Johnnie said grimly. "Listen, Outlaw. I know how you're feeling—"

"The fuck your ass do," he sneered, throwing the cigarette on the floor and crushing it beneath his boot. "How the fuck I'm feelin', John Boy? My girl almost fuckin' dead and my kid in her. How the fuck my ass feel?"

"Like you want to take the fucker out. But not right now. She needs you here."

"Accordin' to Val waitin' too much longer, and he a dead fuckhead. I ain't gonna make him fuckin' suffer the way I wanna."

For her sake, he'd left that motherfucker alive, but he should've known better. Thomas fuckin' Nicholls had been a fucking loose end that needed to be dealt with. Just as Snake and Rack had been, but Christopher had left it all hanging. His indecisiveness hadn't helped one fucking bit. It made him look like a weak fucking pussy and had led to his ma's death, as well as Kiera and Ellen's. And possibly his girl's.

No, fuck. She couldn't die and he couldn't stay in this fucking hospital, waiting around, fearing for news he didn't want to think about. It made his fucking skin crawl.

Christopher turned, heading for the exit. This was just another fucking example of why he was no good for Megan. Nothing should've pulled him from the place until he knew whether she'd live or die. He just wasn't that type of man, though. He was on the verge of going ape-shit crazy if he just stood the fuck around, picturing how small and lifeless she looked.

He clenched his jaw, the cool night air hitting him. Boots pounded behind him and he glanced over his shoulder. Digger and Val were on his heels.

"Here," Digger said, throwing a set of keys to him. "Johnnie said to take his ride."

Christopher nodded but didn't speak.

"She a strong chick," Val said quietly. "And she love you. I heard you and Johnnie talking about the baby. If that's true, then she'll fight double hard. You have to just believe that."

He didn't respond to what Val said. Just gave instructions. "Digger, a grave needed. Usual spot."

"Live body or dead ass?"

"Ain't sure yet," he admitted. "Just get the motherfucker fuckin' ready."

Chapter Forty-Four

Meggie

MEGGIE GAZED AROUND IN HAZY CONFUSION, listening to the steady beeps and the low hum of conversation. Fatigue filled Christopher's voice and she frowned, trying to make sense of what was going on.

The antiseptic smell of a hospital filtered in her head. Her body felt heavy. It took her a moment, but everything came rushing back and she attempted to sit up. Thomas had attacked her, tried his best to kill her. He'd probably already gotten to her mom and was somewhere waiting for her, too. She groaned.

Abruptly, the talking ceased.

"Megan?"

"Christopher," she squeaked in response. He placed a hand on her shoulder, holding her in place. "I need to…Thomas did this. I have to get to my mother. He's probably already hurt her." Her chest throbbed as bad as the hand holding the IV catheter. And God… "The baby!"

"Shhh," Christopher soothed, leaning over and kissing her forehead. "The baby fine. Your ma, too. She downstairs in the cafeteria."

"But Thomas—"

"Ain't botherin' no motherfucker ever afuckingain," he finished.

"Don't worry about that right now, Megs," Johnnie said from her other side.

Looking at the fierceness in Christopher's eyes, Meggie decided she wouldn't ever ask about Thomas's fate.

"I ain't ever lettin' you out my fuckin' sight," he said. "You was in surgery for fuckin' hours. Don't ever—"

"Christopher, maybe, we should get a nurse in here to check her out," Johnnie suggested.

"Yeah," Christopher agreed. "Go 'head. Press the fuckin' button."

Although Dinah and Maggie cried upon seeing each other, it wasn't a real happy reunion. Despite Christopher's reassurances that Thomas was no longer a threat, Dinah wanted details. She wanted to know how Christopher could be so certain when not even the police were. Meggie's attempted murder was listed as an open and active case with Thomas being classified as a violent fugitive, possibly armed.

Meggie knew Thomas was dead. She had vague memories of gunshots and stabbing her stepfather. Perhaps, that had been enough to kill him, and Christopher had merely disposed of the body. She shivered at the thought and wrapped her arms around her belly, thankful she hadn't lost Christopher's baby.

"I need to know," Dinah insisted. "If you know where Thomas is, tell me."

Meggie glowered at her mother, wishing she'd left with Christopher and Johnnie. "Does it matter, Momma?" she snapped. "I hope he's burning in hell."

"Is he dead?" she gasped as the hospital room door opened.

"Do you really care? He beat the crap out of you. He tried to kill me. Just as bad was the way he groped me as much as he could."

"What the fuck?"

Meggie ignored Christopher's growl and kept her narrowed focus on her pale-faced, trembling mother. Nausea roiled in Meggie's belly, the taste of medicine drying her mouth. Her head pounded and she felt like crap in general. "Would you just grow a pair?"

"A pair of what?" Dinah asked.

How could this woman be an assistant principal? Shouldn't she be a little more in touch with reality?

"Calm the fuck down, Megan," Christopher warned.

"I love you, Momma, but you need to get a spine. Thomas took everything away from you. All your self-worth. Your pride. He's gone now. Where? I don't know and I don't care. But get over it. Grow a pair of balls and *move on*."

Amusement danced in Christopher's eyes, and he shook his head. Dinah, on the other hand, just looked defeated and wilted.

"Just tell—"

"Look, lady, you workin' on my last fuckin' nerve botherin' Megan with this whiny bullshit." Before either of them could say anything, he scooped Dinah around the waist and carried her to the door. When he opened it, he said, "Take her to the club. Don't let no motherfucker bother her. But she upsettin' Megan and that shit ain't flyin'."

Meggie couldn't see who Christopher spoke to. He reached the side of the bed, bent and brushed his lips over hers, before dropping into a chair.

"That *is* my mother."

"Ain't givin' a fuck. She coulda been your granny. The bit..." He scowled at her look. "She was gettin' you all worked up. Ain't happenin'."

Meggie sighed. "I'm worried she's going to the police. Tell them she thinks Thomas is dead."

Christopher rested his hands behind his head and shrugged. "Who give a fuck? They ain't stupid. And I ain't payin them fuckheads for nothin'. They can *suspect* all the fuck they want. If they take that further, then they gonna have problems."

"You're a psycho. You know that?"

"Ain't nothin' but a thing, Megan. My ass might be a psycho but I'm *your* psycho." Abandoning his deceptive calm, he leaned forward and took the hand without the IV. "I love you. Ima give your way a try. Buy us another house and shit. You can redecorate our room at the club. Whatever. But, baby, I swear to you, the minute I ain't makin' you happy, the minute you ain't able to handle my lifestyle, tell me. And...and we'll do what we gotta do to getcha happy again."

They'd separate, he meant. Which was probably the reason why he hadn't mentioned marriage. If they couldn't handle each other's differences, it would be easier if there were no legalities involved.

Meggie smiled. "I love you, too, Christopher," she whispered, believing they'd get through anything as long as they were together.

Epilogue

SEVEN MONTHS LATER...

Christopher

"PUSH, MEGAN. SCREAM AS LOUD AS YOU WANNA. Call me a dirty motherfucker for doin' this to you."

Megan shrieked, not saying any of what Christopher told her. He wished she would. It would help his conscience to stop beating him up for getting her pregnant in the first place. She fell back against the pillows, panting, her delicate, little hand squeezing his fingers with everything in her. His plain, gold wedding band bumped against her sapphire and diamond engagement ring and matching wedding band.

They'd been married four days and he loved every moment of it. He knew she wanted a big wedding and he'd let her have it, too. Even if, to him, their courthouse wedding had sufficed.

Now, she was bringing his baby into the world. He tried not to think of his mother just then and how much he wished she was still around. He did, however, remember Big Joe. Christopher had finally made peace with himself and the man he'd once loved. Meggie still knew nothing of her father's memorial. Once Christopher decided her recovered from delivering his child, he'd take her. Bring flowers for both Boss and Patricia.

"Christopher!" she hollered.

"The head is crowning, Megan," Doc Will said gently. "You're doing excellent." She nodded at Christopher. "Isn't she?"

"Yeah, baby. Doc right. This almost over." Christopher kissed her sweaty forehead. He looked at Doc Will for guidance. He liked her, Megan's second baby doctor. The first had been a man and there wasn't no way Christopher would allow some fuck to look up Megan's pussy. It was the Promised Land and his alone. Of course, Megan resisted. When Christopher explained what might accidentally happen to her doctor, she came around to his way of thinking. She arched into another contraction, straining so much Christopher knew she'd faint at any moment. Her hair, piled on her head in a messy bun, was soaked with sweat. Tears streamed down her beet-red face.

She fell back again, panting, her chest rising and falling in a hard wave. A high-pitched wail tore through the air and Christopher started.

"Congratulations," the nurse said with a wide smile, bringing a squirming little alien, coated with all types of goop, to Megan and laying it on her heaving chest. "You have a beautiful baby boy."

A son. He had a son. A son whose head looked crooked and squinched but a son all the same. Besides, Megan didn't seem to give a fuck that their son didn't look quite human. The same look of love and adoration she gave the little boy, she turned on him, and Christopher swore he'd turned into a bitch. He actually felt tears in his eyes.

He hadn't wanted to know the sex of the baby in advance, believing his family genes wouldn't allow him to procreate a male and concluding Megan would give him a daughter. *Fuck*! He was happier than a motherfucker, but he'd have to find something to do with all the pink baby shit he'd bought to surprise Megan with.

"All right, Megan. Let's finish up here," Doc said, and the nurse took the baby away from her.

Christopher bent over and kissed her, for once not having words. But Megan didn't need them. She understood him and returned his kiss in a sweet display. He thumbed her tears away and pressed his forehead against hers.

"Thank you," he whispered. "You thinkin' of a name for my boy?"

She caressed away a tear slipping down his cheek. "Christopher Joseph Foy Caldwell."

Christopher Joseph Foy Caldwell. He might not have been a real royal like they had in Britain, but his son was biker royalty and Megan had given him a name to match his status.

"He's beautiful, isn't he?" she continued, exhausted and drowsy.

Christopher chuckled. "If you seein' beauty in the lil' motherfucker, then yeah he beautiful."

She giggled, her little fingers brushing his jaw. "I love you."

"I love you, too, Megan."

"Would you call Momma and tell her?"

Fuck, he'd prefer to slit his fucking wrists than talk to that whiny bitch. But she was his ma-in-law and Megan still gave her respect, although Christopher couldn't understand why. He sighed. "Yeah, fuck, baby. Whatever the fuck you wantin' yours."

Christopher pulled out his cell phone and began to dial. He still heard Megan's soft words. "As long as I have you and the baby, I have everything I'll ever need."

For once, they were in complete agreement.

The End

Dear Reader,

S EPTEMBER 2022 MARKED 9 YEARS SINCE I FIRST met Christopher Caldwell, whom I discovered later went by the road name of Outlaw. Our introduction came via a dream. I didn't know much about him. He was quite tall, very well-built, and oozing sex. He had green eyes, black hair, a Harley, and a cut with a frightening Grim Reaper as the middle rocker. Scary for me because since the age of eight or nine, I've had nightmares about the Grim Reaper coming for me as I waited alone in a bedroom. My first reaction when I awakened was: *what that mean?* Yes, I said exactly those words. My next reaction was his name *Christopher.* Years ago, I dated a guy named Christopher who had green eyes, but he didn't have black hair and he didn't ride a motorcycle. My next reaction to the dream was: *what the ever-loving fuck was that?*

As dreams go, this one was remarkable because I remembered it. Most of them are forgotten. Very few stay with me. I can count on one hand (and maybe an additional finger from the other hand) the dreams I don't forget. Ever. I thought my dream about Christopher

Caldwell was a throwaway. I recalled it because of certain coincidences. But he didn't go away. The motherfucker *stayed.* He was persistent, demanding, memorable. Two weeks later I gave in to him, sat down at my computer and listened to his story.

At the time, I didn't expect that one, nameless book to turn into 15 books of sex, revenge, betrayal and, most of all, love. Johnnie was just Christopher's cousin, a big, sexy biker competing for Megan. His history and his grandfather's tainted love were unknown to me. What I did know was he and Christopher shared women, and Johnnie took it as a given that it would always be so, even when *he* found a woman he refused to share. I also knew he was Christopher's complete opposite, charming, carefree, and college educated. He was also a man that caught Meggie's attention, in spite of her feelings for Christopher. As a matter of fact, for a brief time, I considered a completely different outcome. Meggie ended up with Johnnie, and Christopher would go with Kiera.

Today, in the here and now, I can't imagine that outcome or a continuation of the series.

Love triangles are controversial. Subverting reader expectations are even worse. One of my absolute favorite series was the Francesca Cahill novels by Brenda Joyce. It began with one hero and slowly introduced a competitor. By the end of the series, I was torn over which hero I wanted Francesca with. Calder Hart had begun as the villain but ended up being darkly charismatic. He lured me into his spell as much as he did Francesca, even as we still clung to and loved the upstanding Rick Bragg.

Once a hero, always a hero, and Christopher was Meggie's. Yet, emotions are complex, the nucleus of love. Emotions are messy, drawing us in even when we want to turn away.

As I met each of the characters in Misled, I wasn't aware of Mortician and Digger's history and how they'd grown up. Val and Zoann's individual traumas were unknown to me. Big Joe was the father Meggie admired and needed so she could save her mother, and the man Christopher despised because of who he'd become. Kendall Miller wouldn't be truly known to me for another six months.

Christopher, Johnnie, Mortician, Digger, Val, Stretch, Big Joe, and K-P gave me enough of their history to tell Meggie's story. As the years went on and each character revealed more and more of themselves, I began to consider going back to book one to add scenes as well as other POVs. The idea came and went, but I never acted on it. I thought I did Meggie an injustice by only mentioning in one or two sentences that she called the police for Thomas, but Dinah always sent them away. I realized her reasons for staying and the help she tried to get for her mother had been glossed over, so sometimes didn't register.

Johnnie, once such a beloved character, needed a little more clarity. A paragraph or two telling about his time with Meggie hit much differently than actually showing it.

Questions such as, 'why did Meggie believe Kiera meant so much to Outlaw', 'why was Snake at the mall', 'what was Outlaw doing while Meggie was in the hospital', also struck me. Of course, there's no way I could ever address all the questions, comments, and points of contention or disbelief that's out there. It is just impossible and unrealistic, but some things bothered me too, even as the end of the series finally arrived and something else I hadn't intended came into existence—plans for a next generation.

When Misled was released in December 2013, I was so ecstatic. I know Amazon lists the date as December 19, 2013, but the original date was the 5th of December, then Amazon pulled it. It took another 14 days before it was listed on the site again.

11 months after Misled's release, my grandmother died. 20 months after, I was diagnosed with Stage 2b HER2 Positive breast cancer. At the 21-month mark, I developed a severe bacterial infection from the port. By 25 months, my doggie died. She would've been 14 that summer; I still miss her. 26 months after Misled I went through 11 ½ hours of surgery. Two weeks before Misled's 3rd anniversary, I rang the bell. It was one of the best days of my life. Yet, I don't think my

life ever truly returned to what it had been prior to my cancer diagnosis.

It affected my three daughters terribly. It was also the beginning of my mother's (Memaw Kelly) memory lapses. The coming years also saw her decline physically.

Real-life pulled me from my world of bikers and revenge.

As depression is wont to do, I also suffered major bouts. In my teens, I was diagnosed with Major Depressive Disorder with suicidal ideations.

Yet, my characters, Christopher especially, wouldn't allow me to let go of them. My readers, my beautiful people, sent me words of encouragement and checked in on me. Some of you still do. Misfit was supposed to wrap up the saga of the Death Dwellers. But Roxy tapped me on the shoulder and wanted her own HEA. Next, Jordan's story needed telling. Christopher got a little jealous and decided he needed a Valentine's story. Finally, Roxy wanted to know if Knox would ever marry her.

When I released Misrule in August 2019, I fully intended to drop Reckless within a few months. Then, Covid happened, and the world screeched to a halt.

It should've been easy to finish Reckless. Instead, my girls' depression worsened, and my mother's vertigo returned, along with bouts of asthma, arthritis, and asthma. I didn't have the time or the brain capacity to write. Not even for Christopher.

In early spring of 2021, things settled enough that my thoughts began to return. Most of all, Memaw got on my ass and told me to sit the fuck down and *write*. If you don't fucking write, you're not a damn writer.

So true.

I placed Reckless on preorder; I fully intended to release it in June 2021. Then, another shitstorm erupted. Suddenly, we were all going for tests, seeing doctors and therapists, and purchasing medications. My release date came and went. Depression returned.

As always, I managed to pull myself together and recalibrate. I jotted down notes and ideas for Reckless. I managed to read an *entire* book for the first time in over a year. Perhaps, even longer. *Island Queen* by Vanessa Riley was worth it, and I loved every word.

I read what I had of Reckless, 250 pages; then, I decided I needed to start from the beginning since I had some characters from the original series making cameos in Reckless. As I reread all 15 books, I saw corrections that needed to be done but had somehow been missed by several pairs of eyes. Dates and timelines needed to match, even motivations explained. There were also details in the original series that needed to be clarified, tweaked, or expanded upon to fit what was in Reckless.

Yes, I'm aware Reckless isn't released yet, so it would've been easier to edit that story rather than the original series. However, I've long wanted new covers. It wasn't until I saw a segment from Stephen Colbert naming a man who sometimes modeled for romance covers being involved in the January 6th nightmare that I felt it became imperative. Mr. Colbert broadcast several covers with the guy's image, and I was crushed that my title wasn't amongst them. 😌 I don't want to be accused of supporting his beliefs by not taking him off the cover. Updating the original series as well as the covers appealed to me.

Besides, there were whole generations that needed accounting. Enemies of the fathers, thus enemies of the sons. Some of the guest appearances in Reckless would make more sense if I went back to the original story and rewrote bits and pieces.

So, in preparation for the release of Reckless, and then the Death Dweller Legacy books, I am updating the original 15 books. Reckless IS coming. It is now 475 pages. I should be wrapping it up soon, so the final page count is unknown. But like Misfit, this motherfucker keeps growing and growing, too.

In closing, I want to thank you. If this is your first time reading one of my books, thank you for taking a chance and I hope you enjoy it. If you have read my books before, thank you for your continued support. Most of all, thank you for your prayers, well-wishes, encouragement, and patience.

Ain't nothin' but a thing,

Kat

THANK YOU
FOR READING MISLED.

I hope you enjoyed Christopher's and Meggie's story.

Please recommend Misled to the fellow readers in your life! Reviews at point of purchase and on Goodreads are much appreciated. Your thoughts and opinions mean a lot to me.

Playlist

All the songs in the playlist below aren't mentioned in *Misled*. But I listened to them while writing the story and fleshing out each character. To me, the music I chose for them gave life to the characters in my head.

CHRISTOPHER

Fuck You by Lily Allen
Evil Angel by Breaking Benjamin
Sex Machine by Dope
Die, Bom, Bang, Burn, F*** by Dope
Sympathy for the Devil by Guns N' Roses
Another Love Song by ICP
My Axe by ICP
Voodoo Child by Jimi Hendrix
Every Rose Has Its Thorn by Poison
No Woman, No Cry by Bob Marley
I Don't Care by Fall Out Boy
American Idiot by Green Day
Apologize by OneRepublic
Time Won't Let Me Go by The Bravery
With Arms Wide Open by Creed

Love In An Elevator by Aerosmith

MEGGIE

Girl On Fire by Alicia Keys
Call Me Maybe by Carly Rae Jepsen
Scream and Shout by Brittany Spears
Insensitive by Jann Arden
Daughters by John Mayer
Waiting on the World to Change by John Mayer
Cruise by Florida Georgia Line
Roar by Katy Perry
Breath of Life by Florence + The Machine
When I Was Your Man by Bruno Mars
Rumour Has It by Adele
The Edge of Glory by Lady Gaga
You and I by Lady Gaga
Wrecking Ball by Miley Cyrus
We Can't Stop by Miley Cyrus
Gangnam Style by Psy
Gentlemen by Psy
5 O'Clock by T-Pain/Lily Allen/Wiz Kalifa
Santa's A Fat Bitch by ICP
Twist & Shout by The Beatles
Royals by Lorde
Pour Some Sugar On Me by Def Leopard

JOHNNIE

Hey Jude by The Beatles
Rocky Raccoon by The Beatles
Star-Spangled Banner by Jimi Hendrix
Convoy by C.W. McCall
Achy Breaky Heart by Billy Ray Cyrus
The Most Beautiful Girl by Charlie Rich
Higher by Creed
Home by Daughtry
Come Undone by Duran Duran
Fairytale of New York by The Pogues
The Marine Hymn by Unmarked Cars
Love Will Turn You Around by Kenny Rogers
I Don't Want To Miss A Thing by Aerosmith

God Bless the USA by Lee Greenwood
Always on My Mind by Willie Nelson

MORTICIAN

Buffalo Soldier by Bob Marley
Brandy by O'Jays
Bottoms Up by Trey Songz
What A Wonderful World by Louis Armstrong
Electric Boogie by Marcia Griffiths
Hot Boyz by Missy Elliot
Big Poppa by The Notorious B.I.G.
Dear Mama by Tupac
My Chick Bad by Ludacris
ET by Katy Perry
Meant by Elizaveta
Too Taboo by Maria Haukaas Storeng

DIGGER

Cross Road Blues by Robert Johnson
Boom Boom by John Lee Hooker
Champagne and Reefer by Muddy Water
Mississippi Delta Blues by Muddy Water
Gin Bottle Blues by Lightnin' Hopkins
A Good Man Is Hard To Find by Bessie Smith
Lick It Before You Stick It by Denise Lasalle
Your Husband Is Cheating On Us by Denise Lasalle

Contact Kathryn C. Kelly

EMAIL: katkelwriter@outlook.com

https://www.katckelly.com
https://deathdwellersmc.com

For an autographed bookmark, please send an SASE to:
24200 Southwest Freeway
Suite 402, #353
Rosenberg, TX 77471

Bibliography

ALSO BY KATHRYN C. KELLY

Phoenix Rising Rock Band Series
Inferno
Incendiary
Scorched
Inflame
Ignite

Death Dwellers MC Series
Misled
Misappropriate
Misunderstood
Misdeeds
Misbehavior
Misjudged
Misguided
Misalliance
Misconduct
A Very Christopher Christmas

Misfit
Mistrust
Misgivings
Outlaw's Dictionary
Death Dwellers: The Complete Series
An Outlaw Valentine

DEATH DWELLERS MC LEGACY SERIES
Reckless – The Legacy Begins

Dirty Boys Studio Series
Dirty Boy

COCKY HERO CLUB
Savage Suit

Dirty Boys Studio Series
Dirty Boy

Other Titles
All My Tomorrows
Dangerous
Riveted
Pink: Hot 'N Sexy for a cure: The
Books for Boobies 2015 Anthology
When Clubs Collide
Desire Me
The Marriage Monologues – Forever A Dark Obsession Anthology
Sexy Santa – All I Want For Christmas Anthology
Red Stiletto – Call My Bluff Anthology
Hazel & Grayson – Brothers Grimm Fairytales: An Erotic Anthology
Barebacked – Game Player Anthology
Breakfast & Bedlam – Happily Ever After Anthology
Drifter's Vow: Red Rum MC – Vow of Protection Anthology
How Innocent My Love – Secrets of Me Anthology
My One and Only – Goodbye Doesn't Mean Forever Anthology
Gods & Goddesses – Wicked Realms Anthology

KINDLE VELLA
Urchin of the Court
Ace of Spades – Red Rum MC

About Kathryn C. Kelly

Kathryn C. Kelly is a New Orleans native who has called southeast Texas home since 2005. She had intended to travel the world but always return to her beloved New Orleans. Hurricane Katrina had other plans. She is the mother of three beautiful daughters and the daughter of one gorgeous mother whose footsteps she followed in by becoming a writer.

Kathryn is the former owner and editor of Inside Rose Rich Magazine. She and her mother have been published by Jove Books as Christine Holden. The books have long been out of print but they got the rights back to the five novels and have plans to re-release them soon.

Kathryn is a cancer survivor. In 2010, she felt a small lump in her breast. In 2015, at the urging of her mother, she went in for her bi-yearly mammogram and was diagnosed with Stage 2b/3a HER2 positive breast cancer. On November 30, 2016, she rang the bell. During her treatment, she was also diagnosed with Li-Fraumeni Syndrome.

In 2013, Christopher "Outlaw" Caldwell introduced himself to Kat in the most cliché way *ever*. He came to her in a dream. After the inauspicious meeting, he planted himself in her mind and the motherf...*the gentleman* hasn't left yet. In what was only supposed to be one book about the fictitious Death Dwellers MC, Outlaw has become a source of amusement, a well of frustration, and a bone of contention between Kat and one of her daughters.

She is hard at work on Reckless, the book that will bridge the OGs with a new generation of Death Dwellers. Her work has been included in several anthologies and she is looking forward to other upcoming single title releases, including Savage Suit from the Cocky Hero Club World created by Vi Keeland and Penelope Ward. She is a former RWA member. She also served as Vice President for the SOLA chapter of RWA.

She is a New Orleans Saints fan, but roots for the Texans, the Rockets, and the Coogs (U of H) as long as they aren't playing any Louisiana teams. She loves champagne and sparkling wine. One day, she will try Snoop's brand. She still loves Chivas Regal but had a chance to taste Sassenach Scotch. A #lifegoal is to one day buy herself an entire bottle and keep it all for herself.

In her head, she is a biker babe with a Harley in her garage, waiting for her to hit the road. In reality, she has yet to hop on a bike and ride. She loves Cards Against Humanity, has very strong opinions that she keeps to herself, has to take her time to talk in public so nothing untoward pops out, and always strives to see the best in people and in life.

Made in the USA
Middletown, DE
09 December 2022

17721734R00283